STONE VOWS

samantha christy

Books Publishing Group

Saint Augustine, FL 32092

ISBN-13: 978-1548050924

ISBN-10: 154805092X

For T.J. – one of my oldest and dearest friends.

STONE VOWS

PART ONE

KYLE

CHAPTER ONE

The piercing sound of a pager goes off, echoing around the room as my adrenaline spikes. It's a sound every resident has learned to love. It's a sound every resident has learned to hate. It wakes me from a deep sleep—sleep I only fell into a short while ago based on the hands of the clock on the wall.

I reach over and grab my pager at the same time as I see feet swing down from the bunk above me.

"It's mine," Cameron says, jumping down to grab his lab coat. When he opens the door to leave, light from the hallway illuminates my body and he stops to laugh. He nods at my pants. "Dude, must have been one hell of a dream you were having."

I look down at my tented scrub pants. Then I grab the pillow from under my head and chuck it across the room at him only to have him dodge it before he closes the door behind him.

I lay my head back on the cot in frustration. I'm still tired. I've only had a few hours of sleep since yesterday. And it's Saturday night which means the ER will be busy. It's the calm before the storm. I should try to go back to sleep. But my mind is stuck on a case I had earlier. And my body needs a release. I could take care of it myself, but what's the fun in that when I have Gina? I pull my phone out of my pocket and send a text.

Me: MHO. Room 1320. STAT!

Gina: MHO?

Me: Just get here quick.

Gina: On my way.

Not two minutes go by before the door opens. Gina walks into the residents' on-call room, looking around before she asks, "What is it, Kyle?"

The side of my mouth rises in a cocky smile as I nod to my crotch. "Lock the door and come join me."

She does what I ask, stripping off her scrubs and undergarments, dropping them on the floor as she makes her way to me. My dick jumps in my pants in anticipation. I'm already hard as a rock. I won't last long. I pull my scrub top over my head as Gina peels my pants and boxers off me.

She climbs on top of me, straddling me. She sinks down on me without any foreplay, swallowing me inside her tight walls as I palm her breasts. She moves up and down, undulating her body on me until my balls tighten. I grab her hips, digging my fingers into them as I hold her still while I empty myself into her.

She tilts her head to the side with a sly smile. "Well, that brought new meaning to the word 'quickie'," she says.

My pager goes off and I reach for it. I'm needed in the ER. "Shit," I say, practically dumping Gina off my lap in my haste to get up. I'm on Dr. Manning's service today and he's a real ball-buster. "Sorry, Gina. I'll make it up to you next time."

I quickly dress and then pick up her clothes and throw them to her on the bed as I head across the room.

"Kyle?" she asks, as I'm reaching for the door. "What's MHO?"

I smile and then wink at her. "Major hard-on."

Her laughter trails behind me as I close the door and run through the halls to the emergency room.

I try not to feel guilty about leaving her hanging like that. About using her for a quick release. I tell myself we both know the score. We agreed long ago that this thing we have would be nothing more than booty calls and stress relief. It's not about feelings or emotions. It's about sex. Whenever and wherever.

As second-year residents, we are slaves to the hospital. We're married to the job. Relationships don't work for people like us. People who work eighty-hour weeks—more if you count the hours we troll for cases and finish up paperwork off the clock. I remind myself that this is what we do for each other. Service our carnal needs. She took care of mine just now. It'll be her turn later. Tit for tat, so to speak.

I round the corner to the ER and find one of the male nurses struggling to hold up a man who appears drunk. And homeless by the looks of it. I go over to help as Dr. Manning comes up behind me.

"Took you long enough," he gruffs, as he skirts by us on his way to curtain one.

"Sixty seconds," I tell John, the nurse. "It took me exactly sixty seconds to get here. And that's pretty damn impressive considering what I was just doing."

"Or *who*," John says, laughing as we hoist the man's languid body onto a gurney in curtain two.

It's no secret what Gina and I have going on. It's not that uncommon for interns or residents to hook up with each other given our rigorous schedule. Hell, it's not uncommon for attendings for that matter. They are just more discreet about it than we are—usually because they are sleeping with residents.

John gets the man cleaned up while I go wash my hands and check in on another patient. When I return to curtain two a while later, what I see amazes me. John has washed our patient down, helped him shave, and combed his hair. With the man in a hospital gown instead of ratty clothing, he almost looks like the doorman of my building. He could be anyone. A banker, a construction worker, a father.

I shake my head knowing we're all just one bad circumstance away from being in his worn and battered shoes.

John hands me his chart. Willie James is the name written at the top. "Mr. James has a ten-centimeter laceration on his right shoulder that will require stitches. Says he fell down the stairs at the subway station. He also has some sores on his feet that I cleaned up, and he appears dehydrated which should come as no surprise."

I do my assessment and look over his chart. Then I order a few tests to rule out diabetes. A lot of homeless people have sores on their feet, but if he's diabetic, they could be life-threatening. "Also, hang a banana bag and hand me a suture kit. I can go ahead and stitch him up while I'm here."

Now that Willie is cleaned up and getting hydrated, he's more coherent.

"You look like my son," he says.

"Really?" I ask, throwing in a stitch. "What does he do?"

He shrugs, making me have to pull the needle away. "Dunno," he says. "Haven't seen him in years. But I'd like to think that maybe he's gone on to do something like you. Your father must be very proud of you, son."

"I like to think he is," I say.

By the time I'm done with him, I've learned a lot about the man, and we've had a good conversation. It's amazing to me how people will open up to you if you just listen to them.

"Thank you, Dr. Stone," he says, grabbing my hand to shake it. "Do you know you're the only doctor who has ever treated me like a person and not an animal?"

I try not to show him pity. But I have a hard time not showing my anger over his statement. "If that's true, it makes me ashamed to be called a doctor."

"You are the future," he tells me, before nodding at an attending walking past us. "Not them. They are old and set in their ways. You can change the world if you put your mind to it."

I smile and nod my head. "I plan to, sir."

He laughs, and then he looks at me like a proud father. "I don't doubt you will, son."

"I'll check on you later, Mr. James. If your tests come back alright, you'll be free to go in about an hour."

I stand at the nurses' station, making notes in his chart. I look over at Dr. Manning and watch him interact with another resident. Willie is right. He's old and set in his ways. I vow never to become a bitter, empty soul like he has. Never to be so consumed with medicine that I forget why I'm here in the first place.

Gina swats me on the ass on her way by. She must have been paged here. She's doing a rotation in the PICU now. But the week after next, we'll be back working together again when we both start a four-week OB rotation.

Cameron, Gina and I are all emergency medicine residents. We spend most of our time in the ER, but we also rotate around to other areas. While it's been fun to be largely on the same rotations as my friends, Cameron has no interest in doing a second rotation with 'the vagina squad,' as he likes to call it. We all had to do one our intern year and that was enough for him. Cameron chose plastics, while Gina and I have chosen OB as our second-year elective rotation.

Gina winks at me as she escorts a toddler on a gurney into the pediatric wing of the ER. I know that wink. It means she wants payback later. I check my watch. It's almost ten o'clock. She'll have to wait. It's bound to be a long night. Saturday night tends to bring out the crazies. I watch her walk down the hall, her long legs striding next to the gurney. Her thick brown hair is pulled up into a ponytail, and I watch it bounce from side to side with each step she takes. I do love brunettes. Always have.

Over the next hour, I deal with several minor cases. Food poisoning. Puncture wound. Dislocated shoulder. By midnight, I'm able to clear Mr. James for discharge, happy to find out he most likely doesn't have diabetes.

I walk into the ambulance bay, catching him on his way out. I'm glad to see that John has outfitted him in clothes from the lost and found. But I know shoes and socks are hard to come by. Especially socks, we're not allowed to give out used pairs. I pull out my wallet and grab a few bills.

"Mr. James," I call after him.

He turns around. "Willie," he says. "You've earned the right to call me by my given name."

"Thanks, Willie." I hand him several twenties. "Take this. Buy some good socks and a new pair of shoes."

He looks at what I'm handing him, clearly wanting to accept it, but possibly letting pride get in the way.

"Son, why are you giving your hard-earned money to an old man like me? A complete stranger."

"You said it yourself, Willie. I want to change the world. Just figured I'd start with you."

He shakes his head in bewilderment. Then he nods at me and I can tell he's choking back tears. "It'll be a slow ride if you plan on doing it one person at a time," he says.

"That's exactly how I plan to do it. Slow and steady wins the race," I say, putting the money into his hand.

He grips my hand along with the money. "Son, you don't know this yet, but you've already won."

He walks away, chin up for perhaps the first time in a long while. He thinks I've done him a favor. He thinks that by giving him eighty bucks, I've somehow improved his life. He has no idea how much it's just brought to mine.

Before I go back inside, someone sitting on the bench outside the ER catches my eye. It's a young blonde woman. A pregnant woman. Sitting alone in the dark. After midnight.

I walk over to her. "Miss, are you waiting for someone? Can I help you with anything?"

She looks up at me with teary eyes and a sodden face. "I . . . I'm bleeding," she says, nodding to her protruding belly. "But it's late and the clinics are all closed."

"I'm going to get you a wheelchair," I tell her. "You need to be seen right now."

"But I don't have insurance," she says with tentative eyes.

I shake my head. "Doesn't matter. We're required to treat everyone in the ER."

"You are?" she asks, looking relieved.

"Yes. What's your name?"

"Uh, Elizabeth," she stutters.

"Wait here, Elizabeth. Don't get up. I'll be right back."

I quickly go inside to get a wheelchair and ask a nurse to come with me. I brief her on our way out. "Pregnant woman. Maybe early third trimester. Vaginal bleeding. Name's Elizabeth."

I help Elizabeth into the wheelchair, noting there isn't any blood on the bench where she was sitting. That's good.

"I'm Dr. Stone, and this is Jessica. We're going to get you inside and see what's going on. How far along are you?" I ask, as we wheel her towards an examination room.

"Thirty-two weeks."

"And when did the bleeding start?"

"Earlier today," she says.

"Can you tell me how much blood? Was there enough to soak a feminine pad? More?"

"I—I don't know. I guess I used a couple of pads. It started out light. I noticed a few spots when I used the bathroom. Then it got a little heavier. Am I in labor?"

"We're going to find out. Have you been experiencing contractions? Or have you had any back pain?"

"No contractions. And my back *always* hurts, so there's nothing new about that."

Jessica hands me a chart and I start on it while she helps Elizabeth from the wheelchair into the bed. "You say your back hurts a lot?"

"Yeah, but I think it's because I'm on my feet quite a bit."

"Are you a waitress?" I ask.

"No." She shakes her head, looking embarrassed. "I walk dogs."

"I see." I make some notes in the chart.

I tell Jessica, "Order an H and H, coagulation studies, and get her started on fetal monitoring. And page OB to do an ultrasound."

I turn back to Elizabeth. "Jessica is going to get you into a gown and then we're going to run some tests to see what's going on. Is there anyone you'd like us to call for you?"

She shakes her head and looks at the ground. "No. There's no one." Then she looks up at me with a forlorn face. "It's too early, right? Thirty-two weeks is too early to have my baby. So much can go wrong."

I walk over next to her and put my hand on hers. I notice her skin is velvety soft as I rub my hand on it to reassure her. I look down into her blue eyes, pooling with unshed tears. "We're going to do everything we can to make sure you make it to full term. But if this baby wants to be born today, there might not be much we can do about it. Thirty-two weeks is early, but not too early. Plenty of babies born at thirty-two weeks are healthy. Let us run the tests and then we'll take it from there. Okay?"

She nods, sniffing. I turn to walk away when I realize she has a firm grip on my hand.

"Sorry," she says, her cheeks pinking up. She releases me.

"You're scared," I say, reassuring her. "It's okay to be scared. But know that you've done the right thing for you and your baby by coming here."

"But I can't afford this. All those tests you rattled off, they sound expensive. What if I can't pay my bill?"

"Don't worry, honey," Jessica says, chiming in. "Before you leave, you'll sit with someone from patient billing to work everything out. It's not like they won't let you leave if you can't pay. Indigent people come in here all the time."

I shoot Jessica an annoyed look before she leaves the room to place the orders. "What she meant is that you pay what you can. Believe me when I tell you they slash the prices for self-pay. It won't be as bad as you think."

Elizabeth stares at the door Jessica just walked through. "Does she think I'm indigent? As in homeless?"

"No. Of course not," I say. "We deal with all kinds of people here. She didn't mean anything by it." I vow to pull Jessica aside and tell her to have a little more respect for future patients.

"Do you have an OB that you normally see, Elizabeth?"

She shakes her head. "I go to the free clinic over on 27th Avenue every four weeks. I was there last week and they said everything looked good."

"Have you ever gotten an ultrasound?"

"Yes, when I was eighteen weeks."

"And that was normal?" I ask.

"Uh, I guess so," she says, tensing up. "What do you think is wrong, Dr. Stone?"

"Maybe nothing, Elizabeth. Some spotting can be perfectly normal during pregnancy. But there is no way to tell until we run the tests. Just hold tight and try not to worry." I laugh at my words. "I know, easier said than done, but that's what they always told us to tell patients when I was in med school."

Jessica returns to do a blood draw and put Elizabeth into a gown.

"I'll be back when we have the results of your tests, okay?"

"Okay."

I close the door to give them some privacy. Then I turn my attention to the next chart that gets handed to me. However, I can't help but let my mind wander back to exam room three. To the girl who said she has no one.

CHAPTER TWO

"We still on for dinner at Ethan's tonight?" Cameron asks me in the residents' lounge as we both catch up on paperwork.

"Yup," I answer, not looking up from the pile of charts I'm updating. I stifle my yawn. "After I sleep for about twelve hours today, I'll be ready for some serious drinking."

"I heard that," he says, slapping my arm on his way out of the room.

I look at the clock on the wall. 6:00 AM can't come fast enough. As residents, we are assigned one weekend per month when we're on call from Friday night through Sunday morning. Makes for a long damn weekend.

My oldest brother, Ethan, invited me over for dinner and some much-needed drinks. My other brother, Chad, will also be there. They are both married, so when we get together I usually try to bring Cameron with me just to make an even number.

My pager goes off, so I close the chart and carry the pile with me back to the ER.

Jessica hands me Elizabeth Smith's chart. "All of her test results are in," she says.

"Thanks." I flip through the results, going over her blood work, which looks normal. When I see her ultrasound findings, however, I blow out a deep sigh. "Did they go over it with her yet?"

"Nope. OB was backed up, so they sent a sonogram tech down to do the ultrasound."

"Right." That means Elizabeth hasn't been told anything. Techs aren't allowed to reveal results to patients. "I'll go tell her now. Can you please gather some literature on her condition for me, along with whatever you can find for pregnant women in need of assistance?"

"Right away, Dr. Stone."

"And, Jessica? I'd prefer it if in the future, you don't ever refer to patients as indigent. At least not in front of them."

"I didn't—"

I hold up my hand. "I know you didn't say it about *her*, but it was inferred. Just please don't let it happen again. Their dignity is already compromised when they are sick and in need of medical care."

"Sorry, doctor," she says. "I'll go get that information right away."

I don't know if this patient is homeless or not. On the surface, it doesn't seem like it. She's clean, put together, and she doesn't have any belongings with her other than her purse. Then again, people have a lot of pride. She might just be good at hiding it. It's possible she could be newly homeless, kicked out by a husband who didn't want a child. Or maybe she's living in a shelter. New York City has a lot of shelters for women, and pregnant women would be taken as priority.

I consult with Dr. Manning and then take a breath before I enter the exam room to give Elizabeth the bad news.

"Ms. Smith, I have the results of your tests."

She looks up at me wearily. She looks exhausted. She looks scared. And I'm about to make her day a whole lot worse.

"Your blood tests were all normal. That means you didn't lose enough blood to have consequences for you or the baby. And the good news is that according to the ultrasound, the baby is right on track for thirty-two weeks. It looks completely healthy."

Her hand comes up to her mouth, where she chews on the nail of her pinky finger. Looks like something she does when she's nervous. She takes it out for a second to ask me a question.

"What's the bad news?" she asks. "Whenever someone says *'the good news is...'* that means there's bad news, too. Am I in labor?"

"No. You aren't in labor. We had you on the fetal monitor for two hours and didn't detect any contractions. However, the ultrasound did alert us to a condition that would explain your bleeding. You have what is called placenta previa. What that means is the placenta is attached down by your cervix. There are varying degrees of placenta previa. Yours is called partial previa because the placenta doesn't cover the entire cervix, just a portion of it."

"But the baby is okay?" she asks, chewing on her nail.

"Yes, the baby is fine right now. But there are potential dangers with this condition, and you'll have to deliver via C-section."

She gasps in horror. "C-section?"

"It's a relatively safe procedure, and in your case, much safer than a vaginal delivery."

She closes her eyes. "But a lot more expensive."

"You can't worry about that, Elizabeth. Having a healthy baby is the only thing you should be concerned about. And that means taking care of yourself. I feel comfortable discharging you because the bleeding stopped and you aren't showing any complications. But you'll have to take it easy. Stay off your feet as much as possible, refrain from sex, and don't put anything in your vagina. And come back if you experience more bleeding."

"Stay off my feet? I'm a dog walker. That's just not possible." Her head slumps and her chin falls to her chest in defeat. "How will I make money? I won't be able to afford this as it is."

"Staying off your feet is imperative to your health as well as the baby's," I say adamantly. "You'll have to coordinate more frequent check-ups with the clinic. I'll send you with your records so they can go over them. Jessica will provide you literature on your condition as well as forms for getting possible aid through government programs."

"I can't get any aid," she says.

"Everyone who needs it can get aid."

"I can't," she says.

"Why?"

Jessica comes in with Elizabeth's discharge papers and an armful of pamphlets. I pull out my business card and write my cell number on the back before I hand it to our patient.

"Here's my card. My personal number is on the back. I'm available twenty-four-seven." I point to the literature Jessica put on the side table. "Follow those instructions, Elizabeth. Jessica will get you ready for discharge and answer any more questions you might have. If you need me to explain anything else, have Jessica come get me. I'm here all night."

I step over next to her bed and put my hand on her trembling arm. "Take care of yourself, okay?"

She nods and mumbles words of thanks before I walk out of the room.

I think about how I love being an emergency medicine doctor. I love everything about it except one thing. We don't have the patient follow-up that most other specialties have. Patients come into the ER and we treat them, but then they either go home or get admitted. We rarely get to hear about outcomes.

But the excitement, the adrenaline rush of being the first to deal with the carnage that comes our way, the multitude of procedures we get to perform 'on the fly,' far outweighs the lack of patient relationships that goes along with working in emergency medicine.

I think.

Damn it. Sometimes I hate my job for the very same reasons that I love it.

An hour later, when I'm paged back to the ER for a gunshot wound, my hands wrist-deep in a gangbanger's abdomen until a trauma surgeon can be paged, I remember why I chose this specialty. And I completely forget that I haven't slept in almost two days.

CHAPTER THREE

"Gina was looking for you this morning before you left the hospital," Cameron says, as we make our way from my building to Ethan's.

"I know." I sigh, guilt washing over me because I didn't find her and make good on my promise. "I was beat. It was a long weekend."

"Are you ever going to invite *her* to one of your brother's dinner parties?"

I furrow my brows at him. "It's not like that between us and you know it, Cam. And the last thing I want to do is ask her to go to dinner with me and have her think it's a date. I like things just as they are. No complications. No strings. No added stress in my life."

"There could be worse things than having Gina as your girlfriend," he says.

I study him for a minute, wondering if there is deeper meaning there.

"Don't get me wrong," I tell him. "She's great. A good doctor, a loyal friend. And the sex, it's as good as it gets. I just don't want to send her mixed signals. We have a good thing going."

I wave at my brother's doorman on the way by. Between Chad and Ethan both living in this building, I'm here often. The entire building staff knows me by now.

We're met at the penthouse door by waves of incredible smells. Garlic. *Hell yeah!* I know this smell.

I pull my sister-in-law, Charlie, in for a hug. "You made lasagna?"

"Mallory made it," she says, referring to my other sister-in-law. "She brought it up from her place and used my oven to cook it in."

"Well, thanks to both of you. It's my favorite."

Mallory and Chad live in the same building, just a few floors down. It's a joke among all of us that Ethan owns the penthouse yet Chad is the movie star. Chad, or *Thad* Stone, as he's known in Hollywood, has seven movies and a TV series under his belt. While Ethan, our oldest brother, is a private investigator who owns his own agency. We all inherited enough money from our grandparents that we'd never have to work a day in our lives. But that's not how our parents raised us.

Cameron and I greet Mallory and my brothers before digging into the case of craft beer I brought over. I hand one to everyone but Mallory, who is seven months pregnant with their first baby.

Ethan looks at the bottle of beer I handed him. "Don't you want the good stuff? I've got some bottles of champagne on ice."

I give him an annoyed look. "This *is* the good stuff, Ethan. A case cost me fifty bucks. That's some damn fine beer."

He laughs. "Fifty whole dollars? Are you sure you can afford that, Dr. Stone?"

"Bite me," I say. "And don't knock it 'til you've tried it. It's good shit."

He holds up his bottle and we all take turns tapping ours against his before we drink. I watch his face as he swallows and then works his tongue around in his mouth like he's some kind of beer connoisseur.

"Hmmm…" he ponders.

Charlie swats him on the back of his head. "It's great, Kyle. Thanks for bringing it over."

Chad coughs while saying, "Cheap son-of-a-bitch."

Cameron joins Chad and Ethan as they laugh at my expense. I'm used to it. As the youngest of three brothers, all the teasing fell on me.

"Well, what do you expect," Cameron says. "He spends his real money on his patients."

Mallory smiles at me. She and I got close when she lived at my place for a few weeks while Chad was wrapping up a film in L.A. I think she understands my compassion for others more than the rest of them.

"I saw him handing a homeless guy a wad of cash last night," Cameron tells the group. "And I heard he paid for some old lady's leg brace last week." He turns to me. "You'd better be careful or patients will be hunting you down expecting you to pay their bills."

"I think what he's doing is incredible," Mallory says, getting up to set the table. "Don't ever stop doing what you're doing, Kyle."

Ethan motions for me to give him another beer. "Hey, before I forget," he says, "Mason hooked me up with some pre-season box seat tickets for next weekend's game. You guys up for it? You too, Cameron."

"Hell, yes!" Cameron shouts. Then he lowers his voice and says to me, "Damn, I'm one lucky son-of-a-bitch to have met you our first day as interns. A movie star brother. Friends who play for the Giants."

"Dude," Chad says to him. "Stop kissing his ass or it will give him a bigger head than he already has."

"Oh, *I'm* the one with the big head, Mr. Jake fucking Cross," I say, referring to his award-winning movie trilogy.

Chad punches me in the arm. "That's *Lieutenant* Jake fucking Cross, you tool."

Charlie and Mallory call us to the table for dinner. The girls tell us about the work they've been doing at Hope For Life, a program for pregnant teens who have been kicked out of their homes and have nowhere to go. The residential center helps girls navigate their pregnancy and then gets them back on their feet afterwards. It makes me think of Elizabeth. But as she's in her twenties, she's too old for the program.

"Bro!" I feel a kick in the shin under the table and look over at Chad who delivered it. "Can you tell me why the hell you've been staring at my pregnant wife the whole night? I know she's gorgeous and all, but what's wrong with you?"

"Sorry," I say to him. Then I wince and turn to Mallory. "Sorry, Mal. Uh, I just can't get my mind off a case I had last shift. She was about your age, and at thirty-two weeks, just a little further along."

Mallory looks worried and puts a protective hand on her belly. "Oh, gosh, what happened?"

"She's okay," I tell them. "And so is the baby—for now. She's got placenta previa. But that's not what got to me. First, I found her outside the hospital sitting on a bench. She was scared to come in because she didn't have insurance. And then, when I asked if I could call someone for her, she said she didn't have anybody. But the way she said it was so sad. I actually think she doesn't have *anyone*. Like she's alone in the world." I shake my head and down the rest of my beer. "It just really sucks, that's all."

"Oh, wow," Mallory says. "That's so sad. I can't imagine being pregnant and alone." She reaches over and takes Chad's hand in hers.

"You have to let it go, Kyle," Cameron says. "I know you want to fix everything and everyone. But you can't. You'd better get used to that now or you'll burn out on this job before you know it."

I nod. "I know. For the most part, I can let things go. I do what I can and then the rest is out of my hands. But this girl, I don't know, I just felt like maybe there was more I should have done. She was different. Better. More deserving somehow." I run a frustrated hand through my hair. "Fuck."

Cameron puts a supportive hand on my shoulder. Then I look around at all the fallen faces at the table. "Shit," I say. "I didn't mean to bring everyone down. I'm sure she will be fine."

I nod to the large ice bucket on the bar that's holding several bottles of champagne. "I'm not back on the clock for twenty-four hours. So how about we open those and get shit-faced?"

Chad laughs. "How about the three of you get shit-faced and I'll be the one to make sure you and Cameron get home."

"Sounds like a plan," I say, just as my phone vibrates with a text. I pull it out to check it.

Gina: Enjoy your day off. But I expect payback tomorrow night!

I smile at the text. Best to stick to the things I can control and let the rest go. I tap out a reply.

Me: Looking forward to it.

CHAPTER FOUR

"Oh, God, yes!" Gina belts out in a hushed scream as I work my tongue on her. "Kyle, uhnnnnng . . ."

She tries to be quiet as I make her come, my mouth feasting on her as I work my fingers inside of her. Her hips buck off the bed and her head lashes from side to side on the pillow beneath it. It makes me wonder what it would be like to have her outside of the hospital. I'll bet Gina is a real screamer. Just thinking of it makes me even harder.

I climb up her body before she recovers from her climax. My dick easily glides into her slick channel. Damn, this feels good. It's just what I needed after the difficult cases I had today. I could have gone home. I'm off the clock now. But let's be honest, Gina is a far better choice than my right hand for relieving tension.

In short order, she's making those noises again and I can't help but smile. I wonder if every man can make her come this quickly, or if it's just me. Whatever it is, she's very responsive. Makes our quick on-call room hookups more interesting, that's for sure.

"God . . . Kyle . . . oh . . ."

She writhes beneath me as her second orgasm pulls her under. Her tight walls pulsate around me, taking me right along with her. I bury my face in the pillow next to her head to muffle my own cries.

I climb off her and lay on my back next to her, knowing we'd better get dressed soon. There is only so long we can keep the door locked before another resident pounds on it. This is only one of two on-call rooms available to residents, and it's heading for midnight.

We pull on our clothes but don't get up. It's dark in here. Quiet. And we take a beat to enjoy the peace.

In a matter of minutes, I realize Gina is asleep. I laugh. The girl could fall asleep anywhere. Before she went to med school, she volunteered for the Doctors Without Borders organization. She spent a year in Uganda observing and helping medical personnel. She had to learn to sleep through all kinds of shit. Guess it stuck with her.

I look down at her and study her face in the sliver of moonlight shining through the window curtain. Her hair is messy and coming out of her ponytail. Her makeup is smudged from the sleep I woke her out of. She has a long, elegant nose. One that I know has a small smattering of freckles across it even though I can't see them now. She is beautiful by anyone's standards. Gorgeous even.

I think back to the day we started all this. This, whatever it is. Friends with benefits. Fuck buddies.

We were a few months into our intern year when Gina fell apart after telling a patient's family he had died. Doing that was supposed to be the attending's job, or the resident's at the very least. Interns are there to learn from them. Typically, they don't let us do shit our first year. But Gina had a douchebag resident she was working with who decided to throw her head-first into the deep end. Without warning, the prick walks Gina over to the family and tells them Gina has news for them.

She was a wreck. The patient was sixteen years old and died in a car accident. I was sleeping in the on-call room when Gina ran in and broke down. She was almost in hysterics. She knew she'd have to do things like that. It was part of the job. But what the asshole resident didn't know when he threw her up the goddamn creek without a paddle, was that her younger brother was killed in a car accident when she was in med school.

As interns, she and I had barely gotten to know each other, as our rotations were not on the same schedule. But when she came in the room, it was clear she needed something to help her through it. She needed someone. She needed me. So I gave her the only piece of me I could give.

I don't even think we spoke a word. We just tore each other's clothes off and had sex. Raw animal sex. Totally free from emotion. Quick and dirty. Then she went back to work and I went back to sleep. We never even spoke of it.

Then a few weeks later, I had my own crisis. A four-year-old kid came into the ER in anaphylactic shock from a bee sting. She was all but dead when the child's Hispanic mother carried her in, screaming things in broken English, with the girl's lifeless body in her arms.

We worked for forty-five minutes to try and get the small beautiful brown girl back. I was given point, which surprised me since I was wet behind the ears. I intubated her, which was no easy feat considering her throat was swelling up like a balloon. I performed CPR until my body simply gave out. We pushed drug after drug, pulling any and all stops to try to work a miracle.

In the end, I was told she was gone from the start, but that it was a good teaching case for me.

I was livid. I threw a procedure tray across the room and cussed out my attending and my resident supervisor. I stormed out, sure I'd be fired after my display of insubordination. Gina saw the tail end of my tirade and pulled me into the on-call room where she 'helped' me just as I'd 'helped' her a few weeks before.

After that, it just became a thing. When one of us had a bad case or a stressful day, we'd summon the other to an on-call room. It's been almost a year since it first happened. It's the ideal situation for two second-year residents owned by the hospital. No messy relationship. No complicated feelings.

I carefully climb over Gina, trying not to wake her. She's on until morning. She can use all the sleep she can get. And I've got a six-pack of ridiculously expensive craft beer waiting for me at home.

~ ~ ~

Next shift, I'm finishing up a chart behind the nurses' station when a familiar face walks through the ER doors. I smile when I see her, but then I realize she's got someone with her and she looks worried.

I drop the chart and push through the doors into the waiting area. "Skylar, what's wrong?"

"Oh, Kyle, I'm glad you're here," she says. "This is Jorge, my head chef. An accident in our kitchen caused some burns on his arms."

I quickly assess the deep red flesh on both of his forearms and escort them into the back.

"Where can I put him?" I ask the charge nurse.

"Curtain two," she says, before directing one of her nurses to take the case.

I find one of the new interns and have her follow me. This isn't a complex case and she can easily handle it.

"How did this happen?" I ask Jorge.

"I was stupid," he says. "One of the strings on my apron got caught on the pasta pot on the stove, and I instinctively reached out to try and keep it from falling."

A senior resident comes in to take a look and then lets me continue with my assessment. "It looks like second-degree burns mostly. We can give you some pain relief and salve the wounds, but they may take a few weeks to fully heal."

While my intern, Hannah Clemens, gathers the supplies, I talk to Skylar. She manages a restaurant a few blocks over that bears her maiden name, and that of her parents who own it—Mitchell's. Skylar grew up with Ethan's wife, Charlie. She and her sisters, Baylor and Piper, were like sisters to Charlie. They are one big family into which I'm fortunate enough to be included.

"He'll be okay," I assure her. "Give him a few days off and make sure the burns stay covered with a non-stick dry bandage while working and he'll be good as new."

She breathes out a sigh of relief before she hugs me. "Thank you."

I laugh. "I didn't do anything. Looks like you did all the right things before you brought him in."

"Dr. Stone!" a nurse shouts from the main triage area we call 'ground zero.'

"Sorry, duty calls," I say to Skylar on my way out. "I'll be back to check on Jorge. Until then, Dr. Clemens will get started fixing him up. He's in good hands."

"Dr. Stone, hurry," Joan, the admitting nurse says. "We have a woman in labor who is insisting on pushing."

The double doors open and a young woman gets wheeled quickly through.

"Room five," Joan says, directing us to a private room away from ground zero.

"Get Dr. Neill," I tell Joan.

Dr. Neill is my supervising resident.

"He was called away," Joan says.

"He was just in curtain two thirty seconds ago," I say. Joan shrugs at me. "Shit. Then find Manning. And page OB."

"Doing that now," she says.

Debbie takes over for Joan, helping me put the girl on the bed.

"What's your name?" I ask.

"Susan. Susan Markenson," she belts out during a contraction.

"How far along are you, Susan?" I ask.

"I'm due in ten days. This is my second child. My first came very quickly."

Great. The nurse hands me some gloves. "I need to check you, okay, Susan?" I ask.

She nods.

I lift her dress and Debbie helps me remove her underpants. And, Holy God, she's crowning.

"This baby is coming right now," I say. "Debbie, prep for delivery. Susan, try not to push for a minute. Let us get set up. Is there anyone we can call?"

"My husband is coming, but in this traffic . . . oh, my God, he's going to miss it," she cries.

Another intern comes in to see if he can help.

"Susan, this is Dr. Felder, but he prefers to be called 'Joe.' He's an intern. If you want to give him your phone, he can video the birth for your husband."

"Really?" she says, looking pleased.

"Really?" Joe asks, giving me a crazy look.

"You heard her, she doesn't want her husband to miss it. Now get her phone. This is happening—*now*." I turn to Debbie when she returns with the equipment. "Any word from Neill or Manning?"

"Dr. Neill will be here in ten. Dr. Manning got called into another trauma. He said you can handle it."

"Handle it? Fuck," I murmur under my breath.

"Have you delivered a baby before, Dr. Stone?" she asks quietly so we don't alarm Susan.

"Not by myself," I admit.

"Well, it looks like you will today," she says. "Come on, wash up."

I strip off my exam gloves and wash my hands, then Debbie gowns and gloves me, having arranged all the instruments next to the bed and the panda warmer in the corner.

There isn't a birthing bed in the room, so I have Susan scoot to the end of the bed and have Debbie stack pillows behind her. Then I ask Debbie to grab a few more nurses to hold up Susan's legs.

"Uhhhhhhh," Susan cries. "I have to push."

"Okay, Susan, go ahead."

What happens next is one of the most incredible things in nature. A dark head of matted hair slowly works through her opening. Once the baby's head is out, it rotates up, and I quickly suction its mouth and then check to make sure the cord isn't around the neck.

"Susan, one more big push and your baby will be here."

She grunts as she pushes her legs into the nurses' hands. I watch as first one shoulder, then another comes through. After that, the baby just slides right out.

"You have a son, Susan!"

The door opens and in walks the OB resident followed by Dr. Neill. They take over for me, cutting the cord just as the baby makes his introductory sound in this world. Susan cries when she hears her son for the first time. After they place him on her chest, she thanks me.

But it's me who is grateful. I just had one of the best experiences a doctor can have. With all the sickness and death that surrounds us, it's humbling to be reminded of how wonderful life is. I find myself exhilarated. Pent up. I'm not frustrated or stressed. I'm on cloud nine. I pull out my phone and tap out a text to Gina.

Me: Room 1320 in 15 min.

Joe hands off Susan's phone to one of the nurses who continues to video the baby's first moments for the absentee father. Then he asks me, "Is it too late to change my specialty?"

We walk out of the room together. "Pretty fucking great, huh?" I say.

He nods and tries to discreetly wipe some moisture from under his eyes. "Yeah, pretty fucking great."

CHAPTER FIVE

The only exercise I seem to get these days is walking to and from work. It's two miles one way, a long walk by NYC standards, but the hospital is not in a part of town I'd choose to live in. Every time I can, I skip the subway and hoof it.

Walking home this morning, after watching Susan give birth, I can't help but think of the pregnant patient I had last week. Elizabeth. I hope she followed up with the clinic. There are so many things that could go wrong if she doesn't seek proper medical attention when she needs it. Bad things such as pre-eclampsia for her; and for the baby, cerebral palsy, fetal growth restriction, or even hypoxia.

I almost wish her bleeding wouldn't have stopped. I wish it would have been bad enough for us to keep her in the hospital without endangering their health.

I find myself looking closely at every person walking a dog. I shudder to think she's still out there being pulled along by a gaggle of furry creatures. She could fall. Hell, even if she didn't fall, just the simple act of walking could cause her condition to worsen. But if she feels she has no other choice—if she truly has no one and has to pay the rent, she's more than likely still working.

I see some dogs way up ahead and speed up my stride when I see a blonde head of hair atop a petite frame sporting a sundress on this hot July morning. I follow far behind the woman for a block or two. I suppose it could be her, but I'm not close enough to see.

"Elizabeth!" I call out.

She doesn't turn around. I think I must be imagining things.

I need sleep. These sixteen-hour shifts can be brutal. But instead of hitting my bed after a shower, I get on my laptop and do an internet search.

Elizabeth Smith, dog walker, New York City.

I stare at what's in front of me on the screen and laugh. I swear to God, Elizabeth Smith must be the most common name in NYC. Maybe even the whole country. I shut the lid of my laptop. Maybe a little too hard. Then I draw the curtains and throw myself onto my bed.

~ ~ ~

My ringing phone wakes me up. *Shit.* I forgot to silence it. But the clock on my bedside table tells me I've gotten a good eight hours of sleep. I reach over and grab the phone to see my brother calling. "What's up, Chad?"

"Oh, man, I didn't mean to wake you, bro. Did you just get off shift?"

"Got off this morning. It's okay, I needed to get up anyway. I'm back on later tonight."

"Do you have time to shoot some hoops at the gym?" he asks. "Mal is out with the girls and I'm bored out of my mind. Some of the guys will be there."

Chad's had a thing for basketball ever since he moved back from L.A. last summer. I agree to meet him at the gym after I grab an early dinner. On my way, I once again scan the streets for dogs and any blonde-haired girls on the other end of the leashes. This time I don't see any.

The problem is, I can't decide if I'm disappointed or relieved.

Someone runs up behind me and slaps me on the back. "Hey, Kyle," Griffin Pearce says. "You here to shoot hoops?"

"Yeah, you?"

"Gotta win my money back. Gavin and Mason really took it to me last time. Hey, speaking of winning money, are you ever going to join us for poker on Monday nights?"

"I'd love to, man, but I'm usually working. Maybe in a few years when things calm down."

"We'll be here. And we'd love to have you anytime," he says, opening the door to the gym.

Or should I say *his* gym. The one he owns with Gavin McBride and Mason Lawrence. The three of them are either married or engaged to one of the Mitchell sisters.

"I saw your wife yesterday," I tell Griffin.

"Skylar told me you took good care of Jorge. Thanks for that."

We see the other guys emerging from the locker room just as we head in. Ethan is the only one who's not here. "Three on two?" I ask. "Ethan's not coming?"

"Well, with you playing, it's more like two on two and a half," Chad jokes. "Ethan's stuck working a case."

"It won't be so funny when I'm mopping the court up with your ass, old man," I say.

"Fuck you," he says. "I'm one whole year older than you. And a whole lot better looking."

"According to the guy staring at you in the mirror," I quip.

Mason comes over to shake my hand. "How you been, Kyle?"

"Can't complain. Hey, thanks for the box seats. Great game the other day."

Mason is the starting quarterback for the Giants. Since meeting him last year, I have a renewed love of sports. Medical school and residency don't leave much time for sports, but I try to watch whenever I can. And Griffin is a huge Cleveland Indians fan so I've grown to like baseball as well.

"Hey, man," Gavin says. "Nice to see we could pry you away from the hospital."

"Hi, Gavin. How are Baylor and the kids?"

"Good," he says. "Baylor just published her twentieth novel. It's what the girls are out celebrating tonight."

"Shit, really? Twenty novels? That's great. Will your production company be making this one into a movie, too?"

He laughs. "Who knows. We've done three already. Life's good, that's for sure."

"Are we going to stand here and kumbaya all fucking day, or play some basketball?" Chad asks.

Just as I turn to go into the locker room, my phone rings. I'm not familiar with the number. "Hello?"

"Uh . . . Dr. Stone?" a hesitant voice asks.

"Yeah, speaking."

"This is Elizabeth Smith. I'm sorry to bother you, and you probably don't remember—"

"I remember you, Elizabeth. Is everything okay?" My heart starts to beat a little faster. It's the adrenaline rush.

Her shaky voice replies, "I don't think so. I'm bleeding again. And it's worse than before. It won't stop."

"What's your address? I'm calling you an ambulance," I say, turning around to head back out the front doors of the gym.

I wave at Chad through the glass and point to my phone. He knows what that means. He salutes me in understanding.

"No. No ambulance."

"If you're worried about the money—"

"No ambulance," she says, louder and more insistent this time.

I blow out a frustrated breath. "Where are you? I'll come get you."

"I . . . you can't."

"Elizabeth, you need to get to a hospital." I hear her crying now. She's scared. Maybe I'm scaring her. "Listen, maybe the bleeding will stop once you get there, just like before. But for your sake and the baby's, you need to let someone examine you. Please."

"But I haven't even paid my bill from last time."

"Doesn't matter," I say. "They still have to see you."

"Are you there? At the hospital?"

"No. I'm on my way. I can be there in thirty minutes. Give me your address and I'll pick you up along the way." I hail a cab, wondering if it would be faster to walk considering it's rush hour. But I'm hoping she'll change her mind and let me swing by and get her.

"I'm only a few blocks from the hospital. I can walk."

"You shouldn't be walking, Elizabeth."

"I'll see you there, Dr. Stone."

The line goes dead. I try to call her back but she doesn't answer.

CHAPTER SIX

"Hurry, please," I tell the cabbie after rattling off the address of the hospital.

He waves his hand at the traffic, looking at me like I'm stupid. "I'll do my very best," he says sarcastically.

Damn it! I remember I'm supposed to start my new rotation today. I check my watch. But that's not for a few hours. Surely the ER won't mind if I step in on her case until then. After all, she was my patient the last time she was in.

Thirty-five minutes later—*so much for hurrying*—I walk into the ER. Before I even change into my scrubs, I ask the charge nurse where Elizabeth is. She directs me to exam room six.

When I enter the room, I see she's been changed into a gown. I also see a sundress draped over the chair. The same damn sundress I followed home from work this morning. *Fuck.* It *was* her. I open my mouth to say something, but when I look over at Elizabeth to see her tearful face, I realize she's terrified and she's probably already feeling a world of guilt without me adding to it.

As she's busy answering questions for the admitting nurse, I pick up her chart to read some notes written by Dr. Redman, who will be my attending on my OB rotation.

"Do you have an insurance card?" the nurse asks her.

Elizabeth shakes her head. "No," she says, looking guilty. "I promise to pay what I can."

"Your phone number?" the nurse asks her.

Elizabeth spouts out the number she called me from earlier.

"Your home address?" the nurse asks.

"Uh . . ." Elizabeth shoots a quick glance over at me. "Is that necessary?" she asks her. "I didn't have to give my address after my previous visit."

"Well, you're being admitted now, dear, we have to have your address," the nurse says. Then she studies her. "You do have an address, don't you?" She raises her eyebrows as if to scold her.

"Of course I do. But . . ."

Elizabeth looks terrified. I'm not sure if she really is homeless or if she's just ashamed about where she lives. Maybe that's why she didn't want me picking her up. Her hands start trembling and I swear she's about to hyperventilate. That won't be good for her or the baby.

I walk over to the nurse and ask her for the admissions form. I write my address on it and hand it back. "Is that all you need?" I ask her, staring her down so she gets that I want her the hell out of here.

She closes the folder. "I suppose I can get the rest later."

"Yes, thank you," I say, walking her out and closing the door behind her.

When I turn around, Elizabeth has her head in her hands, crying. She's having a hard time catching her breath. I pull the chair over and sit next to her, putting my hand on her shoulder.

"It'll be okay," I tell her. "This really is the best thing for you and the baby. We can monitor you continuously."

"I c-can't af-afford it," she blubbers. "What am I g-going to do?"

"You're going to stay in bed like we tell you," I say. "You're going to read trashy magazines and watch hours of mindless television. You're going to eat crappy hospital food. You're going to make friends with the residents and the nurses. You're going to look out your window and watch the world roll by. And after all that, the hope is you're going to walk out of here with a healthy baby. And that's all you need to focus on. Not how much it's going to cost. Okay?"

Her breathing slows and her hands stop shaking. She nods. "Okay." She takes some deep breaths. "Can I ask what you wrote on her form that got her to shut up?"

"They can be pushy," I say. "I just wrote down my address so she would quit bugging you."

"Oh. Do you really think I'll have to stay until the baby comes? I'm not even thirty-four weeks."

I nod, looking at Dr. Redman's notes again. "Yeah, I think you'll have to stay. Your condition has become a threat to the baby. We need to keep the bleeding to a minimum, otherwise you'll have to deliver immediately. The hope is to get you to thirty-seven weeks. That's about three and a half more weeks. That's when we consider it safe for the baby to come."

Dr. Redman walks in and sees me sitting next to Elizabeth. She eyes my hand on her shoulder and takes in my street clothes.

"Well, Dr. Stone," she says. "I see you're eager to get started on your rotation. Am I to assume you know Ms. Smith personally?"

I pull my hand away from Elizabeth and stand up, walking over to have a private conversation with my new attending. "No, I don't. I was on call when she came in last week. I heard she was coming back and wanted to follow up myself."

Dr. Redman lifts her brow and steps back to study me. "Brilliant," she says in her heavy English accent. "Then seeing as you have established a rapport with the patient, you're elected babysitter."

"Babysitter?" My forehead creases into a frown.

"Yes. She's your patient now, Dr. Stone. Bed rest patients don't interest me. Not unless their conditions become life-threatening. It'll be your job to make sure that doesn't happen. Are we clear?"

I nod. I'd heard about her unconventional teaching methods. But . . . babysitter? Surely a nurse can do that. I can see it now; Cameron will have a heyday giving me shit about this.

"Good," she says, eyeing me up and down as if I'm an inconvenience. "Get her moved to the floor. And for Christ's sake, find some bloody scrubs."

Dr. Redman leaves the room as a nurse brings in a wheelchair and a plastic bag for Elizabeth's personal things.

Elizabeth looks at me guiltily. "Are you in trouble?" she asks.

"Why would you ask that?"

"I heard her say you've been elected as my babysitter."

I laugh. "No. Not in trouble. Just a second-year resident. We tend to get the jobs nobody else wants."

She looks down at the bed. "Oh."

I berate myself. "Sorry, that came out wrong. What Dr. Redman meant was that your case isn't bad enough to interest her, so she's assigning a resident. That's a good thing, you know. It means she thinks you're not emergent."

She looks up at me and a luminous smile brightens her face.

Holy shit.

I've never seen anything so captivating. Her bright blue eyes are puffy from crying. Mascara is smudged down her cheeks, but her smile, it lights up the goddamn room. And I vow to do everything in my power over the next three and a half weeks to keep it on her face.

CHAPTER SEVEN

"I heard you got stuck on scut right out of the gate," Gina whispers to me as Dr. Redman addresses us, along with the three other residents who are starting a new rotation tonight.

I shrug. "No biggie. I doubt it'll take much of my time."

"Doctors Stone and Lawson," Dr. Redman says, staring us down. "Is there something more important than hearing about what I expect from you over the next four weeks? An interesting case that I haven't been made aware of, perhaps?"

Gina looks at me apologetically before turning back to our new attending. "No, Dr. Redman," she says. "I'm sorry, I was just asking Dr. Stone about his exciting delivery last night. I didn't mean to be rude."

"And yet you were," Dr. Redman says, looking down her nose at Gina before turning to me. "I heard about it as well. You were lucky it all went off swimmingly."

"I'd say our patients were the lucky ones," I tell her. "There weren't any attendings or senior residents to help so I had to fly by the seat of my pants."

"Are you blaming my department for not getting there quickly enough?" she asks defensively.

"No, ma'am, not at all. It happened very quickly. I meant I was flying solo because none of my immediate supervisors were anywhere to be found."

She walks over to me. "First off, I'm not just some lady off the street who is here to teach back-alley medicine. I believe I've earned my title and I expect you to use it."

I furrow my brows at her. I've heard as attendings go, she's a pain in the ass. But I thought maybe she was misunderstood because she's British and sometimes Brits get a bad rap for being stuck-up just because of the way they speak.

"Doctor," she says. "I'm not *ma'am* or *professor* or *supervisor*. I'm *Doctor* Redman."

"Yes, Dr. Redman, of course. I'm sorry."

I resist the urge to turn to Gina and roll my eyes. Misunderstood my ass, she's a certifiable Nazi.

"And secondly. If you have an issue with staffing, you need to take it up with the residency director. But as a second-year, I'll expect you to be able to handle those kinds of situations should you find yourself in the middle of one again."

"I did," I say, defending myself. "I will."

"Very well, then. Would you mind terribly if I continue with your orientation?" she says sarcastically.

"No, ma—" I get a swift kick from Gina. "No, Dr. Redman."

"Brilliant." She walks back towards the other residents. "Now that Dr. Stone has given me permission to carry on, I'll introduce you to your senior resident, Dr. Anders, who will be your immediate supervisor for this rotation. If she is unavailable, you may report directly to me. But *only* if she's unavailable. And only if it's extremely urgent."

An hour later, as we leave orientation with glazed-over eyes, Gina says, "What a grade-A bitch. I wish we could have Dr. George from our last OB rotation."

"I think he only gets first-years," I say. "I'm starting to understand why. I don't think Red would have the patience for interns."

Gina snorts. "Red. I wouldn't let her hear you call her that. She'd assign you to enemas for sure."

"I've had worse. If four weeks with her gets me further in the program, then I say bring it on."

She studies me. "Have you always been this glass-half-full, Kyle?"

I laugh. "I guess I have. Why, do you have a problem with it?"

She shakes her head and wrinkles her nose. "No. I kind of like it."

Her stare lasts a little longer than I'm comfortable with. Her eyes rake over me as if she's looking at me in a new light. We pass by the on-call room and she nods to it before tapping on the charts Redman assigned to her. "Want to meet up later, after we make our nightly rounds?"

I check my watch. "Sure, if we can fit it in."

She smiles. "Page me, okay?"

She scurries off to check on her new patients. Her *four* patients. I meander down the hallway towards my *one*.

I look down at the sole chart Redman assigned to me, wondering what I did to have her dislike me so much. Redman is older, my dad's age. She's a pit-bull. Worse than Manning even. But I can handle it.

Someday I'll run my own clinic and have to answer to no one but myself. This is all a means to an end. A necessary road I must follow to get to where I want to be. But as I walk down the hall, breathing in the sterile hospital smell along with the occasional aroma of flowers, I know there is no other place I'd rather be. Redman can kiss my young American ass. *Ma'am.*

I walk into Elizabeth's room and catch her watching ESPN Sports Center. I laugh. "Can't work the remote yet, huh?"

"I can work it," she says. "I love this show."

I tilt my head and study her. Then I start to ask her a question but she holds her hand out to shut me up. "One second," she says.

I stand back and put her chart on the table. I cross my arms in front of me and watch the television with her as the announcers go over the scores of some baseball games. I'm amused by how her eyes are glued to the screen.

When they go to commercial, she apologizes for being rude.

"No, you're good," I say. "It's refreshing to see a woman so into sports."

"Why can't a woman be into sports?" she asks.

"They can," I say. "But most aren't."

"Then most are missing out."

"I agree," I say. "I missed out for a lot of years myself. My schedule doesn't always allow for sports. But I'm trying to make time for them again."

"Good. You should," she says. "Everyone needs something besides work, no matter how important work is to them. Sports are a good outlet. Even if you only watch."

"Do you play one?" I ask. Then I motion to her belly. "I mean when you aren't almost eight months pregnant?"

"I did a long time ago. But not anymore." She looks up at the TV and then down to her bed, sad, like there is so much more to the story.

I don't want to pry, so I look over at the whiteboard on the wall where her nurse's name is listed. "Has Abby gone over everything with you?" I ask. "Do you have any questions?"

She shakes her head and then nods to the fetal monitor on her right. "Abby said I'm pretty much going to stay hooked up to this the entire time. I guess that means I have to get permission every time I need to pee."

I laugh. "Yeah, you can't do anything here without someone knowing about it. I hope you left your modesty at the door."

She smiles. "Modesty has never been a problem for me." Then her smile fades. "Being held prisoner, that's another thing entirely."

I feel for her. Being confined to a hospital room for weeks, or even a month in her case, has its fair share of issues. "Don't worry, I'll see if I can parole you from time to time. The hospital has a great courtyard."

"Really?" she says, perking up. "With flowers?"

I nod. "Yes. There are flowers and trees and benches and a cobblestone path. Sometimes I sit out there to eat on nice days. I think they wanted it to have a Central Park feel."

Then I look at her hospital gown. I know she wouldn't want to be paraded around the grounds in it. "Do you have a friend or family member you can call to bring some of your things by?"

She follows my eyes down to her gown. "No, that's okay. I'll just wear this. I think I look good in blue."

"You do," I agree. Never have I thought a hospital gown was anything special to look at. And they aren't. But maybe it isn't the gown. Maybe it's the woman wearing it and the way it brings out the blue in her eyes. "But don't you want someone to bring your personal stuff over? You're going to be here a while."

"I'm fine. I don't need much," she says with a forced smile that lets me know it's anything but true.

"You know, I don't mind going to your place. You could give me a list of what you need."

"I'm good, Dr. Stone. I carry makeup in my purse. Like I said, I don't need much."

Much? This girl literally only has the clothes on her back and the small purse she came in with. My eyes are drawn to her wrist when I notice the chunky metal dime-store bracelet on it that reminds me of one of those house-arrest ankle cuffs.

"We're going to be spending a lot of time together, Elizabeth, considering I'm your babysitter and all," I say with a wink. "So how about when no one else is around, you just call me Kyle."

"Kyle." She tries out my name and I find that I like the way it rolls off her lips.

"Yes. And what should I call you? I mean, what do your friends call you? Liz, Beth, Lizzy?"

For a second, she looks like I asked her to explain quantum physics. "Uh . . ."

"Elizabeth," I say, making my own choice in the matter. "Do you have a home?"

She seems scared, protective of any personal details. Protective of her name even. She doesn't look homeless, yet everything points to it.

"Of course I do," she says, shifting uncomfortably in the bed. Her movement dislodges the fetal monitor and I walk around the bed and reposition it on her belly.

"I saw you this morning, walking some dogs," I say.

She puts her hands on her round stomach, looking guilty. "I did this, didn't I?"

"It doesn't matter how it happened. You could have started bleeding again even if you'd been in bed all week. No point in beating yourself up about it now. Maybe it's fate; a blessing in disguise, you being here. It gives you and your baby the best chance at a healthy delivery."

"Do you believe in that? In fate?" she asks.

I think of my friends, Griffin and Skylar Pearce and the horrifying experience they had to go through to get where they are today. I think of the chance meeting that brought Chad and Mallory back together after nine years apart.

I nod. "Yeah, I think I do."

Her lips fold together thoughtfully. "So, you think the things we go through are all just a way of getting us to where we need to be?"

There is so much more to her question than she's asking. Then again, she could just be referring to her having to be here, and I'm reading way too much into it.

I shrug. "I never really thought of it like that, but yes, I think that. I think exactly that."

The smile she wore earlier returns to her face and I get the feeling this girl is not hard to please. And my urge to please her is uncharacteristically strong.

I make a mental note to call Mallory tomorrow. Elizabeth is pregnant and alone. She will be cooped up here for weeks. She needs a friend. And who better than my sister-in-law, who not only volunteers at an organization that helps pregnant girls, but who herself is pregnant. It's the perfect solution.

I roll the ultrasound machine over to her bedside. "I know you had one downstairs, but now that you've been admitted, we're going to do another one for a baseline."

"Do as many as you want," she says, excitedly. "I love watching him or her wiggle around in there."

"Him or her," I say. "So, you don't want to know the baby's sex?"

"No! Please don't tell me. There are so few mysteries in life. I just really want to be surprised."

I smile, pulling a sharpie out of my pocket to make a big bold note on the front flap of her chart. You never know what intern might walk in here and spoil it for her.

Just as I'm finishing up the ultrasound, Abby walks in with a tray of food. I look at my watch and see it's almost nine o'clock. I laugh. "Pregnancy craving?" I ask Elizabeth.

"No. I didn't get a chance to eat earlier." She rubs her belly. "This one's hungry."

"I'll leave you to your dinner then." I nod to the TV. "And your ESPN. I'll see you tomorrow, Elizabeth."

"See you tomorrow, Kyle . . . er, Dr. Stone." She looks over at Abby to see if she noticed the slip. She did.

When I walk out into the hallway, I think about what she said about not eating earlier. Did she not eat because she was bleeding? Or was it because she didn't have any food?

I try not to think of a pregnant woman, who may or may not have enough food to eat, in the home that she may or may not even have.

Then, before I realize I'm doing it, I end up detouring to the billing office. Because, just like the rest of the hospital, even they have a night shift.

CHAPTER EIGHT

"You *what?*" Cameron asks in disbelief as we grab some coffee and a bagel the next morning after rounds.

I blow on my hot coffee, taking a needed pause to gather my thoughts after telling him what I did. Maybe I shouldn't have told him. But Cameron is probably the best friend I have, not counting my brothers. He's been with me through thick and thin this past year of residency. He, more than anyone, would understand why I did it.

But then why do I feel guilty? Like I've done something wrong? Why do I feel like I have to hide the fact that I'm helping my patient? If Redman knew . . . well, I don't even know *what* she'd do. She seems to have it in for me. Maybe giving her ammunition to use against me is not a very good idea at this point in my career.

Shit. Did I just screw up in a monumental way?

Then again, I'm not sure I would take it back even if I could. Elizabeth isn't just any patient. She's different somehow. I could sense from the very beginning that she doesn't want help, but that maybe she needs it anyway.

"You think I crossed a line," I say, prematurely agreeing with him.

"I don't know," he says. "I've come to expect shit like that from you, but paying for an entire hospital stay? She could be here for weeks, Kyle. That'll be expensive."

I stare him down until he realizes the obvious.

"I know, I know," he says. "It's not like you can't afford it, Warren friggin' Buffet, but just because you *can* pay for it doesn't mean you *should*. If you do it for every patient, eventually you *will* run out of money."

"I don't intend on doing it for every patient," I say. "She's pregnant. And she might be homeless. And even if she's not, there's something going on there. I mean she doesn't have anybody. Literally. She has nobody. Who has nobody?"

"She obviously had *somebody*," he says, making an obscene gesture with his hands by putting a finger inside a hole he made with his fist.

I roll my eyes at him as I toss back some much-needed caffeine.

"Maybe that's why she got knocked up," he says. "So she'd have someone."

"Hmmm. Maybe," I say, pondering that possibility.

"Are you going to tell your patient what you did?"

I shake my head. "I don't think I should. She doesn't seem like a person who wants a handout."

"So, you want to be the anonymous white knight," he says. "You could always tell her the hospital decided to take her pro bono."

I raise my brows at his suggestion. "Good idea," I say. "Plus, I wouldn't want it getting back to Red."

"Red?" he asks.

"Dr. Redman. It's my new nickname for her. She got red in the face when I called her *ma'am* last night. Plus, the name fits."

He laughs. "Ah, the English rose of the vagina squad."

"More like the British bitch, I'd say."

"Yeah, but she's hot."

"She's our parents' age, Cameron."

"Doesn't mean I wouldn't do her in the on-call room," he says.

The visual gives me a bad taste in my mouth. "You are seriously twisted," I say.

"Speaking of on-call rooms, you tell Gina what you did?"

Oh, shit. I completely forgot to page Gina last night. I got pulled in to help on a few cases and then snuck in a few hours of shuteye. "No."

"Why not?" he asks, pensively.

I shrug an unknowing shoulder.

"Maybe you didn't tell her because you think she'd be jealous," he says, eyebrows raised in inquisition.

"Why would Gina be jealous? It's not like I haven't done something like this before," I say.

"Not on this level," Cameron says. "And not for a beautiful young woman."

"How do you know Elizabeth is young and beautiful?"

He smiles deviously. "I didn't. But now I do." He looks down at his beeping pager. Then he gets up and tosses what remains of his breakfast into a trashcan. "And maybe the fact that you want to keep this from Gina means you've crossed the line even more than paying the bill does."

CHAPTER NINE

While I finish my breakfast, I tap out a text to Mallory. I ask if it's possible for her to come by the hospital to meet one of my pregnant patients who seems to have nothing and no one and could she just hang out with her and talk pregnancy or something.

Then I sit back and wonder if Cameron is right.

I'm paying Elizabeth's hospital bills and now I'm trying to get her to make a friend. Neither of those are my job. But isn't being a doctor more than simply treating illness? Isn't it about treating the whole person—mind and body? And her whole person is more in need of a friend than anyone I've ever met.

My pager goes off and I glance down at it. I'm being paged to ground zero. When I get there, Dr. Anders and I get a quick history from the ER resident about a patient who just came in.

"Female, twenty-nine years old, nineteen weeks pregnant. Presented with moderate vaginal bleeding and cramps. Initial exam indicates slight thinning of the cervix and absent fetal heartbeat. I'll leave it to you guys to confirm with ultrasound and then break the news."

My heart climbs into my throat knowing what the woman in exam room three is about to go through. I've witnessed a few miscarriages over the past year. But none have been late miscarriages—those occurring after twelve weeks' gestation. Hell, five more weeks and the baby might have had a fighting chance. Five short weeks.

Fuck.

Sometimes I hate this job. I peek through the window into the exam room, relieved she's got someone with her. Looks like her husband. He's sitting on the bed, no doubt trying to reassure her. They are in for a world of hurt.

I can't help but think of another woman upstairs in OB. My patient. My *only* patient according to the bitch who owns me for the next four weeks. She's much further along than the woman in the ER, and her baby, even if born today, would have an excellent chance of survival. But I can't imagine what would happen if Elizabeth had miscarried, or God forbid, if anything bad happens while she's here in the hospital. She has no one to comfort her. No one to go through it with, to support her and reassure her. No one to sit on her bed and tell her everything will be okay even when they know it might not be.

A nurse wheels the ultrasound machine around the corner and waits for us to go in.

"Are you ready for this, Dr. Stone?" Dr. Anders asks. "I'm going to let you take point on this, but I'll be right by your side. Just nod and I'll jump in if you need me."

For the patient's sake, I'm grateful that Anders was paged to ground zero instead of Red. Then again, it might just be residents that bitch has an aversion towards. I can't imagine she'd get as far as she has if she doesn't have compassion for her patients.

We perform the ultrasound, confirming everyone's fear.

"I'm so sorry, Mr. and Mrs. Beaumont, there isn't a heartbeat and there are no fetal movements. That combined with your thinning cervix and I'm afraid you are having a miscarriage."

Mrs. Beaumont breaks down in her husband's arms. I give them a minute to absorb what I've said. I give myself a minute to gain composure.

"I'm sorry, but you're going to have to make a difficult decision. We can perform a D and C, or if you prefer to hold the baby, we could induce labor. You could also choose to go home and see if labor starts on its own over the next few days. The bleeding is minimal and doesn't pose a risk to your health."

"Go home?" Mr. Beaumont asks, his voice thick with emotion. "Why? Our baby is . . ."

He can't bring himself to say it.

"I know it seems unconventional," I explain. "But some people find they need the time to deal with their loss."

"No. Please, let's just do it now. But I don't want the D and C," Mrs. Beaumont says, looking at her husband. "I want to hold her."

I nod to the nurse, who then goes out of the room to start the admissions process.

Three hours later, I'm delivering my second baby in a week. This time, it's anything but a happy occasion. The miniature body is easily pushed through the birth canal and into my hands.

It's a girl. Her tiny red body is barely bigger than one of my hands, but she's perfectly formed. Her eyes are fused shut and her arms and legs are curled up against her body. She has ten fingers and ten toes, and one of her hands is no bigger than the nail on my thumb.

As I snip the small umbilical cord, my heart breaks for the life taken too soon. It breaks for these parents who have no doubt already envisioned everything from preschool to their daughter's wedding.

Dr. Anders hands me a towel and I clean up the tiny body before wrapping her up and giving her to her mother.

There's not a dry eye in the room, including mine.

I take some deep breaths and try to push my emotions to the side as I get back to work, making sure all the placenta gets delivered. Then we leave them alone to grieve their child.

Dr. Anders tries to catch me before I walk off. I shake my head at her. I need a minute. I know she wants to make sure I'm okay. Maybe even talk about what happened. But that's not what I need.

I take out my phone and tap out a text. Then I plow through the door of the on-call room and kick a chair into the bed. Then I curse myself for hurting my foot. But no amount of hurt can compare to what the Beaumonts are dealing with right now.

The door swings open and Gina comes through. I stride across the room and almost tackle her into the wall. I lock the door next to her as I devour her mouth, her neck, any exposed skin I can get my hands and mouth on.

"I heard," she says into my hair. "I'm sor—"

"Less talking," I interrupt. "More fucking."

She grabs the hem of her scrub top and pulls it over her head. Unlike her usual sports-type bra, she has a lacy white bra on underneath. One of those push-up bras that has the flesh of her breasts spilling over the top. It makes me wonder if she wore it specifically for me or if this was the only clean one she had. I couldn't care less what the hell her bra looks like, especially right now. The only interest I have in her bra is seeing it on the floor.

I reach around and undo the clasp, my lips meeting the soft flesh of her breasts before her bra even lands on the hard tile. I suck on each nipple until they are erect, hard as a rock. Just like my dick.

I pull my shirt over my head, followed quickly by the removal of my pants and boxers. Gina follows suit and rids herself of her bottoms. I push her against the wall. Hard.

"Ugh," she breathes, before she wraps her long legs around my naked body. My dick strains against her stomach, pulsing between us, begging to be inside her.

I carry her over to the table and set her down on the edge. I spread her legs wide and pull my scrubs over so I can cushion my knees on the unforgiving floor. I work my tongue on her. In her. I work it until she begs me to fuck her. When I push inside her, I do it so hard, the table hits the wall behind her and the lamp falls to the floor.

"That's it, baby. Let it go," she says.

My eyes open and snap to hers.

Why the hell did she have to say baby?

I try to pull out of her, but she grabs my ass, holding me inside. "Finish it, Kyle. I know you need to."

She's right. I do. The stress. The frustration. The sheer heartache. I need this. I need it so badly, it could just as easily be Red on this table and I'd still fuck her.

Gina reaches down and rubs herself. Watching her do it brings me back to where I need to be. She throws her head back and bites her lip as she comes quietly but forcefully. When her walls pulsate around me, I push deep one last time before I grip her hips and find my much-needed release.

I pull out of her and go sit on the bed, elbows on my knees, head slumped down in front of me. I should feel better. That's why we do this, to feel better after a shitty case. Maybe this one was just so shitty, no amount of fucking can help.

I pick up my scrubs and put them back on.

"Better?" Gina asks, as she cleans up at the sink.

"Yeah, thanks," I lie.

"Anytime," she says. She gets her clothes off the floor and comes to sit next to me. "I mean it, Kyle. I'm here for you. Whenever you need me. *Wherever* you need me—even if it's outside the hospital."

"Yeah, okay." I push myself off the bed and head for the door. "I have a patient to check on. I'll see you later, Gina."

I run my hands through my hair and realize the smell of sex is still on them, so I head for the nearest bathroom to wash my hands. I look in the mirror and study my face.

"Stupid bastard," I say to my reflection. "She's handing herself to you on a goddamn platter and you couldn't get out of there fast enough."

Gina is great. Smart. Beautiful. Fun. And she's obviously ready to take this to the next level. Maybe she has been for a while. Maybe I've just been too stupid to see the signs. Maybe I need to give this a chance. We're good together. She could be my Mallory, or my Charlie.

Do I want a Mallory or Charlie?

I stare in the mirror and wonder if my sisters-in-law would be able to console my brothers after a similarly-horrible experience. Yes. They would. They pretty much have.

I wash my face, and then stare at my hands. I start to shake thinking of what I held in them not even an hour ago. I look around, seeing if there is another chair I can kick. There's not. So I suck it up, put my lab coat on and compose myself enough to go check on my patient.

CHAPTER TEN

When I get to Elizabeth's room, it's empty, but I hear the shower running in her bathroom. I sit down on the chair next to the bed and close my eyes for a minute. Then I smile when I hear the familiar "Da-da-da-daaaaa" sound coming from the TV and look up to see she'd been watching ESPN again.

Then I look at her bedside tray to see it piled high with various flavors of Jell-O.

Then I look at the fetal monitor next to the bed and all I can see is Jenny Beaumont's face when I told her her baby was dead.

I hear the bathroom door open. I scrub my hands across the two-day stubble on my jaw, trying to rid my head of the painful memory.

"Oh, hi, Kyle," Elizabeth says, walking across the room fresh from a shower. Her blonde hair, that falls just below her chin, is darker and wavier when it's wet; and her face, devoid of all makeup, looks fresh and almost adolescent.

I stand up and help her back into bed. Then I get the fetal monitor hooked up again.

She looks at the clock on the wall. "Yes!" she shouts. "Eight minutes."

I look at her in confusion.

"Abby said I had ten minutes to shower, but I did it in eight." She gives me a triumphant smile.

I shake my head in awe at her excitement. I guess I was right about it not taking much to please her.

"What?" she says. "If I'm going to be stuck in this place, I might as well make the little things count, right?"

"I like your attitude," I say, walking back to the table where I left her chart. "No more heavy bleeding?" I ask.

"Nope," she says with another pleasing smile. "Just some spotting."

"That's good." I open her chart and read the nurse's notes. I catch a glimpse of her recent ultrasound and let out a deep sigh as it has me thinking about earlier.

I don't usually sit down in patient rooms, but I do now. I sit down and pinch the bridge of my nose. Maybe I'm getting sick. I just feel—off.

"What's wrong, Kyle?"

I shake off the feeling and look up at her. "Aren't I supposed to be asking you that?"

"You just seem different," she says, studying me.

"I'm fine," I say. I nod to the television. "What's with you and ESPN? You really are a sports junkie, huh?"

She laughs. "I am. I'm trying to catch up on all the scores. I don't own a TV. I usually go to Sal's to catch the highlights."

"Sal's on 52nd?" I ask.

"You know the place?"

"Best egg rolls in New York," I say.

"Oh, my God, right?" Her eyes roll in appreciation. "I walked his dog for a week when his regular guy went on vacation. After that, he let me come in and watch TV even if I couldn't buy anything." Her eyes snap to mine and she shuts up as if what she said was too revealing. "Um, he had a beautiful Wheaton Terrier named Wonton."

"Wonton?"

"Yeah. A dog named Wonton owned by a guy named Sal who runs a Chinese food restaurant. Pretty crazy. You'd think he'd own a pizza place or something with that name. Sal's Pizza," she muses.

I eye her tray table. "Speaking of food, what's with all the Jell-O?"

She laughs. "Abby said Jell-O is pretty much a staple here at the hospital, and since I'm going to be here a while, I might as well figure out which flavor is my favorite. So, she brought me all of them to try. I really like her."

"Oh," I say, looking out her window to check out the approaching summer storm.

"Kyle?"

I look back at her and see the concern etched in her face. "Something's wrong, isn't it?" she asks.

She looks worried and I realize that maybe she thinks I'm here to give her bad news about her or the baby.

"Everything is fine. You're doing well and so is the baby."

"Not with me," she says. "Something is wrong with *you*. What is it?"

I shake my head. "Just a difficult case, that's all. Nature of the job."

"I'm sorry." She reaches over and touches my shoulder in the same way I comforted her the other night. She studies me. "You need a distraction. Something to get your mind off whatever is bothering you."

"Let me guess," I say, looking up at the TV. "ESPN? Or maybe you had something else in mind. One of those survivalist programs perhaps? Bare-ass naked guy climbs into volcano whilst trying not to roast his balls?"

She laughs for the third time. *Why am I even counting?* Then she asks, "Whilst?"

"Sorry, I guess my British attending is rubbing off on me."

She nods. "Oh, right, the one who sentenced you to babysitting duty."

"Not a sentence," I say. "A privilege."

She rolls her eyes. "Whatever you say, *Dr. Stone*. And no, I wasn't referring to watching television to get your mind off things. I was thinking of a game my friends and I used to play in college when we were stressed out over an exam." She frowns. "But now that I think of it, it wouldn't work in this situation."

"Why not?" I ask, intrigued.

"Well, because for one, I'm pregnant; and two, you're working which probably means drinking alcohol would be frowned upon."

"Probably," I say sarcastically. "What game was it?"

Her face pinks up. "It's totally juvenile. But it was fun. I don't know why I even thought of it. It's stupid."

"After the way you just blushed, now you *have* to tell me, Elizabeth. What is it?"

"Fine. But don't say I didn't warn you." Her face breaks into an adolescent smile. "Have you ever played 'Never have I ever'?"

I draw my brows together thinking of the games my brothers and I would play in the old neighborhood. "Is it anything like 'Spin the bottle' or 'Truth or dare'?"

She giggles. "Not *that* juvenile," she says. "In 'Never have I ever,' you say something you've never done before and if anyone else in the room has done it, they take a drink. It's fun." Then she looks embarrassed again. "Well, it was when I was nineteen. Sorry, it was a stupid idea."

I smile. She doesn't know what a great idea it really is. Elizabeth is a closed book. Not once has she ever given anyone details about her except where her pregnancy is concerned. And I could use something to get my mind off things. Every time I look at my damn hand, I think of the tiny girl I was holding in it earlier. "No, I want to play," I tell her.

She looks at me awkwardly. "What don't you understand about the whole drinking thing?"

"We're not going to drink alcohol, Elizabeth. Although I do have a damn fine bottle of champagne in my locker."

"Why do you have a bottle of champagne in your locker?" she asks. "Hot date after work?"

"Ha! Hardly. I'm a second-year resident. There isn't any time for dating. No, I had a professor in medical school, Dr. Williston, who said every new doctor should keep a bottle handy because you never know when you are going to want to celebrate that one great thing. He said for some it would be the first time they do a solo surgery. For others, the first time they deliver a baby. Or maybe for when you save a life by making a difficult diagnosis."

"And you haven't opened it yet?" she asks.

I shake my head. "Haven't felt the urge."

"It'll happen," she says, encouragingly. "Probably when you least expect it."

"I suppose," I say. "Anyway, alcohol is not required under *my* rules of the game."

I look around the room for ideas when my eyes land on the tray table beside her bed. I stand up and walk around the room to examine the Jell-O cups. There are six different flavors. Six possible things I can learn about the girl lying in this bed. My mind starts to go over all the possible questions.

"We'll play for Jell-O," I tell her. "And we play until each of us has tried every one."

"Jell-O?" she asks, like I'm off my rocker.

"Why not? Abby said you need to pick your favorite flavor; and I, as the great babysitter I am, will play the stupid, juvenile game just to make you happy." I wink down at her.

She smiles and tucks a lock of wet hair behind her ear. "Fine," she says, pretending to pout—but I know better. She's happy.

She reaches over and grabs a couple of spoons encased in plastic. She hands me one. "I'll go first, just so you'll know how to play."

"You better," I say. "This medical degree I have might not qualify me to understand the rudimentary rules of a childhood game."

"Shut up," she says, laughing at me. "Okay, I'm going first anyway. Um . . . let me think." She looks at me and scrunches up her nose to form a small wrinkle. "Never have I ever been a doctor."

I roll my eyes at her. "Really?"

"Just trying to make sure you get how to play. Now pick your flavor."

I open the tinfoil top on the yellow one and take a bite. Lemon—not my favorite.

"Okay, now it's my turn. Never have I ever been out of the country."

Her hand doesn't move at all. "Back to me," she says. "Never have I ever ridden a horse."

I pick up the light-green cup and take a bite. It's friggin' gross. "Tenth grade," I say, choking the bite down. "The horse's name was Beauty. She bucked me off and I broke my damn leg. Alright, let's see . . . never have I ever had stitches."

She picks up the yellow one and takes a bite. "You must have led a sheltered life," she says, pulling her leg out from under the blanket. She points to her ankle. "Scooter accident when I was eight." Then she shows me her left elbow. "Softball field. Fourteen years old. Didn't know there was a break in the fence when I dove for a ball. Ripped my elbow from here to here." She runs her finger along the faded scar.

"And this one?" I ask, touching the faint scar on her collarbone.

She looks up at me, frozen. *Damn it.* I shouldn't have touched her.

Why the hell did you touch her?

I pull my hand back as she clears her throat. "Uh, I forgot about that one. It's not nearly as interesting, I—I fell into the corner of a table."

"Age?"

"Huh?" she asks.

"You were eight when you fell off the scooter and fourteen when you dove for the softball. How old were you when you fell into the table?"

"Oh . . . uh, twenty-three," she says.

"After a night of playing 'Never have I ever'?" I joke.

She smiles morosely. "Funny, but no." She pushes the yellow Jell-O across her tray table with her nose in the air. "Definitely not that one," she says. "Okay, never have I ever flown in an airplane."

I pick up the red cup and open it before dipping my spoon in. "Mmmm, pretty good," I say, swallowing the strawberry confection. "My parents moved us from New York to California when I was fifteen. They still live there so I fly out when I can, which isn't much these days."

"It's nice that you get to see them," she says sadly. "Even if it's only occasionally."

The look on her face. *Jesus.* She really doesn't have anyone, does she?

"My turn again." I can't think of one. My mind is blank. She's going to think I'm a lame doctor who can't think up a stupid question. I just spout out the first thing that comes to mind. "Never have I ever been married."

"I, uh . . ." She looks at the cups in front of her and then out the window.

Damn it. I went too far. I *am* a lame fucking doctor. What was I thinking?

There's a knock on the door. I turn around to see Mallory standing in the doorway with a few bags in her hands. I walk over to help her with them, relieved to be saved from my stupidity.

"Hi, Mal. Thanks for coming. Elizabeth, this is my sister-in-law, Mallory. I thought that since you two are about the same age and you obviously have something in common, you should meet."

Mallory rubs her pregnant belly as she walks over to the bed. "Hi, Elizabeth. It's really nice to meet you."

"You, too," Elizabeth says, looking confused.

Mallory notices her reaction, too. "When Kyle said he had a pregnant patient who was on bed rest for what could be weeks, I told him I wanted to stop by and keep you company. I can't even imagine what it must be like to be quarantined away from the world. Would you mind if I sat with you for a while?"

Elizabeth smiles, looking more at ease. "Mind? Not at all, it would be great to have some company."

She looks guiltily at me. "Not that you aren't good company, Kyle, uh . . . Dr. Stone, but you have no idea what it's like to be pregnant."

"It's still Kyle," I tell her. "Mal is family." I walk around the bed to clean up the Jell-O. "We'll finish our game another time, okay?"

She nods.

"I'm off after rounds, so I'll see you tomorrow, Elizabeth. Thanks again, Mal."

"Anytime," she says.

I walk out the door and stand there for a minute, eavesdropping.

"My brother-in-law is a pretty great doctor, don't you think?" Mallory asks.

"He is," Elizabeth says. "He's a lot nicer than most doctors I've met."

"He's a lot nicer than most *people*," Mal says. "You won't find a better breed than the Stone brothers. Then again, I may be a bit biased. So how far along are you?"

I leave them to their conversation, walking down the hall with a huge smile on my face, realizing just how much better I feel leaving her room than when I first entered it.

CHAPTER ELEVEN

"Sorry I bailed on you the other day. Would have been nice to play ball with the guys."

"Not a problem," Chad says, taking a bite of his dinner. "It's what you signed up for. It's not like it hasn't happened a thousand times before with Mom and Dad."

I nod, laughing. Many dinners, soccer matches, and family outings were interrupted due to my parents' chosen careers. They are both doctors. I know they like to think they influenced me to follow in their footsteps, but the truth is, I'd have become a doctor anyway. I think I was born for it. There was never even a choice in the matter.

Mallory starts to get up from the table. "You need a refill," she says, nodding to my empty wine glass.

I put my hand on her arm to stop her. "Stay put, Mal. I'll get it."

"Thanks," she says, rubbing her growing belly.

"So, how long are you in town for this time?" I ask Chad.

"Well, since *Defcon Three* is pretty much wrapped up, I'll only need to head back to L.A. for some voice-overs and promo spots. *Dark Tunnels* won't be released until after the baby comes, so that means press junkets won't start until early next year. And filming for *Out of the Deep* starts in the spring."

He puts a hand on Mal's pregnant belly. "All in all, I don't think we could have timed this better."

"You're forgetting how we'll need to go to L.A. to collect your Golden Globe and your Oscar," Mal adds.

Chad smirks at her. "Yeah, right."

"That's no joke, bro," I tell him. "Don't sell yourself short."

My uber-famous brother, who was going to be a school teacher like his wife, was randomly discovered while saving my ass at a shopping mall shortly after our parents moved us to L.A. It was tough on Chad, leaving Mallory, who was his best friend; which is why when the opportunity presented itself, he turned to drugs. And women. And gambling. Pretty much anything to distract him from the girl he'd left behind. But in the end, they found each other. And they've never been happier than they are right now.

I can't help but think of Elizabeth and how she asked if I believed in fate.

As if reading my thoughts, Mallory says, "I really like Elizabeth."

"Yeah. She's one tough chick," I say. "I can't begin to thank you enough for going by the hospital."

"I hope I didn't offend her by bringing her a few things."

I remember the bags she showed up with. "The bags were for her?" I ask.

She nods. "When you told me she literally had nothing and no one, I had to ask myself if I were in that situation, what would I need. And since your generous mother keeps sending me maternity clothes that I will never be able to wear due to the sheer numbers of them, I thought I'd take a few things to her."

"You brought her clothes?"

"It was just a few nightgowns and a cute pajama set. And a robe. Everyone in the hospital needs a robe. Those blue hospital gowns are simply hideous."

I laugh, thinking Elizabeth looked quite good in them. Blue is definitely her color.

"Oh, and I took her some packs of maternity underwear. She probably thinks I'm a freak, showing up at a stranger's hospital room with underwear."

"Either that or a Godsend," I say in appreciation. "What did you guys talk about?"

She smiles and gives Chad a look. "Are you asking me if we talked about *you*, Kyle?"

"No, of course not." I take a drink of wine to mask my blatant lie.

She laughs. "I'm only teasing," she says. "The girl is pretty tight-lipped and I got the feeling she didn't want me to ask about her. We mostly talked about being pregnant. And she asked a lot of questions about me and how I like being a school teacher. She seemed really interested in it, almost sad in a way, like maybe it's something she had wanted for herself."

"She walks dogs," I tell them. "For her job."

"Yeah, she did tell me that, rather hesitantly," she says. "But, hey, don't think less of her for it. People love their pets. They pay a pretty penny to have them walked. She's probably not as destitute as you're thinking."

"I *don't* think less of her," I say, defensively. "But I'm not sure about the destitute part. I mean, she wouldn't even give us her address when she was admitted to the hospital."

"You're a doctor, Kyle," Mallory says. "She was probably embarrassed to reveal where she lives, knowing the doctors and nurses surrounding her live a far better life."

"Maybe," I say. "Or maybe she doesn't have a home. Or she could live in a shelter."

She shakes her head. "I don't think so. I mean, I work with homeless girls at Hope For Life. No, Elizabeth just seems like one of us. Heck, she'd probably fit right in at girls' night." Her face breaks out in a slow, growing smile. "Oh, Kyle, I have a great idea. I'm sure the girls would love to help her out. Think about it, we can all take turns visiting her. Between all of us, there is no way she'll get bored or depressed, or whatever bedridden patients get."

I study my altruistic sister-in-law. "You think they'd really do that for her?"

"Have you met any of them, dude?" Chad asks, raising his eyebrows at me.

"I don't know," I tell her. "Elizabeth seems like a private person."

"Maybe that's just because she doesn't have anyone, Kyle."

I nod in agreement. "Let me see how she felt about your coming in today. I don't want to overstep my bounds. I'll let you know what I think."

Mallory bounces in her seat as much as a pregnant woman can bounce. She claps her hands giddily. "Oh, good. I'm going to call the girls. It'll be fun."

"She's not a project, Mal. She's a person."

She shoots me a distasteful look. "Of course she's not a project," she says abhorrently. "Kyle, you've always said we're all just one bad circumstance away from being homeless. Well, maybe we can be her *good* circumstance. With all our connections, maybe we can be what helps her turn her life around."

"Alright," I say. "I'll talk to her."

Chad's phone rings. He looks down at it. "It's Dad," he says. He swipes his finger across the screen. "Hi, Dad, you're on speaker. Mal and Kyle are here."

"Hello, everyone," he says. "How's my granddaughter doing in there, Mallory?"

"She's doing very well, Marc, thanks for asking," Mal replies. "Please thank Jackie again for sending another care package."

"She loves doing it, Mallory. So, how are my boys?"

"Good," Chad says.

"Can't complain," I add.

"Except that you do," Chad says.

"What?" I ask.

"Oh, come on, you nearly made my ears go numb with all the bitching you did about your new attending," he says.

"What's this?" Dad asks. "You having trouble with one of your attendings, son?"

I shoot Chad a look of death. He doesn't need to be bringing this shit up with our dad. "No, sir. No problems at all."

Chad blows out something that sounds like, "Pfffffft."

"You need to learn to get along with your attendings, Kyle," Dad says. "Not all of them will share your 'save the world' philosophy."

"I know, Dad. And I do get along with them for the most part. But this one didn't even give me a chance."

"What's his name?" he asks. "Maybe I know him."

I sigh. "It's not a him," I say. "I started my OB rotation this week. I'm working under Dr. Redman. She decided on day one to put me on scut. She assigned me one patient, Dad. *One*. Then she has me running around doing menial crap that interns should be doing, not second-years. Oh, hey, but I did get to deliver a baby the other night. Solo."

I don't tell him about the second one I delivered just this morning.

When I stop talking, I realize Dad is laughing on the other end of the phone.

"Dad?"

"Huh? Oh, sorry. I think that's great, son. Your first solo delivery. Fantastic. Being in emergency medicine, I'm sure it's just the first of many you'll have over your career." He clears his throat. "And, Kyle, I'm pretty sure Dr. Redman's aversion to you is not your fault."

"No, I'm pretty sure it is. She singled me out over all her residents. I just wish I knew what I did to piss her off."

"It's not anything you did, son. It's what *I* did."

"You?"

"Dr. Redman and I did our residencies at the same hospital," he says.

"You know her?"

"Yes," he says. "I dated her."

"You *what?*"

I hear more laughter. This time, it's not only coming from Dad, but Chad and Mallory as well.

"Sorry, son. It appears you've been getting the wrath of a woman scorned. Although you think she'd have long gotten over it by now."

"Scorned?" I ask. "What did you do to her?"

"I broke up with her to date your mother."

I roll my eyes and let my head fall back as I look up at the ceiling. "Great. Just absolutely fucking perfect."

"Don't curse in front of Mallory," Dad reprimands me.

"Sorry."

"Details, Dad," Chad says. "How long were you and Dr. Redman together?"

"Not long, a month or so," he says. "It was near the end of our third year. We had different specialties, obviously, but it was a smaller hospital, so residents pretty much all knew each other, despite their different fields of study. But when your mom joined the program as an intern, I only had eyes for her. I ended it with Louise before I asked your mom out. But she always knew why I left her."

"One month?" I ask. "She's making my life a living hell because she dated you for one month over thirty years ago?"

Dad laughs again. "It appears I'm a hard man to get over."

Great. I have to spend the next four weeks with a woman who hates my father. How'd I get so lucky?

But then I think of all the experiences I've had this week. Tiny, lifeless babies that fit in my hand notwithstanding, I'd say it's been one hell of a week. And I surmise that despite the wicked witch of OB, I am, in fact, pretty damn lucky.

CHAPTER TWELVE

Gina climbs off me and blows out a long breath. "Wow," she says. "Thanks, doctor, I needed that."

I laugh. "I'm here to serve."

"And serve me well, you have," she says, lying down beside me. "Twice."

For once, neither of us is in a hurry to get anywhere. No pagers are going off. Rounds don't start for fifteen minutes. It's quiet. Almost eerily so.

Red runs an even tighter ship than Manning down in the ER. She has us pulling on-call duty every third night. Gina was on call last night, and based on her ragged appearance, it doesn't look like she had much sleep.

"Busy night?" I ask.

"You have no idea." She buries her head into the crook of my neck. She's never done this before. This is dangerously close to cuddling.

We don't cuddle.

I take a beat and try to decide if I like it. But while the jury is still out, I figure I should test the waters, so I slip my arm around her.

She sighs audibly into my shoulder. I take that to mean she's already decided *she* likes it.

I stare down at her long brown hair before I pull it from the confines of her hair tie. I run my fingers through it. I'm not sure why I've always been attracted to brunettes. Maybe because, like every other kid on my street, I had a crush on Mallory Shaffer growing up—the girl who is now married to, and having a kid with, my brother.

I never told Chad that. He'd probably have kicked the shit out of me if I had. He was always super protective of her, even though they were nothing more than best friends back then.

And although I don't share my middle brother's infamous and highly-televised sexual promiscuity, I've dated my fair share of women. Or should I say, I've dated my fair share of brunettes. I twist a chunk of Gina's dark hair around my fingers. Yes, I'm definitely a brunette man.

Gina cranes her neck to look up at me. "We can tell each other stuff, can't we, Kyle? I mean, we've got each other's backs, right?"

My body stiffens. "You didn't kill a patient last night, did you?"

"No, nothing like that. Not yet anyway. But I did disobey an order Dr. Anders gave me. Or rather, I ordered labs she told me not to order. I know it could cost my patient a lot of money. But I really felt strongly that she needed them. I'll take the heat. Even if I'm wrong and the labs don't show anything, I still stand by my decision. But I was too chicken to tell Dr. Anders what I did. I figured I'd just wait for her to see it in the chart. Dr. Redman will probably have my ass when Anders tells her."

"I did something I haven't told anyone about, either," I say.

"Really?" She puts her hand over my heart and holds it there. "Will you tell *me?*"

While it's not entirely true about me not telling *anyone*, I figure we're sharing here. So I decide to bite the bullet and see how she reacts to my revelation.

"I'm paying for a patient's entire hospital stay."

"And by entire stay, you mean . . ."

"I mean my patient, my *one* patient who is pregnant and on bed rest until she delivers. I think she might be homeless, although she won't admit it. She walks dogs to get cash, Gina. She was admitted with only the clothes on her back. She has nothing. And nobody has come to visit her."

"Oh, my God, that's so sad," she says. "But if she's homeless, what's the point in paying her bill? You can't squeeze blood from a turnip. We have to treat her anyway."

"I don't know. Just a feeling, I guess. I didn't want her stuck in some shared hospital room without windows for weeks on end, which is what we both know would have happened."

"So you're saying she's better than the other homeless people we treat?"

"No, of course not," I say. "I don't know why I did it exactly. I can't explain it. She's not telling me her whole story. But I get the idea that there's more to her than meets the eye."

She wraps her leg around my leg and squeezes me tightly against her.

Yeah, definitely cuddling.

"You are a bleeding heart, Dr. Stone."

"So, you don't think I crossed a line?" I ask.

"We wouldn't be good doctors if we didn't cross the line sometimes," she says.

I nod, somewhat relieved that Gina doesn't have a problem with this.

"Oh, and I found out why Red has it out for me. She was my dad's girlfriend during residency. He broke up with her for my mom."

She laughs. "Seriously? Oh, Kyle, it sucks to be you right now. Good thing obstetrics isn't your specialty."

"No shit," I say.

Gina's pager goes off. She stretches up to kiss me. This is new, too. I mean, we kiss all the time. But only when we're fucking. Never after.

"I might miss rounds. Depends on what's up," she says. "So, I'll see you later?"

"Yeah, see you later," I say, gathering my scrubs off the floor.

We don't ever round on Elizabeth. And we won't unless anything changes. As Dr. Redman said, her case doesn't interest her.

As it turns out, Gina does, in fact, miss rounds. *Damn.* Must mean she has a good case. I don't ever get paged. Not unless the other residents are busy. It was just my luck that they were all fucking busy when the Beaumonts came in. I mainly spend my days fetching labs, drawing blood, and covering non-emergent cases. I'm nothing more than a glorified nurse. I'm the low man. And now I know that's how it'll be.

Three and a half weeks of being Redman's slave. Then I'll be free from her.

Then something happens. My heart misses a beat. And if I'm not mistaken, it happened when I thought that in three and a half weeks, I'll not only be free from Red, but from my one and only patient.

I shake off the notion and head to the cafeteria after rounds for a quick breakfast of a bagel and some coffee. On my way out, something on the dessert cart catches my eye.

I walk over and pick out six various cups of Jell-O, earning me an amused look from the cashier.

"Research," I say.

She furrows her brow at me as I laugh, grabbing two spoons before I head out the door.

CHAPTER THIRTEEN

I stop at Elizabeth's door before I enter her room. I'm awestruck by what I see. I was wrong, blue is not her color. It's green. Definitely green.

I'm assuming she's wearing something Mallory brought her yesterday. It's hot today, and she's not beneath the bed sheet, so I can pretty much see her from head to toe. Her tanned legs are crossed at the ankles and I follow the shapeliness of them until my eyes meet the frayed hem of the sleeping shorts she's wearing. The matching top is riding up on her stomach where the monitor is strapped around her, showing off the flesh of her ribs. The top, also frayed at the hem, boasts a pattern of hearts over her left breast.

I finish my perusal of her when my gaze reaches her face, where I find her eyes glued to the television.

"Yes!" she yells suddenly, causing me to jump out of my skin.

Having been pulled out of my trance, I finally cross the threshold into her room. I look up at the TV to see what's so exciting. Baseball scores. She's excited over baseball scores.

Her eyes flitter briefly to mine and she smiles before focusing on the screen once again. "Highlights are next," she says. "Want to watch them with me?"

"Sure." I put the cups and spoons on the table next to her bed and sit down in the chair.

We silently watch the highlight reels of yesterday's baseball games. I'm about to say something, when she sits up suddenly and cheers.

"Oh, my God, did you see that? That was a double play!" she squeals, her face beaming.

The reel plays two or three more times because I guess it's a contender for their play of the week. A catcher for the New York Nighthawks dances backwards, tripping over the umpire to get to a high-tipped foul ball, catching it before throwing it to second base to get out the runner, who apparently didn't think the catcher would get to the ball, so he was just walking back to the base.

"Impressive," I say.

The program goes on to show highlights of other MLB games and Elizabeth becomes uninterested, turning the volume down before she notices the Jell-O cups stacked on the tray table. She questions me with raised brows.

"For round two," I say. "Unless you've already picked your favorite."

She smiles sadly. "I haven't, but I'm not sure I'm up for that game again."

Damn. I did go too far with the whole married question. But it makes me wonder just what's going on with her. Was she upset because she *is* married, or because she *isn't?*

"Not to worry, I'll go easy on you." I nod to a robe tossed over the back of the chair. "Now let's get your robe on, I'm breaking you out of this popsicle stand."

"Really?" Her blue eyes light up.

God, I'm going to miss those amazing blue eyes in three and a half weeks.

Wait . . . what the hell, Kyle? She's your patient. You're with Gina. You are with Gina, right?

"The wheelchair you requested, Dr. Stone," Abby says, bringing it to Elizabeth's bedside. Then she walks around her bed and takes the blood pressure cuff out of the basket and proceeds to place it on Elizabeth's arm. "If you're going on an outing, we need to make sure you're all good. And you should visit the bathroom first to make sure you aren't bleeding."

"Slave driver," I say to Abby with a wink.

After Elizabeth uses the bathroom, I hand her the lightweight robe from the chair. "This is nice," I say, running my hand over the soft material.

"I know, right?" she says. "Your sister-in-law gave it to me, along with this sleeper set and a few nightgowns. She said your mother spoils her and she had too many to wear. She even brought me a few books on what to do when you're bedridden during pregnancy. I like her. She seems pretty great."

"Mallory is one of the good ones," I say. "You know, I have another sister-in-law who would love to visit you as well. And a few friends of mine, three sisters actually, who could keep you company."

I help her into the wheelchair and then hand her the spoons and the Jell-O.

"I'm not a charity case, Kyle." She looks up at me in a huff. "Oh, my God, did you tell them I'm homeless? I'm not, you know. I have a place. It's nothing special, but at least it's mine."

A wave of relief courses through me knowing she wasn't living on the streets.

"I didn't tell them anything, Elizabeth. There are rules, you know. But when I was having dinner with Mallory and my brother last night, she mentioned how much she thought you were like her group of friends. Said you'd probably fit right in. She thought maybe they could each come meet you, you know, to break up the monotony. Keep you from going stir crazy."

"I guess it might be nice to have some visitors," she says as I wheel her into the hallway.

"Then it's okay if I tell them they can stop by?" I ask with a hopeful grin.

She nods hesitantly. "I'm just not sure what they expect to get out of it."

"How about a new friend?" I ask.

"Friend," she muses mostly to herself as if it's a foreign concept.

I push the down button for the elevator. "Elizabeth, I'm glad to hear you have a place, even if you think it's nothing special. But I have to ask—you'll be here for a long time, how are you going to make the rent?"

"Luckily, I paid it the day before I was admitted. That was on the second so it will get me through to the end of August."

"What about after that?" I ask. "You aren't working now. What'll you do when you get discharged?" I crouch down beside her and keep my voice low. "I'd like to help. You know, just until you get back on your—"

"Kyle, stop," she says, disapprovingly. "I'm not about to take any handouts. Besides, you're a resident. I've seen *Grey's Anatomy*. I know you probably don't make much more than what covers your own rent. Thank you, but no. I'll be fine. I'll figure it out."

I nod, not wanting to push her on the subject. "Okay, but the offer stands. If you get home and you realize—"

She stops my words with her venomous stare. "What about me not taking handouts do you not understand, Dr. Stone?"

Shit.

STONE VOWS

"Sorry," I say, putting my hands up in surrender. "Not another word. I have no doubt you'll figure it all out. You're a strong woman, Elizabeth."

The elevator arrives and I push her in, pressing the button for the ground floor.

"Why would you say that? That I'm strong," she asks. "You don't even know me."

"Yeah, but I know *people*," I tell her. "A lot of people come through the doors of this hospital. As doctors, part of our job is to read the signs, learn what they can and can't handle. My instinct tells me that you've probably already handled a lot. Becoming a single parent can't be easy, yet I've never heard you complain about it."

She rubs a hand across her belly. "Not much I can do about it now," she says. "This is happening whether I had planned on it or not. Might as well make the best of it."

I roll her through two sets of double doors to the courtyard in the center of the hospital. All the wings of the hospital are built around the large arboretum that is lined with trees, benches and decorative sidewalks.

They can't build hospitals like this in the city anymore. But this one was one of the original hospitals in New York, built over a hundred years ago. It's considered a historic building, in fact, so it can't be torn down to maximize space.

Being in the courtyard is nothing like walking around the city. It's quiet. Peaceful. Serene. I remember spending hours upon hours out here studying for my intern exams last spring.

"Oh, wow," Elizabeth says, as I push her down the path towards a seating area. "The flowers are amazing."

"Would you believe the hospital employs its own gardener?"

89

"I believe it," she says. "Normally these types of flowers wouldn't grow without full sunlight." She looks up at the eight-story building that surrounds the courtyard. "A good bit of light is blocked by the building. He must work very hard."

"You garden?" I ask.

"Oh, yes," she says. Then her smile falls. "Well, I used to."

I stop pushing her when we reach my favorite bench. "This okay?" I ask.

"Perfect," she says. "I would have picked this bench, too."

I tilt my head at her. "Why?"

"See those flowers? They're lavender, a calming flower. Their scent is supposed to help with stress. A lot of people spray it in their bedrooms at night to help them sleep."

"Ahh, well, that explains it then."

"Explains what?" she asks.

"How I passed my intern exams. I used to sit here on this bench every chance I got to study for them."

She laughs. "How did a plant that makes you sleepy help you pass your tests?"

"You said yourself it helps with stress."

"By making you sleepy," she says with an eye roll.

"Oh, well whatever it was, it worked because I rocked my exams."

She smiles. "I can see that about you. You look like you are very dedicated to becoming a great doctor. I'll bet you'll be one of the best male obstetricians at this hospital."

I guffaw loudly. "Oh, hell, no. While I want to learn everything I can about delivering babies, I've no intention of doing it for my career. And thank God for that because my attending hates me, or rather, she hates my father."

She shakes her head. "What? Why does she hate your dad, and why are you working on the OB floor if you aren't going to be an obstetrician?"

"First, my dad slept with my attending—over thirty years ago, mind you. Then he left her for my mother. Guess she holds a long damn grudge. Second, my specialty is emergency medicine. The first time you came to the hospital, I was on an ER rotation. That is where I'll spend more than half of this year. When you came back, earlier this week, I was starting my OB rotation where I'll be for the next several weeks. I'll also do rotations in pediatric intensive care, trauma, and critical care."

"So, you'll only be babysitting me for a few weeks?" She sighs and looks down at the sidewalk, biting the nail of her pinky finger.

"Three and a half more weeks, to be exact. I think you'll more than likely deliver before I'm done with my rotation. Thirty-seven weeks is when we'll schedule you for a C-section if it doesn't happen before then."

She rubs her belly protectively. "I hope it doesn't happen before then. He or she needs more time in there."

"He or she is getting the very best care possible, Elizabeth. Don't you worry."

I reach over and take the cups of Jell-O from her. "I believe it's still my turn," I say, handing her one of the spoons.

She looks at me wearily, with trepidation. I know she thinks I'm going to ask her the same question we ended on yesterday.

"So, Ms. Smith, never have I ever read a romance novel. And if you knew who my friends were, that might surprise you, because one of them is an author."

Elizabeth picks up the purple container. "I'm only taking one bite, even though I've read about a thousand of them. What's your friend's name? Has she written anything good?"

"She's pretty successful," I say. "Some of her books have been made into movies. Her name is Baylor McBride, but she writes under the name Baylor Mitchell. My sister-in-law, Charlie, was practically raised with her and her two sisters."

She swallows her Jell-O before her jaw hits her lap. "Shut up!" she says. "You know Baylor Mitchell?"

"You've heard of her?"

"Heard of her? I have several signed copies of her books." She frowns. "Well, I used to. But, yes, she's one of my favorite authors. Wait . . ." She looks at me all wide-eyed before bouncing around in her chair. "Don't tell me she's one of the sisters you were telling me about who you wanted to come visit me."

I nod in amusement at her giddiness.

"No way." She looks down at her robe, smoothing it onto her legs. "I mean, I don't have any clothes. I can't meet her. Oh, my God, Kyle. Really?"

I laugh. "Yes, really. And believe me when I tell you she won't give a shit what you wear, Elizabeth." I hold up my unused spoon. "Now, come on, it's your turn."

She tries to tamp down her ear-to-ear smile but doesn't do a very good job of it. Damn, I love pleasing this woman.

"Um . . ." She bites down on her lower lip in thought. And, Christ Almighty, if watching her do that doesn't do something to me. "Never have I ever written my name in the snow with pee," she says.

I laugh, grabbing the purple Jell-O cup. "That was way too easy," I say, before taking a bite. Then I take my turn. "Never have I ever eaten oysters."

She looks like she swallowed a bug before she picks up the red cup and takes a bite.

"Not an oyster fan?" I ask.

She shakes her head. "I never developed a taste for them, not even after having them dozens of times."

I cock my head to the side. "Then why keep punishing yourself by eating them?"

She shrugs. "Sometimes it just wasn't worth an argument."

I nod in understanding. "Parents torture you with slimy sea creatures?"

"Something like that," she says with a sad smile. "Kyle, I'm kind of tired, would you mind taking me back up to my room?"

"Of course," I say, gathering up the spoons and cups and tossing them into a nearby trashcan.

She's silent the entire way back to her room, making me wonder if talking about her parents is a difficult subject. Maybe they're dead which is one of the reasons she's alone.

When I get her hooked back up to the fetal monitor, she looks up at the TV and then back at me. "Kyle?" she asks. "Would you watch a baseball game with me tomorrow night? I mean, since you're required to babysit me and all?"

"I'm not on duty then, so—"

"It's okay," she cuts me off, trying her best not to look sad. "Never mind then."

"Elizabeth, would you shut up for a second," I say, my lips twitching in amusement. "I was going to say that since I'm not on duty, I can stay for the whole game without being interrupted by pages and scut work."

"I would never ask you to stay here on your night off," she says, looking guilty. "You probably work too much as it is."

"Watching a baseball game with my favorite patient is hardly work, Elizabeth."

"I thought I was your *only* patient," she says.

"You are. That makes you my favorite." I wink at her.

She rolls her eyes just as my pager goes off.

"Get some rest," I tell her. "I'll be back to check on you later."

"Doctor's orders?" she asks.

"Doctor's orders," I say, walking out her door.

As I make my way to the nurses' station to answer my page, I realize I'm excited about tomorrow night. And for the life of me, I can't remember anything I've looked forward to as much as this.

CHAPTER FOURTEEN

I haven't had time to check on Elizabeth since I did her daily ultrasound this morning. I've been slammed with patients because one of the other residents went down with a stomach bug and I had to take over all her cases. But I take a minute to stop by the nurses' station to look at her chart.

"She's doing great," Abby says. "Still some minor bleeding today, but her BP is good and fetal heart tones are normal."

"Good," I mumble, perusing the chart. I flip to the back of the file and look at the pictures from her first ultrasound in the ER a few weeks ago. It was an extensive one. One that clearly shows the baby's gender.

Elizabeth doesn't know it, but she's having a girl. I've had to catch myself sometimes when referring to the baby, and of course there is that note I wrote on the inner flap of her chart to alert staff that she doesn't want to be told.

I try to picture her as a mom. My gut tells me she'll be a good one. She's calm, collected, and funny. And she loves sports, well baseball anyway. But she never talks about becoming a mother. She's only ever mentioned the one time that this was unexpected. Maybe it's because I'm a guy. Perhaps she'll talk about it more when the girls come to keep her company.

"Someone special finally coming to visit her?" Abby asks, nodding down the corridor.

"What?" I ask, closing the chart and putting it away.

"Elizabeth," she says. "She's seemed giddy all afternoon, and she put on makeup and fixed her hair. Figured someone was coming to see her. The baby daddy maybe."

I look down the hallway, not able to help the smile that overtakes my face. Elizabeth's room is right at the end of the hall, so I have a clear view into it. I can see her sitting on the bed reading one of the pregnancy books Mallory brought her.

Abby must follow my gaze. "That girl is a strange breed," she says, narrowing her eyes as she studies Elizabeth. "Every other patient spends hours a day on their phone or laptop. I'm not even sure Elizabeth *has* a phone. And the girl never complains. Not when I wake her up at six in the morning to take her vitals. Not even when she gets served crappy hospital food." She laughs. "Oh, Lord, today is meatloaf day—bless her heart if she doesn't complain about *that*."

Abby gets called away and I'm left staring down the hallway.

I'm pretty sure Elizabeth has a phone. She called me once. But maybe she borrowed one. I pull mine out and scroll back to the day she called me. I find the number and tap on it to place a call.

Elizabeth looks up from her book. She looks scared. Shit, I didn't mean to scare her. I guess she's not used to hearing her phone ring. She lets it ring a few times, then she puts down her book and reaches over into her side table drawer.

She pulls out something that looks like a discount store phone, definitely not a smartphone, but one that probably only calls and texts. She closes her eyes briefly before answering. Maybe she's saying a prayer. Maybe she wants it to be the baby's father. Maybe she's about to be heartbroken that it's just me calling.

I see her bring the phone up to her ear. "Hello?" she answers tentatively.

"I forgot to tell you not to eat dinner," I say.

"What?" She looks anxious as her pinky finger finds her mouth.

"Elizabeth, it's Kyle. I wanted to make sure you didn't eat the meatloaf. It's horrendous. I'll take care of dinner, okay?"

"Kyle," she says my name in a rush of air that sounds an awful lot like a relieved sigh.

Then she looks at the ceiling and smiles. She smiles big.

Lucky fucking ceiling.

"The game starts at seven," she says. "I'll be starving by then. I might have to break out some Jell-O."

I laugh. "Don't you dare. We're going to finish what we started. No cheating and doing it without me."

"Okay. See you at seven," she says.

"See you then."

I disconnect the call and watch her stare at her phone. She runs her fingers across the keys longingly. Lovingly. Maybe she's hoping someone else will call.

But that smile. That sigh. Could it be *mine* was the call she wanted?

"Kyle?"

I look up from my trance to see Gina trying to get my attention. She looks down the hall to where I was staring. "That your homeless patient?" she asks.

"She's not homeless, Gina," I say defensively. Maybe a little too defensively based on the look on Gina's face.

"Is that so?" she asks, studying me.

"Hey, have you seen Cameron today?" I ask, trying to distract her. "I heard he was going to assist on a reconstructive surgery."

"I think he's doing it right now," she says. "Hey, maybe the three of us should go celebrate his accomplishment later. I mean, I'm on call tonight, but I could sneak across the street to Happy's and toast him with a Diet Coke or something."

She wants to see me outside the hospital? Well, not just me, me and Cam, but still . . . *me.*

I peek down the hallway to see Elizabeth reading her book again. "Uh, can't tonight. But yeah, some other time maybe. That could be fun."

She smiles at the prospect. Then she looks around to make sure we're alone. "Room 1320?" she asks with a raised brow.

I can't help but steal another quick glance towards the room at the end of the hall. What is wrong with me? I've got all kinds of shit going through my head right now. I can't think straight. My thoughts are all over the place. I'm thinking of blurred lines that have already been crossed. Vows I've made to help those I can. Unspoken promises between Gina and me.

"Sorry, I'm swamped," I say. "With Morgan out sick, I've got a lot on my plate. Rain check?"

She studies me again. Then she looks down the hall. "Yeah, I can see how busy you are, Dr. Stone. I guess I'll catch you later."

As she walks away, my eyes ping-pong between her and Elizabeth's room.

Fuck.

My uncomplicated life just got a lot more complicated.

CHAPTER FIFTEEN

I step into the elevator and turn around to watch the doors close. Then I study myself in the reflective chrome.

Shit.

What I see looks an awful lot like a guy going to a girl's house for a date.

I showered. Shaved even. I used cologne for Christ's sake. I can't even remember the last time I did that. I have a bag full of Sal's Chinese takeout that could feed an army.

Yeah, definitely crossing a line.

But is it a line I want to cross? I know nothing about Elizabeth. Except that she has three scars, hates oysters and has never been out of the country.

She could be anyone. A girl on the run. A criminal.

No. No way.

I can see it in her eyes. She's no criminal. But she's . . . something. A closed book, that's for sure. I've never seen someone so strong yet so helpless at the same time.

And she's not even my type. Gina—she's my type. Elizabeth is so far removed from my type, she's not even in the same damn ballpark. My girlfriends have all been scholars. Glass-ceiling types who won't take shit from anyone.

But then again, Elizabeth doesn't take shit from me. Every time I try to pry, she puts me in my place.

And she's pregnant. Soooo not my type. I need a family as much as I need a hole in my head. And what the hell has she done to make me even think she's the least bit interested?

Okay, so she smiled when I called her. Maybe she was just so glad it wasn't her landlord or a bill collector that she had no choice but to crack her face in two with a smile that could brighten a room at midnight.

She's not a brunette. There, that proves it. I'm only attracted to brunettes.

This is just a friendly dinner with a patient who needs friends. And by the time I reach her room, I've all but convinced myself of it. But then I stop in the doorway, my breath hitching when I see her.

I was wrong. Green isn't her color, either. It's pink. Definitely pink. But hell, she looks good in anything. Maybe *every* color is her color.

She's talking to someone, but I don't see anyone in the room. Then I see her rub her belly and it dawns on me that she's talking to the baby. I've never wanted to hear a conversation as much as I want to hear this one. And then, Holy God, I realize she's not talking at all. She's singing.

I lean in further and catch a few words, just enough to recognize the tune.

"Blackbird singing in the dead of night . . ." she sings sweetly.

Damn it if my dick didn't just swell in my pants.

This is wrong, Kyle. You should turn around and go find Gina. Page her and meet her in the on-call room and fuck her brains out. Fuck all this . . . whatever this is . . . out of your system. She's your goddamn patient. And she's pregnant. She's off limits.

But my feet are cemented to the floor and I strain to hear her soft voice sing that sweet melody.

Turn around, Kyle. Walk away.

I will my feet to shuffle backwards, inch by slow inch until I've backed up a few feet from her room. Far enough so I can't hear her sing. I close my eyes and breathe. I can breathe better if I'm not hearing her sing. I convince myself to walk away. I can do this. I'm a doctor. I get called into emergencies all the time. Hell, maybe I can go downstairs and find a case to work on. Then it wouldn't even be a lie when I tell Elizabeth I was working.

"Dr. Stone, you're still here?"

Shit.

I see Elizabeth's head snap towards the door as I look behind me to see Abby questioning me. Too late to get out of this now.

"Hi, Abby. I thought I'd save our patient from meatloaf night," I say, holding up the bag of food.

"Is that so?" she says, giving me a look. A look of disapproval. A look that says I should be home sleeping. Or hanging out with the guys. Or paging Gina.

A look that says I'm crossing the line.

"I think I went a little overboard," I tell her, nodding to the large Sal's bag. "You want to join us?"

"No, thank you," she says. "In my experience, three's a crowd." Then she looks into Elizabeth's room with raised brows. "And with those *two* in there, things are already looking a bit crowded, don't you think, Dr. Stone?"

I lower my eyes to the floor and nod like a dog with my tail between my legs. What the hell was I thinking?

"Dr. Stone?" Elizabeth calls out from behind me.

I could pull out my pager and fake a 911 call. I could just walk over to her and hand her the food and walk back out. No harm. No foul. I could man up and tell her this was a mistake and doctors shouldn't be bringing dinner to their patients. I could do all that.

But I don't.

"See you tomorrow, Abby," I say, crossing into Elizabeth's room.

"That you will, Dr. Stone," Abby says, before I close the door on her.

I don't need anyone else looking in on me and judging me. I'm only helping out a patient. I've done that dozens of times before. I've even brought food to some. It's not uncommon for interns or even second-years to sit and socialize with patients. It's all part of the job. Just because this *one* patient happens to be my age, young and attractive, and, I don't know, mysterious . . . just because she's all those things doesn't mean I can't sit with her like I have some others. Right?

"Oh, my gosh. Is that what I think it is?" Elizabeth squeals.

I smile at her as I walk across the room. She holds out her arms, her hands beckoning me closer. Or beckoning the *food* closer.

I laugh. "Patience," I say.

"Screw patience," she says with a giggle. "I'm starving. And maybe salivating."

I roll her tray table over to the side of her bed and unload the bag, her eyes going wide at the smorgasbord I've brought her. I have Lo Mein, Chow Mein, Kung Pao chicken, shrimp and broccoli, white rice, fried rice, and of course, egg rolls.

She leans over as far as she can with a thirty-four-week belly and inhales the aromas coming from the little white boxes.

"Oh my God, I love you," she says. "You are my favorite human being that is not currently residing inside my body."

I laugh, mesmerized by her sheer joy over Chinese food.

I reach inside to pull something else from the bag. I get all serious. "I have a question to ask you," I say. "And your answer will tell me a lot about you as a person."

She sits upright and looks taken aback. It's the same look she gave me when I brought up marriage in the 'never' game. I hold up some forks in one hand and chopsticks in the other. "Which do you want?"

The sigh that comes from her practically echoes throughout the room. The smile that follows lights it up.

"What self-respecting American would eat Chinese food with a fork?" she asks.

I toss the plastic forks over my shoulder, hearing them bounce off the floor as I hand her a pair of chopsticks. "My kind of woman," I say.

She takes the chopsticks from me and when our hands touch, she blushes. I made her blush. Women don't blush unless . . . hell, I don't know. *My kind of woman*—did I actually just say that to her?

I look at her as she tears open the paper package and removes the chopsticks from it. She breaks them apart and rubs them together as I take in her appearance. Her chin-length hair is pulled back in a clip with wisps of tendrils falling around her ears. Her blue eyes stand out even more with the makeup that she's used to highlight them. Her cheeks and her lips are pink, matching her nightgown.

Even her toenails are painted pink, as I see them peek out from under her bed sheet. Have they always been painted? Maybe I've just never noticed before.

This woman—she looks anything but homeless.

She looks dangerous.

Dangerous for me. Dangerous for my career.

Then I think of my brother, Chad, and what he used to say when we were kids. "I eat danger for breakfast," he'd say.

Breakfast, dinner, it's all the same. I pull an egg roll out and hand it to her.

CHAPTER SIXTEEN

"He was SO out!" Elizabeth screams at the television. She turns to me, a bit of soy sauce dotted on her chin. "Did you see that? He was out. Blue better have his eyes checked."

Before I even realize I've done it, I've reached over and used my thumb to wipe the brown sauce from her face.

She picks up a napkin to finish the job I started. "Is something on my face?" she asks, wiping it.

"It's gone now," I tell her. I nod to the TV. "I thought he was out, too."

"Stupid ump," she says, pouting.

"You seem to know an awful lot about baseball. Did you grow up around it? You said you played softball, is that what got you interested?"

She looks up at the TV sadly and nods. "I've always loved softball, so I guess watching baseball just seems natural."

"Did you grow up in New York?" I ask, thinking this is a good opportunity to discover more about her.

She shakes her head then conveniently takes a bite of food to keep from answering.

"But you love the Nighthawks," I say.

"Who doesn't love the Hawks?" she asks.

I laugh, but on the inside, I'm upset that she keeps deflecting personal questions. "My friend, Griffin, actually. He's an Indians fan. He got me watching baseball. Even took me to a few games."

She looks up at me like I said I walked on the moon. "You've been to some games? Hawks games?"

"Yeah, last spring. One of their first games of the season I think."

"Who won?"

"Not the Indians. Boy was Griffin pissed. He doesn't get to go to many Cleveland games so he really wanted them to win."

"Was it . . . was it amazing? Seeing it in person?" she asks, longingly.

I furrow my brows. For someone who loves baseball and seems to know the game so well, you'd think she'd have been to at least one game. They practically give away tickets from time to time.

"You've never been?" I ask.

She shakes her head.

"Well, you have to go," I say. "There is nothing more American than baseball. The whole experience from the funnel cakes to the hot dogs and beer. The fights over the foul balls and home run hits. The seventh-inning stretch. We should go sometime—"

I shut up when I realize what I said. When I realize she looks downright fearful, and I curse myself.

This is not a date, Kyle. She's not your girlfriend. She doesn't want to *be* your girlfriend. She's here to have a baby and you're here to make sure she has a healthy one.

"Uh, what I mean is, you should go. You and the baby."

She nods, rubbing her belly. "Maybe we will one day."

When we've eaten all we can, I pull a handful of fortune cookies out of the bag. Elizabeth eyes them and smiles. I put them on her tray and pick one for myself.

"You can only have one," she says, choosing hers carefully among the three others that remain.

"Why?" I ask.

"Because only the first one you pick will be your fortune. The others don't count."

I feel my face break into a boyish grin. "I didn't know there were rules."

"Oh, yes. Just ask Sal," she says. "You can't trade fortunes with someone else. You have to eat the entire cookie before reading the fortune. And if your cookie is empty, that's a sign of good luck."

We both open our cookies, taking great care not to peek at our fortunes while we eat them. "You first," I say, nodding to her hand.

She opens her slip of paper. *"Your smile will tell you what makes you feel good,"* she reads.

She looks up at me and smiles. Then she realizes what she did and she blushes.

I read mine next. *"Love is like war, easy to begin, but very hard to stop."*

"Huh," she says, musing over the saying. "Did you ever wonder who makes these up? Probably some guy who lives in Boston."

I laugh as I pick up her fortune to toss it in the trash.

She reaches out and grabs my hand, forcibly taking it back from me. "I want to save it."

I raise my brows at her. "Another one of Sal's rules?" I ask.

"No. It's *my* rule," she says. "I only throw out the bad ones."

I watch as she puts the piece of paper on the side table next to her bed. Then I tuck my fortune into my front pocket.

I clean up her tray and box up the leftovers. There are a lot of leftovers. Maybe I can give them to someone on the street later. I put the food by the door so I don't forget to take it when I leave.

"Yes! Go, go, go, go, go!"

Elizabeth is screaming at the television, practically standing on her knees on the bed, having dislodged the fetal monitor as she cheers on a player. It's the same player who had that crazy double-play the other day. His name comes up on the screen as they show the replay of his triple that just landed him on third base, resulting in an RBI. His name is Caden Kessler. I recall the name. There was some press coverage about him early in the season as he changed his number, something that rarely happens in the majors.

"You seem kind of obsessed with number eight," I say, teasingly. "But seriously, you should calm down, you don't want to start bleeding."

She sits back down, looking embarrassed as I walk around the bed to readjust the monitor.

"It's not just him," she says. "I like *all* of them. They're a great team."

As I fix the strap around her belly, the door opens and Gina walks in. Her eyes quickly shift around the room, first looking at me, then the television, then the bag of Chinese food.

"I was walking by the nurses' station when I heard her monitor alarm," she says. "But it looks like you have it all under control, Dr. Stone."

I finish adjusting the strap as Gina's eyes burn into me. I can tell she's taking in my appearance. My street clothes. My clean-shaven face. My extreme guilt that I wouldn't be feeling if I wasn't doing anything wrong.

"Elizabeth, have you met Dr. Lawson yet?"

She holds out her hand to Gina. "No, it's really nice to meet you."

Gina walks over next to the bed and shakes Elizabeth's hand, finally tearing her eyes away from me. "You, too."

I resume my spot in the chair next to the bed and pretend like me being here is a perfectly normal thing. "Gina and I are doing our residencies together," I tell Elizabeth. "She's also in emergency medicine."

"That's nice," she says. "Did you get assigned a babysitting duty as well?"

Gina steps behind me and puts a hand on my shoulder. Then she rubs it around to my back. "No, Dr. Stone was the only lucky one. We've had some good times in the program, haven't we, Kyle?"

My head is so messed up right now. Gina is touching me inappropriately in front of a patient. And she used my first name. Is she trying to stake her claim on me? Or is she simply reacting to the already inappropriate situation I've put us all in?

Elizabeth is staring at Gina's hand on my shoulder. She doesn't seem upset about it. Doesn't seem happy either. She just seems . . . pensive. Then she turns back to the television.

"Do you like baseball?" she asks Gina after an awkward few moments of silence.

"Sports aren't really my thing," Gina says.

"That's too bad," she says. "I was going to ask you to join us. We have a ton of food leftover."

Elizabeth doesn't seem nearly as uncomfortable as I am. Maybe I was reading this wrong all along. She hasn't given me any indication that she sees me as anything more than her doctor. I'm overworked. I'm tired. I'm taking pity on a girl who has nothing and no one and it's clouded my judgment.

They warned us about this in medical school. Getting too involved with our patients. Making things personal. Damn Dr. Redman for putting me in this position.

"I can see that," Gina says, eyeing the mostly-full food containers. "Dr. Stone is always doing such nice things for his patients."

"I'll bet he is," Elizabeth says, eyeing me with a bit of a smart-ass smirk. "Do you take them all Jell-O?"

I can't help my laugh as I shake my head at the private joke.

Gina's pager goes off and I've never been so relieved to be saved by the proverbial bell. She bids goodbye to Elizabeth and then leans down to whisper something in my ear. "I know something we can do with Jell-O later. You can eat it off me. Or maybe out of me."

For the second time tonight, my dick twitches. And I watch her leave the room, wondering why I would ever dream of messing up the good thing I have going with her for a crapload of complication.

"She seems nice," Elizabeth says. "And she's pretty. Is she your girlfriend?"

My eyes snap to hers at the unexpectedly personal question. She doesn't ask personal questions. Not even when we play 'Never have I ever.'

"Girlfriend? No. Gina is . . . to be honest, I don't know what she is." I sigh.

"From the looks of it, I'd say she wants to be."

I nod hesitantly. I know. I've known for a while now. But for the life of me, I just can't figure out if it's the relationship I don't want, or the woman.

CHAPTER SEVENTEEN

"Did Dr. Redman finally give you more patients?" Elizabeth asks when I check on her a few days later.

"Nope," I say, looking over the notes in her chart. "It's still just you."

"Oh," she says. "I figured since I haven't seen much of you for the last couple of days that she must have finally let you out of the doghouse."

She's right. I haven't been to see her much. In fact, I've done everything I can *not* to see her. I've done my duty, making sure she and the baby are okay, but other than that, I've all but relinquished my babysitting duties to the nurses.

I've even gone so far as to seek out more scut. Labs, blood draws, hell, even enemas. Anything to keep me busy enough so I don't have time to socialize.

I went too far. I'm sticking to professionalism from here on out.

"No new patients," I tell her. "Just a lot of busy work."

"Your other sister-in-law came to see me yesterday," she says.

I look up from her chart. "Charlie was here?"

"Yeah, I like her. She watched a whole game with me."

I feel guilty that I left early the other night. But I had to. It wasn't fair to Gina to have to watch me like that with another woman. It wasn't fair to Elizabeth when what I was doing was crossing the line. It wasn't even fair to me—putting myself in that situation.

I'm grateful to my sisters-in-law for stepping up. Especially now that I'm stepping away.

"That's great, Elizabeth. You've got as many as two and a half weeks left here, so I'm glad to see you are keeping your spirits up."

"Two and a half weeks." She puts her hands on either side of her growing belly. "Seems a long time to be here, but not nearly long enough to prepare for this one."

I put down the chart as something dawns on me. "Are you prepared, Elizabeth? I mean, when you leave here with the baby, are you going to be able to take care of it? Of yourself?"

She gives me a sad smile. "I told you before, Kyle. I'll be okay. You said yourself that you thought all things happen for a reason. There is a reason for this," she says, rubbing her hand across her abdomen. "And I know everything will work out."

I can't help the thoughts racing through my head. Thoughts of her taking a newborn to some low-rent crack-house apartment. Thoughts of angry drug-head neighbors who pound on her door in a rage because they hear the baby crying through the paper-thin walls. Thoughts of that baby crying because her mom isn't producing enough milk due to her poor nutrition.

A knock on the door keeps me from stepping back across the line. I look behind me and smile. Baylor is standing in the doorway with a basket of some sort.

"Is this a good time?" she asks.

Elizabeth sees who's at the door and her face falls into that of a star-struck adolescent. Her eyes blink repeatedly.

"Baylor, come on in," I say. "Baylor Mitchell McBride, I'd like you to meet Elizabeth Smith." Without thinking, I add, "Sorry, I don't know Elizabeth's middle name."

I stare at her in question.

"Uh, no. No middle name," she says. "Just Elizabeth."

"Well, it's nice to meet you, Elizabeth with no middle name," Baylor says. "Technically I'm just Baylor McBride, but most people know me as Mitchell, so I'm good with either."

"It's an honor to meet you," Elizabeth says, offering Baylor her hand. Baylor dumps the basket on me so she can shake it. I stare at the contents. Books. A lot of them. And what looks to be a tablet.

Baylor nods to the bounty she brought. "Kyle said you like to read romance novels, so I brought you some. I didn't know if you like paperback or digital, so I brought both."

Elizabeth's eyes bug out as they peruse the basket. I place it on the bed between her legs and she picks up one of the books. It's Baylor's newly-published novel. She opens the cover. "You signed it?"

Baylor laughs. "Sure did. Maybe it'll be worth something when I'm dead."

"Are you kidding?" Elizabeth gushes. "I'll bet it's worth a lot *now*."

"You're sweet to say so."

Elizabeth looks through the basket, pulling out not only books written by Baylor, but other authors as well.

"Oh, my gosh, these are great." She opens the cover on another and gasps. "Are they *all* signed?"

Baylor nods. "Yup. I was at my publisher's the other day and grabbed a handful for you. I hope you like them."

"I'm sure I'll love them, just like I love yours. I've read all of them, well except the new one that just came out."

Baylor picks up the tablet and shows Elizabeth how to sign on to it. "I've loaded it with tons of books. I know you must be going out of your mind being stuck in here."

Elizabeth swipes her finger across the tablet, paging through the titles Baylor put on it. I watch the ease with which she uses the device. Like she's done it a thousand times before. Yet . . . she has nothing. The girl is an enigma.

She looks up at Baylor with sad eyes. "I appreciate this more than you know, but I can't accept the tablet. It's too much."

Baylor waves off Elizabeth's apprehension. "Do you know how many of these things my publisher gives away? It's considered promotional."

"Still, it's too much," Elizabeth says. "But I'd be grateful to borrow it during my stay."

"Of course," Baylor says, winking at me. "Whatever you want."

I put my hand on Baylor's shoulder. "Nice to see you, Baylor. I hope we can catch up later, but I have to run now and take care of some things."

"Sure thing, Kyle. Maybe we can grab a coffee later on my way out."

"Sounds good, just text me. See you later, Elizabeth."

Elizabeth barely acknowledges my departure as she's enamored with Baylor.

I walk down the corridor and plant myself at the nurses' station, pretending to chart when all I'm doing is staring at the room at the end of the hall. Who am I kidding? I don't have anything meaningful to do. I just needed to get out of there. Distance myself.

Yes. Distance is exactly what I need. I pull out my phone and tap out a text.

Me: On-call room in 10?

CHAPTER EIGHTEEN

Gina doesn't respond to my text. Probably because she's got an actual patient who needs a doctor instead of a babysitter.

I head down to the ER to see if I can lend a hand. I find myself uncharacteristically happy to get to throw some stitches in a kid who fell off a scooter. I find myself unusually upset that I don't get in on the gunshot wound that rolls through the doors.

I look around the ER longingly. I need to be back down here. Where I'm actually useful.

Someone slaps a chart on the counter in front of me. I spin around to see Dr. Redman.

"The OB floor not exciting enough for you, Dr. Stone? Are you down here trolling for cases?"

I shrug. "Just trying to keep busy, Dr. Redman."

She nods to the chart. "I've got a complete hysterectomy at four o'clock. Think you can be prepared to assist?"

I try not to pump my fist and yell, *'fuck, yeah!'*

"Of course, Dr. Redman. I'll be ready."

She eyes me up and down like she's trying to decide if I'm worth her time. "Fine, then," she says before walking away.

An hour later, my eyes are bugging out after reading everything I can to brush up on hysterectomies when my phone vibrates.

Baylor: Do you have time for a quick coffee?

Me: Meet me in the courtyard. I'm buying.

Five minutes later, I hand Baylor her cup of coffee. Milk and no sugar, just like all the Mitchell sisters take it. "Thanks for bringing Elizabeth those books. I know she's a huge fan."

"No problem. She's incredible. Nothing like I thought she'd be."

"How so?" I ask.

"Well, I know how Mallory described her, but we all know Mallory is a saint disguised as a school teacher. I guess I expected her to be, I don't know, some shrinking violet who was cowering in the corner wearing nothing but rags. But she's quite the opposite. She's funny, beautiful, and very smart."

"Smart?" I cock my head to the side. "I mean, yeah, of course she's smart, but what makes you say so? She's pretty closed off."

Baylor laughs. "Yeah, I sensed that. But when she was talking about my books, it became obvious she knows a lot about literature. Turns out she has a degree in it. That and elementary education."

My unbelieving eyes snap to hers. "She does? And she *told* you about it?"

"Yes. Why wouldn't she?"

"I don't know. She doesn't ever give personal details. I have no idea where she's from or where she lives or if she is or was married. Nothing."

She raises her eyebrows at me. "Are those things patients usually tell their doctors, Kyle?"

Shit.

"No, I guess not. But I've had to spend quite a bit of time with her since she's my only patient. And getting her to reveal personal details is harder than giving a bald man a haircut."

"Well, she didn't tell me much more than that. She went to the University of Maryland, but that's about all I know. When I asked about the baby's father, she clammed up. I didn't want to pry. But I think there's a story there."

I nod. "I *know* there's one."

"She really hasn't had anyone else but us visit?"

"Nope. She's been here for a week. Not one friend or family member. She literally was admitted with only the clothes on her back and a few personal items in her purse."

"There is no way that girl is homeless, Kyle. I can't believe she is."

"She says she's not. And she does have a job. Although I'm not sure how she'll be able to walk dogs with a baby."

"Where there's a will, there's a way," she says. "She could always push a stroller, or put the baby in one of those Snugli things." Her face suddenly lights up. "Oh, my gosh, we should have a baby shower for her."

"Did you not hear the part where she won't give out her address? How do you expect to throw her a shower?"

She jumps up and down in her seat. "Not after the baby comes, silly. Here, in the hospital. Think about it. She has nothing and I have a ton of stuff my kids have outgrown. I mean, three is enough—just ask Gavin." She laughs. "Mallory said Elizabeth was okay accepting her maternity hand-me-downs, why not used baby items? Some of this stuff is really quality stuff, Kyle, and it's just sitting in my garage. It's perfect. All the girls could come and we could each wrap some of the things. We'd make a day of it."

I shake my head. "I'm not sure she'd go for it, Baylor. She doesn't like hand-outs. Believe me, I've tried."

"What, you've tried to give her money? Of course she won't take money, Kyle. No self-respecting woman would. And we just won't tell her. We'll spring it on her. Later, after we've gotten to know her better. How long is she here?"

"She's here until the baby comes," I say. "If all goes as planned, that won't be for another couple of weeks. But if her condition changes, it could be any time."

"But she'll have to be here for at least a day or two after the baby comes, right?"

I nod. "She'll have to deliver by C-section, so it'll be two or three days."

"Perfect. Why don't we schedule it for two weeks from now and if she has the baby by then, we'll just do it before she gets discharged. But let's keep it on the down low."

I eye her in amusement. "The down low?"

"Yeah, it'll be fun. A clandestine operation. You know, figure out her favorite foods and stuff so we can do it right."

"Chinese," I say.

"Huh?"

"Her favorite food is Chinese. Sal's Chinese to be specific. She loves the egg rolls. And the Lo Mein. And chopsticks."

"And yet she doesn't tell you anything." Baylor studies me curiously. "Yup, definitely a story there."

I shake my head. "What? No. No story there."

"Oh, come on. Doctor falls in love with homeless pregnant patient. That's good stuff."

I choke on my coffee. "Better get your head out of the clouds, Baylor. Life isn't always a romance novel, you know."

"No, it's not. But you have to admit, there's a premise there. She's young and beautiful. You're young and handsome. You are saving her life."

"You forgot one very important detail," I say, stating the obvious. "She's pregnant, Baylor. That means there is a husband or a boyfriend or a baby daddy. Even an *ex* one of those poses a problem."

"Exactly," she says. "No romance novel is good without a crisis."

I roll my eyes at her. "How about you stick to your day job and get out of the matchmaking business?"

"Fine." She blows out a conceding breath. "I have a shower to plan, anyway. I'm going to call the girls. I'd expect to see more of us over the next few weeks. I think Elizabeth might be more likely to accept our generosity if we become better friends." She points a finger at me. "Don't you dare say anything to her."

I hold up my hands in surrender. "I wouldn't dream of it."

Baylor gathers up her things and we hug before she walks away. I watch her walk through the doors, grateful that people such as her exist in this world.

CHAPTER NINETEEN

I wheel the ultrasound machine down the hallway and find it hard to contain my smile. It's the best part of Elizabeth's day. Those few moments when she can see her baby. Every time we do a sonogram it's like the first one she's ever seen. She gets all teary-eyed.

Every time.

And it's become a joke about her not wanting to see what may or may not be between the baby's legs. Although that's not what we're looking for, we're looking closely at the placenta. But I still take a few extra minutes and show her a hand or a foot. Yesterday, the baby looked to be sucking her thumb.

It's the only time Elizabeth talks about the baby. It makes me wonder if she's scared about becoming a mom. Or maybe she's scared about what's waiting out there for her when she leaves the hospital. An old apartment with broken-down appliances perhaps. Or maybe it's drafty in the winter. Hell, maybe it isn't even heated, although I'm pretty sure that's against the law. But slumlords these days don't really give a shit what squalor their tenants have to live in as long as they're making a buck.

Damn it. I wish she would let me help her.

I see someone walking around Elizabeth's room as I make my approach. It's Skylar Mitchell. I park the ultrasound machine outside the doorway and lean against the door jam, quietly observing them before I go in.

Elizabeth takes a bite of something from a Mitchell's To Go container. She rolls her eyes to the heavens. "Oh, my gosh, this is the best lasagna I've ever tasted. It's my favorite homemade meal, you know."

"Really?" Skylar says with a huge smile, winking at me when she sees me in the doorway. "Imagine that."

"Imagine what?" Elizabeth says, shoveling another huge bite into her mouth.

"Nothing. Now that I know you love lasagna, I'll have to bring by some more next week. If that's okay with you."

"Can you bring your chef, too?" Elizabeth asks. "I'd like to keep him. Hospital food sucks."

"Speaking of hospital food, what's with all the Jell-O?" Skylar asks, pointing to her side table.

Elizabeth laughs. "Nothing. Just a game I'm hoping to play later."

"A game? With Jell-O?" Skylar puts her hand up to stop Elizabeth from speaking. "Wait! I don't want to know. Sounds kinky. But somehow I think I like you even more now."

"It's not like that." Elizabeth giggles and damn it if the sound doesn't make my heart skip a beat like a teenage girl at a rock concert.

She's hoping to play the game with me? But she *hates* the game. It seems like every time, I either get too personal or bring up something painful.

She pushes the lasagna away. "I'm stuffed," she says. "I wish I could eat more. It's a shame to let it go to waste. I'll bet if Kyle were here, he'd box it up and take it to some homeless person around the corner."

Skylar looks up at me and smiles. "I bet he would."

They are talking about me. I feel like I should enter the room, but at the same time, I think Elizabeth is more open with the girls than she is me, and I don't want to miss an opportunity to learn something about her.

"He did that with some Chinese food he brought me the other night."

"That's Kyle. He wants to feed the world. And cure it of disease."

Elizabeth starts chewing on her pinky nail again. She only does that when she's nervous.

"Is he . . . a good guy?" she asks hesitantly. "I mean, he's a doctor, so that probably means that inherently he's good, wanting to help people and all. But is he good? Like deep down?"

Skylar puts her hand on Elizabeth's arm. "You'd be hard pressed to find a better man anywhere."

Elizabeth nods.

Skylar stands up and grabs her purse. "I'm off to get my hair done. Griffin is coming back in town after being gone for a week on a photo shoot. I want to look my very best."

"I love your hair," Elizabeth tells her.

"Thanks." Skylar studies Elizabeth for a second. "You know, I might be able to help you out with your roots if you want. I have a great hairdresser who makes house calls." She pulls a piece of paper out of her purse and hands it to Elizabeth. "Here, write down what brand and color you've been using and I'll give it to her to match. If you want, I can see if she can come with me when I bring next week's lasagna."

"You don't have to do that, Skylar. It can wait until I get home."

"I know I don't. And I also know how tired you'll be once the baby comes. This may be your last chance for months to have a touch up. So, unless you plan on going full-on brunette . . ." She nods to the paper.

Elizabeth smiles and writes something down.

I feel like a brick wall just slammed into my chest.

She's a fucking brunette?

Someone drops something in the hallway behind me and Elizabeth finally notices I'm standing here. "Oh, hi, Kyle. Skylar just brought me the best lasagna. Have you ever had Mitchell's lasagna?"

Skylar and I share a look. "Once or twice," I say. *Or a hundred times.*

"I'm out of here," Skylar says, stopping to kiss me on her way by.

I nod in thanks as I wheel the ultrasound machine into Elizabeth's room.

"Will that thing see all the lasagna I just ate?" she jokes. "Because it might be embarrassing. I ate a lot."

"You're allowed to," I say. "You are eating for two."

"I don't know." She looks down at her leftovers. "More like three or four if you ask me."

I stare at the dark roots beginning to show in the part of her hair, wondering how I've never noticed this before. She looks like a blonde with her sun-kissed face and striking blue eyes. She looks good as a blonde. Then again, I thought she looked good in blue when it wasn't her best color at all.

I find myself trying to picture her as a brunette—but I stop. I stop when I realize I'm getting dangerously close to that line again.

"Ready?" I ask.

"Are you kidding?" She squirms in the bed like it's Christmas morning.

I smile as I unhook her from the monitor and then squirt the gel onto her abdomen.

"Don't—"

"Show the salami or the cheeseburger," I say, finishing her words for her. The same words she says every day when we do this.

Last week on my day off, the resident assigned to her saw the note in her chart and made a joke about not showing her the salami or the cheeseburger. On an ultrasound, a girl's parts resemble the layering of a burger. I'd call it more of a hamburger myself, but whatever.

I quickly locate the placenta and make sure it's not tearing. Everything looks good from a medical standpoint.

"What's it going to be today?" I ask. "Hand, foot, face?"

"Yes," she says, with a hopeful grin.

Not able to deny this woman anything, I begin from the top down. The baby is opening and closing her mouth as if she's chewing. "Looks like he or she wants the lasagna," I say.

Elizabeth laughs, causing her belly to jiggle which in turn has the baby moving.

I find one of her arms and work down toward the hand. I know how much Elizabeth likes to count the fingers. She raises her hand to the monitor and traces the outline of her tiny fingers.

"Still five?" I ask.

She rolls her teary eyes at me before she looks back at her daughter.

But I'm still looking at *her*. Jesus Christ, she's beautiful. The way she looks at her baby. I've never seen so much love on someone's face before. I try to look away, but I can't.

The baby starts to jerk around.

"Baby's got the hiccups," she says, laughing. "Must've eaten too much."

I find the baby's head again and we watch her jump around on the monitor.

"Can you feel it?" she asks.

"No. But I can see it on the monitor."

"You have to feel it. It's the best feeling. Here, give me your other hand."

I hold my free hand out and she takes it, placing it on the left side of her belly. My eyes close momentarily as flesh touches flesh and I feel her taut skin under the palm of my hand. When I feel the tiny jerking movements, my eyes fly open to meet hers.

"Pretty great, huh?" she asks.

Life. There is a new life under my hand. A girl who might someday look just like her mother. She could have short brunette hair, falling just past her chin in soft waves. She could have stunning blue eyes that can draw any man's stare like a tractor beam. She could have soft hands and perfect pink toenails and full pouty lips. She could have that curve to her smile that lets you know you are important. She could have that giggle that brings you to your knees.

Suddenly, the walls of the room start closing in on me. My heart starts pounding. I can't breathe. I'm suffocating.

I pull my hand away and take the wand off her belly. I hand her a towel to wipe the gel off. "I'm sorry. I just remembered I have somewhere to be."

"Oh." She looks sadly at her tray table where the cups of Jell-O sit untouched. "I was hoping . . . never mind, you need to go."

"Yeah, I need to go."

I walk out of her room, not even bothering to bring the ultrasound machine with me. I need to go. I need to go like I've never needed to go before.

I need to go, because what I just experienced in that room was something I've never felt.

What I just experienced in that room was so wrong I can't even begin to list all the ways.

But how come what I just experienced in that room feels nothing but so fucking right?

CHAPTER TWENTY

Hot air rolls across the nape of my neck as I fill out a chart at the table in the resident's lounge. "I've got a few free minutes. You?"

I don't have to look up to see that it's Gina. I recognize her whisper, the touch of her hand on my shoulder. Her scent. I close my eyes and sigh. This is the right call, Kyle.

I nod before turning around. "Let me drop off my chart. Meet you there in a second."

She smiles before she heads out the door. It's a nice smile. Gina has perfect white teeth. Almost too perfect. Everything about Gina is perfect for me. She's a doctor. A second-year. She understands my schedule and the demands of my time. She's driven by her job like I am. She doesn't have time for things like watching baseball games and reading romance novels. Let alone time for kids. As far as I know, she doesn't even want kids. *I* don't want kids. Not yet anyway.

We're perfect for each other.

Yes, this is the right call.

I drop my chart off at the nurses' station and head to the on-call room. When I arrive, Gina is already undressed and under the covers. I lock the door and strip myself naked on the way to her. I rip off the sheet and gaze down at her body—her large breasts that don't even fit in my hands. Her trim waist. Her toned thighs. Her triangle of brown curls.

It's there where I focus my attention. I catch myself wondering if Elizabeth has brown curls as well. Maybe not as well manicured as Gina, but brown none the less. I quickly look up at Gina's face—if for no other reason but to remind myself exactly who I'm here with.

I climb on the bed with her and palm her breasts. She pulls my head down until our lips meet. She kisses me hard and with more feeling than she's ever kissed me. And I let her. I let her because this is the right call.

"You feel so good," she says, squirming underneath me. "God, I needed this. I've missed you this week."

"Mmm," I mumble, working my mouth down to her chest so I can suck on her nipples. She grinds her hips into me from below as I take one into my mouth while I pinch the other. My free hand traces a line down her flat stomach, down past her patch of curls to find her wet and ready. I slip in one finger, then another as she moans under my manipulation.

I work my thumb around her clit and she bucks her hips into me. She's close already. It won't take much to get her there. I increase the pressure I've got on her nipple, pinching and twisting as I continue to work the fingers of my other hand inside her.

"Yes. Oh, Kyle. Oh, God!"

I watch her face as she comes. I've always watched her. It gets me hot. But as her head whips around on the pillow and she bites down on her lip to suppress her screams, I realize I'm barely more than lukewarm.

She reaches down to grab me, surprised I'm not rock hard. "Everything okay, Kyle?"

"Yeah, just tired and overworked, I guess."

"Well, I'll just have to wake you up," she says with a sultry smile.

She sits up and pushes me down on the bed. She takes my near-flaccid dick into her hands and works it up and down. When that doesn't produce results, she climbs her way down my body and takes me into her mouth.

Nothing.

I stare down at her. There's nothing more erotic than watching a woman suck you off. I watch her long brunette ponytail bob back and forth as she tries everything she can think of to 'wake me up.'

Nothing.

For the life of me, all I can see when I look down at her is blonde hair with dark roots. Blonde hair that is almost too short to be held back in a ponytail. Blonde hair that would curtain the sides of her face and tickle my thighs if she did this to me.

If it were Elizabeth and not Gina.

And damn it if I don't want that with everything inside me. With everything that I am.

Fuck.

Gina stops her futile efforts and looks up at me in question.

"Sorry," I say.

"Don't be sorry. It happens," she says. "Like you said, you're tired and overworked." She reaches over to grab her scrubs. "Although with your *one* patient, it seems like you'd have time to catch up on your sleep."

Her curt words annoy me, but I hide it with a careless shrug. "Red has been letting me help out on other cases."

"Right. I heard you got an assist the other day."

"It's more than just that, Gina," I tell her. "And I've been spending my spare time down in the ER."

"Oh, well that explains it." She finishes dressing and heads for the door. "Page me after you've had a rest. We'll finish what we started."

I nod, watching her walk through the door.

Then I send a text to Cameron.

Me: Meet me at Happy's after shift.

~ ~ ~

"So, let me get this straight," Cameron says, slamming his second shot glass down on the table. "You have a hot chick desperate to screw you anytime, anywhere, and you're telling me you don't want to anymore?"

He looks at me like I'm ten cards shy of a full deck.

I toss back my own second shot. "I do and I don't, man. I mean, it's always been great with her. No strings. No commitments. I know it's crazy. It's every guy's dream. But today, I couldn't . . . when I was with her I couldn't—"

"Dude, you couldn't seal the deal?"

I shake my head in shame.

He motions for the waitress to bring us more shots. "That really blows." He laughs. "Or I guess maybe it didn't. Next round's on me," he says, grabbing my shoulder supportively.

The alcohol from my third shot burns my throat on the way down. "I don't know what's wrong with me."

He studies me. "Maybe it's not a what. Maybe it's a who."

"A who?"

"Come on, Kyle." He raises his brows at me. "Your patient. The one you talk about incessantly."

"Well, she *is* my only patient," I say. "Who the hell else am I supposed to talk about?"

"It's not that you talk about her, it's *how* you talk about her. It's been obvious to me from the beginning that you have a thing for this girl. First you arrange to pay her hospital bill, then you have your sisters-in-law and your friends come and keep her company. Hell, you get a stupid shit-eating grin on your face every time you talk about her, bro."

"I do?"

He nods.

I run my hands through my hair in frustration. "Shit, Cameron. What the hell is wrong with me? She's my patient. And she's pregnant. And I don't know the first thing about her. But I can't get her out of my goddamn head."

"Does this infatuation go both ways?" he asks.

"No. I don't know. It's obvious she wants me there with her, but for all I know she might want Jack the Ripper there, too, if it meant he'd keep her company."

He tosses a few peanuts in his mouth. "I checked in on her the other day," he says, to my complete surprise.

"You did? But you're not on Red's service."

"I know. I made up a lame excuse about looking for an ultrasound machine."

"Why would you do that?"

He stares me down. "Why do you think, Kyle? Because my friend is seriously close to fucking up his life and maybe even his career. What if she's a con artist and she's after your money? Did you ever think of that?"

"What the hell, Cameron? That's ridiculous. As if she planned her pregnancy and then willed herself into placenta previa so that she could scam me. What's your problem?"

"Okay, you have a point," he says. "But I'm just looking out for you, bro. Anyway, I'm pretty sure she's not a con artist. In fact, she's just about one of the nicest people I've met."

I nod, absently tracing the rim of my shot glass.

"Hot, too," he says, laughing. "If you take away the hugely pregnant belly. And I'm no Jack the Ripper, but she didn't try to get *me* to stay and keep her company. I'm also fairly sure she mentioned '*Dr. Stone*' no less than five times in the two minutes I was in her room."

"What do I do, Cam?"

"She's your patient, Kyle. You take care of her and make sure that baby is healthy. She'll only be here for a few more weeks, right? After that, it's no one's business but yours if you want to see her, fuck her, or raise a child with her."

"Do you have to be so damn crude?" I ask, giving him a look of disdain.

"Oh, what, you can fuck Gina to kingdom come, but when I mention fucking Elizabeth, you look like you want to pin me to the damn ground."

"I don't think of her that way," I say.

"You don't think about fucking her?" He winces when he sees my angry stare. "Sorry, you don't think about *being* with her?"

I blow out a long breath and run my hands through my hair once again. "Therein lies my problem, Cameron. That's *all* I think about."

CHAPTER TWENTY-ONE

"You know what today is?" Elizabeth asks with a smile.

"Your birthday?" I ask, even though I know it's not, because her date of birth is written right here in the chart, and it's only a week away from mine. That makes her two years and one week younger than I am. But who's counting?

"No. Two weeks, Kyle. Today marks the two week point from having the baby. I'm thirty-five weeks today."

I flip through the chart. "So you are. That's good, you know. Even if the baby came today it would have an excellent chance of being perfectly healthy."

She nods. "I know. I read that in my book. But I'd just as soon have it stay where it is for the next few weeks. I can't take any chances with his or her health." She looks at me wearily. "That's okay, isn't it? Do you think the hospital wants me to have it early so they don't have to pay more for my stay?"

"That's ridiculous. Everyone here wants you to get as close to term as possible. Don't worry about any of that other stuff. You haven't mentioned your pro bono status to Dr. Redman, have you?"

She shakes her head and furrows her eyebrows. "I just assumed everyone knew, like it was in my chart or something."

"No. Your chart has no billing information in it."

"You mean to tell me you went over your boss's head to get me in?" she asks playfully.

"I didn't need her approval either way, I just submitted it to the committee. But best not mention it to her, you know how she can be."

"It makes sense now that I think about it," she says. "Everyone up here treats me like a paying customer, not some moocher off the streets like that nurse did my first time in the ER."

"Everyone deserves to be treated the same, Elizabeth, regardless of their financial status or ability to pay."

"Sadly, not everyone shares your philosophy, Kyle."

"Well, then *everyone* can take their misplaced righteousness and shove it up their tight narcissistic asses."

She giggles. "Why, Dr. Stone, I don't think I've ever heard you speak so harshly."

"Sorry, it just makes me angry. In my book, everyone is just one unfortunate circumstance—"

"—away from being in someone else's shoes," she finishes my sentence.

I cock my head to the side and study her.

She laughs. "Mallory pretty much told me that's your motto."

"Did she now?"

"She came for another visit last night. So did your friend, Piper Mitchell."

"Busy day, was it?"

"Yes, but Nurse Ratched didn't let either of them take me for a walk because I was bleeding the day before yesterday. But I haven't so much as spotted in over twenty-four hours. Can you get me out of here for a while? Please?"

I page through her chart, looking at the notes that cover the last thirty-six hours when I wasn't on duty.

"It says here you experienced bright-red blood over the period of about six hours. They did a blood draw. Results look normal. Ultrasound was good. And you say no bleeding since?"

"Nope, none." She looks proud, like it's an accomplishment she had control over. "Please, Kyle. I'm going stir crazy. There is only so much baseball I can watch. A lot of the games aren't even televised, I just have to wait for highlights. And I've read five books since Baylor came to visit. That's five books in less than four days, Kyle. I need fresh air. I need to smell lavender. I need to eat Jell-O. Please?"

So many things are running through my head right now. Things like how I should get a nurse to escort her to the courtyard. Things like how I should turn around and walk out of this room. Things like how I can remember every detail of her face when we walked into the gardens last week and she smelled those purple flowers. Things like how her piercing blue eyes are begging me to take her.

And I know that, despite all the reasons I shouldn't, I'll say yes anyway.

I put down her chart. "Don't go anywhere, I'll find you a wheelchair."

She claps her hands like an excited school girl. "Oh, thank you!"

When I return a few minutes later with a wheelchair, I see she's removed the strap from the fetal monitor, turned the machine off, and put on her robe. I admonish her with my stare.

"What?" she says. "Abby taught me how to work the monitor. It was always slipping off me. It's just easier if I know how to do it myself."

"And the robe?"

She rolls her eyes at me. "It was two feet away on the chair, Kyle. Geesh, and I thought Nurse Ratched was bad."

"Exactly who is Nurse Ratched?" I ask. "I know it's not Abby, since she taught you how to work the monitor and all."

"Her name is Rachel, but she's a slave driver. She was here filling in for the night-shift nurse."

I get her situated in the wheelchair and walk her out to the elevator. Abby and another nurse follow us with their eyes. Elizabeth seems to notice as well.

"What's their problem?" she asks.

"Don't mind them. They just think we're having a torrid affair."

She guffaws. "They *what?*"

I laugh. "Haven't you learned by now that nurses gossip about everything? Patients. Doctors. Other nurses. They work long twelve-hour shifts. I suppose it keeps things interesting or something."

She joins my laughter. "I guess my room is too far away from things to hear the good stuff. Darn."

On our ride down to the main floor, the elevator stops and the doors open. Cameron walks in. He looks down at Elizabeth and then up at me. His face cracks into a huge smile that only I can see. We ride in silence to the ground floor, then we all get off.

"See you later, porn star," Cameron says as he walks away.

"Porn star?" Elizabeth questions me. Then her jaw drops. "Kyle," she says, before clearing her throat. "Did you pay your way through medical school making adult movies?"

I look around to see if anyone heard her ask. Then I lean down and explain, "I have the unfortunate honor of sharing my name with a famous adult film actor."

She covers her mouth and belts out a laugh. "Oh, no. That *is* unfortunate."

"You have no idea," I say. "Growing up with two older brothers, I never heard the end of it."

"Your parents didn't realize what they'd done, obviously."

I shake my head. "That was over twenty-seven years ago. People didn't do internet searches to pick the name of their kid back then. It wasn't until I was in middle school when some idiot friend of my brother mentioned it to him. My brother researched it for accuracy and then proceeded to wallpaper my bedroom with photos of the guy."

"As in naked photos?" she asks.

"Not just naked photos. Action photos," I say. "I was barely twelve. I didn't even know what the hell was going on in most of the pictures. He practically scarred me for life."

She laughs again. "Which brother, Chad or Ethan?"

I'm impressed she remembers both of their names. "Ethan."

"It sounds like you had a lot of fun growing up," she says. Then she looks down the hall and beckons me down to her level where she whispers, "Isn't that Billy Hainey?"

I look in the direction of her gaze. "So, it's not just baseball you like. You're a hockey buff, too?"

"Is that *him?*"

"Looks like him," I say. "It's not unusual to see famous athletes around the hospital. They do a lot of goodwill work."

"That's nice of them. I'll bet the kids love it, and maybe even some of the adults," she says, as I wheel her past the cafeteria. "Hey, aren't you forgetting something?"

"Right. Jell-O." I back up and push her into the cafeteria, parking her to the side while I gather up our supplies.

"More research?" the cashier asks with a smirk.

I laugh and nod.

Out in the courtyard, we resume the same spot we had last week. And just like last week, she takes in a huge breath through her nose, savoring the aroma of what must be her favorite flower.

I sit on the bench and take the Jell-O cups from her, making a pile next to me. "Whose turn is it?" I ask, as if I don't know. As if the memory of every minute I spend with her isn't chronicled in my head.

"Mine," she says. "I've had a lot of time to sit around and think about it, you know."

"Fire away," I say.

"Okay. Never have I ever been arrested."

I chuckle. "Good one, but not good enough." I leave the cups sealed and untouched. "Although I did have a few near-misses back in high school. One time, a bunch of guys and I got drunk out on a golf course. The night watchman chased us all over the back nine before he pooped out. Damn, I haven't thought about that in a while. Good times."

"Now you go," she says.

I don't miss the fact that she doesn't ask me any questions about what I just said. Questions like where was the golf course or what high school did you attend. She doesn't ask me questions like that because she knows I'd quid pro quo.

I try to think of a question that won't stir up bad memories. "Never have I ever kissed someone of the same sex on the lips."

Her face pinks up and her eyes close briefly as she grins and shakes her head back and forth. "Give me the orange one, please," she says, holding out her hand.

My jaw drops.

She rolls her eyes. "Tenth grade. Her name was Jewel. Let's just leave it at that."

I open the orange Jell-O and hand it to her along with a spoon.

"I'm a guy, Elizabeth. I can't just leave it at that."

She laughs right before taking her bite. "Eww," she says, making a face. "Definitely not my favorite."

"Did this kiss involve Jell-O?" I ask. "Or perhaps melted chocolate?"

"Oh, my God, Kyle. No. It was a dare. But I got the idea she liked it way more than I did. She stalked me for weeks after. It was humiliating. Rumors started. Apparently, I was the only one in tenth grade who didn't know she liked girls."

"Was she blonde or brunette?"

"What?" she asks, scrunching her nose. "What does that matter?"

"I have a thing for brunettes," I say. "Was she blonde or brunette?"

"Oh, *I'm* . . . I mean, uh . . . *she* was brunette."

I can't help my smile. She was about to tell me she's a brunette.

"My turn again," she says. "Never have I ever stolen anything."

"Doesn't that kind of go along with being arrested?" I ask.

"No, not necessarily," she says.

"You're right, it doesn't." I pick up a spoon and take a bite of the orange goo.

She's raising her eyebrows at me, waiting for an explanation.

"I was fifteen. We had recently moved to L.A. and I was going through a rebellious phase. We were in the mall and I swiped a pair of sunglasses. Funny story, it's actually how my brother, Chad, got discovered as an actor."

She looks vaguely embarrassed. "I know, Mallory told me."

"Told you my brother was an actor, or told you I stole something?"

"Both. I just wanted to see if you were an honest thief," she says. She nods to the two remaining cups. "You only have one left to try and I have two."

"Better choose our questions wisely then," I say with a smirk.

"Do your worst," she says.

"Never have I ever cheated on a test," I say.

She shakes her head. "Nope, sorry, me neither. Um, never have I ever played strip poker."

I don't touch the Jell-O cups. "Sorry, but no. Never have I ever gotten a tattoo," I say.

She looks down at the ground and huffs out an unhappy sigh. Then she holds out her hand. "Let me try the lime-green one."

"Wait," I say, holding it back from her. "That's not how this game works."

She looks apprehensive and she nervously twists the thick bracelet around her wrist. "I'd show you," she says. "But then I'd have to kill you."

"Oh, it's one of those, is it?" I say, handing her the cup as I wonder just where she has a tattoo. Her inner thigh, maybe. Or perhaps low on her back near the globes of her ass. I find myself shifting around in my seat thinking about it.

Maybe I'll get to see it if I assist on her surgery. Surely Dr. Redman will let me do that after looking out for her all this time.

"This is it," she says, giving me back the container. "Only one last flavor for us to try."

"You're up," I say. "Make it a good one."

She looks around the courtyard in thought. I follow her eyes. She stares at an older couple strolling hand-in-hand, the woman in a hospital gown. The man stops their progress and kisses the woman chastely on the lips. Then he takes her hand again and brings it to his mouth, kissing it as well before they continue their stroll.

Elizabeth brings her pinky finger to her mouth and starts chewing on the nail. She looks almost scared when her eyes come back to meet mine.

"Never have I ever wanted something I can't have," she says, her words hooking me somewhere in my chest.

We share a long look. Not just any look. A deep, powerful, all-encumbering look.

Volumes are spoken between us in these few seconds. Her eyes are more expressive in this moment than I've ever seen them. She's trying to tell me something without actually telling me something. And ethics be damned, I'm all too willing to let her.

She's not looking at me like I'm her doctor. She's not even looking at me like I'm her friend. She's looking at me like the old man was looking at his wife. With sincerity. With reverence. With passion.

"Elizabeth," I whisper.

I don't even break our stare when my hand fishes around for the remaining container on the bench. I open it, surely spilling some as I blindly stick my spoon in for a bite. Without any words, I bring the spoon up to my mouth and eat the brightly-colored blue Jell-O. Then I nod my head at her. I nod my head in answer to the silent questions in her eyes. The questions she doesn't have to ask because I've already answered them all with my stare.

"On second thought," she says, finally breaking eye contact. She grabs the container from me and silently finishes every last bite.

CHAPTER TWENTY-TWO

We haven't talked about what happened in the courtyard a few days ago. But something definitely changed between us. And despite the fact that Dr. Redman has started assigning me more cases, I find myself making excuses to spend more time with Elizabeth.

And Elizabeth, she seems . . . happier.

It's not that she was depressed before. In fact, she's been a joyful person for the most part. But she just didn't seem happy. Not until now.

I'm spending my lunch break in her room, catching up on some medical journals while she reads one of her pregnancy books.

"Are you going to deliver the baby?" she asks, looking up from her book.

"I probably won't be doing the C-section, but I'm hoping to be in the room to assist. Since this is a teaching hospital, the consent forms you'll sign for surgery will give residents permission to participate in your care. But if you don't want me to . . ."

"No, it's not that." Her pinky finger finds its way into her mouth. "How much, uh . . . how much of me will you see?" She blushes, her eyes not meeting mine.

I try not to laugh. "I'm a doctor, Elizabeth. I've pretty much seen it all, you know."

She nods. "I know that. I'm just not sure I want you seeing me. Not *that* way. Uh, not that I think we'll . . . Ugh!" She throws an arm over her head to cover her embarrassment. "Forget I said anything. I'll just stop talking now."

I realize we're in an unusual situation. Most obstetric patients have periodic vaginal exams. But due to her condition, those are contraindicated. The most I've ever seen of her is her belly, and maybe a flash of under-boob when I was adjusting her monitor.

I close my magazine and put my hand on top of hers. "It's okay, Elizabeth. I know what you mean. And just so you know, by the time the doctors get into the operating room, you will have been prepped and draped and pretty much the only thing we'll see is your abdomen."

She sighs in relief. "Oh, okay."

Her hand rests under mine, and I realize we're dangerously close to holding hands. She senses it too, sharing a look with me like the other day. We both stare at each other wondering who will be the first to pull away.

I hear a noise behind us. We simultaneously pull our hands apart as we turn around to see Charlie standing in the doorway. She has a huge, knowing smile on her face, and I say a silent prayer of thanks that it wasn't someone else who caught us sharing a moment. Someone like Abby. Or Gina. Or, God forbid, Dr. Redman.

I've got to be more careful. I can't have this—whatever this is—ruining my career or getting in the way of Elizabeth's care.

"Hi, Charlie," Elizabeth says, embarrassed that we were caught.

"Hey, guys." Charlie walks across the room, putting a bag of food in front of Elizabeth.

Elizabeth smiles, thanking Charlie for the meal as she tears into the bag, pulling out a greasy fast food burger. She bites into it as if she's never tasted food before. I have a hard time pulling my eyes away. I've never before wanted to be a piece of meat like I do right now. The noises she's making. The look on her face. *Damn.*

"As your doctor, I'd be remiss if I didn't bring up the amount of cholesterol you are ingesting."

She rolls her eyes at me and pats her belly. "Baby had a craving," she says around a mouthful of food.

"Oh, it's the baby's fault," I say, sarcastically.

"Totally," she replies.

Charlie laughs. "Don't even think of arguing with a pregnant woman, Kyle."

I hold up my hands. "I wouldn't dare."

"Are you going to watch the game with us?" Charlie asks.

"Game?"

"The Nighthawks game. I'm here to watch it with Elizabeth."

"No, I have to get back to work. Dr. Redman has been assigning me more cases lately."

"Too bad," Charlie says, turning to Elizabeth. "Guess we'll just have to drool over Caden Kessler ourselves."

Elizabeth scrunches her nose in disgust. I guess she doesn't think I should be drooling over him, either.

"What, you too?" I ask Charlie. "What is it about that guy that makes chicks go wild?"

"Other than the fact that he's a hot young baseball star?" Charlie asks.

I gather my magazines to leave when I hear pagers going off all over the OB floor. Mine goes off, too. I check it to see it's an 'all-hands-on-deck' page. My adrenaline starts pumping.

"What is it?" Elizabeth asks, looking concerned as people run past her doorway.

"I'm not sure. Everyone's being paged to the ER. The last time this happened, it was a school shooting."

Her hand comes up to cover her mouth. "Oh, my God. I hope everything is okay."

"I might not be able to check on you later," I say, hooking my pager back onto my pants. "It all depends."

"Of course," she says, looking concerned. "Go."

I run into Gina at the elevator. I can see it on her face, the same expression that I know is on mine. We don't know whether to be excited or saddened that there has been some kind of mass casualty event. As ER doctors, we live for this shit. The blood. The carnage. The trauma cases that we hope we can help.

But as human beings, we know this page most likely means death and destruction.

A few others pile into the elevator.

"I heard it was a building collapse," someone says.

"My cousin just texted me about a huge fire," says another.

When the doors open, we can already hear the commotion coming from the ER. We run around the corner and are met with nurses handing us gowns and gloves. People are pushing gurneys, lining them up along walls in preparation. Nurses are wheeling carts heavy with procedure trays, and techs are bringing massive quantities of blood.

Gina and I are told to join the other residents over by curtain one. Dr. Neill, one of the supervising residents, is already addressing the others when we join in.

"There was a fire in a clothing factory. Early reports from FDNY say chemicals were present that accelerated the spread, causing major structural damage and partial collapse of the building. Prepare yourselves, people. There are a lot of casualties. Some children even. Mostly immigrants. Remember your trauma protocol. Each arrival will have been tagged by EMTs in the field. We're the closest hospital, so we're getting the majority of the critical cases."

Gina grabs my hand in fear and we look at each other knowing what's about to happen. Knowing we are about to witness people dying in one of the most horrible ways.

"Your first priority as residents is to help clear out existing patients to make room for the incoming ones. After that, it's all hands on deck. Make yourselves useful wherever you can."

He throws a couple small vials of Vicks rub to some of the residents. "Put this under your nose. The smell of burnt flesh can be nauseating," Dr. Neill says, heading for the ambulance bay doors. "Remember your training, doctors. And good luck to us all."

We silently pass around the container, each putting a dab under our nostrils.

This is going to be bad. This is going to be very bad.

CHAPTER TWENTY-THREE

We quickly clear the waiting room of non-emergent cases. Then we help the nurses move existing patients into the outpatient and ambulatory wings. Anyone who can be admitted, is done so swiftly, and anyone who can be referred to another hospital or clinic, is asked to leave to make room for the trauma cases headed our way.

Within fifteen minutes, everything is cleared out and ready. We worked like a well-oiled machine. And now we all stand here, gowned and gloved in the calm before the storm. We look at each other, knowing full well we will lose patients today. We look at each other knowing some of us may be changed forever by what we're about to experience.

Gina grabs my hand again. "We'll get each other through this," she says. "We always do."

I walk out to the ambulance bay expecting to hear sirens. But—nothing. I look around at the other residents and attendings who are all standing at the ready. We quietly wait for the shitstorm we know is coming.

The charge nurse pushes out through the double doors, carrying her emergency radio. She shakes her head. "Many of the injuries were fatal," she says, clearly feeling emotional pain. "They are still pulling people out, but I was just told not to expect more than two dozen or so."

Faint sirens in the background get louder and overtake the collective gasps and cries of everyone absorbing the nurse's words.

"Okay, people," Dr. Manning says, shouting over the sirens and sad murmurs. "We still have twenty-four people who need our help. Let's not let this tragedy take any more than necessary. Deal with your emotions later."

Three ambulances pull up one after the other. "Nelson, Jameson, and Stone, you're with me," Dr. Neill says, opening the back of the third one.

There is a rush of acrid smell. Burning hair and flesh that even the Vicks can't mask.

I've smelled minor burns before; and in surgery, they sometimes use electrocautery to cut tissue, but it's nothing like this. It's not like burnt pork or beef as most people imagine, it's a charcoal-like smell with a sulfurous odor that has a fog of humanity to it. And because you know it's human flesh, it's haunting. The smell is so overwhelming I know it will be burned into my memory forever.

Craig Nelson, a first-year intern, runs to the outer wall of the ambulance bay, bracing himself with his hands as he vomits onto the concrete.

My own stomach turns due to the vile smell, not to mention the horror of what we're seeing. I can't even tell if our patient is a man or a woman due to the extensive burns. But as we wheel the gurney through the doors, I can see long hair matted against the shoulder of what I assume is a woman's body. The other half of her hair is gone, burned off along with much of the skin on her scalp.

The entire left side of her body is charred, her clothes having melted right into her flesh. She's conscious and in pain, but probably not in excruciating pain. Not from the burns anyway. Her nerve endings are most likely deadened.

She reaches up with her good arm and grabs onto me, her eyes filled with fear.

One of the EMTs briefs us on her condition as the charge nurse directs us to an open room. As I listen to the EMT describe her injuries, I once again feel ill. He estimates third-degree burns over seventy percent of her body. He shakes his head at us.

It's a death sentence.

"What's her name?" Neill asks.

"I think it's Rosita," the EMT says.

Neill looks at the commotion behind us as more critical cases are being wheeled into the ER. People are starting to arrive to look for loved ones. Many are crying, some screaming, patients are yelling out in pain, hospital staff are scrambling about. It's a scene from a war zone.

He looks at our patient and then at me. "Dr. Stone, Rosita is your patient now." He pulls me to the side. "I need to be out there helping those who might survive. There is nothing we can do but make her comfortable. Start her on oxygen. Give her morphine and cover the burns with towels soaked in saline. Debridement of the wounds would just cause her unnecessary pain, and an IV would simply lead to more swelling. It's possible you'll have to perform a fasciotomy, but we'll play that by ear. Keep her warm—she'll feel chilled. And contact family if you can."

I nod. "Yes, sir."

He takes Nelson and Jameson with him. Probably to find the next dying victim to assign them to. He closes the door behind him, closing us off from the mayhem beyond.

Rosita is crying, rattling off words in Spanish that I fail to understand.

"Do you speak English, Rosita?"

"Yes."

"You've been badly burned, but we need to see if you have other injuries. Can you tell me where it hurts?"

"Here," she says, putting her hand over her lower right-side ribs where a large bruise is forming.

"I'll give you something for the pain. Is there anyone we can call?"

"Sí, my husband, Raul," she says in a heavy accent muffled by the oxygen mask I put on her. Her voice is hoarse as her throat is most likely swelling from smoke inhalation.

I write down the number she gives me and hand it to the nurse who comes in.

We get busy cutting off what clothing we can so we can get Rosita into a gown. Then I give her morphine to take the edge off her pain.

"See if we can get an ultrasound machine," I ask Sandra. "And call her husband, please."

I remove the mask and look down Rosita's throat. It's bad, but not bad enough to intubate her yet. She needs to be able to speak to her husband. Once she gets intubated, that's it, there's no going back.

I make her as comfortable as I can. She looks down at her burned arm. Then her good arm comes across her body to feel the horribly disfigured left side of her head.

She gasps. "¡Dios mío!" She grabs my hand and looks at me. "How much is burned?"

"Don't worry about that, Rosita. Let us take care of you."

She squeezes my hand. "How much, doctor?"

I blow out a deep sigh, trying to keep the awful truth out of my eyes. "Over seventy percent."

She nods, failing to fight back her tears. "I don't have much time, especially if my liver is damaged."

I stare at her, confused. She was working in a garment factory. "Are you a doctor?"

"I was a nurse," she says, taking a big breath that I know is hard for her. She removes her mask so she can speak more clearly. "Fifteen years ago in Guadalajara, before we came to America. But Raul wanted our child to be born here." She covers her mouth to muffle her cries. "¡Oh, mi hijo! Julio will be devastated. He is so young."

I sit with Rosita as she breaks down and comes to terms with what is happening to her. I don't tell her it will be okay, because she knows it won't be. I just hold her hand and let her go through all of the emotions.

Sandra finally comes back with the ultrasound machine. "You have to be quick. They need it elsewhere."

It doesn't take me long to confirm Rosita's self-diagnosis. She has a substantial laceration on her liver. She's right. She doesn't have much time.

"And her family?" I ask Sandra.

She shakes her head sadly. "I left a message."

"My Raul is good man. He won't waste time on phone when at work." She looks at the clock on the wall. "Two o'clock is his lunchtime. He will call then. He always call me then." Then she looks around frantically. "¡Mi teléfono!"

"I'm sorry," I say. "We don't have your phone, but Sandra told him how to contact us."

I pull Sandra to the side. "Call him back, have him bring their son, Julio, if he can. She doesn't have a lot of time. Maybe a few hours at best."

I make note of the time. It's 1:50. I pray Raul is a man of his word.

"Doctor," Rosita calls me back over.

"Dr. Stone," I tell her, taking her hand in mine. "What can I do for you, Rosita. Anything."

She must be in a huge amount of pain because of the injury to her liver. I up her morphine, hoping that will help.

"Just sit," she says. "Back in Guadalajara, I sit with dying patients. Talking helps. You talk."

Normally, I'd encourage *her* to talk. In medical school, they taught us it's good to have terminal patients reflect on their lives. It helps them make the transition. But whenever Rosita speaks, it puts strain on her already swollen airway.

So, I put the oxygen mask back over her mouth and do what she asks. I talk. I tell her about my childhood and some of the antics my brothers and I had shared. She smiles weakly and I know she's thinking of Julio and how she hopes he will still have a normal childhood despite the fact he's about to lose a parent.

I tell her about my mom and dad and my nephew, Eli. I even tell her about Elizabeth. I tell her much more than what I shared with Cameron. I'm not sure why. Maybe I just needed to tell someone. Like a confession to a priest.

Rosita pulls down the mask and then grabs my hand. "Don't wait, doctor. Life is too short for worries about such things. Love will find a way, even if you no want."

Her breathing becomes more ragged and I check her throat. "Rosita, I may need to intubate you."

Sandra comes back in the room. "Her husband is on his way." She looks sadly at Rosita. "I'm sorry, but your husband can't get in touch with your son. He said something about a field trip."

Rosita nods. "Sí, Sí. Better this way." She turns to me. "No tube."

"But—"

She grabs my hand again, firmer this time. "I know you want to do everything to help. But I tell you—no tube. My Raul come. He is all I need."

I nod at her, my own throat becoming thick with tears.

"No heroic measure," she says, looking me square in the eyes. "Do you understand? I cannot put Raul through that."

"I understand," I say, making the note in her chart. "You heard that, Sandra, right?"

"Yes, Dr. Stone."

I watch Rosita try to fix her hair with her good hand. Hair that is matted and singed and only half there. It's surreal watching people die. Once they accept it's going to happen, they are only worried about those around them. And Rosita, being a nurse, knew the score immediately.

She knows that even without the laceration on her liver, it won't take long for the lactic acid building up in her body to cause major cell damage. She knows she'll go into hypovolemic shock due to reduced blood circulation. She also knows it won't take long for her organs to start shutting down, starting with her kidneys.

I steal a moment away from her bedside to talk with Sandra. "What's it like out there?" I ask.

Sandra shakes her head. "It's better now, but it got really bad for a while. Mostly because we don't know what to do with all of the friends and family who are demanding answers. There were so many dead at the scene, a coroner went over there to pronounce them. People are scrambling to find their loved ones. And some people are still trapped in the rubble."

"How many did we get?"

"Two dozen or so, but several of those died en route. We've lost a few more since. But the remainder are stable."

"Children?" I ask. "I heard Dr. Manning say there were children there."

She nods sadly. "A few."

Her pager goes off. "Looks like her husband is here," she says, reading it. "I'll go get him."

I walk back over to the bed. "Rosita, Raul is here. Sandra is bringing him back."

A tear trickles down her cheek and she removes the oxygen mask, taking it completely off her face for what we both know will be the last time.

"Do I look okay?" she asks, trying to pretend she's not in terrible pain.

I grab her hand. "You look beautiful, Rosita. Raul is a lucky man."

Through the window, I see Sandra escorting a man to the door. I slip out and tell him what's going on and what to expect, including his wife's wishes for us not to use heroic measures.

He starts to break down, chanting something in Spanish as his back meets the wall and then his hands meet his knees.

"Raul," I say, holding him up as he peers through the window at his dying wife. "You can fall apart later. Rosita needs you now. She needs to say goodbye. *You* need to say goodbye. I'll be right there if you need me."

He straightens up and wipes his tears. Then he takes several deep breaths and walks through the door.

I go into the room with him and stand over in a corner. They both start speaking in their native tongue, but I don't need to speak Spanish to know they are saying words of love and comfort and sorrow.

Raul climbs onto the bed next to her, on the side with the fewest burns, and he cradles her in his arms. I hear their son's name several times. I hear him sing to her softly. Then, her breathing becomes labored, and the monitors start to beep.

I quickly shut the monitors down knowing there is no use for them anymore.

As Rosita struggles to take her last breaths, Raul leans down and kisses her. He kisses her as she passes from this world to the next.

When her body goes limp, he screams out in pain, burying his head into her chest. I walk over and put a comforting hand on him. There are simply no words.

I give him a few minutes. He needs this time. I need this time. I'm not even sure I could use my stethoscope with the way my hands are shaking.

Finally, he pulls himself together and lifts his head. "I need to make some calls," he says.

"There is a family lounge down the main hallway. It should be quiet in there."

He nods, peeling himself away from his wife. He leans down to give her one last kiss and then he walks out of the room.

I go to the bedside and listen to her heart. Sandra walks in just as I pronounce Rosita dead. Then I sit in the chair and put my head between my legs.

"I'll finish up in here, Dr. Stone."

I nod, taking a few deep breaths before heading out to ground zero, where I see that over the past few hours, everything else has been handled. There is nothing left for me to do. Gina sees me from across the room and runs over.

"Manning's telling the residents to take a break. Re-group. Even go home if we need to. This was a lot to handle."

I turn away from her, walking and then running to the residents' lounge where I just barely make it to the bathroom before I wretch into the toilet.

I wipe my face and then use mouthwash to rinse out my mouth. Then I sit down in a chair and breathe.

Gina comes up behind me. She runs her hands down my chest and then walks around and kneels between my legs. She takes my head in her hands.

"It was a tough day," she says, right before kissing me.

I should want this. This is what we do for each other. This is how we numb the pain. This is how we handle our stress and our grief. So why can't I kiss her back? Why can't I do what we've always done?

She pulls back, sensing my hesitation. She stands up and holds out her hand. "Come on, Kyle. Let's find an on-call room. We both need this after what we've seen."

I let her pull me up. Her hands in mine don't feel right anymore. Her fingers are long and slender, her hands a bit dry from all the washing we do, her nails short and bare.

I find myself needing different hands. Ones that are soft and small. Ones that have pink nails to match a certain pair of pink pajamas.

"I'm sorry, Gina. I can't do this anymore."

I break her hold on me and walk out the door of the lounge.

She calls out after me. "Kyle!"

But I keep walking. I walk to the elevators, but when I see they are all up on top floors, I walk to the stairway. Then I walk up the stairs. Then I run up the stairs, taking them two at a time. I race up to floor seven and don't stop running until I hit the very end of the hallway.

I barge into her room and shut the door behind me.

"Kyle. Oh, my God, what's wrong?" Elizabeth asks.

I don't even hesitate before walking over to sit on the edge of her bed. I can't stop the tears from falling. Painful tears that I held in all afternoon. Sobs bellow out of me as Elizabeth runs a soothing hand down my back.

Small arms come up to embrace me when I start shaking uncontrollably. "Shhh," she whispers, her hot breath flowing over my ears. "It's okay, Kyle. It's okay. Whatever it is, it'll be okay."

She consoles me like this for what . . . minutes? Hours? I lose track of time being in her arms. I lose myself in them. And by the time I come around and realize the colossal inappropriateness of the situation, I know—I know for sure this is the only fucking place I ever want to be.

CHAPTER TWENTY-FOUR

It's been two days since the fire at the factory. Two days of Gina giving me the cold shoulder. Two days of Elizabeth and I not talking about what happened when I broke down in her arms.

Two days of me trying to figure out my life.

"You holding up okay?" Ethan asks after dinner.

My brothers thought I could use a night with family and friends after what happened. And I think the girls are using this as a chance to plan that baby shower Baylor was talking about.

I nod. "I'm fine."

I don't tell him I haven't slept since that day. Not well, anyway. Because every time I close my eyes, I see Rosita. I see her burned and broken and trying to be strong so she could say goodbye to her husband. I see her telling me life is too short. I see her *showing* me just how true that is.

I hold my twenty-month-old nephew, Eli, on my lap and bounce him around. I take in his fine blonde hair, his chubby cheeks, and his hazel eyes and wonder what Elizabeth's daughter will look like a year or two from now. Will she have blue eyes like her mother? Some shade of brown hair, perhaps?

Or will she resemble the bastard who helped make her, but who wasn't man enough to stick around for the big show?

The past few sleepless nights, I've found myself wondering what life would be like if I brought Elizabeth and the baby home with me. What would my apartment look like with diapers, highchairs, and toys strewn across the floor?

It's not something I've ever allowed myself to wonder.

I want kids, yes. But I'm not even twenty-eight years old. Not even a bonafide doctor yet. I have so much more I need to accomplish before I do that.

Like what? I ask myself.

Like becoming an attending. Like working in the ER for a few years and then opening my own clinic.

I stare at the cute kid drooling onto my lap. Who says I can't do all that *and* this?

"Who, indeed," I hear behind me.

I whip my head around to see Charlie standing over my shoulder, staring at me while I play with her son.

"Did I say that out loud?" I ask.

She laughs and sits down next to me. Eli reaches out for her and crawls onto her lap, yawning at the late hour.

"It's okay, Kyle. You went through a very stressful situation. It's only normal you'd readjust the way you look at the world. But I get the idea you were thinking about doing that even *before* the fire."

I look at her and cock my head. "What do you mean?"

"Oh, come on. I've seen the way you look at Elizabeth. I've seen the way you *touch* her, Kyle. I've heard the way she talks about you. There is definitely something there if you want it to be."

"You've been to see her a lot, Charlie. Has she ever said anything about the baby's father?"

"No, she hasn't. I don't think she's spoken to any of us about him."

"It could be a big issue," I say.

"Yes, it could be. Some of us do tend to have those," she says, with a loving glance over at Ethan. "But you just have to figure out if those issues are worth overcoming."

"How can I, if I don't even know what they are?"

"Have you tried asking her outright?" she asks.

I shake my head. "No. She clams up whenever I make any references to her past. She's got enough on her plate right now. Maybe after the baby comes she'll be more willing to talk about it."

"I'll bet she will be," Charlie says. "It's amazing how having a child can make you want to change your entire world."

A bottle of beer gets handed to me. It's the same craft beer I brought Ethan a few weeks ago. I turn around and raise my eyebrows at him. "You *do* like it," I say.

"It's his favorite now," Charlie whispers to me. "But don't tell him I told you that."

She puts Eli down for the night and then the girls get together and plan Elizabeth's baby shower as the guys gather around the television to watch the sports highlights.

When the baseball reels come on, I can't help my smile. When I see the Nighthawks won their game today, I might even shout out.

"Wait, what?" Griffin says with a sour face. "So now you're a Hawks fan? Traitor."

I toss a bottle cap at him. "How can I be a traitor when I'm not even from Ohio?"

"What's wrong with the Hawks?" Mason asks Griffin. "Some of my good buddies are on that team."

"What's wrong with them is that they aren't the Indians," Griffin says.

"Care to make a friendly wager on who wins out at their next meeting?" Mason asks.

Gavin gets out his wallet. "I want in on this action," he says. "I'm with Griffin. Put me down for a hundred on Cleveland."

"Hell, yeah," Chad says. "I'm good for a bill on my home team."

"Wait." I put a stop to their schoolyard betting. "You have friends on the Nighthawks?" I ask Mason. "Do you know number eight?"

"Kessler? Yeah. I've met him a couple of times. Had drinks with him a few weeks ago, when he and some of his teammates showed up at a Giants' benefit. Why?"

The wheels in my head are spinning. "Is he the kind of guy who would do a favor for a friend?" I ask. "Like a big favor?"

"I don't know," he says. "Guess it depends on the favor."

"Elizabeth, my pregnant patient in the hospital, loves the Hawks, and him in particular. She's been stuck on bed rest for weeks and still has a while to go. Do you think—"

"Dude," Chad says, interrupting me. "You want to impress your girlfriend by bringing her a baseball star?"

"Fuck you," I say, shooting him a death stare. "She's not my girlfriend, Chad. And if all I wanted to do was impress her, I'd have shown up in her hospital room with *your* sorry ass."

While the guys share a laugh and continue to talk about their moronic bet, Mason pulls me to the side.

"I'll give Caden a call," he says. "How long will she be laid up?"

"Only until she has to deliver the baby. Could be tomorrow. Could be next week. The sooner he could get there, the better."

"I'll see what I can do," he says.

"Thanks, man."

"Not a problem," Mason says, giving me a supportive squeeze of my shoulder. "Sometimes we have to pull out all the stops for the ones we think are worth it." He looks across the room to his fiancée, Piper.

I look around at the couples sitting in Charlie and Ethan's living room, thinking of all the shit they had to go through to get where they are today. My life has been a walk in the park compared to what some of them have endured.

Then I think of what Elizabeth is going through. What she might have gone through to get here. What I don't ever want her to have to deal with again. And I know with one hundred percent certainly that she's worth it.

CHAPTER TWENTY-FIVE

"Thank you so much for doing this," I say, shaking Caden's hand at the entrance to the hospital. "You'll never know how much this means to me and my patient."

"Happy to do it," he says. "Especially as a favor to Mason Lawrence. He's a great guy. He makes all pro athletes look bad with his portfolio of causes and foundations."

"Yeah, I'm honored to have him as a friend." I open the doors and escort him through. "I can't believe you could do this on such short notice."

"Our rain delay turned into a cancellation," he says, gesturing to the storm outside. "So as luck would have it, my afternoon is free, thanks to mother nature."

A few kids horsing around in the atrium see Caden and get all bug-eyed as they run over to us.

"Mr. Kessler, can I have your autograph?" one asks.

"Sure, slugger. What can I sign for you?" He points to the kid's ball cap. "How about this?"

"Oh, yeah," the boy says. "That would be sweet. Thanks."

Caden scribbles his name on the kid's hat and then turns to the other one. "How about you? Your shirt, maybe? Unless you think your mom will get mad."

The boy, who is maybe twelve years old, looks over at a woman who then nods her head.

"Looks like Mom's okay with it," Caden says, kneeling down to sign the back of his shirt across one shoulder.

"James is gonna die," the kid says. "He'll never believe he missed this."

I laugh as the boy tries to see the autograph without having to remove his shirt.

"Who is James?" Caden asks. "Your friend?"

"Our brother," the small one says. "He got sick and is having surgery. App . . . uh, appendus . . ."

"Appendicitis, stupid," the older one says.

Caden looks at them in thought. "Is James a Hawks fan?" he asks.

"Oh, yes. We all are," the younger one says.

Caden takes off his own hat and writes *James – get well soon, Caden Kessler #8'* on the bill. He gives it to the smallest boy. "Give this to James when he wakes up, okay?"

"Wow," the kid says in awe. "He gets your hat? He's lucky."

They thank Caden and run back to their mom who smiles over at us.

"Do you get that wherever you go?" I ask him as we walk away, thinking how my brother, Chad, has the same problem.

"Pretty much, but it's okay. I don't mind. I'm still getting used to it all."

"How long have you been with the Nighthawks?" I ask. "Sorry, I don't have much time to follow sports these days."

"This is my first full season. They drafted me when I was a junior at UNC. I started with their single-A team in Tampa, and then I was lucky enough to skip right to triple-A out in Las Vegas where I played until they called me up late last summer. It's been a wild ride."

"Wow, you've moved around a lot," I say.

"I go where they tell me. But I really like New York, so I hope they'll let me stay."

"Based on what I've seen, they'd be fools not to. You're a great player."

"Thanks. I've worked my whole life to get here," he says.

I nod. "I know what you mean."

We step into the elevators and I hit the button for the seventh floor. "Well, for being so new, you seem to have quite a following." I nod back to the kids in the atrium. "And my patient, Elizabeth, she seems to know all about you. She won't let any of the staff do procedures if you're in a game or being featured on the highlights."

He laughs. "I'm really just happy to do what I can. It's surreal. It's everything I dreamed of since I was a kid. The only thing missing is . . ."

He looks down at the elevator floor and blows out a breath.

"Is what?" I ask.

He shrugs. "People to share it with," he says. "Family."

"I guess with your sudden fame, you have to be careful, huh? But, hey, you're way too young to consider settling down with a family. What are you, twenty-four?"

"Twenty-three," he says.

The elevator dings and the doors open as we reach the seventh floor. I find myself getting excited knowing I'm about to blow Elizabeth's mind when I walk in her room with Caden Kessler. I wonder what she'll do.

I'm glad she'll be lying in bed, otherwise she might faint. I can't wait to see the look on her face. That smile that makes her eyes light up. That blush that reddens her cheeks and neck. Damn, I love making that woman happy.

Caden gets recognized by one of the nurses and we stop so he can say hello. I look down the hall into Elizabeth's open doorway, my heart pounding with excitement.

I catch a glimpse of movement, her pink pajamas slowly moving past the doorway as she makes her way to the bathroom. She looks up and catches my eyes.

She smiles.

Caden laughs behind me and I start to turn around to see what's so funny when I see Elizabeth's face become filled with fear. She puts a hand on her belly and closes the door. Before I have a chance to process it, the call light for her room goes off at the nurses' station.

Oh, shit. Maybe her water broke.

"Wait here," I say to Caden, right before I race down the hall alongside Abby.

I burst into her room to find the bed empty. I walk to the bathroom. "Elizabeth!" I shout through the door. "Are you okay? What is it?"

I hear her faint sobs though the door.

"I . . . I don't feel very good."

"Are you bleeding? Did your water break?" My heart is pounding thinking of what is happening on the other side of this door. "Can we come in?"

"Who's out there with you?" she asks.

"It's just Abby and me," I tell her. "What's wrong?"

I hear the water turn on and then off. Then she cracks the door and looks out at us. "I'm not bleeding. But I don't feel well. My stomach hurts. Maybe I ate something bad. I don't know. But I'm sick. I think I need to lie down and sleep."

"You need to come out and let us check you over, Elizabeth." I turn to Abby. "Please go get the ultrasound machine."

"Can you shut the door, please?" Elizabeth asks her, wiping the corner of her eye. "I look a mess. I don't want anyone to see."

"Of course," Abby says on her way out.

"Come on." I hold my hand out to her. "Let's get you back to bed."

As we pass the door, Elizabeth strains her head to look out the small window. God, if she only knew who was out there. *Damn it.* I can't bring him in now, not with her feeling ill. And I can't tell her about him being here either, it would only make her feel bad that he came all this way for nothing.

Abby comes back in with the ultrasound. We quickly do the sonogram and confirm the baby is okay and the placenta is intact. I take Elizabeth's vitals, and although her heart rate is slightly elevated, everything seems normal.

I hook her back up to the fetal monitor and she lies on her side, pulling the sheet up to her chin.

"I just want to sleep," she says. "Can you please turn off the lights and make sure nobody disturbs me for a while?"

"Yes. We can do that," I say. "Lie on your left side. And have me paged if you feel any worse or if anything changes. Okay?"

She nods. Then she closes her eyes tightly like she's wishing something away.

It kills me to think of her in pain. "Are you sure you don't need me to stay?"

"I really just want to be alone and rest," she says.

"I'll check on you later then."

As Abby and I walk back to the nurses' station, I ask her to keep Caden's visit a secret. I don't want Elizabeth to get wind of it. Maybe I'll be able to get him back another day.

"Caden, I'm sorry, the patient I invited you to see has gotten sick and can't have visitors."

"I'm sorry to hear that," he says. "Maybe I could send some stuff over instead. You know, a jersey, a couple of signed pictures. You said her name is Elizabeth, right?"

"Yes. That would be great, man. I'd really appreciate it."

After he leaves, the nurses stand around and swoon over him. I roll my eyes. Maybe it's a good thing he didn't get to see her. I sure as hell don't want Elizabeth swooning over anyone.

Not unless that someone is me.

CHAPTER TWENTY-SIX

I spent the better part of the afternoon down in the ER, having been paged for a consult. Dr. Anders and I attended to a few pregnant women who were involved in a car accident.

By the time I make it back to check on Elizabeth, there is a package waiting for her at the nurses' station.

I pick up her chart, relieved to see no new notes after I'd left her. I grab the package and head to her room.

The lights are back on and when I peek through the window, I see her sitting up and reading. I knock once and open the door.

"Feeling better?" I ask.

"Much," she says, putting the book on her tray table. "What's that?" She eyes the box I'm carrying.

"Guess you'll have to open it to find out."

She cocks her head to the side in disapproval. "Kyle, I wish you wouldn't—"

"Just open it, Elizabeth," I say, putting the package next to her on the bed.

She opens it slowly, thinking it's from me, no doubt. I've never seen a woman so hesitant about getting gifts. I mean, she doesn't seem to want handouts from *anyone*, least of all me. It makes me wonder how she'll react when she finds out about the baby shower.

There's a card inside the box, sitting on top of some tissue paper. I peek over her shoulder and read it.

Elizabeth – sorry we didn't get a chance to meet when I stopped by earlier. I hope you are feeling better. – Caden Kessler #8

Her hand comes up to her mouth to muffle a gasp.

"Caden Kessler was here to meet *me?*"

She looks up at me not in excitement or giddiness; she looks up at me in . . . horror. "Oh, my God, do you know him, Kyle?"

"No, I don't know him. He's a friend of a friend. I wanted to surprise you."

She looks pale. I remember how she was scared to meet Baylor at first, too. Maybe she's just embarrassed to be seen lying in a bed wearing pajamas.

"I'm sorry you couldn't meet him."

"No, it's okay. Actually, I'm glad. I'm not one of those obsessed fans who wants to meet ball players, you know. I'm sure there are lots of women who'd want that. Not me. I'm happy to watch the games and cheer them on, but I don't want to *meet* them. God, no."

I laugh. "Elizabeth, I hate to break it to you, but you *are* an obsessed fan. Are you sure about not meeting him? Because I could probably get him back."

Once again, she gives me that deer in headlights look. "I'm sure, Kyle. Please, don't try to bring him back."

"Fine. I was just trying to do something to break up the monotony. Something to make you happy."

"I don't need *him* to make me happy," she says, looking sad. "I just need . . ." her voice trails off as she looks into my eyes, then she shies away and looks out the window.

"What, Elizabeth? What do you need?"

My words draw her gaze back to me and we share a moment. A moment of what, I'm not sure, but I think it resembles something like a moment of need. Her needing me. Me needing her. Us needing this.

I want nothing more than to sit on her bed and take her in my arms. I already know what it feels like to be in *hers*. What it feels like to have her touch me, run a hand down my back. Speak soft words into my ear.

Hell, I want more than to just take her in my arms. I want to kiss her. I've never wanted to kiss anyone so badly before in my life.

It's fucking crazy. She's pregnant. She's so pregnant, she's about to pop. Yet she's the most beautiful thing I think I've ever seen.

I have to reel in my emotions. Get control of myself. She's my patient. The other stuff—if there is any other stuff—will have to wait. I've got a million questions to ask her. There aren't enough flavors of Jell-O to find out everything I want to know about this woman. But damned if I'm not going to try.

Later. After the baby comes. Maybe then she'll be more amenable to letting me help her.

I nod to the package. "Are you going to open it, or what?"

She carefully removes the tissue paper and pulls out one of those onesie baby outfits. She turns it over and sees the #8 on the back. She traces it with her finger and then brings the onesie to her chest, hugging it.

I get the feeling this might be the first piece of clothing she's gotten for the baby. I have to hold in my chuckle, knowing she's having a girl. Then again, knowing Elizabeth and how obsessed she is with baseball, she'll only be too happy to dress her daughter in such things.

She unpacks the rest of the box, pulling out a ball cap, an adult-sized jersey also with his name and number on it, an autographed picture of Caden, and four box seat tickets to a late-season game.

She looks at the tickets hungrily. Then she hands them to me. "Why don't you take these," she says.

"What? No." I point to the date on the tickets. "You'll be fully recovered by then," I say. "Sleep-deprived, but recovered." I laugh, pushing the tickets back to her.

"I don't want to go," she says, clearly lying to me. "I prefer to watch the games on TV."

"Keep them," I tell her. "Maybe you'll change your mind."

She tucks the tickets back into the box along with the rest of the things he sent over. She puts the lid on it and runs her hand over the box longingly. Then she places it on her side table and looks back at me. "Dr. Lawson came to see me earlier."

"Gina?" I ask, surprised.

We haven't crossed paths for days. And I haven't figured out yet if it's me who's avoiding a confrontation, or Gina. I need to have the conversation with her. She knows something's up. I think she's known for a while. But I owe it to her to be honest. I need to tell her it's over.

"She was asking all kinds of personal questions about what I'm going to do after the baby comes. Things like where I'm going to live and how involved the baby's father is going to be. Non-medical questions. It was strange, she was trying to make it seem like she was doing her job. She even had my chart and looked to be writing stuff down, but Kyle, I got the distinct impression her visit was anything but professional."

Shit.

"I'm sorry. I'll talk to her."

"No, don't. She likes you. I can see that. I think she was just trying to, I don't know . . ."

"Size up the competition?" I ask.

Her eyes snap to mine. It's the first time either of us has really acknowledged this, whatever this is. Other than the mutual bite of blue Jell-O we shared last week.

"Am I . . . competition?" she asks.

"Do you want to be, Elizabeth?"

She rubs her hands across her belly in thought. I wish I knew what was going through her head right now. I damn sure know what's going through mine. I haven't ever held her in my arms. Haven't kissed her. Hell, I don't even know where she lives, or where she grew up, or what the name of her first pet was. But one thing is for sure, I don't want her leaving the hospital without me.

"It's a lot to think about, Kyle. Can we just take this one step at a time?" she asks.

I nod in agreement. "Yeah. We can do that," I say. "Let's make sure this little one arrives safely. The rest can wait."

"The rest," she whispers under her breath.

Then she looks up at me and smiles.

CHAPTER TWENTY-SEVEN

I try to schedule my time so I can pop in to see what Elizabeth thinks of her baby shower. With the increasing number of cases Dr. Redman has assigned me to, it's been harder to spend the hours per day I was spending with her just a week ago.

I'm happy my attending has decided to quit punishing me for my father's indiscretions. But at the same time, being sentenced to spend my days with Elizabeth was the best kind of resident torture.

I'm relieved when I hear nothing but delightful conversation and laughter as I make my way to the end of the hallway. I was worried she'd be upset by the outpouring of their generosity.

"Did you know about this?" Elizabeth asks with a smile when I walk into the room.

"I plead the fifth," I say with a wink. "Plus, baby showers are for chicks."

Several small stuffed animals are thrown at me by my sisters-in-law.

"They are not," Baylor says. "You should have seen the combined shower our friends and family had for Skylar and me."

"It was epic," Piper says, laughing at the memory. "They even hooked some guys up to a machine that simulated labor. It was hilarious."

I shudder thinking of it. Definitely for chicks.

I look around the room to see what they've brought her. I know they were only planning on bringing a few things to the hospital. They didn't want her to have to take much home. They told me they were hoping to have the rest delivered to her apartment.

I just wonder if that will happen. Will she tell them where she lives? Will she tell *me?*

I see several small outfits that could be used for either a boy or a girl. There is one of those Snugli things that allows a woman to 'wear' her baby on her chest. The largest thing in the room is an all-in-one car seat/stroller that looks like the Cadillac of all strollers.

I'm glad they didn't overwhelm her with gifts. All in all, everything they brought her could easily fit in the under-compartment of the stroller. But Elizabeth is smiling. That must mean they haven't yet told her about the garage full of other crap Baylor has accumulated for her.

"You've all done so much," Elizabeth says sadly, looking down to fiddle with her chunky bracelet. "I don't know how I can ever repay you."

"See, that's the thing about friends," Mallory says. "You don't *have* to repay them."

Elizabeth shakes her head. "It's so much."

"You realize we were just going to give this stuff away or donate it, right?" Baylor asks.

Elizabeth looks at Mallory, who is about as pregnant as *she* is. "But Mallory is about to have her first child. She needs all this stuff, too."

Mal laughs. "Do you know how many baby things Chad's mom has sent to us? I think we're going to need to get a bigger apartment just to accommodate all of it."

Elizabeth nods in acceptance. "Well, thank you all. I'm not sure how I would have gotten through these weeks without you."

The words she spoke were meant for everyone, I know. But she was looking directly at *me* when she said them.

My pager goes off. It's not an urgent page, just some labs I'd ordered that came back. Either way, it's a good excuse to leave them to their party.

"I'll check back on you later, Elizabeth," I say, walking out the door.

She calls me back. "With all your new patients, I bet you haven't eaten all day, Kyle." She reaches into a Sal's container and pulls out an egg roll. She puts it on a napkin and holds it out to me. "Come on, I know it's your favorite."

Five pairs of eyes watch as I cross the room to take it from her. Five mouths curve up into a smile as I bite into it on my way out the door.

"Wait," she says, before I get very far down the hallway.

I turn around and put my hand up to catch the fortune cookie she threw at me before it hits me in the head. I laugh, sticking it in my pocket.

"Seriously?" I hear someone say as I'm walking out to the nurses' station.

It's the voice I've dreaded, coming from the person I've avoided for the past week. I turn around. "Hey, Gina."

"Do you really mean to tell me your sisters-in-law and their friends are throwing your homeless patient a baby shower?"

I look down the hall and hear more laughter coming from the room at the end. "It looks that way," I tell her. "And for the umpteenth time, she's not homeless."

"Really? That's interesting coming from the guy who had to list *his* address on her hospital forms because she doesn't have one."

I give her an incredulous look. "How in the hell did you know that?" I ask.

She shrugs. "Nurses talk. Abby knows all the admissions nurses. I'm friends with Abby. You should know by now, nothing that goes on within these walls is secret."

"Whatever," I say, pulling her along behind me into an empty procedure room. "Gina, we have to talk."

She crosses her arms, eyeing me up and down. She's studying me.

"Oh, my God," she spits out. "Are you in love with your patient, Kyle?"

"What? No."

"You are," she says. "I knew you were taking pity on her. I may have even known you were smitten with her, but this? Kyle, you're not thinking clearly. I mean, she walks dogs for a living."

"What the fuck does it matter what she does? It doesn't make her any less of a person, Gina."

"What are you planning on doing, taking her and her baby home with you like strays?"

My blood starts to boil. "You and I are friends, Gina. We've been friends for a long time now, which is why I'm going to let that one slide. But you talk shit about her again and all bets are off."

She walks around the procedure bed, putting it between us. "If you want to end this," she says, pointing between us, "that's fine. I like you, Kyle, but I'll move on. But falling for a patient? Paying her bills? Bringing your friends and family in to befriend her? That's crossing the line."

I sit down on the stool, running a hand through my hair.

"I'm not in love with her," I say, trying to sound convincing. To her or to myself, I'm not sure. "At first, I guess I was just taking pity on her. But the more time I spent with her . . ."

Gina walks to the door. "Just tread carefully, Kyle."

"You won't say anything to anyone about this, will you?"

She shakes her head. "I won't tell Anders or Redman, if that's what you mean. But I can't guarantee they won't find out. Nurses talk."

I watch Gina walk through the door, leaving me alone in the room with my thoughts. There is nothing my supervisors can do to me if they found out about all of it, is there? Technically, I'm not doing anything wrong. Maybe, ethically, it's wrong to pay her hospital bill. But how can it be the wrong thing to do, when it's saving her from a lifetime of debt?

I took a vow, an oath to help people. How can I be faulted for sticking to it?

As I leave the procedure room, I glance down the hallway to see a couple of the girls sitting on the foot of Elizabeth's bed as they all admire baby clothes.

I study her. I watch her talk with my friends. Friends who are now *her* friends. She fits in well with them. She fits in well with *me*.

Love? I don't know. Is it possible to love someone you know so little about? Someone you've only seen for a few hours a day over the period of a few weeks? Someone who is pregnant with another man's child?

She looks my way to catch me staring. Our eyes meet. She holds my stare like a tractor beam. An earthquake in New York couldn't tear my eyes from hers. *Damn.* I wish I had some Jell-O. Because never have I ever fallen in love.

Not until right fucking now.

CHAPTER TWENTY-EIGHT

A few days later, I'm checking on Elizabeth when she catches me by surprise. "Did you know Skylar and Baylor were going to offer me jobs?"

I put down her chart and look up in wonder. "*That* I didn't know about," I tell her. "Really?"

She nods. "They both came by last night to bring me dinner. Skylar offered me a job as a hostess at Mitchell's."

"It would be a nice place to work," I say. "It's a great restaurant."

"I'll bet it is, based on the incredible food she's brought me. But I can't be a hostess. Not with a baby."

"What about Baylor's offer?"

"She says she needs an assistant. Said I could even bring the baby to work." She shrugs. "I think she was just making the offer to be nice."

I shake my head. "No, she wasn't. Gavin is always saying how busy she is. She could use someone to keep everything in order."

"I don't know." She twists her bracelet around her wrist.

"Hey, you don't have to give her an answer today, right? It's not like she's needing to replace someone. I'm sure she'll let you think about it."

"That's what she told me. They both did. They said I didn't need to make a decision now since I couldn't work for a while anyway."

I sigh and run my hand through my hair. Four weeks minimum. That's how much time she'll need to recover from her surgery. Six would be even better. "Elizabeth, what are you going to do about paying your bills until you can work again? You'll need to take time off."

She laughs half-heartedly. "Time off from what? I don't even have a job anymore."

"I can help—"

"Stop." She looks at me with distant eyes. "You aren't giving me money, Kyle. I don't take handouts."

I look to the corner of her room where baby clothes are piled into the stroller. "You don't take handouts from *me?*" I ask. "Or from men in general?"

She looks out the window. "I'll be fine. Everyone has been more than generous. And I still have something I can sell."

I'm not sure if she realizes, but as she says that, her thumb and forefinger come up to rub the ring finger on her left hand. *Shit.* Was she engaged? Married?

I want so much to ask her these things, but she's already getting worked up. And like Charlie said, maybe she'll see things differently after the baby comes.

"Okay," I say. "But Elizabeth, if you find you need anything, not just now, but ever, all you have to do is ask."

She shifts uncomfortably on the bed and her hand comes up to her belly. I look at her stomach, and through the thin fabric of her pajama top, I can see the baby moving.

"The baby is really kicking today," she says. She looks up to see me studying her belly. "Do you . . . do you want to feel it?"

"Can I?"

She takes my hand and places it underneath hers. Then I feel a hand, foot, knee, or elbow poke me and I find it hard to keep my emotions intact. There is a person in there.

I know this. As a doctor, I know this. And almost daily, especially working in OB, I see babies coming into the world. But that doesn't stop me from feeling overwhelming emotion at the thought of there being a little version of Elizabeth in there.

My other hand finds a place on her stomach and I sit on the bed next to her as we both feel her child kick and squirm inside of her.

"Pretty great, huh?" she asks, looking into my eyes.

I've touched her before. When I've put the monitor on her. When the baby had the hiccups. When she held me after Rosita died. But this, this is the most intimate moment we have shared. I want to kiss her. I want to kiss her so badly it physically hurts me.

I glance at the open door to her room, weighing my options. But at this point, I'm not sure I even care if anyone sees. I want her to the very core of my soul. My job, ethics, the line I'm about to cross, they can all be damned as I lean in closer to her.

Then, suddenly, she looks up at me with wide eyes. Scared eyes. And I admonish myself for misreading the situation. Maybe she doesn't want this. Maybe I was about to take advantage of her in the worst way.

"Kyle! I just felt a pop," she says. "I think my water just broke."

I pull my hands away as my heart starts racing. "Did you feel a gush?"

She squirms around. "Yeah, and it's still coming. I feel like I'm wetting the bed."

I get up off the bed. "Elizabeth, I need to look at the sheet under you to see if there's any blood."

She nods, scooting up a little so I can see the wetness. It's clear. I'm thankful for that. I press the call button for the nurse just as the fetal monitor shows increased fetal heart tones.

Elizabeth looks terrified.

I grab her hand. "It's going to be okay," I tell her. "You're just a few days from thirty-seven weeks."

"I'm not ready," she says, a tear running down her cheek.

I reach out and wipe it with my thumb. "I know you're scared. I promise I'll be there with you." I take her face in my hands. "You're going to be an incredible mother."

"That's not it," she says, her chin quivering as she swallows hard. "I'm not ready."

Not ready for what, I wonder? To have the baby? To leave the hospital? To leave *me?* To face her past?

I hear footsteps out in the hallway, and I remove my hands from her just as Abby appears in her doorway. "Do you need me, Dr. Stone?"

"Elizabeth's water broke. Clear fluid. Prep her for surgery and page Dr. Redman."

"Yes, Dr. Stone."

Elizabeth cringes as her hands grasp her belly. I look at the monitor that confirms she's having a contraction.

"Elizabeth, we need to do this now. We don't want the placenta tearing as your cervix opens. I have to go get ready for the surgery. It'll all be okay. You can do this."

She nods, more tears streaming down her face. I want to hold her, comfort her, kiss the tears away. But more than that, I need to do my job so she and the baby are safe. And it takes everything I have to walk away from her.

CHAPTER TWENTY-NINE

Twenty minutes later, I enter the OR to see Elizabeth draped and ready. The epidural has been administered. The instruments are all in place. A nurse is adjusting her nasal cannula.

I follow the nurse's movements as she clips the pulse-ox sensor onto the finger of Elizabeth's left hand. My eyes come to a stop when I see that Elizabeth's chunky bracelet has been removed to reveal the tattoo that was underneath it.

As Dr. Redman talks to Elizabeth, I take the opportunity to get a closer look at the tattoo. On the inside of her left wrist, there are intertwining hearts with a name scripted over them.

Grant.

I've never despised a name so much.

Grant, her husband or boyfriend. Grant, the father of her child.

"Dr. Stone?" one of the nurses says, bringing my attention to the fact that I'm standing at the wrong end of our patient.

I look down at Elizabeth to see that she's caught me staring at her wrist. But she's too scared to care. I put a huge smile on my face as I look into her eyes. She can't see it beneath my mask, but that's okay, I tell her everything I need to tell her with my stare. I don't care if the nurses see it. I don't even care if Dr. Redman does. In this moment, I need to reassure Elizabeth that everything will be okay.

I take my position opposite Dr. Redman and watch her slice into the woman I love.

Less than two minutes later, Dr. Redman instructs me to reach in and pull out the baby. I tell Elizabeth that she will feel some tugging and pulling. I put my hand under the baby, forming a cradle for her head so I can pull her out as the nurse pushes down on Elizabeth's abdomen. The tiny body that emerges is gooey and messy and . . . absolutely perfect.

"Elizabeth, you have a daughter," I tell her, my voice cracking with emotion.

I can't begin to describe how I feel being the one to bring her baby into this world. To be the first one to hold her. See her. To instantly fall in love with her perfect little face, her tiny button nose, and her matted head of dark hair.

"It's a girl?" she asks excitedly from behind the drape.

"It's a girl." I suction her mouth and hand her off to the nurse. "Give us a minute and we'll bring her over."

The baby takes her first breath and starts crying to the smiles of everyone in the room. Elizabeth cries out in happiness when she hears her daughter's first sounds.

I lean over the drape to look at Elizabeth. "You did great, Mom."

"Dr. Stone, when I'm done stitching up the uterus, would you care to close?" Dr. Redman asks me.

"Absolutely."

I'm glad she asked. If I'm great at anything, I'm great at suturing. And I'm going to make sure I do my very best work.

After the nurse finishes the first APGAR test on the baby, she puts a tiny pink hat on her head and swaddles her tightly in a blanket. She walks the baby over to Elizabeth, holding her close to Elizabeth's face so she can see, smell and kiss her new daughter.

It kills me that I can't be on the other side of the drape to see every nuance of Elizabeth's face as she sees her daughter for the very first time. I want to kiss her. Cry with her. Laugh with her. Celebrate with her. I've never wanted anything so badly before.

I can't see her, but I can hear her.

"Oh, my gosh. Hi, baby girl," she says. "You're so beautiful."

She cries and mumbles words of love to her daughter.

After a minute, the nurse tries to take the baby away.

"Wait!" Elizabeth says, prompting the nurse to put the baby next to her head again. "I swear I will always protect you."

Those seven words resonate in my head. Protect her from what? From the world in general? Or protect her from someone in particular? Protect her from *Grant*.

My blood boils. Maybe she wasn't kicked out or left by the baby's father after all. Maybe she's running from him.

Fuck.

I have so many questions I want to ask her. But she's lying on the operating table, literally exposed to me right now. And she just had a baby. I need to give her time. She'll be emotional. She'll need to bond with the baby.

But then—then I'm going to get answers.

"We'll wash her up and have our pediatric resident check her out," the nurse tells her. "By the time you are back in your room, we'll probably have her all ready for you."

Another nurse puts an ID tag on Elizabeth's wrist. "The baby has one just like it on her ankle. It's to make sure we know who she belongs to."

"Okay," she says, kissing the baby's head before the nurse takes her away.

Then Elizabeth falls asleep. It's not unusual for that to happen. After the excitement, the epidural, the emotional drain of meeting your child for the first time. Dr. Redman finishes her job, and then I finish mine, taking extra time to make every stitch perfect.

But then my job is done. It's not my job to take her back to her room. It's not my job to be there when they bring her the baby. I've got other patients. Lots of other patients, thanks to Dr. Redman's renewed confidence in my abilities.

And when I scrub out, all I can think about is how I'm going to get through the next few hours without seeing her. Seeing *them*.

~ ~ ~

The past four hours have felt like some of the longest of my life. Seconds were like minutes. Minutes like hours. Every hour felt like an eternity.

When I finally get a break from my other patients, I make my way to her room. I stand in the doorway, mesmerized by what I see.

Elizabeth has the baby propped up on a pillow on her lap. She unwraps her daughter's blanket and silently counts every toe. She wraps her back up and then moves to her fingers. I smile, wondering how many times over the past hours she's done the same thing.

She lovingly strokes the baby's cheek, lulling her back to sleep.

Tears roll down Elizabeth's face as she admires her daughter.

I have to swallow my emotions as I watch the love emanating from her.

I wondered. For weeks now, it has seemed like Elizabeth was in denial. She never wanted to talk about the baby. Never wanted to plan for it. Sometimes I wondered if she really even wanted it.

But now that I see them together, I wonder if she was just scared to become a mom. A single mom, no less.

My pager beeps, alerting Elizabeth to my presence in her doorway. I make sure the page is not emergent before going in.

"Why didn't you tell me?" she asks.

"That you were having a girl?" I say, walking to her bedside.

She shakes her head, more tears spilling from her eyes. "That I would fall in love with her," she says. "Why did I ever think I didn't want this?" She brushes her thumb across the soft skin of her daughter's cheek. "I was made to be her mom."

I smile down at the gorgeous sleeping baby. The baby I helped bring into this world. I can't help wanting to hold her. Claim her as mine. Just like I want to claim her mother.

I see Elizabeth's eyes start to close with exhaustion.

"You need your rest," I say. "You should sleep whenever she does."

Her eyes pop open. "But all I want to do is look at her."

I pull the bassinet around next to Elizabeth's bed. "We'll put her right here. You can stare at her all you want."

She nods, refusing to take her eyes off her daughter. But then she looks up at me. "Do you . . . want to hold her?"

"More than you can imagine," I say, my voice strained with need.

She smiles brightly as she gathers up the baby to hand over to me.

I situate her in my arms and then lean down to smell her, closing my eyes as I take in the unmistakable scent of baby.

"You know, I was the first one to ever hold her," I say. "I was the one who pulled her out of you."

Elizabeth's eyes shoot to mine. "Really? They let you do the C-Section?" She looks embarrassed. "You had your hands *inside* me? Oh, my God. That's incredible. Sometimes I forget you're a real doctor."

I laugh quietly. "Dr. Redman made the incision. But I delivered her. And I got to sew your skin up after."

"I hope you did a good job," she jokes. "You never know who might be seeing it."

I raise my eyebrows at her. "Not too many people, I hope. Actually, not *any* people," I say. "Well, except *one* person." I stare at her, letting her know I want to be that person.

She nods weakly at me before her eyes can't stay open any longer.

I watch Elizabeth drift off to sleep. I watch her baby's little lip quiver in her own slumber. I look up to see my reflection in the dark window of night. The reflection of a man with a family. A family he never knew he wanted. A family that didn't exist mere weeks ago.

I walk over and carefully put the baby in her bassinet.

Then I head to my locker to get the bottle of champagne so I can chill it.

Dr. Williston was right when he said I'd know for sure when it was time to celebrate that one great thing.

CHAPTER THIRTY

I checked on Elizabeth again after my shift last night, but she was sleeping. I watched her sleep. I read a magazine. I held the baby.

Then I went home and dreamed of birthday parties and vacations to Disney World. Anniversary trips to Paris. Warm family fires on cold nights.

For years—as far back as I can remember—I've only dreamed about one thing: medicine. Going to a good college. Scoring high on the MCAT. Getting into a top med school. Matching at a desirable hospital. Running the ER. Opening my own clinic.

I still have those dreams, only now, they include having someone to go home to. *Two* someones.

Today, as I make my way to work with a rather large basket in my hands, I'm taking a rare ride on the subway.

"My, what an interesting bouquet of . . . Jell-O?" a woman standing next to me asks.

I smile and offer her my standard line. "Just doing some research."

"Oh," she says, nodding as if she understands.

I had to stop at four grocers last night on my way home to get everything I needed. Who knew there were so many flavors we haven't tried.

I drop the basket off in Elizabeth's room before rounds. It's early. I was hoping to sneak in and out without waking her. But when I get there, she's not in her bed and the bassinet is gone.

I hear the toilet flush and a minute later, she emerges from the bathroom looking refreshed. Glowing even.

"Oh, hi," she says, smiling.

"Wow," I say, staring at her.

She looks down and fixes her robe to make sure everything is covered. "Wow, what?"

"You look incredible," I say, putting the basket on her side table. "I expected exhausted, drained, emotional. But you look great."

"Thanks. They kept the baby in the nursery all night, only bringing her to me when she needed to eat. It really helped me get some sleep."

She slowly makes her way back to bed, slightly hunched over with her hands low on her belly as if to hold it in place. I rush over to help her, but she puts out her hand to stop me.

"No. I can do it," she says.

"Elizabeth," I admonish her.

"Kyle, I need to be able to do this on my own. Please let me."

"You don't have to, you know. Do it on your own."

Her eyes close briefly as she makes it to the bed and slowly sits herself down. I can tell she's struggling to lift her legs up and swing them onto the bed. I don't care what she says, I'm helping.

I walk over and help her with her legs. Then I go wash my hands and put gloves on.

"As long as I'm here, I'll check your incision."

I lay her back and pull up the sheet so that when I lift her nightgown, her panties remain covered. I open up the belly binder she's wearing and remove the gauze over her incision. "It looks good," I tell her, covering it with new gauze. "The stitches will come out in ten days."

"How long do I have to wear this binder thing?" she asks, as I pull it back around her and fasten the Velcro.

"That's up to you. It's really about your comfort. Most women say they feel like their insides will fall out if they don't wear it for at least a week. After that, your skin and your muscles start to tighten up again."

I raise the head of her bed and then toss my gloves in the trash.

"It's true," she says. "I feel like I've been eviscerated."

She nods to the basket, smiling. "Is that for me?"

I pick it up and put it on the bed. "Unless junior has acquired the ability to eat solid food, I'm going with yes."

"Junior?" she says with raised brows.

"Well, you haven't told me her name yet."

"She doesn't have one. I thought I'd live with her for a few days and see what she looks like."

I laugh. "You think she'll *look* like a name? As in, she'll make a face and you'll think *'oh, yeah, she's a Monica,'* or she'll snore in her sleep and you'll think *'wow, she's definitely a Lisa'.*"

Elizabeth rolls her eyes at me. "I just don't want to screw it up," she says. "A name is with you for life. I have to make sure she won't be made fun of at school. Or that her initials don't spell something outrageous. Or that I don't name her something so girly that she won't be taken seriously as the first explorer on Mars."

I bite my tongue to keep from laughing again. "First explorer on Mars, eh?"

She shrugs. "It could happen."

"You're right, it could. And names *are* important," I say. "Just please be sure to Google it to make sure you don't name her after a porn star or a serial killer."

Elizabeth laughs, and then winces as she puts a hand on her tender belly. "I promise I'll do that before making a decision."

"She's a beautiful baby. She deserves a beautiful name. Like yours—your name is beautiful."

"Thanks," she says sadly, as if she doesn't agree.

She rifles through all the cups of Jell-O I brought her. "Someone wants to play a game," she says, smiling.

"Did you know there are nineteen flavors of Jell-O?" I ask. "That's thirteen flavors we haven't tried."

"That's a lot of 'Never have I evers'," she says.

"Well, I have a lot of questions."

She looks out the window sadly, taking a deep breath. Then she looks down at her tattoo. The tattoo she didn't bother to cover up again.

"The bracelet is too hard," she says, when she sees me looking at her wrist. "It would hurt the baby's head when I hold her."

"Good call," I say, staring at some bastard's scripted name on her wrist, hating him with everything inside me even though I've never met the man.

She covers the tattoo with her other hand. "I'm not with him," she says. "I'll never be with him again. But I'm not ready to talk about him. Please just give me time."

I pick up one of the Jell-O containers and read the expiration date. "Looks like we have about three months."

She sighs with relief.

I, on the other hand, am kicking myself for not pushing a little harder. I promised myself I was going to ask for answers. But maybe when her child isn't even a day old yet is too soon.

A nurse wheels the baby in. "This little one is hungry," she says.

"My cue to leave," I say. "I'll check on you later, Elizabeth."

"Egg rolls!" she calls out after me.

I turn back around and cock my head at her in question.

"It's Meatloaf night." She scrunches her nose in disgust. "I'd kill for some Sal's."

"Are you asking me on a date, Ms. Smith?"

The nurse chuckles as she picks up the baby from the bassinet.

Elizabeth shrugs as her pinky finger finds its way to her mouth.

I leave her room with a huge damn smile on my face.

CHAPTER THIRTY-ONE

Ten hours have passed, and I'm so busy I haven't found any time to check on Elizabeth. I even got to deliver another baby today. This time, I was the one who made the incision and Dr. Redman supervised.

I'm glad Elizabeth wasn't my first. I'm confident in my abilities and all, but still, the thought of pressing too hard with the scalpel and cutting into a perfectly formed baby is more than a little daunting.

Next week, I'll be back in the ER. But I know I'll miss obstetrics. What are the odds that I was in the ER when Elizabeth first came to the hospital and then I was doing my OB rotation when she got admitted a week later?

It makes me think back to one of the first conversations we had about fate and how we both seem to think all things happen for a reason. One thing's for sure. I was meant to meet her. I was meant to be her doctor. And I was damn sure meant to fall for her.

It's more than the obvious fact that she needs someone. She needs *me*. And I never knew it until just a few days ago, but I need her. And now, in some strange way . . . I need the baby, too.

After my shift, I pick up some takeout from Sal's and head back to the hospital. When I get to Elizabeth's room, I find her asleep.

I put the bags down and walk over to the bed to study her. Despite the fact that she must be exhausted, I see she took the time to put on makeup. *For me?* She's beautiful without it, but I know the light shade of blue shadow will bring out the color of her eyes. Her pink lips look even more luscious than normal.

Her lips. I stare at them. I've wanted to kiss them for so long. Maybe even since I first met her. I have to hold myself back every day. I work here. It would be unprofessional. Then again, I'm not on duty now. Doctors have every right to visit their loved ones when not on shift. And they have every right to kiss them.

Don't they?

I take in the dark, thick stripe of the roots of her hair, hoping that maybe she'll let it grow out into her natural brown color. I can't help myself when I reach over and take a lock of her hair between my fingers.

"Hey, you," she says, catching me worshiping her.

"I didn't mean to wake you."

"You didn't. I was asleep for a few hours. The baby will probably want to eat soon. They took her to the nursery to let me rest."

I nod to the bags of Chinese food. "Then maybe we should feed her mom first."

She smiles, shaking her head in wonder. "It still sounds so strange, me being a mom. I'm not sure I'll ever get used to it."

"Well, you are, and you will. And you're going to be a great mother, Elizabeth."

I put all her favorite dishes on the tray table and move it over her bed. I've learned what she likes and what she doesn't. And as we eat, I lean over and pick the slices of watercress out of her food. She smiles every time I do it.

"When do you think I'll be released?" she asks.

"Day after tomorrow," I tell her. "Since you delivered late in the day on Monday, we'll keep you that extra night just to make sure you're okay."

"Oh, good."

Good why? Because she gets to see me? Or because she doesn't have to go back to . . . wherever she's going back to. I shudder at the thought.

"It's my day off, you know, the day you get released." I push some food around with my chopsticks. "I was hoping you'd let me take you home. Get you settled."

She shakes her head sadly. "No, Kyle. I don't want you to take me home."

"I don't care where you live, Elizabeth. Don't you know that by now? You don't have to be embarrassed. But you're going to need someone to help you. Do you have stairs? You can't possibly navigate them with the baby in your condition."

"No, Kyle. I can't. I'm sorry. Don't worry. There's an elevator."

I'm not sure why that makes me feel better. Maybe because I've imagined her living in a building without electricity and running water. Still, even slums have elevators.

"If you won't let me take you to your house, then let me take you to mine," I say, my heart thundering in my chest.

She looks at me in surprise. "Why would you do that, Kyle? You've only known me a few weeks. I have a baby. A baby that will cry a lot. And spit up everywhere."

"Because I want to. Because I have a spare bedroom for the baby—for *you*. Because I believe we were meant to meet, Elizabeth. Because I . . ."

I can't bring myself to say it. I've never said it before. Plus, I think I've already freaked her out enough for one day.

"Thank you, but no," she says, picking at her food.

"Why, Elizabeth?"

She pushes what's left of her dinner away. "Because everyone wants something in return."

"What?"

"Well, hello, Mommy," the nurse says, pushing the bassinet through her doorway. "Ready to feed this little one?"

"Just think about it, please, Elizabeth?" I ask as I clear away her dinner.

The nurse hands her the baby and then glances at me. "Would you like some privacy, Elizabeth?" she asks.

Elizabeth looks up at me shyly. "Uh, I don't know, I'm . . ."

"I'll go wash up in your bathroom," I say, getting up to cross the room.

I stay in there longer than necessary, giving her time to get the baby situated. I hope she knows she doesn't have to be embarrassed to breastfeed in front of me.

When I come out of the bathroom, I see that the nurse has closed the door to give her privacy. I stand across the room, leaning against the wall to give her some space.

"I think I'm getting pretty good at this," she says, looking down at her daughter.

"You're a natural," I say.

She nods at the chair next to the bed. "You don't have to stay over there, Kyle. I was being silly. You're a doctor. You see this all the time."

I resume my seat in the chair next to the bed, trying not to stare at her as she feeds her daughter, but finding it completely mesmerizing at the same time.

"Tell me about your day," she says. "Anything to take my mind off the fact that I'm half naked and you can see my boob."

I laugh along with her.

"Well, I got to do my first solo C-section from start to finish. I guess Dr. Redman was impressed by what she saw when I helped out with you."

"Kyle, that's fantastic. I'm glad I could be your test case."

I frown. "You weren't my test case, Elizabeth. I never would have assisted in your surgery if I didn't think I could do it flawlessly."

"I know. That's not what I meant. You're a good doctor, Kyle. The best."

"Thanks. That means a lot to me."

I spend the next ten minutes telling her all about it as I watch her burp the baby and then switch to the other side. When she's done feeding her, Elizabeth asks, "Do you want to burp her?"

"Sure," I say. "I never liked this shirt very much anyway."

She giggles and hands me a burp cloth. "Use this. I love that shirt, it really brings out the green in your eyes."

I carefully pick up the baby and rest her on my shoulder as I lightly pat her back.

"You like green shirts," I say. "Duly noted."

"I like your eyes when you wear scrubs, too," she says. "The blue brings out the blue in your eyes. In fact, your eyes are amazing. They seem to change colors based on what you wear."

It's the eyes. Girls have always loved them. It's one thing I got from my mother that my brothers don't also possess.

"Technically, my eyes are hazel. But yes, they do seem to take on the color of my clothing, especially if I'm wearing brown, green, or blue."

"I love that. I wish *she* would have eyes like that," she says, nodding at her daughter.

I wish she would too. I wish she had *my* eyes.

Elizabeth seems to understand what I'm thinking. Or maybe I'm understanding what she was insinuating. Either way, we stare at each other as I bounce and pat, bounce and pat.

She reaches over into the Sal's bag and pulls out a fortune cookie. "I'm opening mine," she says with a smile. This has become the favorite part of our dinners together.

After she eats the cookie, I watch her face as she reads her fortune. *"Two days from now, tomorrow will be yesterday."* She studies the slip of paper. "Wow, that's so simplistic, yet so deep."

I laugh. "That guy in Boston must do a lot of Googling."

"Want me to do yours?" she asks, pulling another cookie from the bag.

"No. I want to open my own," I say, laying the baby down in her waiting arms and then sitting on the edge of the bed next to her. "Plus, isn't that against the rules, to open someone else's fortune?"

"What are you, ten?" she asks, giggling.

"Hey, don't come between a guy and his fortunes. When I was seven, I got a fortune cookie that told me I would heal the world. Maybe that's why I'm a doctor. What if someone else had opened my fortune?"

She holds one out to me. "Well, now that I know your fortunes dictate your destiny, I wouldn't dream of interfering."

I open the cookie and pop it in my mouth before I glance at the words. I can't believe what I'm reading. I look at Elizabeth. I look at the baby. I look back at the little slip of paper.

"Well, what does it say?" she asks.

"Uh, it says, *'Your future is right in front of you'.*"

Her mouth hangs open. Just like mine is.

I look into her eyes. The damn thing is right. I swear I can see my future in them.

I want to kiss her. No—I *need* to kiss her. I need to kiss her like I need air.

So I do.

I lean over and take her face in my hands. She looks at me with bated breath. She knows what I'm about to do. Her eyes close and her lips part ever so slightly. It's an invitation. One I don't hesitate to accept.

When my lips meet hers, I wonder why I ever wasted time kissing anyone else. Because these are the lips that were made for me. They're plump. They're soft. They're small. And they fit perfectly against mine.

I kiss her top lip. I kiss her bottom lip. My tongue comes out and requests entry into her mouth that she's quick to allow. A faint mewl escapes her throat as our tongues meet and mingle. The tiny sound travels through me and goes all the way to my groin. But not before taking up residence in my heart.

Our kisses are gentle, not demanding. They're soft. Meaningful. They speak more between us than any words ever have.

I kiss her unlike I've ever kissed anyone before. Because it feels unlike any other kiss. It feels like the first. It feels like the last. It feels like nothing I've ever felt and nothing I'll feel again.

When we're out of breath, our lips part, but our foreheads meet as we breathe into each other.

A cry from the baby pulls us apart, and I look down on Elizabeth's beautiful daughter. Then I lean down and kiss the soft brown curls on her head.

A noise coming from the door makes me turn my head in its direction. And when I do, I see Gina standing in the open doorway. The door I know was closed moments ago.

I try to figure out how long she's been standing there. But I quickly get my answer. The look on her face and the disapproval in her eyes say it all. They let me know the line has been crossed. Hell, it's been shattered. I'm so far past the line, I can't even see it in my fucking wake.

CHAPTER THIRTY-TWO

"Are you in trouble?" Elizabeth asks, when I come to examine her the next day.

"No. I'm pretty sure Gina won't say anything. Plus, I didn't do anything wrong. I wasn't on duty when I came to see you last night."

"Oh. Good."

"I brought you something," I say, pulling a small bag out of my lab coat pocket.

"Kyle, you've done too much already."

I hand her the bag. "Just open it, Elizabeth."

She looks inside hesitantly, as if she thinks it might be an engagement ring or something. Then she pulls out the contents and holds it up to me in confusion.

"It's a wristband," I tell her. "People use it for working out. It's soft, so it won't hurt the baby."

Her face breaks into a smile as she pulls it on her left wrist. She admires how it covers the tattoo.

"And it's pink," she says. "My favorite color."

"I know."

She looks up at me. "You do?"

"You tend to favor the pink pajamas, so I kind of figured."

"Thank you. That was really thoughtful."

The baby makes a noise in her bassinet and I walk over to see her. "How's she doing today?"

"She's great. She seems more aware today. I was staring at her before you came in. It's incredible how she's such a little person."

"I'm not sure I've ever seen a baby with so much hair," I say, admiring her soft fine curls. "And with those long eyelashes, you'd better watch out for this one, she's gonna break some hearts."

Elizabeth laughs. "I know," she says. "I'm already jealous of those lashes. I always wanted long eyelashes like my brother, but I was never lucky enough to have them."

My eyes snap to hers. "You have a brother?"

"Uh . . ." She glances over at the baby and then she looks sad. "Did. I did have one."

She closes her eyes and leans back onto her pillow.

I sit down on the bed. "Elizabeth—"

"I can't talk about it," she says, huffing a deep sigh out of her nose.

I take her hand, wanting to console her for a brother I never knew she had. Because I know nothing about her. Her family. Her past. But it occurs to me that it doesn't really matter. It occurs to me that what happened in her past is just that, the past. The only thing I want from her is her future.

"Have you thought about what I asked you yesterday?" I ask.

Her eyes open and with the way she's looking at me, I already know what the answer is. And damn it if it doesn't make my heart ache.

"Elizabeth, before you say anything, just hear me out. Leave here with me tomorrow. Let me take you to my place. Just so you can see it. Check it out. See if it would work for you and the baby. You don't have to make any commitments today. And I promise, if it's not what you want, I'll put you and the baby in a cab and send you back to your place."

She looks over at the baby and studies her. I can see the struggle going on behind her eyes. She's wondering if I'm doing this just for the baby. Out of pity. But then she's probably wondering that even if she *is* a charity case, shouldn't she do what's best for her child?

I squeeze her hand. "I want this. I want you. I want *her*. And, Elizabeth, based on that kiss, I'm pretty sure you want me, too. But we can take it slow. I'll give you all the space you need. I'll be working most of the time anyway. My building is nice. It's safe. Please, just come take a look."

She looks down at our entwined hands and slowly nods. It's not a happy nod. It's not an excited nod. It's a nod of acceptance. Defeat even.

"Okay," she says. "I'll come for a look. But no promises."

I want to jump off the bed and pump my fist in the air. But I don't. Because although this might be a fist-pumping moment for me, it looks to be anything but that for Elizabeth.

Instead, I lean down and place a kiss on her forehead. "Thank you," I say. "It will all work out, Elizabeth. I promise."

The door to the room swings open and Abby walks in with a folder of papers.

"Your discharge papers," she says, handing them to Elizabeth. "And the mother/parent worksheet you need to complete for the birth certificate. If you can get them all filled out today, it will help things run smoothly for your discharge tomorrow afternoon."

Elizabeth stares at the paperwork long after Abby leaves the room. She leafs through the pages looking carefully at each one. She holds up one of the discharge forms. "Is this *your* address?"

I look at it. "Yes. They got that from the admissions form. Remember?"

"Oh." She rifles through a few more pages. "This is a lot of stuff."

"It's mostly after-care instructions for you and the baby. Abby or one of the other nurses will go over it all with you before you leave. Those are just reminders."

She looks down at the application for a birth certificate. "Do I have to fill this out?"

"Yes. The baby needs a birth certificate. But if you still haven't picked a name, that's okay, leave it blank. Once you pick a name, just come back and tell the hospital and they can submit it for you without charge for up to one year."

"There are so many questions," she says, looking it over.

"You can use my address if you want. It's fine. Even if you don't end up staying with me."

She nods.

"You really haven't thought of a name yet?" I ask, lacing my fingers through hers.

"It's not easy," she says. "It needs to be perfect."

Someone clears their throat behind us and we turn to see Gina standing in the doorway.

"Why don't you let Dr. Stone pick the name? After all, he's paying for all this," she says, waving her hand around Elizabeth's hospital room.

Oh, fuck.

Fuck, fuck, fuck.

Elizabeth drops my hand like it burned her. "He's *what?*"

"Oh, sorry," Gina says, not looking it in the least. "I figured with you being discharged tomorrow, he'd have told you."

"Gina, get out," I say. "And close the door behind you."

She shrugs and turns around to leave.

When I look at Elizabeth, there are tears running down her cheeks. And tension tightens the delicate features of her face. I reach out for her, but she pulls away.

"I'm sorry," I say, not knowing if I should be mad at Gina or myself. "I should have told you. But I didn't want you to think I saw you as a charity case, because that is not what this is about."

"What *is* this about, Kyle?"

The door opens again and Baylor, Skylar and Piper walk in with flowers and food.

Elizabeth quickly wipes her face and pastes on a smile as she greets them.

I get up off the bed. "I'm glad you guys are here," I tell them. "I've got to wrap up a few cases before my shift is over."

I hug the three of them and then turn back to Elizabeth. "I'll come back later? To say goodnight?"

She shakes her head softly. "No, that's okay. You've had a long shift," she says. "After dinner with these guys, I'm going to be pretty tired. I'll just see you tomorrow, okay?"

I want to argue, but not in front of everyone. She's pissed. And we didn't get a chance to talk it out. Maybe it's better to let her sleep on it. Everything will be okay tomorrow. When she comes to my place, everything will be alright. I'll make sure of it.

Then I get an idea. I pull Baylor aside and tell her my plan.

CHAPTER THIRTY-THREE

Heading to the hospital this afternoon, I can't help my smile when I pass by young families walking their kids to school. Or pushing a baby in a stroller. Or stopping to get a breakfast burrito from a street vendor.

I try to imagine what it'll be like for us one day. If she decides to live with me, that is.

I spent hours this morning trying to make everything perfect so Elizabeth will have no choice but to agree to stay with me. Gavin and I moved all the stuff from his and Baylor's garage into my spare room. There is a crib, a changing table, and one of those gliding chairs.

On one side of the room, I put a futon that could be used as a bed for Elizabeth if she's uncomfortable sleeping in mine. I didn't want to presume. After all, we've only just kissed. And we have never talked about us having a relationship. But the looks, the banter, the way we are with each other—they all seem to confirm what neither of us has come out and said.

I know she might still be upset with me. When I talked to Baylor late last night, she told me she could sense something was wrong. Elizabeth gave Baylor the tablet back, insisting she wouldn't have time to use it with the baby. Baylor wrote it off as post-partum depression. Maybe that's part of it, but deep down, I know I'm the cause of Elizabeth's sadness.

I just hope after she sees everything I've done, she'll realize how serious I am. She's not a charity case. I would never look at her as such.

I stop in the residents' lounge to grab the bottle of champagne from the refrigerator. I carry it, two plastic champagne glasses, and a giant stuffed bear with a large pink bow around its neck up the elevator to floor seven.

People look at me and smile.

"Congratulations," one of the elevator passengers says.

"It's a girl, huh?" asks another.

"Thank you. Yes, it's a girl."

I don't tell them it's not my baby. Hell, I practically feel like she's mine anyway. I delivered her. I've held her, burped her, rocked her to sleep. I'm already in love with her and I don't even know her. I laugh to myself. Because I could say the very same thing about her mother.

I can't wait to bring them home with me.

I smile at how my whole world is about to change. How it changed a month ago, when Elizabeth first walked into the ER.

As I make my way down the long hallway, something feels off. Nurses are looking at me oddly as I pass their station. I quicken my steps to get to Elizabeth's room, but when I arrive, everything's wrong.

There is no bassinet. No stroller in the corner. No balloons or flowers. No collection of Chinese proverbs on the side table.

No Elizabeth.

An orderly excuses himself around me with a bucket of water and a mop.

"Where the hell are they?" I ask, as if he'll know the answer.

He shrugs at me and continues his work.

Abby comes up behind me. "Dr. Stone?"

"Where is she?" I ask.

"Elizabeth was discharged this morning," she says.

I shake my head in confusion. "She wasn't supposed to be discharged until late this afternoon."

"Elizabeth asked to leave early and Dr. Anders signed off on it," she says. "She said she would follow up with her own pediatrician in a day or two for the tests we didn't get to complete due to her early release."

"But . . . where did she go? Was anyone with her?"

"I don't think so," she says. "And I suppose she went home. Where else would she go?"

"How could you let her leave without anyone to help her?"

Abby scolds me with her stare. "That's not our job, Dr. Stone. She was healing nicely. The baby was doing well. There was no medical reason to keep her. She'd already long passed the forty-eight-hour mark. Don't worry, I'm sure they will be fine."

They won't be fine, I want to yell at her. I want to wring her neck for allowing Elizabeth to leave.

Abby doesn't understand what she may have done, allowing her to go back to some crack house or shelter . . . or to *him*.

But I know it's not Abby's fault. It may not be anyone's fault but mine.

I lied to Elizabeth. I paid for her hospital stay, and then I lied about it. How could we build a relationship when it began on a bed of lies? Why didn't I tell her sooner? It's not like she could have left, she was on strict bed rest. She wouldn't have run back then and risk hurting her baby. Not like she ran now.

I'm such an idiot.

I never should have left last night. I should have come back after my shift and made her listen. Hell, I should have slept here. I *would* have slept here had I known what was at stake.

I put everything down on the plastic mattress of her empty bed. I run my hands through my hair. Then I pull out my phone and dial Elizabeth's number.

I know she won't answer. But at least I can leave her a voicemail. Try to explain things. Appeal to her motherly instincts. I'll leave a hundred messages if that's what it takes to get through to her.

When it rings, however, I hear a noise in the room. I follow the sound over to the trashcan.

Shit.

I reach down and pull out Elizabeth's phone.

Then I rifle through the rest of the contents of the trash. The birth certificate application. The Nighthawks tickets. And Jell-O.

Lots and lots of Jell-O.

CHAPTER THIRTY-FOUR

Six months later . . .

"Tonight's the night," Cameron says as we walk through the halls of the hospital. "I'm going to tell Gina I love her."

"Seriously?" I stop walking and think about what he's saying. They've been joined at the hip for five months now, I guess it was bound to happen sooner or later. "I think that's great, Cam."

"Do you?" he asks.

I pat him on the back. "Of course, I do. Gina and I haven't been together for a long time. I told you back then it was all good. Plus, I owe you big time. When you guys started hooking up, it took a lot of the heat off me. I'm just glad we can all still be friends."

He studies me. "I know you are. But I've always wondered if you regret pushing her away. Especially after Elizabeth split."

I feel like I've been punched in the gut at the mention of her name. I start walking again.

"Hey, man. I'm sorry," Cameron says. "I didn't mean to bring her up. I know it's a sore spot with you. I know you've been trying hard to move on."

"It is what it is," I tell him. "It's all good, Cam. Go have a great night with Gina."

On my way to the cafeteria, I think of how I *am* truly happy for him. For *them*. Gina and I were never right for one another. We got each other through some stressful times, and for that, I'm grateful.

I was pissed at her for weeks. I blamed her for Elizabeth running away. But in time, I forgave her. After all, *I* was the one who lied. *I* was the one who crossed the line.

Before I'm finished with my meal, I get paged back to the ER.

Diane hands me a chart. "Dr. Stone, we have a young man with an open wound in curtain six. Man versus Cujo."

I open the curtain to find a nurse setting up a procedure tray.

I look at the chart to see the patient's name. "Mr. Howard, I'm Dr. Stone. It says here you've suffered a dog bite."

He nods. "Danger of the job," he says. "I walk dogs."

I turn my head to the side and study him. I can't help but think about her. *Elizabeth.* I want to ask him if he knows her. Maybe all dog walkers hang out in the same circles.

If she's still doing it, that is.

I've looked. I've spent hours upon hours walking the streets of New York looking for her. I've followed other dog walkers, run up on every woman pushing a stroller, eaten at Sal's so many times I'm sick of Chinese food.

I called every number in her phone. All fifteen of them. Every single one was a dog-walking client. None of them had heard from her.

I even used Ethan's agency to try and track down Elizabeth or Grant Smith, but they couldn't find any solid leads when we didn't have much to go on. What they did tell me, however, is that no Elizabeth Smith attended the University of Maryland around the time she could have gone there.

There are a lot of Elizabeth Smith's in the world. Just not *my* Elizabeth Smith.

It's as if she never existed.

Diane pops her head around the curtain as I'm finishing up with Mr. Howard. "There's someone to see you out in the waiting room."

My heart pounds. *Someone to see me?* Could it be her? Everyone else I know would text me.

I rip off my gloves and head out past ground zero, looking through the glass to see if it's her. But she's not there.

I walk through the doors.

"Dr. Stone?" a man asks.

He's a big guy. Intimidating. Taller than me and heavier by a good fifty pounds. He has a crew cut and is clean shaven, with a few scars on his face that reek of fist-fights.

"How can I help you?" I ask.

He pulls a picture out of his pocket. "Your receptionist said she recognized this girl. Said you might have treated her some time ago."

I look at the picture and try not to react. It takes all my willpower to hold in my emotions. My questions. Because I'm staring at a picture of Elizabeth. Only she's a brunette. And, Jesus, she's even more beautiful than she was as a blonde.

"I'm sorry, I didn't get your name," I say.

"Grant," he says. "Grant Lucas."

Holy motherfucker.

I try to stay calm. "Why are you looking for this girl?" I ask, my heart beating so fucking loud, I'm positive he must hear it.

He pulls out a badge and flashes it at me. I grab it before he can put it back in his pocket.

I examine it and then look up at him with a hard stare. "Your badge says Chicago P.D. Looks like you're a little out of your jurisdiction."

"Have you seen her or not?" he asks, getting pissed as he rips his badge out of my hand.

The wheels in my head are spinning. I don't have to reveal any patient information. Not even to a cop. Especially not to a *Chicago* cop. Then again, if this guy is her husband, he might keep pressing the hospital for information until he gets what he wants.

I study the picture some more, as if I'm trying to remember her. "You know, I do remember her. I mean, she's hot, what's not to remember?"

He snorts in amusement. Good, I need him on my side.

"How long ago?" he asks.

I shrug. "A few months. Maybe more. She had a cut on her face," I lie. "Said she was mad because she was heading to . . . I'm not sure, but Boston maybe? Said she was going on some job interview there."

"A cut huh?" he asks.

"Yup. Four or five stitches if I recall."

He scrubs his hands across his face and I get a glimpse of a tattoo on his right wrist. *Oh, shit!* It looks just like Elizabeth's.

I try to keep him talking so I have a chance to get a better look at it. "Hope her job wasn't for a modeling contract," I say, laughing. "Shame really. She had a great face, too."

"I'm going to need to see her hospital records," he says.

"Do you have a subpoena?" I ask.

"No."

I shrug nonchalantly like I don't really care. "I wish I could help, but hospital records are sealed records. And since it was so long ago, it's not like I can just get her chart. It's been archived."

I look around the room, pretending I'm making sure we're alone, like I'm about to give him sensitive information. "But, hey, to tell you the truth, I'm not sure you'd get much out of seeing her chart. If I recall, the girl didn't give us any information. She was a closed book. Maybe she got clocked by a john and was afraid to give her address. Whatever it was, she was in and out quickly. Hell, I don't even remember her name."

He sighs in frustration. Then he reaches into his pocket and pulls out a business card.

It's now when I realize he hasn't mentioned her pregnancy. Or a baby. *Does he not know?*

"If you ever see her again, give me a shout. It's important. She has something I can't get from anyone else."

"Hey no problem." I take the card and extend my hand to him.

When he shakes it, I don't let go. I turn his hand so I can see his wrist. "Great ink, man. I've been thinking of getting one myself. You don't happen to know of any good places here in New York, do you?"

I check out his tattoo as I speak to him. It's the same fucking one *she* has. Except his is more manly. And his has a different name.

Alexa.

CHAPTER THIRTY-FIVE

I shake my head. *Elizabeth Smith.* It's hard for me to think of her with any other name. But that's *not* her name.

Alexa Lucas—that's who she is.

I sit here and stare at a copy of her Illinois driver's license. It's her. It's definitely her.

"She went missing more than a year ago," Ethan says. "Just up and disappeared without a trace. Family members have been searching for her ever since, but with no leads, the case went cold."

I called Ethan as soon as Grant left the hospital a few nights ago. I knew if anyone could get to the bottom of this, he could. Now I sit across the desk from him at his agency as he explains that the woman I thought I loved was not who she said she was.

And all at once, every fear I've ever had about her is coming true. Especially when he hands me her hospital records. Multiple records from different ERs around Chicago with Alexa's name on them. Facial contusions, a broken rib, a deep laceration on her collarbone.

I shake my head thinking of the game 'Never have I ever' when she didn't want to talk about that particular scar.

My blood starts to boil when I think of that scumbag from the other night laying a hand on her. Why didn't she tell me? She was in a hospital. A safe place. I could have protected her. Ethan has lots of connections. We could have made it work. But she never gave me the chance. She just ran.

All this time, I thought it was because I lied. But maybe it's something more. Maybe she got spooked—saw someone from her past whom she couldn't risk recognizing her.

Maybe it wasn't *me* at all.

All of a sudden, there is way more to her story than I thought possible.

He slides another piece of paper across his desk. "Here's their wedding announcement," Ethan says, pointing to the photocopy of a page from a Chicago newspaper.

I pick it up and study it, reading every word carefully. Then my eyes shoot back to Ethan. "Kessler? Are you fucking kidding me? Her maiden name is *Kessler?*"

Ethan cocks his head to the side. "Is that significant?"

My head is shaking in disbelief as I try to process this information. "Elizabeth, er, Alexa, told me Caden Kessler was her favorite baseball player. I thought she was just a super-fan, Ethan. He's her goddamn brother!"

Ethan pulls more papers out of a folder, nodding his head as he reads something. "Yup," he says. "Caden Kessler grew up in Baltimore. He has one sister, Alexa. Two years older."

Suddenly, everything makes sense about the day I invited him to meet her.

I can't believe Caden was right down the hall from her. Fifty feet from seeing that his sister was alive and well and about to give birth to his niece.

I replay the day in my head. She looked out the door at me. Maybe she saw him. It's the only explanation for her mysterious sudden illness. I knew it didn't add up. Her interest in baseball. In him. And then her unwillingness to see him.

But not everything makes sense. "Why was she hiding from her brother?" I muse aloud.

Ethan shrugs. "If she wanted to hide the baby from Grant, it may have been her only choice. Alexa's father is out of the picture and her mother is deceased, so Caden is probably the first person Grant would have gone to in order to find her. Abused women often have to cut off ties with their entire family in order to protect themselves and their children."

I run my hands through my hair. *Shit.* My instinct is to find her. Protect her. But I already tried protecting her once and she didn't let me.

Things are different now. Six months ago, if I'd found her, I think I would have thrown her over my shoulder and dragged her to my apartment, baby stroller and all.

But now—I've had time to think about things. And even with knowing her identity and more details of her past, it's obvious my feelings were not reciprocated. She was nice to me. She even kissed me when I kissed her. But I was her doctor. And patients sometimes mistakenly see their doctors as saviors. Not men they can build a life with.

The fact is, she didn't trust me enough to tell me the truth. She didn't love me enough to trust me.

She stole my heart and then she tore it to shreds. Even if she didn't mean to.

I gaze through the window of Ethan's office. I can't keep doing this. I have to move on. I *have* moved on. I've gone back to basics. My job. *That* is what I'm living for. I never should have lost focus. I've vowed never to allow myself to get close to a patient again. Get close to a *woman* again. At least until I've accomplished my goals.

"Caden should know," I say, gathering up all the paperwork and putting it into a folder. "I need to contact him and tell him everything. But then I'm done."

~ ~ ~

I pick up my third beer of the night and crack it open, waiting for my pepperoni pizza to arrive.

I'm spent. Exhausted from my meeting with Caden. When he was here earlier, we put all the pieces together.

Caden never liked Grant. He didn't think he was right for his sister. He and Alexa would get into arguments about him from time to time. But Caden was young and focused solely on baseball. He blames himself for not seeing the signs. For not being there for her when she needed him.

Since Alexa's disappearance, he'd been suspicious of Grant, but without evidence to go on, there was nothing he could do. Grant kept showing up at Caden's door, always wanting to come inside to talk—to 'touch base' with the brother-in-law he never gave a rat's ass about before Alexa went missing.

We surmised that Grant could be holding something over her. Blackmailing her maybe, which is why she's running but didn't seek out her brother. It's obvious, however, that Grant doesn't know where she is, only that perhaps she's in New York to be closer to Caden. But that seems to be the extent of his knowledge of her whereabouts.

Ethan thought contacting Grant would be counterproductive. Our hands are tied. We have no way of knowing if she's okay, but we can't go to Grant without him finding out we know something, which could make it worse for her in the long run.

When my doorbell rings, I put down my beer and grab a twenty from my wallet for the pizza guy. I swing the door open to see a petite redhead holding a small child. Before I can get the words out to tell her she's got the wrong apartment, my heart lodges in my goddamn throat.

It's her.

PART TWO

ALEXA

CHAPTER THIRTY-SIX

He looks at me like he's seen a ghost. He looks down at a sleeping Ellie on my shoulder. He sticks his head out into the hallway and checks both directions before he grabs my arm and pulls me inside, pushing the stroller in after us.

"What are *you* doing here?" he asks, closing the door behind me.

I find it hard to speak, looking into his eyes. I've dreamed about these eyes. The eyes that can't seem to decide on a color. His dark-blonde hair is longer than it was last year. Edgier. And his five o'clock shadow . . . He's everything I remembered and more.

And for the millionth time over the past six months, I scold myself for leaving the hospital the way I did. For leaving him.

But I did what I had to do. What I thought was right at the time.

He sighs and runs his hands through his hair. I don't know him well enough to read what's behind his eyes. He looks angry. He looks relieved. He looks confused.

"Are you in trouble?" he asks, holding out his arm in an invitation for me to go into his living room.

I look around the expansive room. Oh, my God. I knew this building was in a nice area, but this is . . . I don't even know. This is unreal.

"Kyle, do you live with your parents?"

He shakes his head. "No. I live here alone. Can we not change the subject, please? Are you in trouble?" he asks in an irritated and impatient tone.

Still distracted, my jaw drops as I look around and take in the floor-to-ceiling windows that overlook the city, the chef's kitchen with oversized refrigerator, the big-screen television.

Ellie squirms in my arms trying to get comfortable, causing me to break my gaze of our surroundings. "Uh, sorry. No," I tell him.

He blows out a breath as if he's relieved. "Do you want to lay her down?" he asks, pointing to the sofa.

I nod and gently lay her down on the exquisite soft leather, propping up pillows to keep her from rolling off.

"What's her name?" he asks, looking down at her. "You know, since you ran off without ever telling me that—or *anything* for that matter."

I close my eyes in shame. I know I have a lot of explaining to do. It's just that I still haven't figured out how. After all, how do you tell the man you want to be with that you're married? And that your husband beat you, demeaned you, raped you. And that you'll always be married to him so you can protect your daughter.

"Her name is Ellie," I tell him.

"Nice name," he says. "I guess there were already too many girls named Alexa."

My eyes widen in horror when he says my real name. I instinctively reach for Ellie so I can pick her up and protect her, but Kyle stands in my way.

"No," he says. "Let her sleep."

"I . . . how?" My heartbeat is pounding in my ears. My throat becomes thick, and tears pool in my eyes, threatening to spill onto my cheeks.

How could he know? I was so careful. More than a year and nobody has recognized me. *He* hasn't found me.

"Eliz—" He shakes his head. "Alexa, it's okay. You're safe here. I know everything."

"I don't understand," I say, biting back the sob rattling in my chest.

I eye the front door and then the balcony. I wonder if there is a fire escape. I find myself needing to know where all the exits are in case I need to run. Old habits are hard to break.

"Sit," he says, pointing to the sofa Ellie is lying on. "I'll tell you what I know. But first, let me get you a drink. Water? Beer? Something stronger?"

I look around his place again. It's nice. Christian-Grey nice. He's got money. People with money think they can buy anything. And if they can't buy it, sometimes they just take it.

Stop it, Lexi, I tell myself. Kyle is not Grant. Back at the hospital, he was nothing like him. He was helpful and kind and funny and . . . everything I didn't know I wanted in a man. And I left. Then I started to make a life for myself and for Ellie.

And now I might be risking everything to come back.

I trust my instincts and sit down on his sofa. "Water is fine."

He walks to his kitchen, never taking his eyes off me as if he thinks I'm going to run away again. After he reaches into his refrigerator, he pulls out his phone and taps the screen a few times. It looks like he's sending a text. I want to ask to whom, but I lost the right to that information when I walked out of the hospital.

Then his doorbell rings and I jump to my feet, ready to pick up Ellie and make my escape.

"Elizabeth, it's okay—sorry . . . Alexa. I ordered a pizza. I thought *you* were the pizza guy."

I let out a long breath. "Oh."

I sit back down as he hands me my water and makes his way to the door.

He puts the pizza on the coffee table and sits in the chair next to the couch. He leans forward, putting his elbows on his knees. "Grant came to the hospital a few days ago."

My heart stops. It stops beating and I die for a second.

I look over at Ellie, small and innocent, her little chest rising and falling as she sleeps peacefully. I don't want her to live in a world where men like her father even exist. I'm scared for her. Everything I do is about this girl. Loving her. Protecting her.

I wipe the tears that cloud my vision as I watch her sleep.

Then my heart starts beating again. It thunders in my chest as I realize what is happening. I stand up, ready to pull Ellie in my arms and race out of here. "Is that who you just texted? Oh, God, Kyle, did you tell Grant where I am?"

"No," he says, standing up with me. "Hell, no. I would never do that, Elizabeth—*Damn it!*—Alexa. I told you you're safe here. Sit down and let me explain."

Maybe I was wrong to come here. I waited too long. Just another mistake in the long list of epic mistakes I've made in my life. Marrying Grant. Letting him control me the way he did. Being naïve enough to think things would get better.

"Alexa," Kyle says, motioning to the couch. "Please."

I take a deep breath and sit back down on his sofa, bracing myself for what he's about to tell me.

"He didn't tell me he was your husband. He flashed his badge, making it seem like he was on the job even though he wasn't NYPD. I gave him a made-up story about you coming in for stitches. I said you were heading out of town for a job interview. The only reason I know your real name is because I saw his tattoo. He didn't mention the fact that you were pregnant. Did he not know?"

I shake my head.

He lets out a sigh. A sigh so deep it looks like he's in pain. "He hurt you," he says.

It's not a question.

I nod.

"And you left him when you found out you were pregnant." He looks over at Ellie. "You left to protect her."

I nod again.

"But why, Alexa? Why didn't you tell me? Why didn't you *trust* me? Why the hell did you just run off and leave me?" he asks, his voice cracking in anguish. "I could have helped you, you know."

"Kyle, I'm sorry. You're frustrated with me. I deserve it. I know you have a lot of questions and I have a lot of explaining to do, but no, you couldn't have helped me. You still can't. Not when it comes to Grant. He's a cop, Kyle."

"Yeah, I know, in narcotics," he says.

My eyes shoot to his.

"My brother is a private investigator, Alexa. It wasn't too hard to put everything together once I knew your name."

"Lexi," I say.

"What?"

"My name. It's Lexi. It's what everyone has always called me." I look at the floor. "Everyone but *him*."

There's another knock on the door, and again, I look at it in trepidation. Yet I also feel a sense of relief, because now I have a few more moments to gather my thoughts. To figure out all that I need to tell him.

"Relax," he says, sensing my fear. "It's all good."

I watch him cross the room, my heart pounding as I try to figure out if I can trust him. I want to trust him. I might even need to trust him. But trusting men is not exactly my strong suit.

He opens the door and I cry out. I cry out as I race across the room and jump into the arms of my brother.

I look back at Kyle, tears streaming down my face.

"It's okay, Lexi," Kyle says, smiling at our sibling reunion. "Catch up with Caden. There will be plenty of time for us to talk later."

CHAPTER THIRTY-SEVEN

I jolt awake, darkness surrounding me. But I feel safe somehow. The scent of the pillow is familiar. It smells of him. Of Kyle. It's the smell I dreamed about all these months. The smell I craved.

Moonlight shines through the bedroom window. Kyle's bedroom window. And I see the silhouette of my daughter sleeping on the bed next to me. I must have fallen asleep after the excitement of seeing Caden.

I hear voices beyond the bedroom door. He must still be here. The clock tells me it's just after midnight.

My head falls back on the pillow when I remember the dream that woke me. The nightmare. Seeing my brother brought it all back as if it had happened yesterday. I squeeze my eyes tightly closed as if that will somehow ward off the bad memories.

It doesn't.

Nothing can.

And I find myself reliving it all over again.

"Is it that fucking hard to iron out all the goddamn wrinkles, Alexa?" Grant yells. *"A fucking five-year-old could have done a better job."* He looks at his watch. *"Shit, we don't have time now."*

He rifles through my dresses and pulls out the shortest, tightest, most revealing one. I haven't worn it in years. He thrusts it out to me. "This one."

"Grant, no," I beg. "It's too tight. Too revealing."

He laughs. "Maybe you should lose some fucking weight then. You'll wear it. My wife is going to be the hottest one at the Policeman's ball."

"Please," I say, hanging it back on the rack and pulling out the green one instead. "This one is more appropriate."

He rips the green dress—my favorite dress—out of my hands. Literally rips it out, tearing the bodice so that it's unwearable. He throws it down on the floor and pins me against the wall with his hand to my throat.

"Maybe we need to go over the rules again," he says.

That was the day my fate was sealed. That was the day I knew I couldn't leave him. I'd had it all planned out. I had been stashing money away for months. I'd sewn it into the lining of my purse, along with some random pieces of jewelry he'd given me over the years. Jewelry that a narcotics officer from a blue-collar family shouldn't be able to afford. Jewelry that, after presented to me, it was expected I'd give something in return.

But that night, I fought back. I was done with his rules. I broke away from him and grabbed a suitcase, throwing my things into it as I screamed at him that I wasn't going to take it anymore.

It was a mistake. I should have known better. I should have played the good little housewife that night and then left quietly when he was at work the next day.

As it turns out, we never made it to the ball. Instead, I ended up in the hospital with a fractured rib. And a broken will.

I should have kept my mouth shut. I told him I would go live with Caden. I reminded him that Caden was doing well in minor league ball and would soon be called up to the majors. He'd be able to easily afford to take care of me. I told him I didn't need him anymore.

That's when Grant told me what he would do if I ever left him and ran to Caden. He said he would break his arms. Break his legs. Make it so he'd never be able to play ball again. He said he knew people that would do it for him no questions asked. It would be as easy as making a phone call.

I knew he wasn't bluffing. I'd seen some of the people he associated with. Cops mostly, but working in narcotics, he was around criminals. Gangs. Probably even mafia.

So I stayed. I stayed to protect my little brother. I stayed because without going to Caden, I had nowhere else to go, Grant made sure of that. He made sure our only friends were *his* friends. He even made sure I never got a job—sabotaging any interview I'd ever gotten by making sure I couldn't show up because he knew I wouldn't—not with a black eye.

I stayed until one day, I threw up for no reason. Then I peed on a stick and the stick turned pink, and I knew I had someone else to protect. Then I picked up my purse and walked out the door on my life.

The bedroom door cracks open and a sliver of light shines through, illuminating more of the room as Kyle peeks his head in to see me sitting up.

"You're awake," he says. "Do you need anything?"

"No," I whisper, looking down at Ellie. I'm not sure why I tend to do that. A freight train couldn't wake her up. It looks like she's down for the night. "Is Caden still here? I heard voices."

"Just left," he says. "He's coming back after his practice tomorrow."

I get up off the bed and put my pillow alongside Ellie, just as someone had on the other side of her so she wouldn't fall off the bed. I walk out to the living room with Kyle, leaving the door cracked so I can hear if Ellie wakes.

"What do you mean he's coming back?" I ask.

"I want you to stay here, Eliz—uh, Lexi. This building is secure . . ."

He stops talking and studies me.

"What?" I ask.

"This building is secure," he says again. "How did you get up to my door without being announced?"

I sigh. "I've gotten very good at being invisible."

He looks at me sadly. "I'm so sorry," he says.

He heard it all. Well, not *all* of it. But he heard enough. When Caden came to the door, I knew the jig was up. I told them how Grant threatened Caden and how he hurt me.

Kyle had to physically restrain Caden from leaving to go kill Grant. He even told us that when he left Kyle's place earlier today, after finding out about me, he was plotting to get even. So, it's a good thing I chose today to make an appearance. I can't imagine what trouble Caden might have gotten into, getting tangled up with Grant and his cronies.

It took some convincing, but Kyle and I were able to reason with him. Grant is a cop. One with lots of connections. And right now, he doesn't believe Caden had any hand in my disappearance. I begged him to keep it that way.

Caden told me that when I first disappeared, Grant came to him, asking lots of questions and acting strangely. There was a police investigation, of course, but that quickly became a cold case.

When I left, I walked out the door with nothing but my purse and a few changes of clothing that Grant wouldn't notice had gone missing.

I walked three miles to the shopping district, took a cab to a sleazy hotel where I cut and colored my hair, and then I made my way to New York on buses.

New York. Where I'd be close to Caden.

Kyle's words about Grant being in town a few days ago flash through my head. My hand flies to my mouth to cover a gasp as the sudden realization hits me like a ton of bricks. "Oh, my God! What have I done? Caden is the one in danger now," I cry. "If Grant finds out he's helping me—"

"Lexi, he won't find out. That's why you can't stay with Caden. Who knows if Grant is having him watched."

"I've put him at risk," I say, berating myself for my stupidity.

"Caden's a big guy. He can take care of himself. He's smart. He'll take precautions. He's coming back tomorrow so we can get your stuff and move it here."

"You want me to *move* here? I thought you meant you just wanted me to stay here for the night." My heart beats faster as I imagine being here with him. In his apartment. On his couch. In his bed. But then I think better of it. "I can't move here, Kyle. I've built a life for myself. It may not be much to someone like you, but it's nice. And I was starting to feel safe. Like maybe everything else was in the past."

"You *can* move here," he says, giving me a no-nonsense look that says he's used to taking charge. "You have to. Has it not sunk in yet that Grant was looking for you a few days ago? He's *here*, Lexi. In New York. You are anything but safe."

"All the more reason for me not to stay here," I say. "I have a place outside the city, about an hour from here."

"No. We can't protect you there. He tracked you here. To *my* hospital. Who knows how long it would take for him to track you to your new place. Caden and I agree that it's best for you to stay here, with me. You and Ellie can stay in the second bedroom. It's not set up like a nursery anymore, but we'll make do."

"What do you mean, *anymore?*"

"The day you left the hospital, Gavin and I moved everything from his garage into my spare bedroom. He gave me a crib, a changing table . . . everything."

I look at him with wide, undeserving eyes. "You did all that for *me?*"

"Why wouldn't I, Lexi? I wanted you. I wanted Ellie. And you just left. I know it wasn't because Grant found you, so tell me, why did you leave without so much as a word?"

His intense gaze is fierce. It's demanding. It's begging for the truth. The truth I was unwilling to reveal until now. But that's why I came here, isn't it? To tell him the truth. To get him back—that is if I ever really had him.

"When I found out you had paid for my hospital stay, everything changed. I know how much that must have cost. I knew I'd always be indebted to you. It felt like *him* all over again."

He pinches the bridge of his nose, sighing in frustration. "I would never expect anything in return. I didn't even want you to find out about it. And, God, I would never lay a hand on you. On *any* woman."

I nod, finding it hard to keep tears from pooling in my eyes. "I know. I think I always knew. I panicked, Kyle. But these past months, I've had a lot of time to think about things. And I had to come back. I had to find out."

"Had to find out what?" he asks.

"If . . . if . . ." I look into his eyes and then down at the floor.

He scrubs a hand across his jaw and shakes his head. "Lexi, it's been a long time. And you weren't the only one who had time to think. Before I met you, I was one-hundred-percent focused on my career. I didn't have time for relationships. It was hard enough to find time to keep up with my brothers. I can't do that again.

Relationships cloud judgment. They take away from what's most important to me. I have to put my career first. I'm sorry."

I swallow the colossal-sized lump in my throat, biting back the tears that threaten to fall. "It's okay," I say, walking to the massive wall of windows to gaze out onto the city below.

It's not okay. I love you. I've loved you ever since you made me play that stupid Jell-O game.

"Lexi," he says, his reflection looking guilty as he comes up behind me.

He holds his arm out as if he's going to touch me, but at the last second, he pulls back. He squeezes his eyes shut and mouths a cuss word. He runs his hands through his hair again. He does that when he's frustrated. He looks up at the ceiling and blows out a long breath. He's completely unaware that I'm seeing all of this. He thinks I'm looking out the window when I'm really looking at him. His reflection. And I can see it as clear as day. And it tells me the opposite of what his words did. It tells me that he's not over me, that maybe I still have a chance.

Instead of touching me, he stands next to me. "I still want you to stay here. Until we can figure this Grant thing out. We'll meet with Ethan, he's a private investigator. He can tell us what to do."

I shake my head. "No. I don't want anyone contacting Grant. I'm not putting Ellie at risk."

"But—"

"Nobody is contacting him, Kyle. Or I'm getting Ellie and we're walking out that door."

"Fine," he says, frustration spilling out of him in a fiery sigh. Then he puts his hands on my shoulders and turns me so we're facing each other. "If that's what it takes to get you to stay."

I want to smile. I want to smile, because even though he doesn't want me, he's willing to do anything to have me here.

CHAPTER THIRTY-EIGHT

Sunlight shines through my eyelids, causing me to wake from one of the best sleeps I've had in a long time. I almost forgot where I was. But even before I open my eyes, the smell reminds me. I'm in Kyle's apartment. In Kyle's bed.

He insisted on taking the futon in his guest room. He didn't want to disturb Ellie.

I reach out my arm to find my daughter, but all I run into are pillows. My heart races as I quickly crawl to the side of the bed to see if she's fallen off. But the floor is empty. I hop out of bed and go out in the living room, stopping in my tracks when I see Kyle holding Ellie.

He's sitting on the couch, his back to me. He's singing that song, *'This is the way the ladies ride . . .'* as he bounces her on his knee.

And I know he must be making funny faces as he sings, because Ellie is laughing.

She's laughing. At him. A stranger.

I'm mesmerized watching him interact with her. He doesn't have kids, yet he's a natural. So calm and confident. I guess it comes from being a doctor.

I quietly walk around the back of the couch, over to the kitchen where I grab a bottle of water from his refrigerator. Kyle hears me open it.

"I hope you don't mind," he says. "I heard her wake up, but you were dead asleep. I wanted to give you a few more minutes of shut-eye. I know yesterday was a big day for you, seeing Caden and all."

"It's fine," I say, admiring the way he's holding Ellie. "She seems taken with you."

He shrugs. "I have that effect on all the ladies."

I roll my eyes. "But at least you're humble about it."

He laughs and then turns back to Ellie, who is playing with the buttons on his shirt. "Case in point," he says. "She doesn't even care that you are over there talking to me."

I come out from behind the kitchen counter and Kyle's jaw drops. He rakes his eyes slowly up my body, starting at my bare feet and ending with what is most definitely a bad case of bed head.

I look down at myself, realizing that in my haste to get to Ellie, I forgot pants. The t-shirt Kyle gave me to sleep in covers my undies and hits me mid-thigh, revealing a lot of leg. Nothing he hasn't seen before, but still, the way he's looking at me—he's a starving man and I'm filet mignon.

It makes me wonder what he's been doing all these months. He says he's focusing on his career. But he's a man. A man in his twenties. A gorgeous man. Men like that aren't celibate.

Ellie starts to squirm around in his lap. She throws her head back and cries. She's hungry.

"I think she must want breakfast," he says. "Are you hungry, Ellie? Do you want Mommy to feed you?"

She keeps crying.

I walk around the sofa and tell him, "Put your thumb opposite your fingers and open and close your fist, like you're milking a cow." I demonstrate how to do it. "Like this."

He looks at me in confusion.

"It's the sign for milk," I say.

He looks down at Ellie, studying her. I expect him to look sad, take pity on her perhaps. But he doesn't. He looks surprised, yes, but he doesn't look at her like she's any less of a person. "She's deaf?" he asks me.

"Yes."

He uses his hand to sign to her as I instructed, and Ellie immediately calms down. Then I walk over so she can see me and she raises up her arms to me.

I sit on the other end of his couch, pulling a blanket over me so I don't reveal too much when I lift my shirt to nurse her.

"I had no idea, Lexi."

"I know you didn't. I left the hospital before they did her hearing test. I promised them I would have my pediatrician do it."

"And what did her pediatrician say?"

"That she is profoundly deaf."

"Did he talk to you about cochlear implants?"

I nod. "Yes. But I'm choosing not to go that way. I know most people wouldn't understand my reasons, least of all doctors who want to fix everything. But, Kyle, she doesn't need to be fixed. She's perfect just the way she is and I won't have anyone telling her she's not."

He holds up his hands in surrender. "I would never try to talk you into something you didn't want, Lexi. As her mother, you know what's best for her. And I happen to agree with you. In med school, I wrote a research paper on this very subject. Children who are profoundly deaf have no concept of sound. They are visual learners. Having an implant might actually confuse their senses and delay learning."

I look up at him, floored by his understanding. His unconditional acceptance of her.

"That's part of why I didn't want to do it," I say. "So many people look at deaf people as if they aren't normal. They try to make them fit into the hearing world. I didn't want that for her. Being deaf *is* normal for her."

"I applaud you for handling it so well," he says.

I laugh. "You didn't see me six months ago when I found out." I look down at my nursing daughter and remember the day I got the devastating news. "I was a wreck, Kyle. I thought I was being punished somehow. That Ellie was deaf because of something I did. Maybe I took an Aspirin early in my pregnancy. Maybe I didn't eat enough vegetables."

"There is nothing you did to cause this, Lexi."

"I know that now. I've done a lot of reading on the subject. I could probably write my own research paper."

"I don't doubt it," Kyle says. "I know how smart you are. Literature *and* education. Double major. Impressive."

I furrow my brow wondering if I'd ever told him that. I was so careful not to reveal any personal details.

"My brother is a private investigator," he reminds me. "Once I knew your real name, he dug up whatever he could find on you. Grant, too."

I gaze down at Ellie, feeling sorry for her not because she's deaf, but because she got dealt the shitty hand of having the world's worst father.

"Did you find anything on him?" I ask, wondering what Grant has been up to since I left.

"We found plenty," he says, shaking his head in disgust. "I'm surprised he's still working in law enforcement with how dirty he is. You were right to do what you did, Lex. You were right to leave him and protect Ellie."

I smile because he called me *Lex*. He's giving me a nickname for my nickname. He wouldn't do that if he didn't like me. The way he looked at me wearing his t-shirt. The way he was playing with Ellie.

He *must* like me.

Maybe he just doesn't realize it yet.

CHAPTER THIRTY-NINE

"What other signs does Ellie understand?" Caden asks me from the front seat on our way to collect my things.

I look between Caden and Kyle, wondering how I ever got so lucky—how Ellie got so lucky—to have two accepting men in her life. Grant would never be happy with her. He'd insist she get the implant. He probably wouldn't even bother to learn sign language. He would no doubt make her feel like less of a person.

"I know for sure that she understands milk, eat, more, all done, and no. I'm working on sleep, dog, cat and mom. But mom is hard since I'm referring to myself."

Kyle glances back at me. "Maybe we can help with that, what's the sign for mom?"

With my fingers spread open, I tap my thumb to my chin and show him. Then I watch him sign it back to me and my heart melts.

"When do you think she'll start signing back?" Caden asks.

I shrug. "Who knows? She's six-and-a-half months old and I've been signing to her since I found out she couldn't hear. I know they say it's pointless to sign to a baby younger than four months old, but it just felt wrong speaking to her knowing she couldn't hear me. Even if I was only doing it for me, at least I felt like I was communicating with her on her terms."

"Do you know a lot of signs?" Kyle asks, turning his head to speak to me.

"Yes, I pretty much know all of them," I say and sign at the same time.

Kyle turns around in his seat. "You know *all* of them?" he asks.

"I've been practicing for six months, Kyle. Sometimes four or five hours a day. There isn't much else to do in the country, you know. It's not like I'm proficient at it or anything. I'm still kind of slow, but I'm improving every day."

"In case you haven't figured it out by now, my sister is pretty much a genius," Caden says, with a proud smile. "Maybe now you'll get to use those awesome brains of yours, Lexi. You know, get a real job like you always wanted?"

"Maybe," I say, gazing out the window, knowing it's anything but true. I can't get any sort of meaningful job. Not if I want to remain anonymous.

After riding in Caden's truck for more than an hour, we come up on the train station where I left my car.

"What should I do about my car?" I ask them. "I parked it there and took the train into the city."

"You have a car?" Caden asks. "How?"

"It's not a nice car," I tell them. "I bought it for five hundred dollars off a nice old man who owns the corner grocery. Turn here," I say, seeing my street.

"I've got GPS, Lexi," Caden reminds me.

Of course he does. I sometimes forget about GPS, what with my twenty-one-year-old car that doesn't even have working air conditioning.

Kyle looks back at me. "How did you buy a car without identification?"

"I gave him cash and explained I didn't have enough left to pay for the tag, so he let me keep his tag that he had recently renewed. I guess I just figured I'd deal with it later."

"What if you'd gotten pulled over or been in an accident?" Kyle asks.

"I only drove it when necessary. To Ellie's doctor. To a big box store once every few months. We pretty much walked everywhere when the weather allowed. And we stayed at home if it didn't."

"We'll take care of the car," Caden says.

A few minutes later, Caden pulls into the driveway of my cozy little cottage. It needs a paint job. One of the shutters is falling off its hinge. And the yard is in terrible disarray. But it's been home for over six months.

"How can you afford this, Lex?" Kyle asks, getting out of the truck.

"Do you remember how I told you I'd be okay, that I still had something to sell?"

He nods.

Then Caden says, "Your engagement ring."

"Yes."

"I always wondered if it was real," he says.

"It was. And he never let me forget it."

Caden shakes his head in disgust. "I should have paid more attention. I was so stupid. So focused on playing baseball that I let him . . ."

"You didn't let him do anything, Caden," I say, pulling Ellie from her car seat. "If anyone is at fault here, it's me. I knew what he was doing to me was wrong. Yet I stayed. I have no one to blame but myself."

Kyle kicks a rock across my yard. "I'd say there's no one to blame but that bastard who calls himself a man."

"Hey there, Miss Elizabeth," Mrs. Peabody says, coming over from the main house next door. "Who are these fine-looking gentlemen you've brought with you today?"

Kyle holds his hand out in greeting. 'I'm—"

"Joe," I say, interrupting his introduction. "These are my brothers, Joe and John. And this is Mrs. Peabody. She rents me her guest house."

Mrs. Peabody giggles. "Joe, John, and Elizabeth Smith. Your parents sure were simple folk, huh?"

"That they were," Kyle says. "At least they didn't name us after adult film entertainers."

I cover my laugh and elbow him in the ribs.

Mrs. Peabody laughs at the joke she doesn't understand.

"Well, Mrs. Peabody, we've convinced our sister to move back to Ne—"

"Nevada," I say, glaring at Caden. "I'm moving back home to Las Vegas."

I've had over a year to perfect my ability to lie to people on the spot. It comes naturally to me now. But Kyle and Caden—they don't have a clue how harmful revealing even small, seemingly inconsequential details could be. Regular people might overlook that kind of stuff. Cops don't. Grant wouldn't.

"Oh, how delightful," Mrs. Peabody says. "It will be nice for you and little Ellie to live close to family. But, oh, how I will miss this adorable face." She pinches Ellie's cheeks.

"Yes. I'm looking forward to it," I say, looking at Kyle.

"Mrs. Peabody, how much does Elizabeth owe you for the rest of her lease?" Caden asks.

"Oh, I couldn't ask her to pay six month's rent. No, no. She is such a good girl. Always keeping to herself, but bringing me pies or cookies every Sunday."

"How much is your rent, Elizabeth?" Kyle asks.

"Four hundred," I say.

Caden gets out his wallet and pulls out a bunch of hundreds. He leans over to Kyle. "I'm a little shy, can you spot me?"

They pool their money and hand Mrs. Peabody a wad of bills that makes her eyes bug out.

"Like Elizabeth, we keep to ourselves," Kyle says. "We like our privacy and we hope you'll respect that if anyone ever comes around asking questions."

"Of course," Mrs. Peabody says, practically drooling over the stack of hundreds in her hand.

"It won't take long to get our stuff," I tell her. "I'll leave the key on the counter when we're done."

Mrs. Peabody leans down to kiss Ellie and then she pulls me in for a hug. "You are the best tenant I've ever had. I will miss you."

"We'll miss you, too, Mrs. Peabody. Thank you."

She walks back to her house, shaking her head at the wad of money in her hand. I imagine her walking to her kitchen and putting it in a coffee tin in her cupboard.

"I don't have much," I tell them. "The house came furnished. It's just our clothes and Ellie's crib and a few other things."

Caden pulls the boxes he brought out of the bed of his truck and we walk up the porch steps.

"I'll pay you back, Kyle. How much did you give her?"

"You don't have to do that, Elizabeth." He curses under his breath. "Lexi."

"I do. I still have some money left from selling the ring."

"You do?" he asks, looking surprised.

"It was a nice ring," I say.

He studies me. "Where did you sell it?"

"At a place down the street from the hospital."

He nods. "That must be why Grant came looking for you there. After he found out where you sold the ring, he probably cased the entire neighborhood surrounding the pawn shop. Maybe he'd been circulating pictures of you or your ring to pawn shops since you went missing, hoping to track you down."

"I knew he probably would. It's why I left the city after I sold it. I knew he never believed I was abducted. He knew I ran away from him. But he couldn't tell anyone that. They'd ask too many questions."

Ellie starts to fuss. "Milk?" I sign.

That makes her happy, so I tell the guys what they can box up before I excuse myself to my bedroom to feed her.

I look around the room that has been my home for the past six months. It was quiet here. It was safe. But it was lonely.

I look down at Ellie. Everything I've done is to protect her. Am I risking too much going back? *He* knows I'm there now. He's probably watching Caden. Maybe he even followed us and knows we're here.

What kind of mother puts her own child at risk for love?

I stare at the door and think of who is on the other side.

Maybe the kind of mother who wants her child to see what real men are. What real love is.

And maybe, just maybe, some risks are worth taking.

CHAPTER FORTY

Caden and Kyle are setting up Ellie's crib in Kyle's spare room. The futon is still in there, but they had to move a desk and a chair into Kyle's bedroom to make room. I'm busy feeding Ellie her dinner at the kitchen table where her highchair now sits at one end.

I look around the apartment that is now riddled with our stuff, and I smile. His place looks better with Ellie's things scattered about. It was too clean. Too clinical. But maybe that comes from his being a doctor.

I don't know how long we'll be here. But what I do know is that baseball season is about to be in full swing and Kyle doesn't want me staying with Caden when he's on the road so much. Plus, there is the whole Grant wanting to break his arms and legs thing.

That gives me about six months to get Kyle to come around. Seven if the Nighthawks make it all the way to the World Series.

I turn back to Ellie. "More?" I sign.

She opens her mouth big in answer.

"What was that you just did?" Kyle asks me, coming into the kitchen. "It looked like you were clapping with your fingertips. Is that the sign for 'eat'?"

"No, that's the sign for 'more.' The sign for 'eat' is this—" I bring my thumb and fingers together and make it look like I'm bringing food to my lips.

He copies my movements, doing both the signs for 'more' and 'eat.'

Ellie squeals.

"I think she likes that," I say. "She doesn't see many people signing. And especially not words she knows."

He smiles down on her, her chin orange from drooling carrots. Then he brings his thumb to his chin, doing the sign for 'mother.'

"Mommy," he says, signing again and then touching my shoulder. He does it three more times since he has Ellie's undivided attention.

This man. Does he work hard to be this charming, or does it come naturally?

"Thank you," I say. "Nobody has ever done that for her before. I'm the only one who ever signs to her."

He looks at me in disbelief. "Not anymore," he says. "I know I work a lot, but on my days off, I'd love for you to teach me."

"You want to learn ASL?" I ask, surprised.

"Of course. It won't really be fair to Ellie if you have to tell her everything I say, now will it?"

"Uh, no, but—"

"Good. Then it's settled. I have a thirty-six-hour shift and then I have a night off on Tuesday. We'll start then."

The doorbell rings and ends our conversation. I'm teeming with excitement. He wants to learn sign language. He thinks we'll be here long enough for him to need to communicate with her.

Caden comes out of the spare room—*my room*—and heads to the refrigerator to get a few beers. "The crib's all done. Want a beer, Lexi?"

I haven't had a lick of alcohol since the moment I found out I was pregnant. I look at Ellie and then over at Kyle.

"One beer is fine," he says. "Doctor's orders. You need to relax."

"Okay," I say, holding out my hand to accept it.

Kyle places a giant bag of Sal's take-out on the table in front of me.

"Oh, my God. You remembered?" I ask, smiling from ear to ear.

He laughs. "How could I forget? I'm a bit surprised you didn't name your daughter *Sal.*"

I sneer at him. "I'm not *that* obsessed with it."

"Oh, but you are. Sal's Chinese food and Hawks baseball."

Caden pats me on the back. "That's my sis."

"You should have seen her, Caden," Kyle says. "She wouldn't even let anyone speak if you were at bat. Or behind the plate. Or even on a highlight reel—*especially* then."

"I wasn't that bad," I say, reaching in the bag to get the boxes out and spread them around the table.

Kyle raises his eyebrows in objection. "Eliz—sorry—Lexi, you *were.* At first it was endearing, a woman so into baseball. But then as time went on, I became aware that it wasn't baseball in general, it was one particular baseball player. And I'm not ashamed to say I was jealous as hell."

Caden snorts beer through his nose. "Dude, that's just wrong. Jealous of me and my sister?"

Kyle throws a pair of chopsticks across the table at him. "I didn't know she was your sister back then."

He leans over me to grab his favorite egg roll, and when he catches Ellie watching him, he does the sign for 'mother' and puts his hand on my arm.

He has no idea what his doing that just meant to me.

I watch him take a bite of the egg roll and then wrinkle his nose at it.

"What?" I ask. "Is it not good?"

"It's fine," he says, putting it down on his plate. "It's just, I've had a lot of them over the past several months. They may have worn out their welcome with my taste buds. I might have to move on to spring rolls or something."

"You've eaten at Sal's a lot, huh?"

"Uh, I guess once or twice," he says, looking embarrassed.

He went there. He went there for *me*. It was the only place outside the hospital that he associated with me. I can't help my triumphant smile.

"What?" he asks, annoyed with himself for revealing what he did.

"Nothing," I reply. Then I turn to Caden. "So, are you going to keep number eight, or go back to twenty-seven?"

"I think I'll stick with eight," he says around his food. "It's brought me a lot of luck. I had seven home runs last season. And now *you're* back. Lucky number eight."

"Why did you change it?" Kyle asks him. "I thought it was kind of unusual for a player to change a number."

"It is," Caden says. "I grew up being number twenty-seven. It was the first number they ever assigned me when I started playing T-ball at age five."

"Every year, he just kept getting better," I say. "He impressed his coaches. The other players. He thought it was the number. It got to the point where if he couldn't get number twenty-seven, he wouldn't play for a team. I remember a few travel ball teams he turned down when he was twelve just because they already had a kid with the same number."

"Really?" Kyle asks Caden in amusement.

"It's a superstitious sport, man. People do crazy things in baseball."

"But you changed it halfway through your first year with the Nighthawks. What happened?"

Caden nods at me. "Lexi went missing. It was a tribute to her."

"How was it a tribute to Lexi?"

"Alexa Octavia Kessler," Caden says. He looks over at me and we share a nostalgic smile. "My big sister always thought I should be number eight, not number twenty-seven. She said eight was the better number and that I should listen to my big sister and if I didn't, bad things would happen. I guess my superstition about that overrode my superstition about baseball."

"No shit?" Kyle says. "You'd think that story would have been all over ESPN. I never heard about it."

Caden shakes his head. "I never told anyone why I changed the number. I'm sure my teammates thought it had something to do with my sister going missing, but I kept it to myself. Lexi was the only person who needed to know why I did it."

I reach across the table and touch my brother's hand. "The dynamic duo," I say.

He laughs. "The dynamic duo," he repeats.

"It's what we used to call ourselves when we were little," I explain to Kyle. "Our father took off shortly after Caden was born and our mother bounced around from man to man looking for her next husband—of which she had four. Nobody had time for us. It was us against the world."

"Darn," Kyle says, looking overly dramatic. "You guys are a walking-talking Lifetime movie."

Caden and I both pelt him with fortune cookies.

Kyle catches them and winks at me. "Still my favorite part," he says, keeping one and tossing the other back to me.

"Mine too," I tell him, ripping open the plastic to get to mine.

I can't help but smile as we both hide our slips of paper while we eat our cookies. Caden looks between us, not understanding the private moment.

I read mine first. *"You will be hungry again in thirty minutes."*

We all moan and chuckle as Caden opens his. *"Made in the USA,"* he reads.

"Boston!" Kyle and I shout at the same time, laughing.

"Now you," I say nodding at Kyle.

He opens the slip of paper and reads his fortune to himself. Then he shakes his head and gets up from the table, throwing his food in the trash.

"Dude, did it say you were going to kill a patient or something?" Caden asks, laughing.

Kyle doesn't respond to Caden's laughter. He just keeps walking to his bedroom. We've reminisced a lot tonight about the month I was under his care in the hospital. But it was evident to me that the more we walked down memory lane, the more uncomfortable he became. Maybe all those good memories just reminded him of how I left him without even a word.

There is still so much he wants to know about me. Still so much I should share with him. I wish things were like they were before and I could just show up with a dozen flavors of Jell-O and two plastic spoons. How I long for those days. Before I made the biggest mistake of my life.

Kyle's bedroom door slams shut.

Feeling a bit defeated, I walk over and look at the trashcan, the little slip of paper having fallen off his plate, coming to rest on the floor next to it. I pick it up and read it.

'Everything happens for a reason.'

CHAPTER FORTY-ONE

I hug everyone as they pile into Kyle's apartment. Charlie, Mallory, Baylor, Skylar and Piper have all come over to 'keep me company' while Kyle is at work and Caden goes to a late meeting. Seems I'm not even on bedrest anymore yet I still need babysitting.

I'm not complaining though, I've missed them all so much. Mallory even brought her daughter, Kiera, who is three weeks younger than Ellie. We sit them on a soft blanket next to the couch as I catch everyone up on my life.

"I'm sorry I didn't tell you any of this when we talked on the phone earlier," I say to Baylor after I tell them everything. "But I just didn't have the energy to talk about it more than absolutely necessary."

"Are you kidding?" she says. "I completely understand, Elizabeth. I mean, Alexa. Oh, wow, that is going to take some getting used to."

"Please call me Lexi," I say.

"So you've been running and on your own for over a year?" Skylar asks, her head shaking in anger over what I told them about Grant.

"Just about thirteen months," I say.

"And you supported yourself with no identification, no address and no bank account?" Mallory asks.

"Well, I did some odd jobs before Ellie was born. Walking dogs, cleaning apartments, but after she came along, there was no way for me to work."

"Is that why you came back?" Charlie asks. "You ran out of money?"

I shake my head. "Money was tight, but I was managing. I had sold some jewelry and I was babysitting for some of the moms I met at Mommy and Me."

"Then why come back? Especially if you think he knows you are in New York?" Baylor asks.

I don't even realize it when I look over at Kyle's bedroom.

"Oh, my God!" Baylor squeals. "You're in love with him!"

"I knew it!" Mallory yells.

"You owe me ten bucks," Skylar says to Piper.

My jaw drops in disbelief. "You bet on me?" I ask, watching Piper get out her wallet to make good on her bet.

Skylar laughs. "We all knew you and Kyle were right for each other. Even Piper. But she pegged you for a runner."

I look at Piper and her eyes look sad as they hold mine. But what I see in them is something . . . familiar.

"I'm still running, you know," I tell them. "I'm not sure I'll ever be able to resume my identity. He could come after me. After Ellie. I can't risk that."

"Kyle will protect you. Those Stone brothers are very good at protecting the ones they love," Baylor says.

"It's not like that," I tell them. "Kyle and I aren't together. He's letting us stay here for our safety, not because he wants to get together with me. I blew that chance when I walked out of the hospital six months ago."

"That's ridiculous," Charlie says. "I see that man once a week at dinner. He may say he's over you. He may even think he is. But the eyes never lie. He's lost, Lexi. Those weeks you were in the hospital, he was a different person. He's always been happy, but back then he was, I don't know . . . glowing, for lack of a better word. I'd never seen him like that before and I've not seen him like that since. That is not a man who just wants to be friends with you. Believe me."

"I appreciate your support and optimism," I tell them. "I really do. But I can tell Kyle is still very hurt and guarded, even now that he knows my past. He's helping me because that's who he is—a nice guy who helps people. A doctor who wants to change the world. He'd do it for anyone. Heck, he did it for me before he even really knew me."

Skylar elbows Piper. "Care to make another wager?"

Piper rolls her eyes at her sister.

"Regardless, I'll bet Ethan can help you with your Grant problem," Mallory says. "He has lots of connections. Maybe even at Chicago P.D."

Baylor and Skylar and Mallory all try to convince me to let Ethan help, while Charlie and Piper look at me with sympathetic eyes.

"No," I tell them in no uncertain terms. "I already told Kyle and Caden that I don't want Grant contacted. There are just too many laws that protect those who shouldn't be protected."

"She's right," Charlie says, coming to my defense. "We all know scumbags get away with too much as it is. She can't risk her daughter. Are we in agreement, girls?"

All five of them put their hands on top of one another's. Then they look at me and nod to the top of their hand pile. I place my hand on top and it somehow feels like in doing so, I've become one of them. A sister of sorts. Someone they will protect.

I've always wanted a sister. Now I have five.

Tears spill down my cheeks.

Baylor hugs me. "It's okay, Lexi. We're here for you, whatever you need."

I nod, wiping the wetness from my face. "Thank you. I don't even know what to say."

"Say you'll be my assistant," she says.

I look at her with drawn brows. "What? Surely you've filled the position by now."

She laughs. "I did. And it was a horrible train wreck. The girl didn't know a hyperbole from a simile. She lasted about six weeks before I realized I was spending more time telling her how to do her job than I was doing *my* job."

I shake my head. "I can't," I say with resounding regret. "I can't work as Alexa Lucas. He'll find me if I do. And I can't get paid as Elizabeth Smith—I have no identification. No bank account or social security number."

"I don't care about any of that," Baylor says. "You are exactly the kind of person I need working for me. The way you discussed books with me in the hospital tells me you know your stuff. You have a degree in literature, so I'm assuming you know what hyperbole is without me having to gouge my eyes out trying to explain it to you." She laughs at her own hyperbolic joke. "And you can work part-time from home, right here from Kyle's apartment. I can messenger over everything. And when we need to have meetings, I can come to you. And paying you under the table won't be a problem."

"But that's not fair to you," I say, wanting so badly to accept her offer, but not willing to do it if she made it out of pity. "You wouldn't be able to deduct my pay from your taxes."

"Gah!" Piper bolts out. "Do you know how much money she makes writing sappy love stories? People eat that shit up, Lexi. She's rolling in it."

"Says the fiancée of the football star," Baylor scolds her youngest sister. Then she turns back to me. "I also wouldn't have to pay your social security or your medical and dental. It would save me a lot of paperwork. It's a win-win situation. Will you at least think about it?"

I shake my head. "I don't have to think about it," I say.

She looks sadly at the other girls.

"I don't have to think about it, because I'll do it," I say, smiling. "I'll take the job."

She shrieks and pulls me in for a hug. "You won't regret it," she says. "I'm an awesome boss."

I laugh. "Sure. As long as I know a hyperbole, from . . . what was that other fancy word?" I joke.

"See?" she says. "You're a smart ass like me. I think we're going to get along just fine."

"So, you have a place to live and a job," Mallory says. "Now we just have to work on the man."

I sigh in frustration. "The man who doesn't want a relationship anymore?" I ask her.

"Haven't you learned by now that men don't have the faintest clue about what's best for them?" she asks.

I shrug. "Grant is the only man I've been with. I have no one else to compare to."

"Well, take our word for it," Skylar says. "They are clueless when it comes to matters of the heart. And sometimes we have to nudge their hearts in the right direction."

"I—I don't even know how to begin to do that," I say.

Charlie laughs. "Ethan said Kyle was all frazzled when he called earlier. I'd say you know *exactly* how to do that."

Before the girls leave, Charlie and Piper pull me aside. "We have some idea what you've been through," Charlie says. "If you ever need to talk, you can call one of us. We've both been, uh . . . mistreated by men."

I shake my head in sadness. "I'm sorry," I say.

"We're good now," Piper assures me. "And you will be, too. We just didn't want you thinking you were alone in this. Really, anytime, day or night."

"Thank you. That means a lot to me."

Once they leave and I get Ellie to bed, I sit and stare at the 'fortune' Kyle tried to throw away earlier. Then I think about what Skylar said about men needing a nudge in the right direction.

I send Skylar a text, hoping an offer I never took her up on six months ago still stands.

CHAPTER FORTY-TWO

I stir my eggs nonchalantly when Kyle walks in the door after his thirty-six-hour shift. He must be exhausted and wanting to sleep, but he doesn't get two feet into the kitchen before he stops dead in his tracks.

I pretend like I don't notice his reaction. Like I don't see his eyes take in my legs—legs that are bare from thigh to toe because I still have on nothing but my sleeping shirt—the one that barely covers my ass cheeks.

I pretend like I don't notice how he's checking out my new hair—hair that I let Skylar's stylist return to my natural brown color. Hair that isn't as short as when I was laid up in the hospital. It's grown out from chin-length into longer, flowing waves.

I love my naturally wavy hair. Always have. But Grant insisted I keep it super long and stick-straight, like one of those high-priced runway models. I'm pretty sure I'll never own a flat-iron again. My hand instinctively runs along the inner flesh of my right forearm as I remember how he once punished me with the hot appliance.

I shake off the memory and go about popping some bread into the toaster as if Kyle is not devouring me with his eyes.

"Oh, hi, Kyle," I say, as if I'm just now realizing he's standing there. "Would you like some breakfast?"

He finally tears his eyes from me. "No, thanks. I grabbed a bagel at the hospital." Then he laughs. "You'll never guess who I treated today," he says.

"Let me guess," I say. "POTUS?"

He looks at me in question.

"The President of the United States," I clarify.

"Oh," he says, with a chuckle. "No, not POTUS."

"The Pope?" I ask. "Oh, wait! Was it Liam Hemsworth? I heard he was in town."

He shakes his head and rolls his eyes. "Nope. I treated Elizabeth Smith."

"Really?" I look over at him, amused.

"She was very old," he says. "While I was treating her, she told me that at one point, her name was the most common name for a woman in America, with both Elizabeth and Smith topping the charts."

"She's right. Elizabeth battles with Mary, Patricia, and Barbara for the top spot depending on the year."

"That's why you chose it," he says knowingly. "A common name that couldn't be traced."

I nod.

"Smart move," he says. "Some women would have chosen differently. A unique name that maybe they wanted as a child, or some heroine they read about in a book."

"I wanted to be invisible," I tell him.

"You could never be invisible, Lexi," he says, with a conflicted look on his face.

I walk back over to the stove to check on the eggs when I feel him come up behind me. He touches a lock of my hair, and even though hair doesn't have nerve endings, I swear I can feel it all the way to my toes.

"You shouldn't leave the apartment," he says, concern lacing the deep cadence of his voice. "Not until we have a plan in place for your safety."

I turn around, putting our chests inches from each other. I look up at him. "I didn't leave. Skylar's hair stylist came here to the apartment."

"Good," he says, looking relieved. He brushes a stray hair out of my eyes, but then pulls his finger away like touching me has burned him. He takes a step back, putting distance between us.

I reach over and grab a slip of paper off the counter. It's the fortune from the other night that reads *Everything happens for a reason.'* The one he tried to throw away. "Here," I say, handing it to him. "You dropped this the other day on your way out. It's bad luck to throw away a good fortune."

He silently reads it to himself, then he looks at me. I know we're both thinking of one of the first conversations we ever had.

I point to the fortune. "I asked you once if you thought everything we go through is a way of getting us where we need to be. Do you remember?"

He nods.

"Do you remember your answer?" I ask him.

He nods again, slipping the fortune into his pocket before he walks away. "I'm going to hit the sack. I'll probably sleep most of the day. I had a busy few nights."

"I'll try to keep quiet," I tell him, guiltily looking over at Ellie, who is banging a toy on her highchair.

He laughs, walking over to her. "Don't worry about it. I can pretty much sleep through anything." Then he leans down and gives my daughter a kiss on the top of her head.

I'm jealous. I'm jealous of my own child. *I* want to be the recipient of his kisses.

He walks through the living room towards his bedroom as I pull my eggs off the stove and slide them onto a plate. When I turn back around to join Ellie at the kitchen table, I see Kyle standing in his doorway, staring at me again.

"I like the brown," he says. "You looked good as a blonde. You even pulled off the red, which not many women can do. But brown is definitely your color."

I smile as I place my plate on the table. And before he closes his door, I could swear I hear him let out a big sigh as he quietly says, "And mine."

CHAPTER FORTY-THREE

"What is that incredible smell?" Kyle asks, emerging from his bedroom almost nine hours later.

I put down the picture book I was reading to Ellie.

"Lasagna," I tell him. "I thought you might want a home-cooked meal after eating hospital food for two days. You had all the ingredients. I hope it's okay."

"You don't have to cook for me, Lexi. I don't expect you to do anything."

"I know you don't. That's why I wanted to do it." I trace an invisible line on the couch.

He walks over and sits in the chair next to us. "Did *he* expect you to?" he asks.

"Yeah." I nod sadly. "He expected a lot of things."

"Shit, Lex," he says, shaking his head in anger. Then he looks guiltily at Ellie, who is watching him. "Sorry, I shouldn't cuss in front of her."

I raise my eyebrows at him.

"I know she can't hear me," he says. "But she will eventually learn to read lips, so I shouldn't get into the habit."

Eventually. I try to hide my smile. He thinks we'll still be here eventually—whenever that may be.

"So, what are you doing?" He nods to the book. "Reading?"

"She loves this book about dogs and cats. I read it to her every day and teach her the signs."

He looks into the kitchen. "How long before dinner is ready?" he asks.

"About an hour."

"That should be long enough for my first lesson." He gets up from his chair and joins us on the couch. "So, teach me. Teach me how to sign dog and cat." Then he smiles at Ellie. "Mommy," he says to her as he taps his thumb to his chin while touching my shoulder.

Him teaching Ellie 'mommy' has become the highlight of my day. It's the only time I get to feel his touch. And I find myself hoping it takes her a long time to learn that particular word.

I point to the picture of the dog in the book and then I pat my hip as if calling a dog. "Dog," I say as I sign. I point back to the picture and repeat the motion.

Then I point to the cat as I say the word and pinch my thumb and index finger together next to my cheek and bring it out like I'm teasing my whiskers straight.

Kyle points to the pictures and does the signs. Ellie likes it when he does that.

"So, give me the basics," Kyle says. "But start me off slowly."

"Okay," I say, putting Ellie on the floor next to some of her toys. "ASL is kind of like shorthand writing. All the concepts are there, but not every word is signed. Signing is slower than speaking, so unnecessary words like 'a,' 'an,' and 'the' are not used. There are thousands of word signs, but not all words have signs. Those you fingerspell. Also, nouns tend to come before adjectives because in a visual language, it makes more sense to give details after you have an idea about the subject."

He nods to the cover of Ellie's book. "So, you would sign 'dog' 'brown' and 'bark' to say 'the brown dog is barking'?"

I smile. "You're a fast learner, Dr. Stone. That is exactly right."

"Do I get a gold star from the teacher?" he asks.

"Yes," I say, as I nod my fist up and down to sign the word.

"Another thing that's very important in ASL is the use of facial expressions and body movements. To ask a spoken question, you would raise the pitch of your voice. Using ASL, you'll raise your eyebrows, or widen your eyes, otherwise someone might think it's a statement. As in *'want coffee',"* —I do the signs without any facial expression— "as opposed to *'want coffee'?"* —I do the signs and raise my eyebrows. "The first time I signed it, you might think *I* wanted coffee, but the second time, you would know I was asking if *you* wanted coffee."

"I think I got it." He does the sign for milk and raises his eyebrows.

"That's good," I say, impressed he remembered the sign. "I know you are asking a question about milk, but without an accompanying sign, I'm not sure if you're asking me if I *want* it or if I *have* it. We'll get to that another day. Today I'm going to show you the alphabet. I also have a ton of books you can borrow if you ever want to practice on your own."

"I know," he says, stretching his back as if in pain. "I carried them up here a few days ago."

I laugh. "See, you used body language to get your point across. That's good. Body language is how you make one sign different just by how dramatically you sign it. For instance, the sign 'mad' can also mean 'really mad' or 'furious' based on bigger gestures and more emphatic body movements. And the difference between 'happy' and 'ecstatic' would be demonstrated by the amount of joy in your expression when you sign the word 'happy'."

Ellie pulls a pen off the coffee table and puts it in her mouth. I take it from her. "No," I say, closing two fingers to my thumb as I shake my head back and forth and give her a hard stare.

Kyle mimics my sign until he gets it right.

I spend the next half hour teaching him all the letters of the alphabet. Sometimes I have to manipulate his fingers into the proper position. Whenever I touch him, he looks at my face, as if my touch is doing something to him that he can't quite figure out.

"What's the sign for 'friend'?" he asks, at the end of our lesson.

I show him and he signs it back to me. He signs it back to me using crystal clear facial expressions to get his point across. Facial expressions that tell me he's sorry, but a friend is all he's willing to be.

The kitchen timer goes off and Kyle hops up to take the Lasagna out of the oven for me. Then he sets the table. Then he gets the salad I made out of the fridge and slices the hot bread, putting it into a basket before he carries it all to the dining room.

I walk into the kitchen and perch on a barstool, mesmerized by watching a man serve me dinner.

He notices me as I regard him. "What was it like with him?" he asks, reading the expression on my face.

I put Ellie in her highchair and grab a few jars of baby food. Then I sit at the table as Kyle dishes me out some dinner. "Pretty much the opposite of this," I say.

"It's okay if you don't want to talk about it," he says.

I take a bite of salad, contemplating what or how much to tell him. The first night I was here, he heard the gist of it. He knows Grant hurt me. But that's not what he's asking me now.

"He wasn't always a monster," I tell him. "In fact, he was pretty charming in the beginning. We met on spring break in Myrtle Beach when I was nineteen and he was twenty-five. I was a sophomore at the University of Maryland and he was on vacation with a few of his policeman friends."

I turn my attention to Ellie to give her a few bites. "Yummy carrots," I say and sign, watching Kyle mimic the gesture in my periphery.

"We hit it off right from the start, spending the entire week together. I remember my friends were so mad at me for going off with this random guy who I didn't even know. But he made me feel special." I sigh, berating myself for being so gullible. "My mom didn't bring home the best role models," I tell him. "Her boyfriends and husbands treated her terribly. And they treated me like I didn't even exist. So, when Grant swooped in and made me feel like the most special girl on the planet, I fell for him instantly.

"After I went back to school, he sent me love letters every week. He came to visit me for long weekends in the summer. The next fall, he started flying me to Chicago over my school breaks. He was always giving me gifts," —I bow my head in shame— "and I was all too eager to show him my appreciation.

"I was young and naïve. I didn't even realize a cop shouldn't be able to afford such things. Not an honest cop, anyway. And then when my mom died junior year, he stepped up and paid for me to finish college. He even paid some expenses for Caden, who had earned a baseball scholarship, but was still in need of spending money. Grant took care of everything when I had nothing."

Kyle puts his fork down in disgust. I think he gets where this is going. "Jesus, Lexi, and then I went and paid for your hospital stay." He runs his hands through his hair. "When did you realize he wasn't who you thought he was?"

"When I graduated, there was no home for me to go back to. Mom's fourth husband, the one she was married to when she died, sold their house and moved away. So, when Grant proposed and asked me to move to Chicago to live with him, it seemed the right thing to do. And it was great for a while. He told me to take my time, plan the wedding, get used to the city before I ran out and got a job. So, I did what he asked." I shake my head at myself and how stupid I was back then. "I always did what he asked. Right up until a month after our wedding when he found out I'd lined up some job interviews. He didn't want me to get a job. I told him it was my life and I needed something for myself, apart from him. He didn't like that very much, so he made sure I couldn't go to the interviews."

"How did he make sure, Lexi?" Kyle asks, his hand balling into a fist.

"He said nobody would hire a woman with a messed-up face."

Kyle violently pushes his chair away from the table. He gets up, walks to the kitchen, and throws his plate into the sink. "Fuck!" he yells, facing the other direction as he braces his arms against the counter.

He takes a few deep breaths before turning around. "By then, you felt like you were trapped."

I nod. "It took me another two years to build up the courage to leave him." I look down at my daughter. "It was Ellie. She's what gave me the courage to leave. I'm not sure I would have if it weren't for her."

"I have to ask," he says, looking curiously at me. "Were you and Grant trying to have a baby?"

I shake my head. "No. In fact, I was pretty opposed to it, which wasn't a problem considering he didn't want me to *'ruin my body'* with a pregnancy." I look over at Ellie as she mashes a few

Cheerios into her mouth. "It was my own fault, getting pregnant. I used to swim a lot at the local YMCA and I ended up with a bad ear infection. I stupidly didn't use backup birth control. I didn't even think about it."

Kyle looks annoyed. "Your doctor should have warned you that antibiotics can reduce the effectiveness of the pill."

"Yeah, I realize that now." I laugh.

"And you're sure he doesn't know about you being pregnant?"

I shrug. "I don't see how he could. I left the day I found out."

He grabs a beer from the fridge and sits back down at the table. "I'm sorry I ruined dinner," he says. "Thank you so much for cooking. Lasagna is my favorite."

"I know," I say, spooning more carrots into Ellie's mouth. "Mallory told me."

"She did, did she?" he asks with a crooked smile.

"She told me a lot of things about you," I goad.

"Really?" His eyebrows shoot up. "Such as?"

I wipe Ellie's face as I say and sign, "All done." Then I get up and take my dishes to the sink. "A girl's gotta have some secrets, Kyle."

CHAPTER FORTY-FOUR

"Lexi!" Charlie screams, pulling me into her penthouse after she opens the door. "Get in here, Piper has some great news."

I'm dragged to the sofa where all the girls are sitting, and I put Ellie down where Mallory's daughter, Kiera, is playing.

"What is it?" I ask.

"We've set a date," Piper says, excitedly. "May 14th." She looks over at her fiancé, Mason. "He's finally going to make an honest woman out of me."

Mason tips his beer at his bride-to-be. "Don't let her fool you, Lexi. I've been trying to get her to set a date for three years."

"There was never a good time. Someone was always having a baby, filming a movie, or out of the country," Piper says.

"Congratulations," I say. "That's only two months away. Is that enough time to plan a wedding?"

Baylor, Skylar and Piper all share a look. "You don't know our mother," Baylor says. "When Jan Mitchell puts her mind to it, she can make anything happen."

They start to share stories of the three of them growing up in Maple Creek, Connecticut. It sounds like they had an incredible childhood. I look over at Ellie and watch her play with Kiera. Then I watch Gracie and Caitlyn toddle into the room. Everyone calls them 'the twins,' because Skylar and Baylor had them only days apart. Then I watch Charlie's son, Eli, follow around two rambunctious five-year-old girls—Jordyn, Baylor's daughter, and Hailey, Mason's daughter with his ex-girlfriend. Aaron, Skylar's four-year-old son, sits perched next to her, paging through a book. The only one missing is Maddox, Baylor's oldest. He's away at church camp with his youth group while school is on spring break.

The love and life in this penthouse is amazing. This is what I want for Ellie. I want her growing up with family, friends . . . siblings.

Piper sits down next to me. "I'd love it if you would agree to be a bridesmaid," she says. "And I promise I'm not just saying that because every other woman here will be."

"Me?" I look at her in disbelief.

I had friends in college. Good friends, even. But no one who would have asked me to be in their wedding. No one I even asked to be in mine. Probably because Grant wanted to keep it small and local. In fact, the only guest in attendance who was there for *me* was my brother. Just another way Grant was able to manipulate me.

"Of course," she says. "Will you?"

I look over at Mason and realize what it would entail. He's the quarterback for the Giants. I shake my head. "I would like nothing more, Piper. But I can't. Your wedding will probably be covered by the news. Maybe even ESPN. And pictures will be plastered all over. I'm really flattered that you asked, but I'm going to have to settle for being part of the crowd if that's okay with you."

She nods in complete understanding. She's not one to push. She knows we all have our reasons for why we do things. I know this because just yesterday, she brought Hailey over for lunch and told me her own horrific story. The two of us are bound by similar experiences. Mine, from a man with whom I shared a bed. Hers, from total strangers.

"Will you help me plan it?" she asks.

"I'd be honored, Piper."

Charlie calls the adults over for dinner as the babysitter they hired rounds up all the kids and herds them into the theater room to watch the latest Disney movie. Mallory and I carry our girls back after them and get them situated with some toys on a blanket in the corner.

By the time I make it out to the dinner table, they are already deep in conversation. About *me*, apparently.

Ethan and Kyle are discussing ways for me to file for divorce and get full custody of Ellie.

"Are you guys crazy?" I ask them. "What is it about '*he could sue me for custody*' that you don't understand? I took his baby away. Without his consent. He would have a solid case against me." I look at Kyle in anger. "You promised you wouldn't contact him."

"I won't, Lexi. I would never do that without your okay. We're just tossing around ideas here. When Grant came to the hospital, he said you had something he couldn't get from anyone else. Do you think he was talking about the ring?"

I shrug. "I suppose he could have been. But he never fussed too much over the jewelry after he gave it to me. After he got his way. Anyway, if he came looking for me in New York because he found out I sold the ring, the idea that he needs to get it from me is kind of a moot point. I'm more concerned that he was talking about Ellie. That he somehow knows I had a child."

"How could he know?" Mallory asks. "Didn't you say you ran away the day you found out?"

I nod. "Yes. And I took the pregnancy test and all the packaging with me. I didn't see a doctor until I got to New York."

"Boobs," Gavin says, and all heads turn to him.

Baylor's jaw drops. "You'll have to excuse my husband," she says. "He left his manners down in the building lobby."

Gavin laughs, grabbing his wife's hand. "When you were pregnant, your boobs got bigger almost immediately. Hell, when you got pregnant with Caitlyn, I was the one who told you to take a test, remember?"

"Oh, my God, you're right," Baylor says. She turns to me. "Maybe he suspected."

"No," I say. "No way." Then I think about how Grant loved my boobs. He loved to show them off in tight dresses. He didn't want me wearing bras around the house. He was always touching them. Palming them. Studying them.

Oh, shit. *Shit, shit, shit.*

Maybe he *did* know. "That's all the more reason to keep him from finding me. If he's trying to find me because he knows about Ellie, that means he's after *her.*" I look at Kyle. "You said it yourself, I have something nobody else can give him."

"You realize you'll be a prisoner of circumstance, don't you?" Ethan asks. "You'll never be able to get a passport, or any identification for that matter. You'll never be able to marry. You won't even be able to enroll Ellie in school."

"I'll homeschool," I say. "And marriage is overrated."

"Ethan," Charlie says. "With all your connections, couldn't you conjure up a new identity for the two of them? Say, Elizabeth and Ellie Smith? I've seen some pretty authentic-looking documents pass through our offices before."

Mallory's husband, Chad, points his fork at me. "You know, we have some pretty realistic identification for some of the characters I've portrayed. I wonder if I could find out who does that for the studio." He turns to Gavin. "Gavin? Maybe you can put out feelers, too."

"Sure. I could do that."

"See?" Charlie says. "Problem solved. We'll just have to get used to calling you Elizabeth again."

"Nobody's calling her Elizabeth," Kyle insists. "We're going to figure this out. We just need time." He sighs and runs those large hands through his hair. "Hiding away forever is no way to live, Lexi. You'll be looking over your shoulder your whole life."

For a second, I wonder if he's worried that I'll overstay my welcome.

"Given the choice, I don't really fancy living in hiding either," I say. "But wouldn't you all do anything you had to do to protect your children? What if there was even a small chance one of them could be taken away?"

"She's right, guys," Skylar says, glancing back towards the theater room where her own two kids are safe and sound. "She can't risk it. The guy is a cop. A corrupt one. And he's probably got a lot of other dirty cops in his pocket. Maybe even dirty politicians. You guys might have connections, but my guess is that he does, too."

A lot of heads nod in agreement.

Kyle blows out a long breath. "Okay. We'll all try to figure out how to get you some identification. But you'll still need escorts when you leave the building. I don't want you and Ellie walking around the city."

"I walked around the city for six months without being found, you know," I remind him. "Before I had Ellie."

"That was before Grant knew for sure that you were here. Now he knows. Now that he traced the ring back to New York City."

"I've got wigs," Mallory says. "Remember the wigs you sent to me, Chad, when we first started dating?"

I wrap a piece of my hair around my finger. "Maybe I should have stuck with red."

"No," Kyle says, his eyes burning into mine. "You definitely shouldn't have stuck with red."

In my periphery, I see Baylor elbow Skylar in the ribs as they watch Kyle look at me.

His eyes, the way they look at me. Follow me. His words may say one thing, but if I were deaf, I'd think his actions, his expressions, were saying something entirely different.

CHAPTER FORTY-FIVE

By the time we get back to Kyle's apartment, it's late. He heads straight for his room and I go put Ellie down for the night before I take a shower. As the warm water flows down my body, I think back on this evening. I would have loved to accept Piper's invitation to be a part of her wedding. How I long for that normalcy in my life. Will I ever be able to do things like that without thinking about the ramifications?

For almost a week now, I've been Lexi again. And it's been great. I feel like I can finally be myself. Around them. Around him. And a small part of me, deep down inside, wants to go along with them and file for divorce and full custody. But the very large part— the part that owns my heart—is not willing to take even the smallest chance that Ellie could be taken from me.

I comb through my wet hair and put on my tank top and undies before I pad back down the hallway to my bedroom. When I reach the doorway, I stop. My breath hitches when I see what's inside. Kyle is rocking Ellie.

And he's shirtless.

His head is resting against the rocking chair and his eyes are closed as he glides back and forth. He's completely unaware that I'm standing here staring at him.

I've never seen him without a shirt before. And even though he's mostly covered by Ellie, I can clearly see the outline of his abs, the strong lines of his chest, the low dip of his lounge pants. *Oh, my God.*

I can feel my nipples pebble under the thin material of my shirt and all of a sudden, I'm reminded of my lack of clothing. I start to cross the room to get my robe when I hear his softly spoken words.

"I hope you don't mind," he whispers. "She was crying."

I look over at him to see his eyes taking me in. I might as well be wearing nothing. And with the way my nipples are poking through my shirt, I might as well be wearing a sign that says how much I want him.

Embarrassed, I cross my arms over my chest and finish my walk across the room, hyperaware that he's now seeing my backside, thanks to my teeny-tiny panties.

I put on my robe, that itself, barely covers my thighs. "No, I don't mind. Thanks for getting her back to sleep," I say. "I do that, too, you know—whisper when she's sleeping."

He smiles, looking down on her dark head of fine curls. "It's amazing to hold her, knowing I'm the one who brought her into the world. I literally put my hand inside you and pulled her out. Isn't that incredible?"

I nod, staring at them with tears welling in my eyes. This is how it should be. Ellie should have a man in her life who loves her. Who gets emotional when he holds her. Who thinks she's wonderful just the way she is.

I remember how he was with all the kids at Charlie's tonight. He played with them. Helped feed them. Picked them up and cuddled them when they fell down. He's everyone's favorite uncle. This man was born to be a father.

"You're good with kids, Kyle," I tell him. "Maybe you should go into pediatrics."

He kisses the top of Ellie's head and lightning bolts shoot through me, just as if he'd kissed the top of mine.

"I considered it early on," he says. "But ultimately, my goal is to run my own clinic. Emergency medicine gives me a better background for that."

"Run your own clinic?" I ask. "What does that mean exactly?"

"You know, for people who don't have insurance. So they can get better care than most places are willing to give them. So they can feel like normal people instead of being ashamed of who they are."

"You mean for people like me," I say, trying to keep the self-pity out of my voice.

"There are a lot of reasons people can't afford health care, Lexi. You are just one example. We're all just one bad circumstance away from being in someone else's shoes."

I smile at his motto. "Is that why you wanted to help me, Kyle? Because you thought I was down on my luck? But many people are down on their luck. Surely you don't pay for *everyone's* hospital stay." I motion at our opulent surroundings. "Although it looks like you might be able to afford it. So, why me?" It's a question I've wondered about a lot over the past six months.

He stares at me, gathering his thoughts. He shrugs. "Just a feeling, I guess. You looked so put together, yet you had nothing. You seemed educated, but you walked dogs for a living. Something was just . . . off. I felt it right from the start. From the minute I saw you sitting on the bench outside the ER."

He gets up from the chair and walks Ellie to the crib, gently placing her down to sleep on her back as I watch from over his shoulder. When he turns around, he bumps into me, but I don't move. Our chests are close and his gaze locks onto me as we look into each other's eyes.

His hand comes up to play with a lock of my hair and he stares at it, bemused. He once said he liked me as a brunette. I wonder if he's thinking about seeing me as a blonde. A redhead. He works my hair between his fingers and all I can think about is what it would feel like to have his hands on me, touching my body like he's touching my hair.

His eyes find mine again. They speak volumes. They tell me he wants exactly what I want. To touch me. To kiss me. Kiss me like he did over six months ago on my hospital bed. It was the only kiss we ever shared. The kiss I knew I'd always remember. The kiss that had me seeing my future and forgetting my past. The kiss that had me risking everything to come back and knock on his door.

He looks at me with a possessive, heavy-lidded stare, the intensity of his gaze winding through my entire body. My breathing accelerates. My pulse races. My insides are on fire being this close to him. I want him. I want him more than I want my freedom. More than I want my sanity. More than I want air.

His eyes break from mine when he puts his hand down, dropping my hair as he takes a step back. Emotionally. Physically. And it's now that I notice the front of his lounge pants are tented. I want to reach out and grab him, pull him back against me. Show him how great we can be together. But I don't, because his eyes are now telling me a different story than they were just moments ago. And it's a story I don't want to hear.

He sighs deeply, grabbing the back of his neck. "I—I'm sorry. I have an early morning," he says, his apologetic eyes now dark with pain.

He looks back down at a sleeping Ellie and then pads out of the room, shaking his head along the way.

I shut off the light, close the door and flop down on my bed in frustration. He wants this. It's all too evident by the way he looks at me. By the swell in his pants. Why can't he just let it happen?

I crawl beneath my covers, anxious and confused as hell, my body wired as tightly as a bow string. I let my hand wander under my shirt; under my panties, thinking of those hazel eyes, that unruly hair I'd like to run my hands through, those naked abs, his tented pants . . .

CHAPTER FORTY-SIX

When I get up with Ellie the next morning, Kyle is gone. I sit at the bar, drinking coffee from the same cup he used. It's silly and juvenile, I know—the idea of me putting my lips where his have been.

"Mommy is crazy," I sign to Ellie.

She smiles as if she agrees with me.

"You like him, don't you?" I ask rhetorically, musing over the question while I shovel a spoonful of pears in her mouth. "I mean, he's great, right? Much better than the jerk whose DNA you possess." I wipe her mouth. "I'm sorry, Ellie," I say and sign. "I'm sorry you drew the short straw with your father. I know someday in the far-off future, you might want to meet him. But I hope by then, you've had a good male role model in your life." I look over in the direction of Kyle's room.

"You hit the jackpot with your uncle, though," I tell her, as she babbles between spoonfuls. "Caden is a big baseball player. One day, he'll take us to his games and we will cheer him on. Maybe one day you could play softball, like I did." I ruffle her soft hair. "Never let anyone tell you that you can't do something. Or that you're not good enough. Do you hear me?"

I laugh at my blunder. "You know what I mean," I say to no one, rolling my eyes.

Ellie moves her mouth as if she's talking. She likes to mimic me when I verbalize words. I do the sign for '*I love you*' and then I put my face in front of her face, puckering my lips in waiting. She leans forward and lays a kiss on me with her pear-flavored mouth.

I get up to wash out my cup, realizing just how much time I spend having conversations with my six-and-a-half-month-old daughter who can't hear me and wouldn't understand even if she could. "You need a life, Lexi," I tell myself.

After reading to Ellie and doing our laundry, I spend the rest of the afternoon doing some work for Baylor. I love my job. Not only do I get to use my education and help out a friend, but I get to read the book she's currently working on before anyone else. It's called being a beta reader. She feeds me chapters of her novel as she writes them and I give her my feedback.

Reading for her is not part of my job, per se, *that* I do for fun. I spend most of my working hours answering emails on her behalf, perpetuating her social media presence, organizing orders from her e-commerce site, and researching topics she's asked me to look into for future novels.

Today, I'm gathering all the information I can on Paris. She needs maps, descriptions of historical sites, names of famous streets, commonly-used French phrases. Basically, anything and everything I can find about the city.

I asked her why she doesn't just go to Paris to find all that stuff out. She said one day she might do that, but for now, she's happy being here with the kids. She laughed and said that if I had a passport, she'd probably send *me*.

I can't imagine ever being able to pick up and just fly overseas. I can't even renew my driver's license. Hell, I don't even *have* a driver's license. I dumped it, and everything else in my purse that had my name on it, into the trashcan at the hotel where I cut and colored my hair. I was sure to squeeze a glob of color onto all of it so nobody would be tempted to go through it if they were so inclined. Then I double-wrapped the trash bag and walked it out to the hotel dumpster myself.

I left no trace of Alexa Lucas. A name I despised.

If I ever find myself in a position to get a divorce, even if it's forty years from now, the first thing I'll do is resume my maiden name. Alexa Kessler. I've always thought it had a nice ring to it. Lexi Kessler is even better.

I look down at my note paper only to see that in my mindless doodling, I had written my name. The only thing is, I didn't write it as Lucas or Kessler.

The name I wrote was Lexi Stone.

I tear out the paper and wad it up, ready to throw it in the trash. He doesn't want to date me, let alone marry me. And even if by some miracle, that happened, I'd never be able to marry *him*.

Across the room, my phone chirps with a text and I smile. One of the first things I did after moving back here, was get a phone. Well, technically, it's not *my* phone, it's Kyle's. But I insisted on paying my part of the monthly bill. I can afford it now that I have a job. And it's not one of those old burner phones like the one I picked up at a discount store last year. It's a nice phone. A smartphone. So now I can text or email or Facetime anyone from anywhere. So many people take those things for granted.

I've vowed to take nothing for granted, not anymore. "For granted," I think aloud, pushing aside the soft armband that reveals Grant's hidden name on my wrist. I study it until I remember the waiting text.

I hop up and walk over to the counter to check my phone.

Kyle: I'm going out for drinks with Cameron and Gina after work. Didn't want you to worry if I was home late.

Gina? As in the one who was his maybe, maybe-not girlfriend? I toss the phone back down on the counter, pouting.

Maybe he's with her and doesn't want to tell me. Perhaps he's only using his career as an excuse. Maybe it's not that he doesn't want a relationship. Maybe it's that he doesn't want a relationship with *me*.

I pick up my phone and tap out a text.

Me: I'm not your mother, Kyle. Do what you want.

~ ~ ~

Five hours and half a bottle of wine later, I hear his key in the door. I fling myself on the couch, picking up a book that I'm pretending to read so he doesn't know I've been waiting for him. Doesn't know that I've been picturing those brown-green-blue eyes of his looking at *her*. Those large hands touching *her*. Those dreamy lips kissing—

"Oh, hey, you're still up?" he says, tossing his keys on the counter. The keys slide all the way across the bar and then fall off the counter onto the floor. When he goes to pick them up, he hits his head on the edge of the bar. "Son of a bitch!"

He quickly looks around the room for Ellie as he's done every time he curses.

"She's in bed," I say. "Because it's after midnight. And besides . . . SHE CAN'T HEAR YOU!"

Yes, I realize I'm acting like a toddler, but he's obviously drunk, and he's stupid, and he's a big dumb guy who doesn't know anything—and yes, I realize I might be a little drunk and stupid myself, but that's what happens when the guy you love goes off and sleeps with a smart and beautiful doctor who may or may not be his girlfriend.

I toss my book on the couch and reach over to refill my wine glass, splashing some wine on the coffee table as I do.

"Are you drunk, Elizabeth? Shit—Lexi?"

I hold up the bottle of white wine so he can see how full it is. Or how empty it is. Depends on how you look at it. "Not yet, but another glass ought to do it." It's a lie. I'm already drunk. I haven't had more than a single beer or glass of wine in over a year.

He staggers over and takes the bottle from me, examining it. "Did you drink all this yourself?"

"Don't worry, *Dr.* Stone, I'll buy you a new bottle."

"I'm not worried about the damn wine, Lexi. You're nursing. You can't drink that much." He looks at me like I'm a terrible person. Like I'm hurting someone I love on purpose.

He's looking at me like I used to look at Grant.

I stand up and rip the bottle from his hands. "Pump and dump, asshole," I say.

"What the hell are you talking about, Lex?"

"Pump. And. Dump," I say to him like he's a two-year-old. I put down the wine bottle and my glass, then I grab my boobs. "First I pump them, then I dump it down the drain. Got it?"

He looks somewhat relieved that I wouldn't serve my baby alcohol-laden breast milk. "Well, good," he says. "And you don't need to replace the wine."

"Oh, I'll replace it," I say, resuming my seat so I don't fall over. At least that's what I meant to say, I think it came out more like *I'll replathe it.*' I take another sip. "I don't need anything from you."

"What's going on here?" he asks. "Did I miss something? Are you pissed off at me?"

"I don't know, Kyle. Why don't you go ask little miss . . . little miss . . . oh, hell, I can't think of a stupid name to call her. Just go ask your damn girlfriend."

"My girlfriend?" He looks at me like I'm crazy. "What the hell are you talking about?"

"You know exactly what I'm talking about. Your squeeze. Your, what . . . Your fuck buddy? Did you get some tonight, Kyle? Did you share some Jell-O with her? Or is that only for hospital patients you feel sorry for?"

He cringes, looking hurt by what I said. "You think Gina is my girlfriend?"

"Well, isn't she?"

"No. In fact, she's in love with my friend, Cameron. Has been for months. I haven't given Gina a second look since I fell—" He runs his hands through his hair. "Shit!"

He paces the living room floor, scrubbing a hand across his jaw. The jaw that hasn't seen a razor for days, making him appear even sexier. Then again, maybe my vision is clouded from the wine.

"What does that even matter, Lexi? What the fuck difference does it make to you if I'm screwing Gina? You left me. You left me high and dry. I was all in. I was so in I was furnishing my goddamn apartment. I was planning for the future. I wanted you. I wanted Ellie. But you made your decision. You made it for the both of us. There's no turning back."

I get up off the couch, steadying myself so I can try to stand my ground. "How can you say that, Kyle? You know there is more to the story than me just deciding to leave you."

"Well, there's nothing more to it now," he says. "You being here, I'm just helping out Caden. That's all there is to it."

Tears well in my eyes and my throat stings. "I don't believe you. I see how you look at me. What happened between us back then—it doesn't just go away. I loved that time we spent together. And I know you did too."

He shakes his head in denial. I'm not sure if he's trying to convince *me*, or himself. I'm losing him. And it hurts. It hurts my head. It hurts my heart. It even hurts to breathe.

"Why do you think I named my daughter Ellie?" I cry. "It's short for Elizabeth, Kyle. I named her that because being Elizabeth with you was the best month of my life."

He grabs me, both of his hands on my upper arms. There's so much pain in his eyes. There is a battle raging behind them. One I'm not even sure he knows which side he wants to be on. "Then why didn't you fucking trust me? Why did you leave like that?"

He's angry. But his anger doesn't scare me. It's not directed at me. It's almost like he's angry with himself for not letting himself love me. His eyes are glassy as they beg me for answers.

"I'm sorry," I say, tears spilling over and rolling down my face. "I'm so sorry I left. But I'm here. I came back for you, Kyle. I'm risking everything for you now. Can't you see that? Can't you see I lo—"

Before I can get the word out. Before I can even form another thought in my head. Before I realize what is happening, his lips come crashing down on mine.

CHAPTER FORTY-SEVEN

His kiss is hard and demanding. Like he's claiming me. It's different from the kiss we shared over six months ago. It's not sweet, seductive, and promising like it was back then. It's messy. Emotional. Purposeful.

His tongue comes out, parting my lips as we devour each other. He tastes like whiskey and mint. I'm sure I taste of wine and pizza. He sucks on my tongue. I moan into his mouth. His hands come up to grab my face, holding me in place as if he's afraid I'll pull away.

I won't.

Wild horses stampeding through his apartment couldn't get me to stop kissing him.

My hands are everywhere. On his neck. In his hair. On his back. On his ass. I can't get enough of him. I've never touched him like this before. Not outside of my dreams—the ones that keep me warm at night and haunt me during the day.

Once he's sure I won't pull away, he allows his hands to explore. He runs them down my sides, then around to my back, and finally up to my engorged breasts. When he grabs them, he cries out, "Jesus, Lex."

I'm ripping at his clothes like I want them gone yesterday. He's pulling at mine as if we share a brain. Shirts come off, pants go down, material gets ripped. We don't stop until we are completely naked, all the while kissing, touching, and feeling every inch of flesh we can reach.

I moan loudly when he reaches between my legs, dragging his fingers through my wetness and spreading it over my clit.

"Kyle!" I cry out when he rubs circles over my pulsating nub. I cry out again when he pushes a finger inside of me.

Never has it felt like this. Like my body is being worshiped instead of used. Like I'm giving a gift instead of obeying a command. I can't stand it. I'm building so fast, I feel I'm going to explode.

I wrap a leg around him and he pulls me up into his arms, holding me by my ass as his penis throbs between us. I've never wanted anything so badly before. "Kyle, I want . . ." I can't even explain it. I can't articulate it.

"What do you want, Lexi?" he asks, running his tongue down the side of my neck over to my ear. "Tell me," he whispers.

"Everything," I say, breathlessly. "I want everything."

He walks us over to the kitchen and puts me down on the back corner of the L-shaped counter. He holds my stare with his as he carefully lifts each of my legs to place them outstretched on either side of me. Oh, my God. I'm completely on display for him.

When he looks down at me, before he touches me *there*, he traces a finger over my C-section scar. I remember what he said last night about delivering Ellie; about being the first one to hold her, and I wonder if he's remembering it too.

Then, when his mouth touches me, I shiver. Tingles race up and down my spine as he swirls his tongue around on me. He slides a finger inside me, then two. I grab his hair as he crooks them to find my sweet spot. "Oh, God," I murmur over and over as his fingers work their magic.

His other hand reaches around to my backside so he can hold me against him when it gets so intense I feel I need to pull away. I find it completely erotic to look down on him and watch as he does this to me. Purely for me. For my pleasure and mine alone.

He brings me right to the edge of detonation, and then he pulls back, withdrawing his fingers; his tongue. My body is begging for release. "Kyle, please," I plead.

He smiles as he resumes his ministrations. I pull on his hair, hoping he will hurry this along and let me come. I can't take it anymore. The buildup, the ebb. But I need it to flow. I need it to flow like I've never needed it before. "Do it . . . please!" I yell.

He pulls back once again, looking amused. "Do what, Lex?" he asks with a crook of his finger.

"Make me come!" I shout. "Jesus Christ, Kyle, make me come already!"

He snickers, resuming his tongue on my clit where he licks, sucks and laves circles on it, making me pant and squirm. This time, however, when I reach the precipice, he doesn't stop. He keeps moving his fingers and circling my clit as I buck my hips into him. "Yes," I breathe, holding his head tightly in place.

"Oh, God. Yes! Yes!" I scream at the ceiling as wave after wave, pulse after pulse, overcomes me, sending me spiraling off the cliff and into the crashing whitecaps below as they pound against me, toss me around, and churn me under until they finally let up and I can reach the surface and breathe once again.

I feel like I just ran a marathon. My breaths come fast and my legs are tense. I realize I'm still holding his head hard against me. "Sorry," I say, releasing him.

"Don't be sorry, Lex," he says, standing up to come face to face with me. "That was the hottest thing I've ever seen. Jesus."

He wraps my legs around him and I grab onto his neck as he lifts me off the counter. He walks us across the living room. I think he's going to take me to his bedroom, but he stops short.

"I can't wait another second," he says, pinning me against the living room wall, devouring my neck and shoulders with his mouth.

I reach between us to put my hand around his penis. Oh, God. It's velvety soft. It's hard as steel. It jumps, thick and ready, under my touch.

He breaks the seal his mouth has on my flesh to ask a question. "Condom?"

"I'm good," I say, running my fingers up and down on him. "Nobody since him."

"Me too," he mumbles, finding my neck again with his tongue. "Nobody since her."

I don't even have the wherewithal to comprehend what that means right now. I'm too busy thinking about what his hands are doing to me. And how his fingers are touching me.

"Are you on the pill?" he asks, breathlessly.

Shit! Oh, my God. I didn't even think. I know I'm nursing, but that's no guarantee. "No."

He puts me down and runs across the room, frantically rummaging through his pants to find his wallet. It's almost comical to watch. He's determined. Desperate.

He races back to me, quickly putting on the condom before he reaches me. I boldly jump back into his arms, needing to feel flesh on flesh.

"Now, Lex. Please." His eyes, along with his words, beg me to give him entrance. So I do.

"Now," I say, nodding my acceptance.

He holds me up, pressing me against the wall as he enters me. He takes his time, letting himself get used to me. Letting me completely open myself for him. When he's fully seated, he quickly pulls out to the tip and then pushes back in. He does this over and over until I unexpectedly start building up again. But I can tell he's holding back. He's gritting his teeth. He's concentrating hard. He wants me to come. Again. *Me*. Before he's even had his.

"Don't worry about me," I say.

I don't tell him I won't come this way. That I never come this way. He's using his hands to hold me up, and I'm too shy to use mine to help myself along.

"I'll always worry about you, Elizabeth."

I don't bother to correct him. Maybe I'll always be Elizabeth to him. I don't even mind it when he calls me that. It reminds me of some of the best weeks of my life.

Then my thoughts become muddled and grey as he leans his head in and kisses me. He kisses me hard. He kisses me with tongue and I taste myself on him. It's strangely erotic knowing where he's been. His chest presses against my breasts, rubbing them as his thrusts become more demanding. He licks my neck, all the way around to my ear.

I feel my insides coil. I feel the familiar tug of impending release. Building. Building. *Oh, God*.

"That's it," he whispers, his hot breath flowing over my ear. "You feel so good, Elizabeth." He grunts and thrusts. "Come with me."

On his command, my body pulsates, burning from within as my walls squeeze him tightly. He shouts out as he explodes inside me, our words of ecstasy mingling together as we cry out in tortuous pleasure.

His knees buckle and he falls back onto the floor, careful to keep me on top of him. We lie like this, our chests pinned together, our hearts beating wildly, our breathing labored. We lie like this until my eyes grow heavy.

Maybe it's the late hour. Maybe it's the alcohol. Maybe it's the release he gave me—the two releases—that I've craved for so long. Maybe it's a bit of everything. But the last thing I remember before falling off into slumber is him picking me up and carrying me.

That's not true. The last thing I remember is how I feel in his arms. I feel safe. I feel loved.

I feel home.

CHAPTER FORTY-EIGHT

I wake up to the sound of Ellie babbling in her crib. As I stretch my arms and legs, I feel a twinge down below. A twinge of soreness that reminds me about last night.

I smile.

But then I realize I'm in my bed. And I'm alone.

So many things are going through my head right now. I look at the clock, wondering if Kyle had to work this morning. I look at the empty space beside me, thinking maybe he's not in it out of respect for Ellie. I look at the wall that separates my bedroom from his, and I wonder if he's over there thinking of me.

I look at my bedroom door, praying he's not had second thoughts.

I throw on my robe and go to Ellie's crib, signing *good morning* before I pick her up and change her.

I settle into the rocking chair with a hungry Ellie. But I realize I can't feed her. I never did my pump and dump. However, I'm not sure I want to go out that door to get her a bottle. Right now, I'm in this perfect bubble. Last night was incredible. It was everything I dreamed about. It was *more* than I dreamed about. I didn't know it could be like that. I've never had a man put my needs before his own.

And I want to feel like this as long as I can. Because now that I think about it, I'm pretty sure he didn't have to work today.

Which means he's still in the apartment. And he's not with me. He's not in my bed and I'm not in his. So, this perfect bubble I'm in will most likely break as soon as I walk through that door.

I look down at Ellie. "I'm being ridiculous, right? I mean, last night was great. He probably just didn't want you to wake up and find me gone. And the bed in here is far too small for two adults to sleep on."

I remember the words he spoke last night. *'Nobody since her.'* Has it really been that long since he's been with anyone? Maybe he was telling me the truth when he said he was focusing on his career. I find myself hoping that is the case. If that's all I need to overcome, the odds are in my favor. However, if there's more to it than that; if he truly doesn't want me anymore, that may be a harder battle to win.

But he *does* want me. Last night proved it. The things he said. The way he worshiped me. It wasn't just about sex. It couldn't have been.

When Ellie starts fussing loudly, I stand up and walk to the door. As I reach for the doorknob, I say a silent prayer.

I walk out into the living room to see Kyle sitting on the couch. He's leaning forward with his forearms resting on his knees. His shoulders are slumped and his head is hung low. This is not the posture of a happy man. A man who had sex last night. A man who is excited about his future.

But that's not even what concerns me the most. It's what I see on the coffee table in front of him that makes me want to die of shame. *Oh, my God!* He's staring at a piece of paper on the table. The crumpled paper I had doodled my name on. The one that reads *Lexi Stone.*

He hears me walking behind him. But I only know this because his whole body stiffens. He doesn't say a word. I walk into the kitchen, my heart thundering beneath my robe. It's beating so hard, I fear it's about to break—right along with my perfect bubble.

He's not yet started the coffee. That's unlike him. I do it myself, holding Ellie in one arm. And when I turn around to put Ellie in her highchair, I catch him watching me—staring at me with eyes that are dark and distant.

Hot tears roll down my cheek as I reach into the refrigerator to get Ellie a bottle. As I place it in the warmer, I keep my back turned to Kyle so he can't see how his stare has completely wrecked me. I busy myself gathering coffee cups and then I wait silently for the coffee to finish brewing.

I give Ellie her bottle along with a handful of Cheerios, and then I take some deep breaths before I pick up the two coffee mugs and walk out to the living room. I put his mug on the table in front of him, and then I take the piece of paper and throw it in the trashcan, embarrassed that he found it.

He stares at the empty place on the table. "It can't happen," he says.

My heart breaks into tiny little shards that rip their way through my veins. "I'm sorry about that," I say, nodding to the trashcan as I bite back more tears. "It doesn't mean anything. I was just doodling."

He shakes his head, looking intently at the floor. "It can't happen, Lexi," he says again. "Not even if we wanted it to. You are still married. Married to *him*. And since you're unwilling to do anything about it . . ."

"Is that what this is about?" I ask. "Me being married to Grant?"

"Yes. No." He runs a hand through his hair. "I don't know. Listen, we were drunk last night. And I take full responsibility for what happened."

"Oh, you take full responsibility. Like I had no say in the matter. I was there, too, Kyle. We both made a choice. And you know why I'm still married. I'm doing it for Ellie. Would you really have me risk my daughter just so you don't have to think of me as Alexa Lucas?"

"I don't know what I want, Lexi. I just know this is complicated. It's too complicated for us to go throwing caution to the wind like we did last night. It was a mistake. I have my career to think about. You have Ellie."

"Please don't use your career as a cop out," I say. "If you don't want to be with me, just tell me. But don't hide behind your career. Plenty of men have powerful careers *and* a family. I know I hurt you by running away. I know you think you can't trust me now. Maybe you think I'll leave again. But I'm not going anywhere. Not unless you want me gone." My breath hitches and my heart falls. "Do you want me gone, Kyle?"

He looks over at Ellie, who is now happily mashing Cheerios with her gums while she's playing with a plastic set of keys.

"I'm not about to put the two of you out," he says. "I would never do that."

"That's not what I was asking, Kyle, and you know it. Do you want me gone?" My heart refuses to beat as I frantically hold onto a sliver of hope while waiting for his answer.

He looks at me. He looks into my eyes for the first time since last night. "No. I don't want you gone. But beyond that, I can't say what I want, Lex. I need time. I need space."

I nod my head. Needing time and space are things I can understand. I had over six months of time and space. Over six months to think about my life and come to terms with what I wanted out of it. Over six months to realize it only took me a few weeks to fall completely head-over-heels in love with the man who brought my daughter into this world.

I guess it's only fair that he have his own time and space to come to the same conclusion. And I know he will. I know, because I felt it last night. I felt the way he wants me. The way he needs me. I may have even felt the way he loves me.

"Okay," I tell him. "But if Ellie and I are going to be here, I can't be walking around on eggshells all the time. How about we start by just being friends, Kyle? No more doodling silly names or talking about things we can't change. You do your job and I'll do mine. And sometimes, when you feel like it, I'll teach you more ASL. Sometimes when I feel like it, you'll bring me Sal's."

He looks at me again, this time with brighter eyes. "Friends, huh?"

Ellie drops her toy and starts fussing about it. I get up to retrieve it for her. "Sure, why not?" I ask.

"I think I can do that," he says, finally picking up his coffee to take a drink.

I gather up Ellie and head to the bathroom. When I reach the doorway, I turn around. "But, Kyle . . . I'll never forget last night."

He nods, looking at the wall where we made love. "Yeah," he says, blowing out a deep sigh. "Me neither."

CHAPTER FORTY-NINE

"How have you been holding up the past few weeks?" Caden asks, digging in for another scoop of spaghetti.

"Fine," I say, shoveling another bite of strained peas into Ellie's mouth. "I'm still in the friend zone, if that's what you're asking."

My brother has come over at least once a week for dinner. Always at my place. Never at his. Just in case Grant is watching him. Caden and I have become close since my return, and he's well aware of my feelings for Kyle.

"I kind of figured," he says, glancing around the room. "You know, because he's not here and all."

"We live this symbiotic life now. Sometimes he cooks. Sometimes I cook. Sometimes I eat his leftover takeout. Sometimes he orders pizza for us. He doesn't feel obligated to tell me when he's going out. I don't always inform him when I'm having guests. We're living like roommates," I say, looking over towards Kyle's bedroom. "It's torture."

"I'm sorry, Lexi. I know it's hard for you. You need to give him time. Maybe he just needs to see that you aren't going to leave again."

"I don't want to leave," I tell him. "But if all we are is friends, surely he's going to expect me to at some point."

"I think we are a long way from getting to that point, Lexi."

I shrug negligently. "I hope so," I say, topping off Caden's wine. "But, hey let's quit making everything about me. How are you doing? Why aren't you dating anyone? Surely there is a plethora of women lining up to date a famous young ball player who isn't even that ugly."

He chuckles at my joke before shaking his head in disgust. "That's the problem," he says. "There are so many of them. And they all want something from me. Money. Fame. A baby."

"A baby?" I ask, incredulously.

"You'd be surprised how many players in the league have been trapped by women getting pregnant on purpose," he says. "Some of them end up married to women they don't even like, just to give their kid a family. Others simply fork over eighteen years of child support."

"That's awful. Didn't anyone ever teach them about birth control?" I ask.

"Some women are ruthless. Lying about being on the pill. Poking holes in condoms. When I got called up, they made me sit with their PR rep who basically gave me a talk about how not to get a girl pregnant." He rolls his eyes. "It was humiliating. I felt like I was in middle school. But it happens so often, they've made it part of the transition from the minors. Always carry your own condoms. Never use one a girl provides. Put it on yourself. Make sure to flush it after, don't just dump it in the trash and leave, because resourceful girls might dig it out and use what's inside it."

My hand comes up to cover my surprised gasp. "Oh, my God, Caden, really?"

"Really," he says. "So you can see how it might be hard to trust anyone. Even getting set up with friends of friends is hard. You just never know their true motives. After a scare last year, I decided it just wasn't worth it to try to find a girlfriend."

322

"Scare? Did some girl say you got her pregnant?" I look at Ellie thinking how sad it would be for her to have a cousin she would never get to see.

He takes a big swig of his wine, then places it down on the table, tracing the mouth of the glass with his finger. "She didn't just say I got her pregnant. I *did* get her pregnant."

I look at my brother with wide eyes. "Caden, do you have a child?"

He shakes his head. "No. She had a miscarriage a week after she told me she was pregnant. But the whole thing scared the shit out of me, Lexi. What would I have done with a kid when I was barely twenty-three?"

"Why didn't you tell me?" I ask, hurt that he never thought to pick up the phone and get advice from his big sister.

"It was last March," he says.

"Oh." I disappeared in February. There was no way for him to contact me. "I'm so sorry, Caden. I wish I'd been there for you. Maybe I could have helped."

"*You're* sorry about not being there for *me?*" He looks at me sideways, studying my face. "Lexi, *I'm* the one who should have been there for *you*. I was so wrapped up in my own life—in baseball—that I couldn't even bother to pick up the phone. Maybe if I would have, you'd have told me what was going on. I feel like all of this is my fault. I should have made more of an effort. Can you ever forgive me?"

I reach over the table and grab his hand. "Caden, there is nothing to forgive. You didn't do anything wrong. *I'm* the big sister. You shouldn't have to look out for me. When Mom died, I should have made you my top priority. Instead, I was already in deep with Grant. I let him control me. I let him take me away from my friends. From you. If anyone is at fault here, it sure as hell isn't you."

"It's not you either," he says. "You know that, right? What he did to you—it's not your fault."

I nod. "I know that. I even knew it back then. I only stayed with him because I felt trapped. After he threatened you, I literally had nowhere to go."

He smacks his palm on the table in anger. "You did, Lexi. You did have somewhere to go. You could have come to me anyway. I don't care what he would have done to me. It would have been worth it to get you away from him."

A tear rolls down my cheek as I smile at my little brother, knowing he'd sacrifice his career for me. I feel the same way about him. I'd do anything to keep him safe. "I wasn't going to let that happen," I say. "Baseball is your life."

"But you're my family," he says, trying not to get choked up. "Family will always trump baseball, Lexi. Don't ever forget that."

"I love you, you know that, right?" I say.

"Yeah," he says, getting up to come hug me. "I love you, too."

I smile up at him. "That's the first time I've ever heard you say that out loud."

"Really?" he asks. "Well, shit. Plan on hearing it a lot more." He does the sign for '*I love you*' with his hands. He signs it to me and then he signs it to Ellie.

"You remembered?" I ask.

I showed him a few signs when he came for dinner last week.

"I've been practicing," he says. "I happen to have the best niece in the world who has the coolest uncle who plans on talking with her every chance he gets. Don't be surprised if I get her a phone when she's two, just so we can text each other."

I laugh, happy that he plans to spoil her. "Did you know that texting was invented solely to allow deaf people to communicate on cell phones?"

"No shit?" he says. "And now, it's how *everyone* communicates. Imagine that."

I clean up Ellie and then take our dirty dishes to the sink. When I come back out, Caden is holding Ellie and she's laughing when he makes faces at her.

"Speaking of family," I say. "I have something I've been wanting to ask you, Caden."

He stares at me for a second. "This looks serious."

"It is," I tell him, motioning for him to sit down on the couch.

He puts Ellie between us, giving her one of her plastic picture books which she promptly puts in her mouth to chew on. "Whatever it is, the answer is yes," he says.

"Don't say that until you know what it is. This is a pretty tall order," I tell him.

"I don't care, Lexi."

I nod to Ellie. "If something ever happens to me, will you raise her?"

He looks from Ellie to me and then back to Ellie. I'm not even sure he understands the question. I open my mouth to clarify, but he holds his hand out to shut me up. "In a fucking heartbeat," he says. "It would be my absolute honor to raise her. Of course, yes, Lexi. But *nothing* is going to happen to you. I promise I won't let that bastard hurt you ever again."

"It's not just about Grant," I say. "I could get hit by a bus. Or I could fall down the stairs and break my neck. I could get bitten by a raccoon and die from rabies. Or get run over by—"

"Enough, Lexi. I get it," he says, looking annoyed. "You really don't need to chronicle all the ways you can die. It's so morbid. And raccoons in New York City? I doubt it."

I shrug. "I may not always live in the city."

He looks at me like I'm crazy. "You'll live in the city," he says. Then he looks around the apartment. "If I were a betting man, I'd bet you'll probably even live *here*. Or maybe someplace even bigger. I mean, I thought *I* had money. How rich is this guy?"

"I don't know exactly. But I think it's family money. You should see his brothers' places. If you think *this* place is nice, it actually looks like a dump compared to Ethan's penthouse."

"You could definitely do worse, sis," he says, looking out the massive picture windows.

"I'd love him if he had nothing, Caden."

He laughs through his nose, nodding at me. "I know. That's why he's going to come around. He'd be a fool not to."

CHAPTER FIFTY

"The steak was amazing. Thank you," I tell Ethan and Charlie. "And it's so nice of you to hire a sitter to watch all the kids so we can relax."

"It's our pleasure," Charlie says, refilling my glass of wine. "Most of them are watching a movie, the last I checked, and Kiera and Ellie were playing with blocks."

"What movie? One of mine?" Chad asks, jokingly.

"Of course," Ethan replies. "Don't you know by now that we just love to let Eli watch dudes kill each other. Especially if it involves blood, gore, and guts. And drugs. We love to let him watch people do drugs."

"Oh, and the ones where you shove your tongue in someone's mouth—those are good, too," Charlie says. "I think Eli particularly likes the ones where you grab a woman's bare breasts."

"That's my boy," Ethan says, laughing.

I still can't believe the incredible people I have in my life now. A famous actor, the starting quarterback for the Giants, a best-selling author. Not to mention all the rest of them with 'regular' jobs, who themselves seem larger than life.

How did I ever get so lucky to get Kyle as my doctor so he could lead me to all of these wonderful human beings?

"What do you guys want to do now?" Ethan asks. "The night is still young. Hell, none of the kids have even had an injury yet."

"Now you jinxed it," Griffin says. "Better not be one of mine, or I'll sue your ass."

Ethan reaches into his pocket and pulls out a few quarters. "This is about as much as you'll get out of me," he says. Then he studies the quarters in his hand. "Hey, you guys want to play a drinking game?"

"Quarters?" Charlie asks, looking at his hand. "No way, I was never very good at that game. But I'll play something else. You guys ever played 'Never have I ever'?"

Kyle's eyes snap to mine and we share a quick private moment of nostalgia.

It's strange, being here with five other couples but not being part of a couple. The girls all know the score. Well, maybe not the *whole* score. I failed to reveal to them that Kyle and I slept together a few weeks ago. I can only assume they've told their significant others what is—or *isn't*—going on between us.

But that doesn't stop any of them from inviting *me* over whenever they invite Kyle. Every time, I tell Kyle he doesn't have to drag me along. I tell him he should go have fun with his brothers, but he insists they are all my friends now, too, and it wouldn't be fair to leave me home.

I stare at Kyle, waiting for him to give Charlie a reason not to play the game.

But he doesn't.

Maybe he's hoping to learn more about me. Maybe he's looking for a reason to let me in.

Maybe he's looking for a reason to kick me out.

Charlie doesn't even have to explain the rules. Apparently, Kyle was the only teenager in the history of teenagers who had never played the game.

Ethan brings several more bottles of wine to the table. "Ladies first," he says.

"Age before beauty," Piper says to her oldest sister, who in turn pelts her with a chocolate candy.

"Your beauty is ageless, darlin'," Gavin says to Baylor, leaning down to give her a kiss on the lips.

"Okay, this isn't 'Spin the Bottle'," Skylar says. "Quit being all lovey-dovey and ask your question."

Baylor throws another chocolate at Skylar as they all share a laugh.

They are lucky to have each other. I've never realized that as much as I do now, after being able to spend these last few weeks getting to know my own brother again.

Baylor chews on the inside of her cheek in thought. "Never have I ever been stuck in an elevator," she says.

Skylar takes a drink. Then Mallory and Chad look at each other and burst out laughing before they both have a sip of wine.

"Wait," Charlie says, eyeing them suspiciously. "In an elevator? Seriously?"

Chad shrugs guiltily. "We were stuck. There was nothing else to do."

Ethan high-fives Chad.

"Never have I ever been in handcuffs," Skylar says, looking around at everyone.

Chad takes a drink. No surprise there, we all know about his highly-publicized troubles from years back.

Ethan nudges his wife. "Come on, Tate. Drink up," he says, using his nickname for her.

Charlie rolls her eyes and takes a drink. "They weren't even real," she says under her breath.

Piper laughs. "Eww, I don't even want to know," she says.

"Okay, my turn," Mallory says. "Never have I ever called in sick to work because I had a hangover."

Everyone but Mal and Kyle take a drink.

"Goddamn overachiever," Chad says, throwing a wine cork at Kyle.

"You're next," Skylar says to me.

"Um, never have I ever flashed a bartender to get a free drink," I say.

All the guys look at their significant others. Charlie and Skylar both take a drink.

"Really, Sky?" Griffin asks his bride.

She shrugs. "What can I say, I was a bit of a firecracker before I met you."

"Never have I ever had sex with my best friend," Charlie says, winking at Piper.

"Does that only apply to *when* you were best friends, or *after?*" Mallory asks.

Chad hands her a glass of wine. "Just drink, babe." They share a sweet look as they both take a drink.

"Now me," Piper says. "Never have I ever called out the wrong name during sex."

Everyone looks around, waiting for someone to take a drink, but no one does. I strongly debate telling Kyle he needs to. After all, he called me Elizabeth—in the throes—*twice*. But I guess I'll let it slide, since technically, he was still calling out *my* name.

"Chicks have boring questions," Chad says. "Come on, Gav, give us something we can chew on."

"Okay," Gavin says. "Let's make things a little interesting. "Never have I ever kissed someone of the same sex on the mouth."

Kyle laughs out loud. I shoot him a venomous stare as I quickly take a drink. But I'm not the only one. Charlie does, too.

"It's a good thing we're already home," Ethan says, laughing at his wife. "Because I have a feeling you might be getting drunk tonight."

"And I have a feeling you might be getting lucky," she says to him.

They share a smile. Then I look over to see Kyle watching me from where he sits across the room. He's always watching me. He watches me when I eat. When I clean the apartment. When I work. He especially watches me when I'm with Ellie.

But right now, he's watching me like he's jealous. He's jealous that his brother and sister-in-law have something he doesn't. And I take another drink just for posterity.

"Never have I ever had to do a walk of shame," Griffin says.

Glasses are raised all around the room, with the exception of Piper. Even *I* have to take a drink, from the first time I was with Grant and had to sneak out of his hotel room in Myrtle Beach.

"Never have I ever taken a naked selfie," Ethan says.

Nobody picks up their glass. "Really?" he asks his wife. "I just assumed with all the crazy stuff you did in Europe . . ."

"Oh, my God, Ethan," Charlie says. "No!"

"Okay, well maybe later then, after these freeloaders go home?" He raises his eyebrows at her as we all laugh.

She rolls her eyes at him.

"Never have I ever given a lap dance," Chad says, looking around at all the ladies.

Nobody moves. "None of you? Are you sure?" he asks.

Baylor, Skylar and Piper all throw chocolates at him.

Everyone looks at Kyle. "Uh . . . Never have I ever had sex in public," he says.

Griffin, Gavin and Mason all look at Ethan and Charlie. "What?" the couple says in tandem.

"The pool at the gym," Mason says, staring them down like they just took candy from a baby.

Ethan laughs. "Oh, right." He lifts his glass to his wife and they toast before they take another drink.

I'm starting to get the idea there is a lot more to Charlie than meets the eye.

Mason clears his throat. "Never have I ever had an STD scare," he says.

Charlie rolls her eyes and takes another drink, emptying her glass.

"Really, Tate?" Ethan asks.

"Scare," she says, putting emphasis on the word. She ignores her husband's open jaw as she gets up off the couch. "So, anyone want dessert before round two?"

We all get up and stretch our legs.

Ethan comes over to me. "Lexi, I have something for you. It's in my office. Can you join me for a minute?"

Kyle watches us walk out of the room and then follows behind. Ethan turns on the light in his office and walks around his desk, pulling a large envelope out of his drawer before handing it to me.

"Is that what I think it is?" Kyle asks, leaning in the doorway behind me.

"Open it," Ethan says, nodding to the envelope.

I pull open the flap and pull out the papers. There are two birth certificates issued from the state of New York. In the names of Elizabeth Catherine Smith and Ellie Elizabeth Smith. There is also a New York State ID for me. I don't miss that it's been issued with Kyle's address.

"I wouldn't go using those to get a passport or anything, but if you wanted to open a bank account or get a library card, those should do. I'm working on getting you a social security card, but those are hard to come by and could have major repercussions."

I shake my head. "I don't need a social security card, Ethan. I don't want to steal anyone's identity or get you into trouble. This is all I need. Thank you."

Kyle looks at the documents in my hands and gruffs before turning and leaving the room.

Ethan puts a hand on my shoulder. "Don't worry about him."

I sigh. "I really think he just wants me to contact Grant and let the chips fall where they may. I can't do that, Ethan. I wish he could understand."

"He's torn up inside, Lexi. Confused. You're married to another man. You could never legally be with him. But on the flip side, I think he understands that you have no choice. That you're doing it to protect not only yourself, but Ellie. But it's a big pill to swallow, knowing that the one you love can never truly be yours."

"Love?" I ask, looking up at him with trepidation. With hope.

"I see the way he looks at you, Lexi. He's not fooling anyone—except maybe himself." He puts an arm around me, escorting me back out into the main room. "Just give him time. He'll come around."

I stare at Kyle as he talks to Chad, and it dawns on me how ironic it is that I'm living with a man who I love, who refuses to love me—refuses to touch me; when just over a year ago, I was living with a man I hated, who had his way with me whenever it suited him.

The irony is—I still go to bed every night living a lie.

CHAPTER FIFTY-ONE

I fall to my knees in the dirt, heartbroken to see the remnants of my flower garden scattered all over the backyard. Roots have been pulled out of the ground. Stems bent or snapped in two. Buds and bulbs plucked from their stems and scattered about. It's been completely destroyed.

Who would do such a thing?

My first instinct is to call the police. But then I remember my husband is the police, so I guess I'll just tell him when he gets home. Maybe he can file a vandalism report. I'm not supposed to bother him at work. Not unless it's an emergency. And he wouldn't consider this one of those. My flower garden meant nothing to him. In fact, I think he hated it. In some way, I think he was even jealous of it.

Oh, God.

I quickly make my way to the gate in our privacy fence. The one that is always locked. Padlocked. I find it secure. Either someone scaled the six-foot fence, or . . .

I look around the yard for clues. There are none. I go back into the house and make my way to the garage. What could he have used? I look at my gardening tools. The hedge clippers. The trowels. None of them would have produced the destructive results that litter what was once my pride and joy of a backyard. It's one of the only things that was truly mine and not his. It's how I found peace. Solace. And now it's gone. Beaten down and ripped to shreds—just like I am.

Defeated, I turn to head back into the house, but then I catch a glimpse of something and stop in my tracks. It's his golf bag. The very thing that allows him peace and solace every Saturday morning while I sit at home by myself. I pick up the largest club and pull it out of the bag, examining the clumps of dirt on the club face. Then I look on the ground next to the golf bag and see a mangled petal of my favorite flower.

He didn't even have the decency to cover up his crime.

I race inside the house, wanting nothing more than retaliation. I go into his study—the room I'm not allowed in. I eye his boxing trophies on the shelf above his desk. The ones that are his pride and joy. I pull the biggest one down and throw it on the floor, gaining instant satisfaction from hearing it crack and shatter.

My satisfaction doesn't last long, however, when I realize what I've done.

For the second time today, I fall to my knees. This time to pick up the pieces of his prized trophy. One he likes to show off almost as much as he likes to show off me. That's what I feel like when he parades me around in front of everyone—his trophy.

I sit on the floor with my back to the wall, holding his broken relic in my hands. What have I done?

I look at the clock. He'll be home in an hour. I don't have time to try and replace it. I don't even have time to go to the store to get anything to fix it.

I rifle through his desk drawers, hoping to find superglue. The drawers I'm forbidden to go through, in the desk I'm not supposed to sit at, in the office I'm never allowed to enter. I'm violating so many rules today that my face starts to ache just thinking about what he might do to it.

I do find some superglue. But not before I find a bunch of other things I wasn't supposed to see. Small baggies of what I can only assume are drugs. Rolled-up bills secured by a rubber band. There must be hundreds of dollars here—maybe thousands.

I contemplate taking one or two bills to add to my collection in the lining of my purse. But then I think better of it. He could have it here to test me. To see if I'm snooping. To see if I'd steal from him. To give himself more reason to 'remind me of the rules.' I put the money back exactly the way I found it.

Then I find something you'd think would be the most disturbing of it all, but, oddly, it's not. I find letters written to him from a woman. Love letters. With pictures inside. Naked pictures. Of her. Of them.

My heart races. Not in fear or worry, but in pure unadulterated relief. He's with another woman. He'll want to leave me for her. I close my eyes and say a prayer of thanks. But then I notice the date on one of the letters. It was written over a year ago. I page through all of them, looking at more dates. They range from a few years back to as recently as two weeks ago. I drop the letters onto the desk as if they have burned me.

He's not going to leave me.

I put the letters back, careful to arrange them as they were. Then I take the superglue and the trophy into the kitchen and get to work.

Thirty minutes later, having done a meticulous job to get it back to original condition, there are still some tiny cracks that one could see if they closely examined it. But it's up on a shelf. How often does he really sit and stare at the thing?

I just get it back on the shelf when I hear the door to the garage open. My heart beating wildly, I quickly put the superglue back in the drawer where I found it and take one last look around the office to make sure I didn't miss anything.

I make it out to the hallway, just as he's rounding the corner.

"What are you doing, Alexa?" he asks, looking at me suspiciously.

"I was just coming from our bedroom," I answer, hoping my lie is convincing. "I was reading in bed and had fallen asleep. Time got away from me, I guess. I'm going to go out back and clean up the yard before dinner."

Neither of us bother to mention the condition of said yard. He knows I know he did it. I know he knows there is nothing I can do about it. Same dance, different day. He takes something I love and destroys it. He doesn't want me to have anything that I love more than him.

But what he doesn't know is that I love everything *more than him. Sometimes I think I'd even love death more than I love him. But every time I consider it, I think of my little brother. I swore to myself that one day I'd make my way back to him. I can't make him bury his sister—his only living relative whom he cares about.*

Grant watches me as I pass by him and walk through the kitchen to the garage where I get a rake and some trash bags. He's still standing in the hallway when I come back through. I look at him and paste on a smile as I pass. "Would you mind ordering pizza for us tonight? This might take me a while."

He reaches a hand up to cradle my chin, leaning down to place a kiss on my lips. Lips that want to spit at him; spew words of hate at him. Lips that want to tell him I'm walking out that door and never coming back. But I hold down the bile rising in my throat and let him kiss me. Just like I always do. And later, I'll lie underneath him and let him have his way with me. Just like I always do. Because I know what happens if I don't follow the rules.

"Sure, I can do that. I'll even get it with pepperoni," he says. "I know it's your favorite."

I smile at him before I walk out the back door.

I despise pepperoni and he knows it.

Thirty minutes later, I'm being flung across the yard onto my back with a thud that I know will have my body aching for a week.

He's hovering over me holding his prized trophy. "What the fuck did you do?" he yells at me.

"I just—"

"Shut up!" he yells, grabbing me by one of my arms and dragging me back into the house.

He's dragging me into the house so the neighbors won't hear. That means he's about to yell at me some more. He's about to hurt me. And he's not about to let the neighbors think he's anything less than an upstanding police officer.

One who they can always count on. One whose wife is the perfect little housewife.

He slams the door behind us and he shoves me into the corner of the kitchen. "What the fuck were you doing in my office? Did you really think I wouldn't know? I'm a fucking cop, Alexa. A damn good one. I know you moved my trophy."

"I w-was upset about the g-garden," I stutter through my tears. "My f-first instinct was to go after something you love, too. I'm sorry." I try to shrink into the corner.

"And you thought that gave you the right to go in my office?" he yells, pacing the floor. "A place you are forbidden from going? Because of your stupid flower garden?"

"It's not stupid to me, Grant. It means something to me."

"It's a fucking flower garden!" he shouts, waving his trophy around.

Then, I watch in horror as a piece of the trophy comes apart right where I had glued it. His eyes bulge and the vein in his temple pulsates in anger as he runs his finger across the break, obviously feeling or seeing the glue. He examines it further and pulls on it, causing it to separate in all the places I'd fixed it.

He throws it across the room, shattering what remained of it against the wall next to my head. "You broke my goddamn trophy? You selfish little bitch!"

He walks over to the broken pieces, picking one up before he attacks me with it. I cover my face with my hands, shielding it from him, hoping against all hope that he will hit me once and then leave me alone.

I feel the sharp blow to my upper chest and immediately feel the sting. The burn of tearing flesh. The warmth of blood trickling down onto my shirt.

Strong arms come around me as I lash out, trying to save myself. "Lexi, wake up! Wake up!"

CHAPTER FIFTY-TWO

"It's okay," he says, holding me down so I don't hurt him. "It's, okay, Lexi. It's Kyle. I'm not him. You're safe. You and Ellie are safe here."

He wraps his arms around me, holding me tightly until I calm down. "Shhhhh," he whispers into my ear, his hot breath rolling across my neck.

"Kyle?" I ask, trying to shake the dream away.

"Yes. I'm here. It's okay."

I stop fighting back and he relaxes his hold on me. But he doesn't entirely let me go. He's behind me in my bed, kind of spooning me, but without any of his lower body touching any of mine. His reassuring hand rests on my upper arm.

I crane my head back to see him in the dim light coming from the hallway. "Sorry," I say with a big sigh.

"Bad dream, huh?"

I nod and put my head back down on the pillow. "You could say that. More like a nightmare," I tell him. "One I actually lived through."

"Do you want to talk about it?" he asks.

I shrug noncommittally.

"I did a rotation in Psych, you know," he says, squeezing my arm. "And if I learned anything, I learned it's always best to talk about things that bother you. If you don't, they will grow like cancer, slowly eating away at you."

I turn away, so he can't see the shame on my face. "Grant destroyed my flower garden."

"Why would he want to do that?" he asks.

"Because I loved it."

Those four words tell Kyle more about my relationship with Grant than I could ever tell him in an entire conversation. I can feel him shaking his head behind me. He doesn't know what to say.

"When I took the pregnancy test and found out I was going to have a baby, my first thought was of my flower garden. I planted it right after we moved into the house. It was shortly after we married. He told me it was a great idea. That he would love to have fresh flowers around the house. He even helped me till the earth and haul in fresh planting dirt. He was always nice and helpful back then—early on.

"Then about a month into our marriage, when things had begun to change, he started complaining that I spent more time with my flower garden than with him. And he was right, I did spend a lot of time there. But only because he wouldn't let me get a job. It was the only thing I had that was truly mine.

"Months later, I'd find freshly cut flowers, that I had put in vases around the house, thrown into the trash. He told me they were a reminder of how *he* wasn't enough for me. He actually thought my entire world should be centered around him. So when the pregnancy test turned positive, I knew without a shadow of a doubt that I needed to leave.

"If he destroyed a flower garden because he thought I loved it more than him, I wasn't about to stick around to see what he would do to a child. Because I knew, despite who its father was, that I would love it more than anything in the entire world. And he wouldn't be able to handle that."

"Jesus, Lex." His hand comes around my body to pull me against him, but he quickly realizes what he's done and he removes it, sitting up on the bed to look down at me. "It makes me sick to think there are men like that walking around."

"Do you remember when I showed you my scars that one time we played 'Never have I ever'?" I roll onto my back and look up at him.

"Yeah."

"The night he destroyed my flower garden. That's the night I got this." I run my finger across the scar on my collarbone.

He stares down at the scar. His hand twitches as if he wants to touch it, but he doesn't. He just stares at it, his jaw hardening, his eyes burning with hatred.

"I broke one of his boxing trophies," I tell him. "I did it out of anger when I saw what he'd done to my garden. I tried to glue it back together before he saw it, but I didn't fool him. He stabbed me with a broken metal shard from one of the pieces."

He scrubs his hands across his face. "If I ever see that bastard," he says, shaking his head.

"The plan is to never see him again, Kyle. Now you know why I can't ever contact him. He would destroy everything that I love just to hurt me. I love Ellie. I can't risk it."

He nods his head, looking from Ellie's crib back to me. He nods it as if he finally understands what I've been telling him for weeks. "I know," he says. "I know."

"He was having an affair," I admit. "As far as I could tell, for the whole time we were married he was also with someone else."

"I'm so sorry," he says. "You deserve so much more."

I think I can see regret in his eyes. Regret over what? Grant hurting me? Or him not wanting to be with me?

"She deserves more," I say, glancing over at Ellie.

"You both do," he says. "Are you okay now?"

I nod. "Yeah, thanks."

He stands up and checks on a sleeping Ellie. "I'll bet they don't list that as one of the benefits of having a deaf child," he says.

I look at him strangely. "Benefits?"

"Yeah, you know, that you can have nightmares and you won't wake her up. Or you can fight with your . . . whoever, and she won't even know."

My gaze goes past him, beyond the door where I can almost see the place we made love. "Or have loud animal sex," I say.

His eyes meet mine and I swear he's remembering every second of that night.

Just like I am.

"Yeah, that, too." He pulls a blanket up over Ellie.

"Thanks, Kyle."

"Anytime." He turns to leave, but stops in the doorway. "I'm off at seven. Think you can wait for me to celebrate?"

"Celebrate what?"

He nods to Ellie. "It's her seven-month birthday tomorrow."

I smile. I know it is. Of course I know it is. But I didn't know *he* did. "I think she wants Sal's," I say.

He laughs. "Does she now?"

"Definitely."

"See you at seven-thirty, Lexi."

Then he pulls the door closed, leaving me a fidgety mess. Because for a second, it almost sounded like we just made a date.

~ ~ ~

"I had a deaf patient today," Kyle says, handing me my chopsticks. "He was in his mid-twenties. Broken leg. Interesting guy."

"How so?" I ask.

"I was trying to pick up pieces of the conversation he was having with his friends. I saw them doing a sign I wasn't familiar with. His friends would sign the letter 'R' while simulating the motion of strumming a guitar. I asked them what sign it was and they told me it was his name sign. His name was Ridge and he plays guitar for their band, and they explained to me that deaf people can have name signs which are like shorthand for their names."

"Yeah, that's pretty common."

"Does nothing about what I told you seem unusual?" he asks.

I cock my head to the side, shrugging an ignorant shoulder.

"Lexi, the guy is in a band. He plays guitar. And he's profoundly deaf."

My eyes snap up to his when I realize what he's telling me. "Oh, wow. Really?"

He nods proudly. "He's good. Really good. After I told him about Ellie, he played his guitar for me." He looks over at Ellie who is playing on a blanket on the floor across the room. "There truly are no limitations to what she can do."

"You told him about Ellie?" My mind races wondering just how that conversation went. Did he tell him he has a friend with a deaf daughter? A roommate? I'm dying to know how he refers to Ellie, to *me*, with a stranger.

"Yes. Well, technically, his friends told him. I'm not very good at signing much more than asking Mommy for more milk."

I laugh when he does the signs for those three words. "How can he play guitar?" I ask.

"It was pretty amazing. He holds it tightly against his chest and he feels the vibrations of the different chords. I'm telling you, there is no way you'd know he's deaf when listening to him play."

"Oh, my gosh. That's incredible, Kyle."

"It is. I wish Ellie were older. I'd take her to see his band." He shrugs. "Maybe someday."

I smile thinking that he would do that for her. I smile knowing that he's thinking about a 'someday.'

"It got me to thinking," he says. "Do you have a name sign for Ellie?"

I shake my head. "I can't give her one."

"What? Why not?"

"In deaf culture, only another deaf person can give someone a name sign. It's like a rite of passage into the deaf community. It might happen when they start going to school. Or when they pick their profession. Maybe it's a physical trait, such as long hair, or a dimple, that gets used to make their sign. With that guy, Ridge, he's probably played guitar his whole life and people came to associate him with it."

"So, they take the first letter of their name and then do a sign that describes them?"

"Yup. Sometimes, they don't even use a letter."

"So, what do you think *my* name sign would be?" he asks.

I study him for a minute. Then I sign the letter 'K' before putting two fingers on my wrist as if to feel my pulse.

"Ahhh, good one," he says. Then he signs the letter 'L' and puts his pinky in his mouth.

"What does that mean?"

"That would be *your* name sign," he says. "Because you always chew on your pinky when you're nervous."

I look at my little finger and then back up at him. "I do not."

"Oh, but you do," he says.

"Well, then, it's a good thing you're not the giver of name signs. Because you are terrible at it."

He laughs, holding out the fortune cookies so I can pick one. Just as we always do, each of us only selects one and he pushes the others aside. We'll add them to our collection. The collection we started a few weeks ago. A jar we earmarked for extra fortune cookies. Because you never know when you might need one.

We open them up simultaneously and hide the slips of paper as we eat our cookies.

"Go ahead." I nod to his hand.

He opens up his fortune and reads it. "*He who dies with the most toys is still dead.*" He looks up at me. "Damn, that's deep."

I read mine to myself, crumpling it up and throwing in the trash.

"Hey, that's not allowed," he says.

"Why not? *You've* done it."

"Come on, Lex. What did it say?"

I sigh. "It said '*The world is your oyster'.*"

He looks at me sadly. "It wasn't your parents who made you eat them, was it?"

I shake my head. "He thought they were an aphrodisiac. He made me eat them a lot."

Kyle looks disgusted. "They aren't, you know. Medically speaking, oysters do nothing to stimulate sex hormones. But the theory is, they resemble female genitalia, thus they can increase sexual desire."

"Only if you desire to have sex," I say sadly.

He runs his hands through his hair and I know he's thinking about Grant forcing himself on me. He picks up one of the discarded fortune cookies and hands it to me. "I think we can make an exception," he says.

I take it from him and crack it open, giving him half of it to eat. I stare at the slip of paper, then I glance down at my tattoo before I read my fortune aloud to Kyle. *"Take nothing for granted,"* I say.

Suddenly, I know what I need to do and I vow to call Skylar after dinner to get the ball rolling.

"Holy shit, Lex. Look!"

I look where he's pointing to find Ellie up on all fours, scooting one knee forward and then the other as she attempts her very first crawl. "Oh, my God!"

I sit stunned, my eyes locked on Ellie as she reaches this milestone. I'm mesmerized by watching the careful and meticulous way she tries to move herself forward. After a few failed tries, she manages to crawl a few steps. "She's doing it!" I squeal, excitedly.

I glance over at Kyle to see that he's gotten out his phone and is videoing the entire thing. And I'm not sure which touches me more—my daughter crawling for the first time, or Kyle looking like the proud father while she does it.

CHAPTER FIFTY-THREE

I find myself getting excited when I look at the clock. It's been almost two days since I've seen him. He was on call over the weekend, and the hospital was so busy, he just decided to sleep there. I'm sure he's so used to sleeping at work that it doesn't bother him. Me, however—even though Ellie and I have only been here for six weeks, I find it lonely in the apartment when he's not around.

Nothing has changed between us in the past few weeks. Nothing except I can tell he's fighting his feelings more and more. He has to catch himself sometimes before he touches me. And often when we sit on the couch and watch late-night TV, he absentmindedly plays with my hair. He really seems to like my hair.

He rarely slips up and calls me Elizabeth anymore, which is funny, because outside of our circle of friends, that is exactly who I am. The doormen to our building, the residents who use the fitness room, the little old couple who own the corner market—they all know me as Elizabeth. After all, that's what my birth certificate and photo ID say.

Ellie starts to fuss in her highchair as I'm chopping up vegetables for dinner. Kyle walks through the front door just as she breaks out into a full-on scream. I know this scream. This is her *I've pooped my pants and I don't want to sit in it'* scream.

Kyle watches what I'm doing in the kitchen for a few seconds, then he unstraps Ellie and picks her up. "I'll go change her," he says. "You've got your hands full."

"Thanks," I say, smiling from ear to ear as he carries her away. I smile because he knows that scream, too. I smile because he's not her daddy, yet he's changing her diaper—and not for the first time. I smile because if anyone would look through our window on any given night, they would think we are a family.

But then I frown, because we *aren't* a family. We're roommates. Roommates who give each other time and space, apparently.

I'm *drowning* in time and space. Can't he see that? What will it take to get him to make the decision that he wants to be with me?

Maybe he already has. Maybe the decision is he doesn't want me in his life—not like *that* anyway.

"All clean," Kyle says, bringing her back into the room.

Ellie looks at me as they approach the kitchen. She lifts her hand up and touches her chin with her thumb.

My eyes go wide. "Kyle, did she just . . .?"

Ellie does it again, smiling at me.

"Oh, my God, she did!" I squeal. "She just called me Mommy!"

Kyle does the sign as well and then touches me on the shoulder, just as he always does. Ellie repeats the sign for the third time, looking at me and smiling.

Tears are spilling from my eyes at the first real communication from my baby girl. I hug her in Kyle's arms as we cheer and turn in circles, our arms around each other, Ellie swimming in laughter between us.

"Thank you," I say to Kyle. "Thank you for teaching it to her. I can't believe that was her first word. It never would have happened if it weren't for you."

"Of course it was her first word," he says. "You are the most important person to her, Lex."

We step apart and Kyle puts Ellie back into her highchair, sitting next to her at the table so he can spoon some strained peas into her mouth.

"I really needed that after my day," he says.

I bring a bowl of salad over to the table. "Tough one, huh?"

He nods.

I go back in the kitchen and get the chicken casserole, setting it on a hotplate before I sit down. "You know," I say, with the faintest trace of humor. "Some wise doctor once told me not to keep things inside or they will eat away at you."

"Some wise doctor, huh?" he asks, his mouth twitching in amusement.

"Yeah, well *he* thinks he's wise. But I just think he's a wiseass."

He chuckles, scooping another bite of peas into Ellie's mouth.

"So, this tough day. Was it tougher than Rosita?" I ask.

His eyes snap to mine. "You remember that?"

"Of course I do. That was the day everything changed," I tell him. "Before that, you always went to Gina for comfort. But that day you came to me. That's the day I knew—"

I stop talking. I stop talking because sometimes I forget we're not together and some things are not appropriate for us to say to one another. I busy myself dishing out dinner for the two of us.

"That's the day you knew *what*, Lexi?"

I shrug as I carefully compose my answer. "That maybe there could be something more."

He nods in understanding. Then he studies me. "Wait, you knew about me and Gina? I mean, I know I told you we had . . . *something* maybe, but I don't ever remember getting into the particulars with you."

"What was it you told me once? Nurses love to gossip? I was in the hospital for almost a month, Kyle. I heard all kinds of things."

He takes a bite of casserole. "Wow, this is really good. You know I don't expect you to cook for me. After all, you *are* paying me rent—which I'd like to go on record as saying you absolutely don't need to do."

"I'm glad you like it," I say. "I know I don't *have* to cook for you. That's probably why I like to. And, for the record, the pittance I'm paying you for rent is just a token of my appreciation and we both know it. Anyway, you're missing the point. I was trying to get you to talk about your day."

He blows out a strong breath. "I told you I'm doing my PICU rotation, didn't I?"

"Yeah. Pediatrics, right?"

"Not just pediatrics, pediatric intensive care," he says.

I look at Ellie. "That must be really hard."

"It is. But kids are strong. Resilient. Most of the outcomes are good. But today . . ." He looks over to the window and I could swear he's trying to keep from crying. "Today, there was a kid about my nephew's age. He wasn't even three years old and already he'd had a dozen surgeries. He needed a heart-lung transplant, but he had a very specific blood type and we couldn't find him the organs in time. I sat and watched his parents say goodbye."

He chokes up, getting up from the table to grab a bottle of wine. He brings it and two glasses back into the dining room.

"I know what you need," I tell him.

He raises his eyebrows at me. "You mean besides the wine?"

I stand up and go into the kitchen, bringing the large cookie jar out, putting it on the table in front of him. "You need a fortune cookie."

"I do?" he asks, pouring me a glass of wine.

I nod, taking the lid of the jar off. "You do."

He reaches in and pulls out a cookie. After breaking it apart and popping the halves into his mouth, he reads the fortune to himself, drawing his eyebrows together.

"Well, what does it say?" I ask, curiously.

"It says *'Sometimes you just need to lie on the floor'*."

I take it from him, scanning it over before I laugh. Then I take Ellie out of her highchair and put her down on her blanket with her favorite toys. Then I lie down on the area rug between the couch and the television and I stare at the ceiling.

"What are you doing?" he asks.

"Come on, Kyle. You can't mess with ancient Chinese proverbs."

"That is not a Chinese proverb, Lex."

"Okay, then you can't mess with the guy in Boston who sits around for days on end coming up with deep existential bullshit."

He snorts and then walks over to look down on me. "Fine. In the name of deep existential bullshit, I shall lie on the floor."

He lies down next to me and we both stare at the ceiling, trying not to smile and make each other laugh. We lie here for minutes, silent and anticipating. Anticipating what, I don't know.

"Is it working?" I ask.

He turns his head to look at me. "Hell if I know," he says, his eyes taking in the apartment from this new vantage point. "But the next time I clean the apartment, remind me to move the coffee table. I think there are a hundred Cheerios under there."

I giggle and he smiles. Yeah, I'd say it's working.

He turns on his side and rises up on an elbow, taking a lock of my hair and working it between his fingers. "Thanks," he says.

"Anytime."

He stares at me as his face inches closer. It happens in slow motion—his gaze flitters between my lips and my eyes. His hand moves from my hair to my shoulder. His body moves closer so he's almost on top of me.

When his lips finally find mine, my body heaves at the intimate familiarity. I've only kissed him a few times before, but my body knows what to expect. It anticipates every movement of his lips, and our mouths move together in a synchronized dance only we can perform.

But then, as quickly as it started, the kiss ends and he pulls away, rolling back to where he was as my lips and my body long for more.

"I'm sorry," he says, leaning his head back onto the floor with a thud.

Those two words say it all.

I close my eyes. "You're confusing me, Kyle. Do you want me, or don't you?"

He takes a deep breath. And then another. "Jesus, Lexi, of course I want you," he says. "But—"

"But what?" I ask, keeping my eyes shut to protect me from his words.

"But I want *all* of you, Lex."

"I'm giving you all that I have to give, Kyle."

"I know," he says. "I just have to figure out if that's enough."

Little hands slap my chest and my eyes fly open to see that Ellie has crawled over to join us. I pull her over the top of my chest, positioning her between Kyle and me. She laughs, playing with us on the floor.

Kyle sits up and pulls her favorite book off the coffee table. He reads it to her with the signs I've taught him. Ellie settles into his lap, pointing at the pictures as he tries to teach her the signs.

It makes me wonder if she'll ever need to learn the sign for 'Daddy.'

Kyle looks like a daddy. He even acts like a daddy. But he can never *be* her daddy.

And maybe that's why this will never be enough.

CHAPTER FIFTY-FOUR

"Ouch!" I yelp. "I'd forgotten how much this stings."

I stare down at my wrist as a guy named Spike transforms my tattoo into something that won't have me thinking of the past—only the future.

"Don't be such a baby," Skylar jokes with a wink.

"Actually, it doesn't hurt as much as it did the first time I got it." I close my eyes at the horrible memory. "Probably because I actually *want* this one."

"Oh, my God. Did he force you to get it?" Piper asks.

I shake my head and look at the floor. "He didn't force me to do anything," I say, shamefully. "It was more like he intimidated me into it."

"Is there really a difference?" Skylar asks in disgust.

Two of the three Mitchell sisters have come with me for moral support. Skylar was able to pull some strings with Spike and get me in this week. He's in high demand and is normally booked weeks in advance. But sometimes, when inspiration strikes, you just have to do it before you chicken out.

I reach out and grab Piper's hand, squeezing it when I feel twinges of pain. "Are you ready to become Mrs. Lawrence?" I ask.

The smile that overtakes her face is all the answer I need. "I can't believe it's only ten days away," she says. "You guys will die when you see Hailey in her little flower girl dress. She's adorable. I'm so excited to finally become her official step-mom."

"She's called you 'Mommy' for years," Skylar says. "Will things really be all that different?"

"Of course they will." Piper gives her sister an exasperated look. "Every time I take Hailey someplace new, I have to introduce her as *my fiancée's* daughter. After next Saturday, I'll be able to introduce her as *my* daughter. Huge difference."

I let my head fall back against the headrest and I close my eyes.

"Oh, shit, Lex—uh, Elizabeth," Piper says, cringing at her slip-up. "I didn't mean things weren't great the way they were. I mean, families come in all different shapes and sizes. There are no rules."

"I know, Piper. But I also know that Kyle feels the way you do. About Ellie. About me. He doesn't want to think of us as somebody else's. And I'm just not sure he will ever get past that."

"Give him time," Skylar says. "And maybe give him a little nudge in the right direction."

"Nudge?" I ask, remembering her saying that once before.

"Yeah, there's nothing like a little jealousy to get a guy to admit he loves you. Believe me. I know from firsthand experience."

I raise my eyebrows at her. "You had to make Griffin jealous?"

"I didn't set out to," she tells me. "I thought Griffin was out of the picture when I started dating John. But then Griffin came back, and, oh boy. All I can say is that if John weren't in the picture, I'm not sure Griffin would have been so quick to lay his claim on me."

"Lay his claim, huh?" I ask.

"Oh, he laid his claim alright," Piper says. "I wasn't there, but I have video evidence to prove it. And it was epic."

"Video?" I ask. "I think I might need to see this epic display of claim-laying."

Skylar laughs. "Next time you come over, I'll get it out. It's been a while since I've watched it. Could be fun."

"I feel a girls' night in the near future," Piper says.

"Speaking of which, did you get my email about the bachelorette party?" I ask.

She bounces up and down in her seat. "I did. And I love your idea. How did you come up with it?"

"Are you kidding? Your oldest sister has me researching all kinds of stuff for her books. If you ever want to know how long it takes to crash land a twin-engine plane after it runs out of gas—I'm your girl."

Piper laughs. "Baylor sounds like a slave driver."

"Best boss I've ever had," I say.

"Isn't she the *only* boss you've ever had?" Skylar asks.

I shrug. "If you don't count the yappy four-legged furry types I used to work for."

"She's really happy with you, too," Piper says. "You should have seen her with her last assistant. I thought she might actually pull her hair out in frustration. But these days, Baylor is so relaxed and stress-free. That's *your* doing, you know."

"I'm just glad it's working out so well. At first, I thought she was taking pity on me by giving me a job."

Skylar looks at me like I'm crazy. "But now you know her well enough to see how she didn't do that, right? She hired you because you're good. Because you had the qualifications she wanted."

"I get that now," I say.

"We fought over you, you know," Skylar says. "Back when you were in the hospital. I thought that with your amazing personality and stunning looks, you'd make a great hostess."

"Thanks," I say, trying not to choke up. "I feel like I've hit the jackpot with you guys. I never thought having real friends could be so important. I'm grateful for all of you."

They both put a hand on my arm. "We're the lucky ones," Piper says.

"Okay, young lady," Spike says. "I'm all done. Let me wash it off and cover it and you'll be good to go."

I look down at my new tattoo after he wipes the soap off it. I stare at it, happy to have endured an hour of pain so I don't have to stare at *his* name anymore.

Yes, this will do. This one is much better.

~ ~ ~

As I watch the odometer on the treadmill tick off another mile, I count all the things in my life that I have to be thankful for. Nine months ago, when I was sitting outside the hospital on a bench, bleeding, I never could have imagined what my life would be like now. Despite everything I endured with Grant, I still consider myself a lucky girl.

"Hi," a deep voice says next to me.

I look in the mirror in front of me and lock eyes with the guy who has stepped on the treadmill next to mine. "Hi," I say, breathlessly, not wanting to break my pace.

He quickly works himself up to a fast run, my brisk walk paling in comparison. I find him staring at me often. He's good looking. Tall, with striking brown eyes. I'm sure lots of women would be flattered to get his attention.

But the only attention I want is from the man whose eyes can't seem to choose a color.

Twenty minutes later, when I turn off my treadmill, Brown Eyes does the same. He grabs a towel, wiping his sweaty face before swinging it over his shoulder.

He holds out his hand to me. "Hi, I'm Conner Ridley from 2105."

I shake his hand. "Elizabeth," I say.

"I haven't seen you here before. Did you just move in?"

"I've been here a few months," I tell him.

"Which unit did you buy?"

I stare at him, unwilling to divulge the information.

"Right," he says, cocking a brow at my silence. "You don't know me from Adam. Well, Elizabeth, from somewhere in the building, it's nice to meet you."

Conner spends the next few minutes telling me about the quirky residents who live here. Mr. Jones on the fourth floor is always writing apocalyptic sayings on poster boards and hanging them in his front window for everyone to see. Then there is Mrs. Hannigan up on twenty-three, who brings her Yorkie to walk on the treadmill every day because she's scared to go outdoors. And Hank Anderson, who is on *my* floor, he works on Broadway as a transvestite opera singer.

I look up at the clock on the wall. I told Greta, Charlie's trusted babysitter whom she loaned out to me, that I'd be back by six.

Conner understands my cue. "It's been nice talking with you, Elizabeth. I hope we meet again."

"Thanks," I tell him. "It was good to meet you."

As I make my way up to the twenty-eighth floor, I think about what Skylar said earlier about how men sometimes need a nudge.

Then I wonder what would happen if Kyle thought I might be interested in another guy. A guy like Conner Ridley.

A guy who wouldn't care about a piece of paper. A guy who I would be enough for exactly as I am.

CHAPTER FIFTY-FIVE

"Where's Greta?" I ask Kyle, when I walk through the door and see him holding Ellie.

"I sent her home," he says, without bothering to look at me.

"But I need to pay her, Kyle."

"Do you think I'm stupid, Lexi? Of course I paid her."

He still hasn't looked at me. In fact, he's doing everything in his power *not* to look at me. He's pretending to wipe something off the counter, but I can see from here, the counter is perfectly clean.

"Is something wrong?" I ask, closing the door and walking across the room.

"What could possibly be wrong?" he asks sarcastically. "Ellie's happy. I had a great day at work; diagnosed a difficult case. Oh, and you—there's obviously nothing wrong with you, I mean with all your exercising and all. And there sure as hell isn't anything wrong with Conner Ridley."

I have to pull my lips into my mouth to suppress a smile. He must have seen me talking to Conner. "Oh, you know him?"

He finally turns and faces me. "Everyone knows Mr. 2105."

"What?"

He raises a questioning brow. "Do you mean to tell me he didn't give you his apartment number?"

"He told me," I admit. "But he was just making polite conversation."

"Polite, my ass. He tells *everybody* his apartment number. And he's slept with every woman south of fifty who lives in this building."

My jaw falls open. "Really?"

"Yes, really. So stay away from him, Lex. He's bad news."

"We were only talking, Kyle. He's nice."

He shakes his head in disgust. "Of course he's nice. How else do you think he gets women to follow him home?"

The vein at his temple is pulsating and I have to bite my lip to hold in the laughter. Skylar may have been right. However, he's hardly declaring his love for me. More like looking out for his roommate, I'd say.

"Did you tell him where you live?" he asks, putting Ellie down in her playpen.

I look at him like he's gone crazy. "No, Kyle, I didn't. You know me better than that."

"Do I?" he asks.

I narrow my eyes at him, not bothering to justify his question with an answer. I think he *has* gone crazy. Or better yet, I think Mr. 2105 has *made* him crazy.

I walk over to kiss Ellie before I head to the bathroom to take a shower. "Ellie will be fine in there for a few minutes while I clean up."

I close the bathroom door behind me, but it immediately opens and Kyle walks through, pinning me against the counter with his stare. "Do you want him, Lexi?"

"Do I want the playboy of the western world? No, Kyle. I don't want him. Now would you mind if I shower, please?"

"He was eye-fucking you and you were letting him," he says, crossing his arms defensively.

"Eye-fucking? Are you kidding me, Kyle? What is *wrong* with you?"

He shakes his head. "I think we've already determined that *nothing* is wrong with me. What the hell is wrong with *you* that would make you want to talk to that scumbag?"

I blow out a frustrated breath. "I didn't know he was a player. Give me a tiny break for not being able to read everyone's mind, okay? Plus, I was only *talking* to him. For like two minutes, no less."

"Is that why you have your tattoo covered up?" he asks, nodding to the bandage on my wrist. "So you can *talk* to guys? Or is it so they won't know you have some other man's name branded into your flesh?"

I don't even know what's happening to him right now. Where is my nice, kind, save-the-world roommate? "You've gone mad, Kyle," I say, trying to push him towards the door.

He doesn't budge a single inch. "Tell me the truth, Lex. Is that why you have your goddamn tattoo covered?"

"It's none of your damn business why I have my tattoo covered!" I yell. "And what *if* I was out trolling for guys—why would you even care?"

"Of course I would fucking care, Lexi."

"Then prove it!" I say loudly. "Prove to me that you don't want another man's lips kissing mine. That the idea of someone else's hands on my body doesn't make you crazy. That the thought of me making love to Conner—or any other guy—doesn't make your skin crawl. Because when I think about *you* doing those things with anyone else, I want to die, Kyle."

He takes a single stride, closing the gap between us before he devours my mouth with his. I may even taste a little blood due to the violent way his lips are claiming mine. But I don't care. Because every fiber of my being wants to be claimed by this man. Every beat of my heart and every cell in my body lives for this feeling. The feeling I get when he's touching me. I never felt it before him, and I know I'll never feel it with anyone else after him.

He lifts me up onto the counter, kissing, licking and sucking on my neck. It doesn't even register that I've just been sweating and desperately need a shower. I can't think of anything but what his lips are doing to me.

He lifts my tank top over my head and swiftly removes my sports bra, cupping my breasts in his hands as he leans down to worship them with his mouth.

"Oh, Kyle," I say breathlessly, fumbling with his belt as I try to undo his pants.

He helps me remove his pants and then my running shorts. His hungry eyes run over my naked body, making me feel as if I'm the grand prize; the biggest and best present under the tree; the winning lottery ticket. And I'm fairly certain I return the sentiment with my own heated gaze. Because he's all those things. He's all those things and more.

He runs his thumb across my clit and I shudder. A moan escapes me when he puts a finger inside me. I reach down and grab his manhood, running my hand up and down his length in firm but gentle strokes until his moans of desire mingle with mine.

"God, Elizabeth," he says, gasping.

My eyes fly open when I hear him call my name. But it's *not* my name. Not really. And it dawns on me. I finally understand it. I understand that he only calls me Elizabeth when we do this. When we get hot and heavy together. When we get *real* with each other and let all of our emotions come through.

Because the truth of it is, he wants me to be her again. He wants me to be Elizabeth. The girl with no past. The girl without a predetermined future.

And I know I finally have my answer.

I have to dig deep for my willpower as I push him away. "Stop," I say, my voice cracking with emotion.

His hands immediately fall from my body. Of course they do. Because he's not Grant. Because he's nice and kind and generous and he would never make me do anything I didn't want to do.

"What is it?" he asks, looking me over while bracing a hand on the mirror behind me. "Are you okay?"

I fight back tears as I reach a hand up and trace the hard angles of his face. "Kyle, have you changed your mind? Have you decided that this is enough for you? That this—right here, right now, is enough for you? Because Alexa Lucas has to be enough or this will never work."

He looks down at the floor. It's all the confirmation I need.

I hop off the counter and pull my towel from the hook on the back of the door to cover myself. "I'm moving out."

He looks at me with guilty eyes. "Lex, no."

I nod in affirmation. "After Piper's wedding next weekend, I'm moving in with Baylor. She offered Ellie and me her guest room. It's the right thing to do, Kyle. I have to do it. I have to do it for me."

He backs up against the wall and runs his hands through his hair. "I don't want you to go." His torn voice is rough and thick.

"But that's the thing, Kyle. I don't think you really want me to stay, either."

His eyes fall to my wrist. In the midst of our passion, my bandage came off, revealing my redesigned tattoo. He takes my arm in his hands and examines it. I have to admit, Spike did a fantastic job. You'd never even know this tattoo was created from another one. The entwined hearts are still there, but instead of the single word scripted over them, there is now an entire sentence.

His fingers trace the edges of my reddened skin as he silently reads it. 'Take Nothing For Granted.'

He looks up at me. "Shit, Lex. You have your very own Chinese proverb."

"Nah," I say. "But I think the guy from Boston might just be onto something."

CHAPTER FIFTY-SIX

"You are so beautiful," I tell Piper. "Mason is a lucky man. And Hailey is about to get the best step-mom in the world."

"Thanks, Lexi," she says, trying to hold back tears so she doesn't ruin her flawless makeup.

I leave her and the rest of the girls to their last-minute preparations as I go hunt down Kyle. After all, everyone else I know is in the wedding, so he is the only one I can sit with.

I eye the security guards as I pass by each exit. Mason is a well-known football hero and him tying the knot is sure to draw attention. I'm grateful for the added security at such a high-profile event. But even so, I still refused to stand up with Piper. I couldn't risk any wedding party pictures making the newspaper.

"Mason is going to flip when he sees her," I tell Kyle, when I find him staring at a stained-glass window. "I've never seen her look more beautiful."

He shifts his stare from the window to me. Then his gaze rakes up and down my body, taking in my form-fitting chiffon dress. I realize this is the first time he's seen me all dressed up. He opens his mouth as if he wants to say something. Maybe he wants to tell me he's never seen *me* so beautiful. But he doesn't. He just smiles and shuts his mouth. Much like he's done since I told him I was moving out.

What he doesn't know is that I lied to him. When I told him Baylor had offered me their guest room, it was a complete lie. That night in the bathroom when I finally realized he might never fully accept me, I panicked, saying the first thing that came to mind. And then the next day, I went to Baylor with my tail between my legs, begging her to let me stay with her until I could figure something else out.

She was only too happy to accommodate me. She said we could stay as long as we needed. But with three kids and a husband, I can only imagine adding two more bodies into the mix will be chaotic.

Maybe I can move back into Mrs. Peabody's guest house. I can work for Baylor from there. And it's only an hour train ride so I can come back for meetings and for girls' night.

"Lexi?" He whispers my name so no one will hear, pulling me from my thoughts so he can escort me into the sanctuary.

He won't call me Elizabeth. Not even in public. Not since that night in the bathroom. I guess he realized what he'd done. So now, if he needs to get my attention when we're not around close friends, he'll just say *'hey.'* He may have even jokingly used the name sign he made up for me. But not Elizabeth. Never Elizabeth.

Kyle whispers something to the usher, and then the usher takes us to an inconspicuous spot several pews behind Piper's family. More people funnel in and eventually, we become lost in the impeccably-dressed crowd.

Mason and his groomsmen take their places at the front of the church. Music starts and heads turn to watch an adorable Hailey dropping rose petals on her way down the aisle. Laughter ensues when she reaches the front and turns to Jan Mitchell to ask loudly, "Did I do good, Mema?"

Mallory and Chad walk down the aisle, followed by Baylor and Gavin and then Skylar and Griffin. Then Charlie, Piper's matron of honor, is escorted by Ethan, who is Mason's best man. The organist pauses before starting the processional. We all stand and watch Piper as she's escorted by her proud father. He's smiling from ear to ear, and maybe even crying, at the thought of marrying off his youngest daughter.

While everyone continues to stare at Piper, I look at the front of the church and watch Mason. This has always been my favorite part. Watching the groom as the bride makes her way down the aisle. Mason doesn't even try to hold back the emotions he's feeling. I envy Piper. This is how every groom should look at his bride.

I think back to the way Grant looked at me during our small ceremony that only consisted of my brother and a few of Grant's police buddies. Or should I say, the way Grant *didn't* look at me. He didn't look at me because he was too busy watching the reactions of others as *they* looked at me. He liked to show me off, put me on display. I always thought it was because he was proud of me. I should have seen it that day, the day of my wedding. I should have seen the way he was collecting me like the way he collected his other trophies. I should have turned and run back up the aisle.

I wipe a tear that rolls down my cheek when Piper's dad kisses her and hands her off to Mason. I have to choke back more when I see Mason mouth the words *'I love you'* to her before the preacher gets started.

I want this. I've never wanted anything so badly in my life. I don't care about the hundreds of people. I don't care about the skillfully-decorated church. I don't care about any of the pomp and circumstance. I just want to be looked at like that. To be completely and utterly revered by a man like Piper is right now.

I turn to look at Kyle before we sit, and my breath hitches. Because he's not looking up at Piper and Mason like everyone else. He's looking at me. And maybe I'm dreaming, but I could swear he's looking at me with the same eyes as Mason was looking at his bride. He's looking at me like *he's* never wanted anything so badly in *his* life.

We sit down and I pull a tissue out of my purse to dab my wet eyes. Eyes that won't seem to dry up because I want something I can never have. Eyes that continue to water because I know *he* does too.

Their vows make the congregation laugh. Their vows also make us cry. And as Kyle and I watch two of our friends get married, he reaches over and grabs my hand, lacing his fingers tightly with mine. We've never done this before—held hands. It's nice. I close my eyes and cherish the moment. I'll miss this.

When the preacher pronounces them husband and wife, we all cheer as Mason takes his wife in his arms, kissing her passionately before walking his bride up the aisle.

I feel my arm being tugged from behind. Kyle drags me out of the pew before the applause even dies down. He pulls me to the side of the sanctuary, behind a large support pole that holds up the balcony above. I look up at him, confused.

"Don't move out, Lexi," he says, his eyes begging me. "I thought I needed this." He gestures back to the crowd. "I don't. I don't need *any* of this. I just need you."

Tears well up in my eyes once again and I nod at him as realization dawns on me. "I *do* need this, Kyle. I want this. I want it for you. I want it for me. I want it for Ellie."

He laughs at our unexpected, yet simultaneous changes of heart. "We'll make it happen," he says. "One day, Lexi, I promise we'll make it happen." He takes my head in his hands, rubbing his thumbs gently across my cheeks. "I don't care if you're Alexa Lucas, Elizabeth Smith or Lexi Stone—I love you no matter who you are."

My heart thunders at his words that I'm not sure I heard correctly. I stare up into his eyes, wondering if this moment is real.

"Did you hear me, Lex? I said I love you. I love *all* of you," he says, his voice a low vibration that sends shivers to my very soul. "And I love Ellie. And I want us to be a family, in whatever way we can. I'll take you any way I can get you."

I can't hold back the emotions flowing from my eyes. I nod as I swallow the colossal lump in my throat. I've waited Ellie's whole life to say these words. If I'm being honest, I've even waited all of mine to truly mean them. "I love you, too, Kyle."

His eyes get glassy and he pulls me closer until our lips are almost touching. "Lexi, will you marry me . . . someday?"

I look up at the heavens, thanking God for this man. My doctor. My savior. The man I want Ellie to grow up with. The man I want to grow old with.

I can't speak. I'm overcome with emotion. All I can do is hold up my hand and sign, *"Yes."*

CHAPTER FIFTY-SEVEN

Dancing in Kyle's arms feels unreal. The way his hands run up and down my back. The way they pull me closely against him. The way he rubs tiny circles on the exposed flesh of my shoulders. I feel like it's all a dream. A dream from which I hope I never awaken.

On the drive to the reception, we had decided not to tell anyone. This is Piper and Mason's day, not ours. But who are we kidding? With the way we've been dancing all night, we're not fooling anybody.

Caden asks to cut in and dance with me. I laugh when Kyle hesitates. He doesn't want to take his hands off me. But he acquiesces. After all, Caden is my brother.

"I'm glad you could make the reception," I tell Caden as he spins me around. "How was the game? Did you win?"

He pastes on a big smile. "Five to four," he says proudly. "I hit a double in the bottom of the ninth to drive in the winning run."

I harden my hold on him. "That's great! I'm so proud of you. I wish . . . I wish Mom were here to see what a success you are. Even if she wasn't the best mom, she still would have been proud of you, kid."

"You're all the family I need, Lexi. We've got each other's backs now. I promise I'll never let anything bad happen to you again."

"I'll always be here for you too, you know. I'm not going anywhere," I say.

He cocks his head, looking at me sideways. "I thought you were moving to Maple Creek to live with your boss."

"Nope." I can't help the large smile that travels up my face. I sneak a glance over at Kyle, who is watching me intently.

Caden follows my gaze. "Well, I'll be damned. It's about time Kyle came to his senses. I knew it was only a matter of time." He leans down to kiss me on the cheek. "I'm happy for you, sis."

"Hey, now." Kyle walks up and steals me away from my brother. "I'm the only one who's going to be kissing her tonight."

Caden extends his hand and Kyle shakes it. They nod at each other in that way only males can understand. And I'm not sure, but I think volumes were just spoken between them.

"You told him," Kyle says with a raised brow after Caden walks away.

"He's my brother."

"It's fine. I told Chad and Ethan, too." He gives me an innocent shrug of his shoulders as his mouth curves indulgently.

An hour later, after the cake has been cut, I tell Kyle I simply have to sit down. I'm exhausted and my feet are killing me. I haven't worn heels since the day I ran away from Grant. I always had to wear heels for him. He insisted on it. It's one of the reasons why I haven't bought any since. Well, until now. And the heels are high and the shoes are new—a deadly combination.

Kyle checks his phone for the time. "Ellie will be getting tired and hungry," he says. "We've been here for hours. We've done our duty. Why don't we pick up Ellie from the daycare and head out?"

I love how we've only officially been together for four hours, yet he can already read my mind.

We say our goodbyes to the bride and groom and their entourage and then head down the hall to where a daycare had been set up for small children. We find Ellie asleep on one of the babysitters. I gently pick her up as Kyle gets out his wallet to tip them.

I smile. They probably think we're a family.

I look up at Kyle and he winks at me. Yeah, I'm pretty sure he's thinking the very same thing.

We walk past the security guards who are just inside the front door. Kyle takes Ellie from me and lets me hold onto his elbow as I navigate the many front steps in my ridiculously-high heels.

When we reach the base of the stairs, he nods to a bench by the front walk. "You and Ellie sit here. The car is a half-mile away." He leans down and kisses Ellie on the head before he gives me a warm peck on the lips.

"Thank you," I say, taking him up on his offer.

Almost instantly, Ellie lays her head on my shoulder and falls back to sleep. I gently rub her back, letting my tired eyes close as I daydream about what tonight has in store. What tomorrow will bring. What the rest of my life will be like with Kyle Stone in it.

"Well lookie fuckin' here," a low, gravelly voice rumbles out of the darkness, sending shivers of familiarity up and down my spine.

My heart falls into my stomach. Bile rises into my throat. My eyes snap open, putting me into the nightmare I've always feared. I look over near the bushes to see Grant walking towards me.

I want to get up, but I'm frozen to the bench. And even if I weren't, I can't run, not in these heels. Not with Ellie in my arms. I look behind me, but all I see are empty stairs. Two dozen empty stairs. Too many that stand between me and the security guards inside the building.

I try to calculate how long Kyle has been gone. I think it's only been a minute or two. He parked far away. Too far for me to yell. I look around and see no one else in the vicinity. I'm utterly alone. Alone with the man who's been hunting me.

I start to hyperventilate.

"What's wrong, baby?" he asks. "Feel like you've seen a ghost?" He nods over his shoulder in the direction Kyle was walking. "Looks like we have at least a few minutes to take care of business before your baby daddy comes back. Shit, Alexa, you sure didn't waste any time turning into a little slut, did you?"

I look down at a sleeping Ellie, putting my arms possessively around her.

He draws his eyebrows together and stares at Ellie. "Wait," he gruffs, scrubbing a hand across his jaw. "Wait just a goddamn minute." He points at her. "Just how old is she?"

I don't speak. I can't. I feel myself holding Ellie tightly and she starts squirming in protest under my grip.

Grant paces back and forth on the sidewalk in front of me, pulling a flask from his back pocket. He takes a long drink before looking at her again. "Is that my fucking kid?"

I momentarily hear music coming from inside as the doors to the reception hall open. *Thank God.* Someone must be coming. Maybe Grant will run away. But he doesn't back off. Instead, he sits down next to me and puts his arm around my back, gripping my neck like a vise.

"Say anything and I'll hurt her," he growls at me.

I want to vomit at his words. I've never been so scared in my life. Not when he was hitting me. Not when he was holding me down to have his way with me. Not even when he stabbed me with his precious trophy.

Then I hear a familiar voice. Ethan. *Oh, God, Ethan, please see me. Please don't just walk past me and keep going.*

Ethan is talking, but I don't hear Charlie respond. I come to realize he must be on the phone. Maybe he just slipped out of the reception to take a call.

As his voice comes closer, Grant's hold on me becomes tighter. "Shhhh," he whispers in my ear, the stench of vodka rolling off his breath.

Ethan comes down the last step, barely faltering in his stride as he passes us on the sidewalk. He looks at us as if we're of no consequence, his eyes falling on me for only a second. He even tips his chin at Grant. Barely a minute goes by and he finishes his call and walks over to us. "Hey, buddy, do you have a light?" he asks Grant, while reaching into his pocket.

"Don't smo—," Grant starts to say, when all of a sudden, before I even realize what's happening, Ethan has Grant face down on the sidewalk, his knee in his back as he brings Grant's hands up behind him, securing them with a zip tie.

"Oh, my God!" I scream. "Ethan, it's Grant."

I get up off the bench, holding a still-sleeping Ellie as I back away from the two men.

"Yeah, I figured," he says. "Damn lucky timing, huh?"

He digs his knee into Grant's back, causing Grant to curse. "She's my goddamn wife, you son of a bitch!" Grant yells, a vein near his eye bulging as his face grows red. "Do you have any fucking idea who you're dealing with?"

Ethan leans down, close to Grant's ear. "I know exactly who you are, you piece of shit."

A car pulls up to the curb and Kyle runs out, summing up the situation as he makes his way to me. "Lexi, are you okay? Did he hurt you?"

Ethan pulls Grant off the ground and forces him to sit on the bench that I vacated.

"I'm okay. He squeezed my neck, and he threatened to hurt Ellie, but we're okay," I tell him.

Kyle walks over and gets in Grant's face. "You will never fucking touch her again or I'll kill you. Do you hear me?"

Grant smirks. "Maybe you shouldn't talk that way in front of my kid." Then he studies Kyle. "You're that doctor I talked to a while ago. You lied to me, you asshole." He looks back and forth between Kyle and me. "Have you been fucking my wife?"

Kyle's hands ball up into fists and Ethan puts his arm out to hold him back. "Kyle, why don't you call the police?"

Grant laughs. "I *am* the fucking police." He leans forward and stretches his bound hands out behind him. "None of this is necessary," he says. "I didn't come back for her. I don't even want her anymore. I came here to get her to sign the papers." He nods to an envelope in his breast pocket that is now crumpled and torn.

Kyle takes it from his pocket and opens it, quickly scanning whatever's inside. He looks over at me, surprised. "They're divorce papers," he says, walking them over to me.

"You think I'd want to stay married to that frigid bitch?" Grant spits. "Although, now that I know I have a kid, maybe things have changed. What's my daughter's name, Alexa?"

I squeeze Ellie to my chest, refusing to tell him anything. She wakes up crying. She's hungry. It's late. Behind Kyle's protective stance, I pace around, bouncing Ellie in my arms, but she's inconsolable. Her cries become wails. I try to soothe her, talking to her as I sign my words.

"What the fuck are you doing?" Grant shouts over at me. Then he looks to Kyle. "What the fuck is she doing?"

"She's talking to her, dipshit," Kyle says.

Grant watches me. His eyes ping-pong between my signing hands and Ellie. Then his eyes go wide in realization and his head falls back as he laughs up at the sky. "Are you kidding me?" he asks, shaking his head. "Is the kid fucking deaf?"

Kyle and I both remain silent, Kyle staring at Grant with hatred seeping from his every pore.

"I don't want no gimpy kid," Grant says. "The one I have with Tara isn't defective."

Kyle lunges at Grant, and Ethan has to hold him back once more. Grant tries to get up off the bench to challenge Kyle, but Ethan pushes him back, holding him down by his shoulders.

I stop pacing and look over at Grant. "Tara. She's the one from those letters in your study."

His jaw tightens and his shoulders tense, just like they used to right before he would hit me. He's pissed knowing I went through his things.

"You have a *kid* with her?" I ask, from behind my protectors. "The woman you had on the side all those years?"

He laughs at me. *"You* were the one on the side, baby. Not her."

I study him in confusion. "Then why did you even marry me, Grant? Why not her?"

He shrugs. "She was already married to some rich lawyer from Ft. Wayne, Indiana." He nods to the papers Kyle is still holding. "But when he found out she was knocked up with someone else's kid, he tossed her out and divorced her. I didn't want a bastard kid, so I said I'd marry her. But I had to get you to sign the papers first. Christ, Alexa, you crawled under a fucking rock and died," he says, almost as if he's proud of me for being able to hide from him. "I've been driving here one weekend a month for a year, following your goddamn brother around. I thought I got close when I found out you pawned the ring. Guess I should have given you more credit. I didn't think you were smart enough to dodge me all this time." He looks between Kyle and me again. "But then again, maybe you're not. Maybe doctor-boy here was helping you all along."

"But . . . why wouldn't you just tell Caden you wanted a divorce? You could have saved yourself a lot of trouble," I say. *You could've saved* me *a lot of heartache.*

"And miss this joyful reunion?" he asks with smug smile. "Now what would be the fun in that? I mean, now I get to charge your friend here with false imprisonment. And let's see, I guess I can charge *you* with kidnapping."

I gasp. Tears well up in my eyes as I hold a sniffling, crying Ellie.

Kyle reaches into the diaper bag and gets out a bottle, handing it to her to calm her down.

"You want the gimp?" Grant asks Kyle, laughing. "You can have her."

Venom spews from Kyle's eyes as he walks over and punches Grant in the face. Grant's head snaps to the side and blood flies out of his mouth, spattering the sidewalk. He spits blood onto the ground and then wipes his mouth on his shoulder. "Add assaulting a defenseless cop to that list," he says.

"You want to talk charges? Let's talk charges," Ethan says, hovering above Grant. "How about beating your goddamn wife. Raping her. Assaulting her here tonight by grabbing her neck. And let's not forget threatening her child."

"Rape?" Grant asks, like he honestly doesn't think what he did to me ever qualified. "Yeah right, she was a willing participant."

"And you're sure a jury would see it that way?" Ethan asks. "What do you stand to gain here, Lucas? If you take her to court, what, you're going to ask for custody? Of the kid you don't even want?

"And let's talk about these other charges you say you want to bring against us. The way I remember it, you were holding Alexa's neck and threatening her child. Kyle walked up and hit you and then I cuffed you to keep you from hurting anyone." He turns to Kyle and me with raised brows. "Is that how you guys remember it?"

We both nod.

"So you see, you have a choice here," Ethan tells him. "You can get what you came for, or you can be a stubborn ass and fight us out of spite. But let me tell you something, Lucas, you don't want to mess with us, because I promise you, all your dirty cop connections can't buy you half of what *we* can afford. Between her brother and the rest of us, we can get the best team of lawyers money can buy without even breaking a sweat."

Grant's eyes bounce back and forth between Ethan and Kyle, and then he looks at Ellie. "How much is she worth to you?"

"You really are a sick fuck," Kyle says, running a hand through his hair.

Ethan stands between them so Kyle won't take another swing. "I don't think you understand," Ethan says to Grant, with a harsh chuckle. "Do you really want to be burdened with eighteen years of child support? Deaf children can be expensive. Private schools. Instructional camps. Elective surgeries. Do you really want to take that on?"

Grant looks over at me and his face falls. I've never seen the man look defeated. He's always won. He's won everything he's ever done. The only thing he hasn't won is getting the best of me. And he knows it.

His eyes are cold and hardened with anger when he nods to the papers in Kyle's hands. "So, are you going to sign the fucking papers or what?"

"She'll look them over tonight," Ethan says, tucking one of his business cards into Grant's shirt pocket. "You can meet us at my office at noon tomorrow. At that time, Alexa will sign the divorce papers and you will sign papers recusing yourself from being that child's father."

Grant shakes his head in frustration. He knows we have him beat. "Fine," he says, with a lifeless tone to his voice. "Can you get me out of these fucking cuffs now?"

Ethan looks at us and gestures to Kyle's car. "As soon as they're gone."

Kyle takes Ellie from me and puts her in her car seat. Then we get in and drive away. Kyle reaches over and grabs my hand. "Tomorrow," he says, giving my hand a squeeze. "Tomorrow is when everything changes."

CHAPTER FIFTY-EIGHT

"Oh, my God, Kyle. I'm free. I'm free!" I squeal as we walk through the door to his apartment after our noon meeting at Ethan's office. "Is it wrong of me to want to go down on the street and scream my name for all of New York City to hear?"

He laughs, tossing his keys on the counter. "If that's what you want to do, Lex, I'll go down there with you. Hell, I'll buy you a megaphone. Anything you want to do to celebrate is fine with me."

"Anything?" I raise a sultry brow at him.

We didn't get a chance to be together last night. After we got home, Ethan came over with his high-priced lawyer. At ten o'clock at night, no less. Must be nice to have so many people at your beck and call. We went over the divorce papers Grant gave me. And we drew up papers for him to sign relieving him of all parental rights to Ellie.

There may not even be much red tape to work through since I never filed for an official birth certificate for her. And since she's not yet a year old, Ethan's lawyer said I can still apply for it without any problems. Kyle immediately asked if there was any way he could be listed as the father. I think I fell in love with him even more, if that's possible.

Kyle picks me up, carrying me with one arm behind my back and the other under my knees. The way a groom carries his bride.

He takes me to his bedroom. "When is Charlie bringing Ellie back?"

I smile up at him. "Not for a few more hours."

"A few hours?" he asks with a smirk. "I can think of a lot we can do in that amount of time."

He puts me down on his bed and I inhale the scent of his room. I haven't been in here since the night I showed up on his doorstep over two months ago. "I love the smell of your room."

He climbs on top of me, straddling me. "It's your room now, too, Lexi. Everything I have is yours."

I put my hands on his face, running my fingers across the stubble on his jaw. "And everything I have is yours." I give him an apologetic shrug. "Sorry. I know you're not getting a very good deal."

In the past few months, I've come to have a pretty good idea just what he has. And it's more than I can even comprehend. I'd love him without it, of course. I'd love him if he weren't a doctor. I'd love him if he lived in a broken-down shack.

"That's not true, Lex. I'm getting more out of this than you can imagine. I'm getting you. I'm getting Ellie. And you're both perfect."

"Thank you," I say, a tear rolling off the side of my face. "Thank you for saying she's perfect."

I remember all the hateful things Grant said about Ellie last night and it makes me sick to think he was her father. But he's not anymore. We made sure of that today.

For all intents and purposes, Kyle is her daddy now.

I spread out the fingers of my hand, tapping the tip of my thumb onto my forehead.

His smile reaches all the way to his eyes, telling me he knows exactly what sign I just did.

"Did you know that every time I would teach Ellie the sign for 'Mommy,' I wanted nothing more than for someone to touch *my* shoulder and teach her the sign for 'Daddy'?"

I nod, my throat becoming thick with emotion. "I wanted that, too. I wanted it so much."

"I'm sorry it took me so long to realize what an ass I was being," he says, wiping my tears.

"I understand, Kyle. I understand wanting something so much that you can't accept anything less than having all of it. It's the way I feel about Ellie. It's the way I feel about you."

He leans down and presses his lips to mine. "I love you, Lexi Kessler," he says, rasping my name in heated passion.

I smile against his lips. I had Ethan's lawyer add an addendum to the divorce agreement that restores my maiden name. Not that it matters much, I don't plan on being Lexi Kessler for very long.

"I love you, too, Kyle Stone," I say, kissing him along his strong jaw. Then I pull my head back and look up at him as something dawns on me. "We need to Google it."

He looks at me as if I've fallen off my rocker. "Google what, exactly?"

"Ellie Stone," I say. "You know, to make sure she's not a porn star."

His body shakes with laughter and his radiant eyes shine in the afternoon light coming through the window. "I'll get right on that," he says, fingering the buttons of my blouse. "But first . . ."

He swiftly unbuttons my blouse, moving it to the side. Then he pulls the cups of my bra down, exposing my breasts to his wide and appreciative eyes. He takes one breast in his hand, the other in his mouth, causing my back to arch as I push myself further into him.

I throw my head back against the pillow as I moan, my hands grasping at his shirt, my words begging him to remove it. I need to be closer to him. I need to feel flesh on flesh. I need for there to be nothing between us. Not space. Not time. Not even air.

We make quick work of removing the rest of our clothing, not caring in the least if any get ripped or wrinkled. Then we lie facing each other, side by side, taking in each other's bodies as if it's the very first time. It might as well be. The only other time we made love was when we were fighting. When we were drunk. When we knew we wanted each other, but were afraid of what it might mean.

Now, however, we see each other in a whole new light. The past is behind us. Our future is a clean slate just waiting to be written upon.

"Christ, you're beautiful," he says, his voice slipping over me like crushed velvet as he strokes a hand up and down my bare thigh.

"You are beautiful, too," I tell him. "You're the most beautiful person I've ever met, Kyle. Inside and out. Without you . . . I . . . I don't know what I would have done."

"You'll never have to find out," he says, his teeth nipping at my earlobe. "I'm yours, Lexi. And you're mine."

"Say it again," I beg, needing to savor his proclamation as his lips find mine.

"You're mine, Lexi," he says through our heated kisses. "You're mine."

His hand wanders over my chest, across my stomach, down through my soft patch of curls. I gasp when his fingers graze over my clit, teasing me as he coats it with the wetness he pulls up from beneath.

I reach down and grab his steely length. He twitches at my touch. I run my hand along him, slowly at first, then faster as he writhes against me. "Lexi, Jesus!"

We work each other until we're right on the edge. Then he climbs down my body, making his intentions clear as he looks up and locks eyes with me. He kisses my stomach, kisses my faint silvery stretch marks, kisses my scar—the scar *he* so masterfully stitched to perfection.

When his mouth comes down on me, I shudder. I hold him to me, wanting everything he's giving me. Wanting to give him everything he's taking. Never has anything been this good. Felt this right. And as he makes me come, I cry out his name. And I know—I know it's the only name I ever want to shout for the rest of my life.

"Kyle, please," I beg, needing to feel him inside me.

He climbs up my body, his penis throbbing violently against me. He brushes the tip across my opening. "I want to feel you, Lex. I want to feel you with nothing between us. And if we make a baby, I'm okay with that, because nothing I've dreamed of accomplishing in my life will mean anything without you. Without Ellie. Without whoever else we bring into this world."

"Yes," I tell him, tears stinging the backs of my eyes.

He looks down at me, savoring every second of how it feels when he enters me. He kisses me and whispers words of love and longing in my ear. He takes his time with me, holding off his own release so he can build me back up with him.

"Oh, God, Kyle," I cry, calling out his name for the second time as my walls spasm around him.

When he finally allows himself to come, he shouts out my name. *My real name.* That's when I know for sure that Elizabeth is finally gone. I'll always be grateful to her because she brought me to him, but it's time for me to say goodbye to her. To move on to the next chapter of my life.

As if reading my mind, Kyle brings my wrist up to his mouth, kissing my tattoo. "This is only the beginning," he says.

I nod, biting back tears of joy. "Never have I ever felt this way before, Kyle. Thank you."

A broad grin splits his face. Then he startles me by quickly jumping out of bed. "Wait here," he says, with a devious cock of an eyebrow.

He walks out of the room, not even bothering to put on a stitch of clothing. When he returns, his hands are full of small cups of Jell-O. I laugh, realizing what I had said a moment ago. He puts the cups on the bed and crawls back in next to me, pulling my body firmly against his.

"You forgot the spoons," I say.

He chuckles behind me and then flips me over so I'm pinned underneath him. "We don't need spoons," he says, right before his mouth comes crashing down on mine.

EPILOGUE

6 months later . . .

I don't care about the hundreds of people. I don't care about the skillfully-decorated church. I don't care about any of the pomp and circumstance. All I care about is that I'm being looked at by the man of my dreams. And he's looking at me like I'm the center of his universe. He's looking at me like every bride deserves to be looked at.

As Kyle goes to say his vows, he drops my hands. But I only have to wonder why for a second. Because as he says his vows with his spoken words, he also says them with his hands. My hand flies to my mouth to cover my gasp. He's learned sign language. Not just the few words and phrases I'd been teaching him. He's learned it *all*. And as he says and signs his vows to me, I know he's not just solidifying our bond as husband and wife, he's solidifying our bond as a family.

After the preacher introduces us as Dr. and Mrs. Stone, Ellie toddles over to us as cheers echo throughout the sanctuary. Kyle scoops her up and carries her in one arm as he escorts me past tearful friends and family. When we get out front, we have a second to ourselves before our guests start to trickle out. Kyle leans down to kiss Ellie's head. Then he puts a hand on my belly.

The belly we just found out is carrying his baby. His *second* baby. Because like I am, Ellie was always destined to be his.

I was meant to go through everything I had to go through in order to get to him. I can't regret any of it, because it was the path that led me to where I am today. And it was that path that brought me Ellie.

I look down at my tattoo and vow I will never in my life take any of this for granted.

And I vow to always, *always*, have a jar full of fortune cookies.

Caden's story is

Catching Caden

If you've enjoyed Stone Vows, I would appreciate you taking a minute to leave a review on Amazon. Reviews, even just a few words, are incredibly valuable to indie authors like me.

ACKNOWLEDGEMENTS

With the completion of Stone Vows, I now have two full series of books plus three standalone novels. Nine books! I still have to pinch myself sometimes when I realize I'm an author. How did this even happen? How did a silly New Year's resolution I made over three years ago turn into a career?

Stone Vows never would have seen the light of day if it weren't for my dear friend and beta reader, Tammy Dixon. When I had writer's block, she brainstormed with me. When I needed a nudge in the right direction, she pushed me off a cliff. She kept me on the right track as she always does. Her direction and her vision help me more than she'll ever know.

Thank you to my other beta readers, Laura Conley and Heather Durham. You both have an extreme eye for detail, and for that, I'm grateful.

My hard-working editors, Ann Peters and Jeannie Hinkle, have done it again, allowing me to produce an indie novel that can rival traditionally published ones. Thank you for the countless hours you pour into my books.

Lastly, thank you to my incredible writing buddy, April Barnswell. Your daily emails and never-ending encouragement make this seem like a lot less of a job and more like a journey.

This year has been a year of incredible opportunity for me, and I owe it all to the readers who have stuck with me since the beginning and the readers who are just now discovering me. Providing you entertainment through my books is a real honor.

ABOUT THE AUTHOR

Samantha Christy's passion for writing started long before her first novel was published. Graduating from the University of Nebraska with a degree in Criminal Justice, she held the title of Computer Systems Analyst for The Supreme Court of Wisconsin and several major universities around the United States. Raised mainly in Indianapolis, she holds the Midwest and its homegrown values dear to her heart and upon the birth of her third child devoted herself to raising her family full time. While it took time to get from there to here, writing has remained her utmost passion and being a stay-at-home mom facilitated her ability to follow that dream. When she is not writing, she keeps busy cruising to every Caribbean island where ships sail. Samantha Christy currently resides in St. Augustine, Florida with her husband and four children.

You can reach Samantha Christy at any of these wonderful places:

Website: www.samanthachristy.com

Facebook: https://www.facebook.com/SamanthaChristyAuthor

Twitter: @SamLoves2Write

E-mail: samanthachristy@comcast.net

Printed in Great Britain
by Amazon

84252862R00233